P9-DKE-099

BLIC LIBRARY

Portrait in Shadows

This is a portrait of a professional killer who started killing when he was fifteen: and ruthlessly disguised the crime to land the guilt on his equally young companion. That companion was blackmailed into becoming a slave for life.

It is a story about the killer's attitudes and requirements: about guns, contacts, 'cover' – in this case a very high profile as a fake modern surrealist painter – about laundering the cash paid for killing, and about professional pride and perfectionism.

There are scenes of studied planning and ones of nerve-tingling excitement as the killer smoothly carries out each contract, leaving the police seemingly helpless and inept against such a motiveless killing machine.

It is also a portrait of amorality: of a man with no passion and no soul, and of the people he uses to reach his own goal of perfection.

John Wainwright is renowned as a writer of realistic crime novels which propound motives as much as means. Here he has undertaken a portrayal of the blackest side of human nature and has succeeded triumphantly, while at the same time creating a thriller of true suspense.

R

PORTRAIT IN SHADOWS

John Wainwright

MACMILLAN

First published in Great Britain 1986 by
MACMILLAN LONDON LIMITED
4 Little Essex Street London WC2R 3LF
and Basingstoke

Associated companies in Auckland, Delhi, Dublin, Gaborone, Hamburg, Harare, Hong Kong, Johannesburg, Kuala Lumpur, Lagos, Manzini, Melbourne, Mexico City, Nairobi, New York, Singapore and Tokyo

British Library Cataloguing in Publication Data
Wainwright, John, 1921-
    Portrait in shadows.
    I. Title
    823'.941[F]   PR6073.A354

    ISBN 0-333-41275-3

Typeset by Bookworm Typesetting Ltd., Manchester
Printed by Anchor Brendon Ltd., Essex

Every man's work, whether it be literature or music or pictures or architecture or anything else, is always a portrait of himself.

Samuel Butler, *The Way of All Flesh*

> Between the idea
> And the reality
> Between the motion
> And the act
> Falls the Shadow

T. S. Eliot, 'The Hollow Men'

The author and publishers are grateful to Faber and Faber Ltd. and Harcourt Brace Jovanovich Inc. for permission to quote from 'The Hollow Men' in *Collected Poems 1909-1962* by T. S. Eliot.

ONE

'I want a Browning Mauser, high-powered model. You know the stock-length?'

Pollard nodded and tasted the weird alcoholic concoction he'd brought from the bar.

'Get it to Frisch for a going-over. Single trigger-pull. Not more than half an ounce ... the usual. Tell him I want it calibred and chambered to take a nine-millimetre Mauser, metal-covered, soft-nosed. Two-four-five grains. Nose drilled for dum-dum effect.'

'That's illegal,' smiled Pollard.

'We're not rehearsing a vaudeville act, Pollard,' I reminded him gently.

'I'm sorry.' He tasted his drink again. He seemed to enjoy it.

'Tell Frisch to fit a Bausch & Lomb scope-sight. For ... what distance?'

'We think fifty yards. An average of fifty yards.'

'Assuming you've chosen a good aiming-point.'

'You won't complain.'

'I will,' I assured him, 'unless I'm satisfied. But, for the moment, let's assume fifty yards. That's a straight bullet-rise of two and a half inches, not counting wind deflection.'

'The – er – bullet-*drop*?' Pollard raised his eyebrows a fraction as he murmured the question.

'It rises before it drops, Pollard.' I could feel my brow pucker into a frown of annoyance. '*Then* it drops. Four inches at one hundred yards. Please don't try to tell me my job.'

'Sorry.' He apologised again, and the look of mild panic touched his eyes for a moment.

'How fast does he jog?' I asked.

'Never less than two miles.'

'Not how far, how *fast*? A steady jog? Or does he do sprint bursts?'

'A steady jog. Same pace all the way. Usually Tuesdays and Thursdays. *Always* on a Sunday. He sets off between seven and seven-thirty.'

'When he's at home.' I was fine-combing the details for possible snags.

'Wherever he is. At home. Hotel. Wherever he is.'

'Alone?'

'A Special Branch man goes with him.'

'Always?'

Pollard nodded. 'A Minister of the Crown. It's to be expected.'

'Just the one SB man?'

'They don't expect trouble at that hour,' smiled Pollard. 'It's not as if —'

'Pollard,' I interrupted gently, 'they *always* expect trouble. Twenty-four hours a day. Every day.'

Pollard moved his shoulders, but didn't argue. Once more he tasted his drink.

I voiced my musings aloud. It was a pattern we'd developed over the years. I wasn't asking for observations. Not even reactions. After ten killings, I knew my job, and Pollard's role was little more than that of an animated sounding-board.

'We're up against professionals this time. *Real* professionals. The IRA crowd have forced them to tighten up security. One SB man . . . but there'll be others. Less obvious, but still there. Armed? Probably – some certainly will be. But not long-range stuff. Say, three to do the job.'

'Three?' He sounded surprised. 'Three rounds – dum-dum – a good rifle, with telescopic sight?'

'Pollard,' I murmured, 'you have been watching too many TV shows. Bisley couldn't come up with *that* degree of accuracy. A moving target. The first task is to *stop* it moving. A body-shot. The hip area. Second shot to remove the guard. Put *him* out of action.'

'Kill him?'

'If he's unlucky. But I'm not being paid to kill the *guard*. As long as he's too preoccupied to radio for additional assistance or to throw himself on top of the man he's there to protect. Then third shot to make sure. A stationary target this time. Unless he's Superman, the shock will have knocked him out. *And* a dum-dum. Probably overkill – he might be beyond repair after the first shot – but no matter.'

'Why a bolt-action?' asked Pollard. 'Why not an automatic reload, to save time?'

'Reloaders sometimes jam.' I'd no objection to giving reasons. Pollard, I knew, had a morbid interest. As with all artists, I drew mild pleasure from explaining some of the finer points. 'The less that *can* go wrong, the less that *will* go wrong. A misfire from a bolt-action means the bullet's at fault. Frisch will check the bullets. Three times to work the bolt. Say, five seconds from the first shot. Double that – make it ten seconds, to allow for any hitch. If an automatic reloader jams, it takes longer than ten seconds to clear the breech.'

'So easy,' breathed Pollard.

'It *is* easy.' I allowed myself a quick, unaccustomed smile. 'When you know how, everything's easy. That's what they pay for, Pollard. Expertise . . . and certainty.'

TWO

Without wishing to claim entry in *The Guinness Book of Records*, I think I have some basis for the belief that I was the youngest person to kill a grown man deliberately. In this country, that is, and in contemporary times. What happens outside the United Kingdom does not concern me; the

Continentals are an excitable crowd, and capable of anything; the Americans have gun laws geared to encourage assassination and mayhem from the toddler stage; beyond the Berlin wall and south of the Panama Canal could be on the dark side of the moon for all I care. Equally, what happened in pre-Edwardian days leaves me unmoved. The skin of civilisation was still very thin at the time.

But in 1955 the murder of a gamekeeper by a fifteen-year-old was . . . unusual?

Pollard and I were fellow-pupils at this ridiculous private school. Mother insisted it was a 'public' school. She always referred to it as if it was some sort of Lake District Eton or Harrow. It wasn't. It was in the Lake District . . . just! On the other hand, I doubt whether any of the official Lake District quangos would have agreed. There is a limit to how many rural districts can lay true claim to being a part of one of England's most famous beauty-spots. On the other hand, 'situated within the glorious splendour of Lakeland' was a selling-point. About the only possible selling-point the school could lay claim to. It therefore stretched things a little. It did no harm. University places were not on offer to people able to name the approximate whereabouts of Windermere, Derwent Water and Coniston Water.

From the point of view of weather, if we weren't actually *in* the Lake District, we were remarkably *like* the Lake District. I recall it rained a lot. Almost daily, and whatever the season. The roof leaked in at least a dozen places; not great fluvial leaks, demanding immediate repair but, rather, insignificant, dank leaks which stained the ceilings but allowed those responsible to place the repairing of the roof well down any list of priorities.

The walls were also damp. Again, *always*. Knowing what I know now, I doubt whether the builders had included a damp-course. I doubt whether they'd even *heard* of damp-courses.

It was a most miserable place. Cold as an underground cavern and, no doubt, run on the principle that acute discomfort encouraged academic endeavour.

As a principle, it was a non-starter, but nobody seemed to mind. I think the masters kept themselves one chapter ahead of the pupils in the textbooks covering whatever subject was being taught. Certain it is that the end-product of any moderately well-run grammar school was an Einstein by comparison with what *that* school turned out.

We were neither happy nor unhappy. Physical discomfort has little relationship with genuine joy or misery. I've known tramps of good cheer, and rich men burdened by discontent. And the pupils of that school had had all real emotion squeezed from them long before they became its pupils.

In effect, the school was a high-priced lumber room in which to dump incommodious offsprings.

Not that we minded too much. Parental love was at a premium, and I can't remember anybody being consciously homesick. Other than coughs and snivels, I can't remember any boy being ill, despite the everlasting rain and the perpetual dampness. Illness was actively discouraged, in that the sick-bay was, if anything, even more austere than the cold and uncomfortable dormitories.

Other than when we were being lectured at by academic numbskulls, our time was our own. Beyond the crumbling walls of the school grounds, things were happening. Churchill had been driven into retirement by an illness he'd denied for years, and Eden had taken his place as Prime Minister. Some Russian called Bulganin had succeeded another Russian called Malenkov as the leader of the Kremlin. One of the masters – a fool with far too much compassion ever to instil discipline in a class of self-opinionated hooligans – told us, with tears in his eyes, that somebody called Schweitzer had been appointed honorary member of the Order of Merit. As if *we* cared. We'd never heard of the man, and hadn't the foggiest notion of what was meant by the Order of Merit.

Pollard and I were far more interested in robbing birds' nests of their eggs.

Why birds' eggs, I wonder?

We'd no real interest in the things. We weren't 'collecting'

11

in the true sense of the word. We could identify no more than half a dozen or so. I think it was one of those phases all bored schoolboys have to go through on their way to adolescence. We robbed every nest we could find, bare. We vandalised trees and bushes to reach our quarry.

Our favourite hunting-ground was the estate adjoining the school grounds.

It was a large estate, owned by Sir Somebody-or-other, who was on the school board of governors. Much of the woodland had been let run to seed and there was bird-life galore. Each evening, that summer and early autumn, Pollard and I would climb the wall separating the school from the estate, and we rarely returned without pockets bulging with eggs.

The gamekeeper spotted us a couple of times, and gave chase, but he was a great, lumbering lout and, each time, we gave him the slip.

Then, more by good luck on his part than by cunning, he caught us up a tree. I think it was an elm. Pollard was higher than I – he'd scrambled into the topmost foliage – and he was handing down eggs which I, in turn, was storing in Pollard's cap.

'Right. I've got you young buggers now.'

The gamekeeper was at the base of the tree, and had us cornered. He didn't sound particularly angry. He was far too pleased with himself to be angry.

'Come on, let's have you down. Let's know who you are.'

I think neither Pollard nor I spoke a word. In those days, young teenagers tended to be less verbal than today. We'd been caught. We were (I suppose) stealing. We were certainly trespassing. What was there to say?

I reached the ground first. I bent to place the capful of eggs carefully on the turf – for some ridiculous reason, it seemed important that I shouldn't break any – and, as I bent, the gamekeeper swung his walking-stick and brought it hard across my backside.

That was when the fury hit me. It was a fury I'd never known before. It was almost *physical*. Almost *painful*. I can

12

liken it to a white-hot needle touching some particularly sensitive part of my brain . . . just for one shaved second.

I screamed, 'You sod!' then stepped back as he swung the walking-stick a second time.

Then the fury was gone. In its place was a cold calculation. In retrospect, for a youngster of fifteen – especially for a not very well-educated youngster of fifteen – it was a remarkable degree of self-control.

By this time, Pollard had reached the base of the tree and, unlike myself, he showed every sign of panic. It was panic which made him dive for the broken branch, then swipe the gamekeeper alongside the head. Equally, it was panic which forced the 'Oh, God!' from his lips when he realised what he'd done.

It stunned the man. Knocked him to the ground and, for the moment, knocked him unconscious.

I shouted: 'Run for it.'

Pollard didn't move. He stood there, aghast at what he'd done. Gaping at the sprawling gamekeeper.

'Come on!' I grabbed his arm and jerked him out of his stupor. 'Come on, before he comes round.'

We ran. We ran perhaps fifty yards, and until the trees hid us from the gamekeeper, and hid the gamekeeper from us. Then I stopped and pulled Pollard to a halt.

'Your cap,' I said. I tried to put false concern into the words. 'It has your name inside.'

'What can we . . . ?'

'You run ahead. Get back into the grounds. I'll go back and get it, while he's still groggy.'

Pollard was away, almost before I'd finished speaking. The funk was still controlling his actions and his reasoning.

Not so me.

I hurried back. Quickly, but quietly. The gamekeeper was pushing himself slowly to his feet. Still on his hands and knees, and still groggy. The branch was where Pollard had dropped it. A little more than three inches thick at its heavy end and about four foot long. I picked it up and stepped towards the gamekeeper and, as he raised his head to look at

13

me, I could see in his eyes that he guessed what was going to happen.

The first blow knocked him unconscious again. Thereafter it was a simple matter of pulping his skull. There was no frenzy. Instinct demanded that the matter be concluded deliberately and without room for doubt.

No frenzy, therefore. No hatred. Merely a determination not to be carpeted by the headmaster for a minor offence of trespass.

I placed the eggs carefully into the pocket of my blazer, smeared some of the blood from the gamekeeper on to the cloth of Pollard's cap, then left the scene. On my way to the edge of the wood I threw the filched eggs as high and as far as possible. One at a time. They would fall and smash. There would be no link between the broken eggs and the dead gamekeeper.

Pollard was waiting at the boundary wall.

'Is he . . . ?' he began.

'He was still unconscious.'

'Oh!'

'I got rid of the eggs. Some of the blood splashed on to your cap.'

'I can't see how it. . . .'

'Look.' I held out the cap for him to see.

'Oh, my God!'

'Let's get back over the wall. You cut off to the common room. Act normally.' I stared at him and, for the first time, saw the deep-rooted terror touch the back of his eyes. '*Act normally*,' I repeated . . . and knew he would.

'The – my cap?'

'I'll call in at the boiler house, and throw it into the furnace. Then I'll join you in the common room.'

That should have been the end of it, but it wasn't. We were lucky.

Ned, one of the local poachers, was out that same evening. He was stopped by a passing constable as he left the woods, and before the gamekeeper's corpse was found. As I recall

14

(and the newspapers of the district were, of course, full of it) Ned had a couple of wood-pigeons and a pheasant with him. Dead, of course. He'd used his catapult. Ned was of the old school. He trapped and he snared. He believed in silence. That catapult of his . . . it was said he could knock a perching pheasant or wood-pigeon from its branch at up to twenty yards.

He was known to the police, and the hatred and counter-hatred between himself and the gamekeeper was no secret.

Ned was still in custody on a poaching charge when they found the gamekeeper. And Ned had no alibi. He'd been in the woods. The bad blood was there. More than once, in his cups, Ned had voiced threats against the gamekeeper.

When they hanged him, before the year was out, he left a widow and three children.

Pollard and I argued it out, behind the cricket pavilion, while Ned was waiting his turn in the hanging-shed. It was raining at the time. Pouring down, with a dark grey sky which seemed to promise rain for ever more. The belted macs we wore were of little use. They were described as 'shower-proof', and this was no shower, nor had been for the last hour. I recall the cold wetness which touched my shoulders, through my clothes, and the sight of Pollard's streaming face as the downpour mingled with his tears.

'We've *got* to,' he pleaded.

'No, we haven't.' I was quite calm. He was frightened of me, and my immediate task was to make him even more frightened of me.

'But he didn't do it.'

'He's a scoundrel. He's a drunkard. I expect he beats his wife.'

'What's that to do with it?'

'He'll be no loss. She'll be better without him.'

'But he didn't *do* it.'

'You've left things too late, Pollard.'

'You said. . . .'

15

'The police say he did it. The court say he did it. In a few days' time the hangman will say he did it. After that, it doesn't matter.'

'You – you've – all along you've said they *couldn't* find him guilty. They *couldn't* hang him. That – that. . . .'

'We all make mistakes,' I smiled.

'But, look, we *can't*. I mean *we* —'

'You,' I interrupted. 'Don't drag me into it, Pollard. You hit him. I didn't.'

'I didn't think I'd hit him as hard as that. I didn't think I'd *killed* him.'

'As I say, we all make mistakes.'

His sobbing grew worse. His shoulders shook, his face creased into ugly heartbreak and, for a moment, I thought he might faint.

'Listen,' I said. But he didn't and, because I expected hysteria at any moment, I slapped him hard across one cheek, then snapped, 'Listen, Pollard! Listen, before you make a complete ass of yourself.'

He looked into my face, then wiped the back of a hand across his mouth. He was still snivelling, but he was also listening. He was quite terrified.

The rain came down, and I had to speak a little louder than usual, to counter the soft drumming on the tin roof of the pavilion. It didn't matter. Nobody else was outdoors, and I wanted him to hear, and understand, every word.

'Pollard, the police wouldn't believe you. You've no proof. If you went to the police and told them you'd killed him – that they'd got the wrong man – *they wouldn't believe you*. They'd want some sort of proof – and you haven't any – and even *then* they wouldn't believe you.

'And, Pollard, understand this – I want no part of it. I'd deny being there. I'd deny even knowing about it. So they'd just *never* believe you.

'The police are never wrong, Pollard. Never! And they're not going to let a schoolboy show the world that they *can* be wrong. The police. The courts. Everybody. They'll think you're mad. Probably think it's a jape of some kind. Some sort of a schoolboy joke. Whatever they think, they'll *never* believe you.

'Leave it, Pollard. Leave things as they are. You didn't *mean* to kill him. And now you can't do anything about it. Let the man they think killed him die. Hanging – it's a quick death, or so they tell us. He's a nothing. He's scum. Unimportant. We're more important than him. *You're* more important. Don't let it worry you. Forget it. Have your cry, if you must – then, forget it. Who cares? Who *really* cares?'

Young as I was, I knew Pollard. It wasn't his conscience that was troubling him. Not only his conscience ... not even *mainly* his conscience. He had the fear of every coward. The same fear which had made him attack the gamekeeper in the first place. The fear that, until our conversation behind the cricket pavilion, had urged him to walk into the nearest police station and confess.

The lesser of two evils. *That* was the way he looked at things. To give himself up and, perhaps, be given nominal punishment, because he was 'man enough' to save an innocent? Or to risk being found out, at a later date, and then *really* be punished?

In his own stupid mind, he'd weighed one probability against the other and, because he was a weak person, he'd chosen the soft option. Like the skipper of a vessel caught in a sudden storm. To run for shelter or to battle the weather?

My talk had convinced him that the storm wasn't even in his path. He didn't care about the poacher. The only person *he* cared about was Pollard.

I've no doubt that, after our talk, he slept more soundly.

The day of the hanging came, and went. Pollard didn't even notice it – or, if he did, he made no mention – and I saw no reason to remind him. The boring routine of school life continued. The killing of a gamekeeper and the execution of a poacher did nothing to slow the spin of the earth.

It was about a fortnight later when I dropped the bombshell. I did it quietly. Calmly. But very directly. I'd already worked it out. To approach the subject obliquely

17

would have been a waste of time. It had to be done immediately, but at the right time.

It was mid-morning, one Sunday. Pollard and I had cut church. It was a period when Pollard and I had decided we were 'unbelievers'. Nobody cared *what* we believed ... or whether we believed *anything*. The Holy Joe responsible for our spiritual welfare wasn't a man given to going out of his way to round up lost sheep. It wasn't raining (which itself was a miracle) and we'd wandered into the grounds and well away from the school buildings.

We were talking cricket and, if I remember correctly, Surrey had won the county championship for the fourth time in a row. As supporters of northern counties we were disgruntled and, I suspect, were making all the usual schoolboy excuses.

In a gap in the conversation I said: 'By the way, I didn't burn your cap.'

'Which cap?'

I think (because the topic had been cricket) he thought I meant a *cricket* cap.

'The one you were wearing when you murdered the gamekeeper.'

'Oh!'

'The one with blood on it. Blood from the gamekeeper's head.'

'You said you'd burn it.'

'Yes.' I nodded.

'You *promised* to burn it.'

'I didn't keep my promise.'

'You're a right little ratbag.' His voice was quite hoarse with passion. 'You'd better let *me* have the cap, then *I* can —'

'Oh, no, Pollard,' I smiled. 'That wouldn't be a very sensible thing to do.'

'Look! If they get hold of that cap. . . .'

'"They"? You mean the police?'

His eyes widened. A realisation was dawning.

I said: 'There's blood on your cap, Pollard. The

gamekeeper's blood. The same blood that's on the branch you hit him with. Same group. Same *blood*.

'Now, if *I* go to the police, and take them the cap – that's all they'll need. You'll be the murderer, Pollard. More than the murderer. You'll be the chap who kept quiet while an innocent man was hanged. Two killings, not one. You're in the soup, my son. We'd better stay friends, Pollard. Very *good* friends.'

He nodded. He was licked.

I don't think he trusted himself to speak.

THREE

As the years passed, I gave less and less thought to the gamekeeper. I almost forgot the unfortunate poacher. But, as the years brought a little philosophy, I began to examine myself more closely.

I think I'd always known I was 'different'. Not like other boys. Not like other youths. My enthusiasms were less extreme. What depressions I had were less severe. My plateau of life was just that – a plateau. Except on very rare occasions, I could control my emotions. What emotions I seemed to possess.

I recall. . . .

I was past eighteen – fast approaching my nineteenth birthday – when mother insisted I accompany her to the funeral of her brother. He'd been, I suppose, a good man. What the world judged as a good man. He'd certainly treated me well enough. His presents, at Christmas and on my birthdays – and at other times – had always been carefully chosen, and very acceptable. He'd given me my first ballpoint pen. I remember that quite vividly. Ballpoints weren't common in those days and, unless you bought an expensive one, it either didn't work properly or it leaked like the very devil. Mine worked beautifully, and must have cost a pretty penny.

Looking back, I think he must have thought of me as a surrogate son. He'd never married, and perhaps what paternal instincts he had he channelled in my direction. At school, he'd always sent a weekly letter. Very 'newsy' and, more often than not, with a folded banknote enclosed.

He died before he'd reached the half-century mark. Something to do with his kidneys. Like ballpoint pens, dialysis machines were not as plentiful as they are today.

It was quite a funeral. A real 'send-off', with much sobbing, far too many flowers and a cleric who droned on interminably about the virtues of the corpse when it had been alive.

All around me women (and some men) were weeping. It was either a put-on, or they felt infinitely sad. I felt nothing. Bored . . . if anything. An uncomfortable church. A slow walk behind a wooden container carried shoulder-high. A shoulder-jostling grouping around a hole in the ground, with our feet squelching in slippery mud. It was such a waste of time. Such an accumulation of irrelevancies. The man was dead. Have done with him, forget him, he no longer existed.

On the way back from the grave to the house, Mother said: 'Let it out, dear.'

'Let what out?' I didn't understand.

'The sorrow. Cry, if you want to. We'll all understand.'

'I don't want to cry.'

'If you keep it bottled up like this. . . .'

'Like what?'

'You know. Being a man. Not being weak.'

'I'm not being "weak", Mother. This whole day's been —'

'I know. I know, dear.'

She patted my knee reassuringly, so I didn't finish my remark. The word I *didn't* say was 'inconvenient'. Weeks before, I'd made arrangements to go to a nightclub, and Mother's determination that I attend the funeral hadn't pleased me. I could have been enjoying myself, in a quiet way. I could have been looking forward with some warm anticipation to an evening's drinking. To some sort of floor-show. Perhaps, and if the money would run to it, a pleasant enough night with a moderately accomplished whore.

Instead. . . .

'There's the will,' whispered Mother. 'When we get back to the house, the solicitor will read the will.'

We shared the rear seat of one of the cars. I doubt if the peaked-capped driver heard. I doubt if he was either listening or interested. He was doing his job, and his job was driving one of the cavalcade of cars. What other concern could he have had?

Nevertheless, Mother continued to whisper, as if sharing some important secret.

'He won't have forgotten you, dear.'

I grunted.

'You were *always* his favourite nephew.'

He left me £30,000, which in those days was a small fortune. Various other members of the family, and some of his friends, received odd sticks of furniture ... specifically mentioned. The rest of the money (it amounted to almost another £20,000) he bequeathed to various servants, friends and a whole list of charities ... after having given instructions to pay off all debts.

He also left me the house, and contents not specifically mentioned.

It was quite a windfall.

The solicitor raised token objection when I demanded the keys to the house before he left. But the the-king-is-dead-long-live-the-king brand of argument silenced all opposition and, before *I* left, arrangements had been made for whatever bits and pieces other people could lay claim to to be collected and the house was locked tight against any would-be this-should-be-mine claimant.

Later I was told that various members of the family were somewhat miffed by my attitude. I didn't notice it. Indeed,

21

had I bothered to notice, it wouldn't have mattered. *My* charity is a very homely affair, and always has been.

It took me less than a week to say a relieved goodbye to the snooty department store where I'd been paid near-starvation wages to feed prospective customers verbal bilge about the latest trend in art, to dispose of the few sticks of tat with which I furnished a bedsit and to move into what seemed like a scaled-down replica of Buckingham Palace.

In honesty, it was a huge house. Ten bedrooms, three bathrooms, with attics and ground floor to match. The grounds topped the two-acre mark, with a six-foot-high wall surrounding them. Lawns, flower-beds, a great vegetable-garden, *two* greenhouses and a multi-stalled stable which had been turned into a garden-cum-potting shed. My uncle, it seemed, had been somewhat gaga about all things 'outdoors'.

I wasn't.

I immediately sacked the gardener and his assistant and two of the 'cleaning ladies'. For appearances' sake, I kept on a motherly biddy, who daily called in to stir the dust around. Each morning, I burned my own toast and brewed my own tea. Other than that, I ate out.

It took me more than a month fully to appreciate exactly *what* I'd inherited.

There was a study. I liked that study. It seemed to be the very heart of the house – and probably had been. Glass-fronted shelves lined whole walls, and the books were not there for show. Hemingway, Steinbeck and Caldwell rubbed covers with Priestley, le Carré and Buchan. Shaw's *Prefaces* was there, as was Cobbett's *Rural Rides*. It wasn't a 'collector's' library. It was a *reader's* library. Literally, thousands of books, every one a recognised bestseller, written by a top-class author.

I liked that library. I like it still. I've added to it, over the years – and I wouldn't insult it by including a paperback on its shelves.

One part of the library – one whole corner – was devoted to guns and shooting. Field sport, mainly. Books like Eric

22

Parker's *Shooting Days* and *Game Pie*. But, also, volumes on marksmanship and ballistics, generally and specifically, Cleveland's *Hints to Riflemen* and Mann's *The Bullet's Flight*. There were also ten issues of *Gun Digest*, each carefully rebound in a hardback cover. Since first seeing that collection of near-textbooks, I've added volumes by Ian Hogg and his peers.

I found guns, too. Later, when I'd the deeds of the property – when the solicitor reluctantly dug them from his strongroom and posted them on to me – I found on them what had originally been some sort of butler's pantry. Some sort of spare room in what had originally been the servants' quarters. This uncle of mine had turned it into a gun-room. Racks, shelves, everything. With a barred window, steel lining to the door and two first-class Chubb locks. He knew all about guns. Including how to keep them safe from the wrong hands.

A dozen shotguns were in there. Double-barrel, single-barrel. Magnum, twelve-bore, four-ten, hammerless, repeaters. Churchill, Winchester, Darne, Krieghoff. There was a custom rifle – a Fashingbauer. There was a Smith & Wesson match automatic. There was even a Remington slide-action big-game rifle. Plus, of course, ammunition in plenty for all of them.

I found authority for all those needing authority. The firearms certificates and gun licences were locked away in a tiny wall-safe, inside the safety of the gun-room itself.

Inside that safe I also found a 7.65 mm Luger and a .32 Browning automatic, with ammunition for both. These were *not* authorised.

'Your uncle was a real gun buff.' The local uniformed police sergeant made the observation, with that half-smile peculiar to policemen who haven't yet decided whether or not you're to be trusted. He added: 'He was a nice chap. Never gave us a minute's trouble.'

'Men who understand guns don't,' I fenced.

'That's true enough.'

He'd called to check the guns and documentation. He'd

already counted the weapons and ammunition. (But *not* the Luger and the Browning, or their ammunition. That little lot had been removed from the safe and tucked away in a secure hiding-place.) He was now mulling his way through the certificates and licences.

'He used the Remington in the Highlands, I'm told.'

'Deer-stalking,' I murmured.

I'd briefed myself as much as possible about this uncle of mine. Fortunately, and like all enthusiasts, he'd 'talked shop' to as many people as he could find who were prepared to listen.

I forestalled the next possible question by saying: 'He usually took the Fashingbauer along for long shots.'

'I've never stalked deer,' said the sergeant. 'I've never even tasted venison, come to that.'

'A very dry meat,' I assured him. 'Slightly overrated. That's a personal opinion. Red-deer venison has a very "gamey" flavour.'

'You went with him?'

'As often as possible,' I lied.

We were in the study cum library. We occupied twin wing-back armchairs. It was, it seemed, only a semi-official call, therefore we both sipped good whisky as we talked.

'You'll be wanting to keep the guns, then?'

'If I can get authorisation. It's *my* sport, too.'

'A lot of shotguns,' observed the sergeant.

'He collected them,' I smiled. 'Like a lot of things, their value increases with age. As long as they're kept in good condition, of course.'

'Of course.' He tasted the whisky. 'There's this Smith & Wesson.'

'The match automatic. He was a very good shot. He did a lot of competition shooting, you know.'

'I'm told. . . . And you?'

'Not as good as he was.'

'No. I mean, will you be wanting it for target shooting?'

'If possible.'

We were like dogs, meeting each other for the first time.

Ready to live and let live, but willing to fight. Tiptoeing around each other, each sniffing at the other's anus ... for what?

The truth is, at that time I wasn't too interested in guns. Any guns. Other than at fairgrounds, I'd never handled one. I'd certainly never fired a handgun. But the guns were *mine* – they'd been left to me by this slightly eccentric uncle – and I wasn't going to part with them for the sake of telling a few lies to some tinpot police sergeant. I meant to keep them. Maybe I'd learn to use them – the shotguns, at any rate. On the other hand, if any 'gun nut' (somebody like my uncle) came along and made a handsome offer ... why not? They were mine, and I'd sell them, use them or merely keep them, as I saw fit.

Eventually, the sergeant said: 'You'll need to reapply for certification, of course.'

'Naturally.'

'You should get new certificates, in your name.'

'I hope so.'

He tipped what was left of his whisky down his throat, picked his helmet from the carpet alongside the chair and stood up.

'I'll send the application form round for you to sign.'

'Good.'

'The gun licences. You take them out at a post office.'

'Yes. I know.'

'Thanks for your time, sir. I hope you'll be happy here.'

The house was, of course, far too big. The grounds were too big. Nevertheless, I rather liked the place. It had what estate agents call 'potential'.

I shopped around, and found an architect who seemed to know what he was talking about. One whose ultimate aim was a little beyond bingo halls and supermarkets. He brought his tape-measure and clipboard along and, after spending all morning measuring, sketching and jotting down figures, we both drove to a nearby inn for lunch, booze and some sort of decision.

25

I recall the meal. It was roast duckling, with black cherries, plus all the trimmings. It was the sort of place where businessmen make themselves fat and shiny, on the firm's account. It served expensive lunches – often more substantial than dinners – in a side-restaurant, with the tables far enough apart to ensure privacy of conversation. That we ate there is a measure of the affluent life-style into which I had moved since the timely death of this uncle of mine.

We'd reached the coffee stage – Jamaican coffee, which is black coffee with Tia Maria – before we got down to business.

'Flats,' he said with a smile.

I'd already thought of flats, but I waited.

'Those old stables,' he continued. 'Clean them up, put down a wooden floor, give them a couple of really large picture windows – double-glazed, of course – they'd make a perfect studio.'

'Let's start with the flats,' I suggested. 'How many?'

'At a pinch – six: five, and one for yourself. Assuming you want to live there.'

'I'm going to live there. Let's not "pinch" things.'

'Luxury flats?'

I nodded.

'The attics would make one,' he said carefully. 'Then your own in the middle, with one on each side. It would cut down your own external walls. Shield you from the weather.'

'Cosy.' I rather liked the idea. 'What about privacy?'

'No problem. Each with its own door. Three maisonettes, with a flat above.'

'I live in the middle maisonette?'

He nodded.

'I rather like the idea,' I repeated. 'But you haven't answered my question about privacy. Your own front door doesn't ensure *full* privacy.'

'Extra internal walls. A double floor in the attic, if necessary. Soundproof filling. As much absolute privacy as you're prepared to pay for.'

'Money talks,' I said gently.

'Money.' He chuckled quietly. 'Money doesn't just talk. It sings. With enough money, you can produce your own version of *Così fan tutte* ... on coloured ice, if that's what you want.'

We finished the coffee while I thought things over.

'How long?' I asked eventually.

'Not how *much*?' He raised a quizzical eyebrow.

'Let's assume I can afford what I'm asking for, shall we?'

'Assumption accepted.'

'The stables into this studio thing you've mentioned. With some sort of living-quarters?'

'Of a sort.'

'I live in the house until *that's* finished. Then I move into the studio – what was once the stables – until I can move back into the centre maisonette. By which time the full conversion's almost finished. How long?'

'Quite a decision to make over one cup of coffee.'

'Let's have a second cup.' I raised a hand, and a waiter arrived. Two more helpings of Jamaican coffee were placed on the table. 'I presume I can let the other two maisonettes, and the flat?'

'Of course. *And* the studio.'

'And the studio ... if I want to. Luxury maisonettes. A luxury flat. Everything soundproof. Absolute privacy. The rents will be correspondingly high.'

'The rents', he assured me cheerfully, 'can be positively outrageous. With what I have in mind – with what you seem to want – they'll be queuing up before the paint's dry.'

'Therefore' – I stirred the coffee slowly – 'how long?'

He rubbed his jaw meditatively as he answered.

'I'll need to draw up the plans, get your approval, then submit them to the local authority. I can't see *them* raising any objections. Then the builder. Not just any builder. . . . I know a couple of firms capable of this sort of work. Then the subcontractors. It's wise to check *them* out, too. Quotations. Not estimates. They can always play footsie with an estimate. A quotation pins them down ... especially with a time clause and a quality clause.'

'I want personal supervision,' I said.

'Me?' He looked surprised.

'Every day . . . and more than a quick glance.'

'I – er – I don't come cheap. Not on *that* basis.'

'They could con me.'

'They wouldn't. Not the firms *I* have in mind.'

'I'd feel happier.'

He moved his shoulders.

'How long?' I asked, again.

'Say – what? – a year.'

'Say six months . . . finished and done with.'

'For God's sake!'

'My friend' – I stopped stirring the coffee and placed the spoon carefully on to the tiny saucer – 'let's say I want *Così fan tutte* . . . on coloured ice.'

FOUR

The £30,000 (even in 1959/60) didn't make me a millionaire. If you get the gist of what I mean. But it gave me leeway, and I'd always had the yen to live the life of a gentleman of leisure. I also had a very firm backstop.

A certain amount of family history is called for.

I never knew my father. Never met him. He was an officer (and, I hope, a gentleman) in the British Army. A 'regular'. Which meant he'd landed on French soil before the end of September 1939. Within a month he was dead. He died 'in action' – of a sort! The action was in a French bordello, and with a knife in his guts. I doubt if he felt much. From what I gather, he was blind drunk at the time. That was *his* contribution towards saving democracy from the jackboot!

I was born in 1940, the only child of a comparatively rich

war widow. Father had had money, he'd left it to his wife, and she, in turn, had added to it by marrying an already-rich entrepreneur, wise enough to keep well clear of the sharp end of the war and, instead, to invest in the manufacture of various types of hydraulic jack. The services rather liked these hydraulic jacks. Consequently, my stepfather moved from being rich to being *very* rich.

Despite his busting a gut for a knighthood (which he never got) I approved of the life-style of my stepfather. He was decent enough to house his two mistresses in Switzerland, appeared only occasionally in the William Hickey column and smiled benevolently as he honoured any cheque my mother presented to him to sign.

A very civilised man . . . although I rarely met him face to face.

You will appreciate, then, that although I had never taken previous advantage of the fact I had quite a milk cow at my disposal. I could twist my mother round my little finger, and my mother had my stepfather firmly by the balls.

That £30,000 was really only glorified small change!

Mother was delighted. She called it 'going into the property market'.

'It's high time you branched out, dear. Working in a *shop*.'

'It was rather more than a "shop".'

'You were *selling* things.'

'Hydraulic jacks, for example?' I teased.

'Don't mock your father, dear. He's a good man. He has his faults – like all men, he's very *carnal* – but, basically, he's a good man.'

'He's not my father.'

'You know what I mean. He certainly looks upon you as his *son*.'

'I may want a certain amount of financial backing,' I said tentatively. 'To cover the cost of conversion, and until the rents start coming in.'

'Of course you will.'

'Quite a lot, I think. To prime the pump . . . as it were.'

29

'You see' – she gave one of those high-pitched giggles which made her sound faintly idiotic – 'you're learning the jargon already.'

'Mother, it's likely to be —'

'Let me know how much, dear. I'll have words with your father.'

I left it at that, and let her get on with what she was doing. What she was doing – and what I was supposedly helping her to do – was watching a fashion show. I was bored rigid with the thing, but it was a pastime she enjoyed, and I'd gone along knowing that, at a time like this, she'd be in a receptive mood.

I'd been right, and I settled back to pay the price. A parade of shapeless females, with outrageous 'creations' draped across their skinny shoulders.

Later, in the taxi, Mother frowned and said: 'Nothing really "me" there. Don't you agree?'

'Not unless you've developed the knack of sneering with your hips.'

'Dear, that's not a nice thing to say. Those poor girls work very hard.'

'You know about these things,' I sighed.

'I know what.' She suddenly perked up, leaned forward and gave a new destination to the driver. 'We'll call in and see this new exhibition of cubism.'

'I'm rather busy, Mother,' I protested.

'Busy?'

It was, I agree, a lame excuse, and I thought I detected a slight warning tone in the question. She was a lonely woman and, in her own way, she doted on me. Equally, she must have known she had me over something of a fiscal barrel. I couldn't really blame her for committing a form of minor blackmail.

I smiled, shrugged and murmured: 'Perhaps not *too* busy.'

Cubism. Even today I know little about art, but I knew even less in those days.

Cézanne is, supposedly, the parent – perhaps it would be

30

more correct to call him the *grand*parent – of the style. Picasso is the true parent. The object was (as I understand it) to move away from mere visual effects. To add a certain *sense* to form and colour. I think it was never meant to be other than two-dimensional. Therefore, that late afternoon, I stared at the pictures with open scorn. Colour against colour – shape against shape – made no sense. Had no meaning.

Constable I could understand. Vincent Van Gogh I could tolerate. Rembrandt I could take or leave alone. But this lot!

'Mother . . . what the hell is it supposed to *mean*?'

'Look, dear, you're not supposed to look at these paintings with your *eyes*.'

'That, I'm quite prepared to believe.'

'Not *only* your eyes. With your inner feelings, too.'

'That's cultural crap.'

'No, dear. If you stand a little farther away from them.'

'Two miles . . . thereabouts. That would be *my* distance.'

'Gaze at them, dear. Gaze *into* them.'

'Oh, for God's sake! A three-year-old could make a more understandable mess on canvas.'

A voice said, 'A very talented three-year-old,' and I almost recognised the voice. It added, 'A very wealthy three-year-old,' and, as I turned, I knew I'd be facing Pollard.

We hadn't seen each other since leaving school but, other than fattening out a little and sporting a hair-style which I thought to be on the long side, he hadn't changed. The same timid look about the eyes. The same loose-lipped mouth. The same weakness about the chin.

We grinned at each other and shook hands. I noticed that his grip started firmly enough, then suddenly grew limp.

Mother looked first at Pollard, then at me, then said: 'Do you two know each other?'

'From school,' I explained.

'Good. Good. How nice.' Mother beamed at Pollard, patted his arm, then said: 'Take this son of mine around the pictures, dear. Try to make him less of a Philistine.'

31

She disappeared into the tiny crowd.

'Your mother?' smiled Pollard.

'She lives in her own select world of silks and satins.'

'I've – er – I've never met her before.'

'No.'

'It wasn't that sort of a school, was it?' His smile carried a certain amount of melancholy. 'Parents weren't encouraged to visit.'

'They paid to have us swept under the carpet.' I moved my head. 'This garbage? Don't tell me you profess to understand it.'

'Of course . . . and it's *not* garbage.'

'No?' I mocked.

Thereafter I was gently escorted from picture to picture. Expressions like 'analytical cubism', 'high cubism' and 'synthetic cubism' were used to describe paintings which, to me, meant nothing.

'It all moves to, and from, Orphic cubism,' he explained.

'Great God! You mean to say it *developed*? That something even *worse* came before this crap?'

'It's still developing.' He shook his head wearily. You're still a complete Philistine.'

'I prefer a blank wall,' I admitted.

'Let's have coffee,' he suggested.

'Where?'

'Here . . . in my office.'

'*Your* office?'

'I'm – er – junior partner in this gallery.' He gave a quick, and what seemed to be a slightly shamefaced, smile. 'When we left school. I mean, what *good* were we? What had we been *trained* for?'

'Not a great deal.'

We were moving to a corner of the main hall, and towards a door marked 'Private'.

'I found I had a flair,' continued Pollard. 'I had a natural knack. I could tell the genuine from the counterfeit.'

'Cubism?' I couldn't keep the hint of mockery from the question.

32

'Cubism. Impressionism. Most forms of abstract art. It *can* be beautiful. Controversial.' He opened the door, then followed me into the tiny but pleasant office. As he closed the door, he continued: 'It's not a camera-substitute. That's the basic mistake most people make. It's *not* a camera-substitute . . . and doesn't pretend to be.' He waved me to a very modern, but remarkably comfortable, swivel chair while he stepped across the office and flicked the switch of an electric coffee-percolator. 'The good artists of today – the *good* ones – they paint what they feel, rather than what they see. An obvious example. The female body. It's been reproduced on canvas thousands of times. Legs, breasts, buttocks, belly, thighs . . . everybody *knows*. But what sort of emotions do those things arouse? What sort of thoughts?'

'Dirty?' I suggested.

'All right. Lascivious thoughts.' Damn the man, he was taking me seriously. Too seriously. 'But copulation's been painted scores of times. The so-called "dirty postcards". They're nothing – nothing! – compared with paintings tucked away in private collections. Some of them by great artists. Farouk, when *he* died – God, he'd the greatest collection in the world.'

'Big deal! Dirty pictures,' I grinned. 'Farouk was known for it.'

'Farouk was a primitive.'

'Aren't we all, at heart?'

'No. Try to understand. Damn it, man, you're missing out on one of life's great joys.' He opened a wall cupboard and lifted down two cups and a bowl of brown sugar. 'Forget Farouk. Think about – what? – a horse. Think about a horse. A horse running, a horse jumping, a horse rearing up on its hind legs. Not just the *look* of it. More than that. The emotion it sparks off. The joy, the admiration, the thrill. You don't just *see* a thing . . . period. The sight evokes a mental response.'

'And?'

'That's what the cubist, the impressionist, a whole school of modern artists is trying to capture. The old masters could draw the horse. *They* want to communicate the emotional *response* to the horse.' He began to pour coffee into the teacups. 'You look at one of their abstract paintings. Study it. Touch it with your mind. Then suddenly it happens. You have the same emotion as if you were seeing a horse. Trotting, racing, jumping. That's what you "see" in your mind's eye.'

'Slightly subliminal . . . wouldn't you say?'

'Black or white?'

'Black, please.'

'That's *exactly* what it is. Subliminal.' He carried the cups, the sugar and spoon to a table-desk, then joined me in another swivel chair. 'To see something far more than you *think* you're seeing. To study the painting till you *realise* that – the title sometimes gives a clue – then it *means* something.'

It was all mildly boring, but the coffee was good. By this time, too, Mother would have found some other outlet with which to counter her dreary life, therefore I stayed and chatted.

About thirty minutes later, I said: 'I always thought you lived round Oxford way, somewhere.'

'I did.'

'But you've moved up here? The gallery, I presume?'

'More or less. The chap who owned it – who still owns a major share – was being ripped off.'

'By your buddies?'

'By cheapjack fakes.' He wasn't pleased at my continued non-conversion. 'I put him right. It even got to the point where the police began to take an interest.'

'The good old British bobby,' I chuckled.

'Anyway, he offered me a junior partnership. He was getting a bit old. I jumped at the chance . . . of course.'

'Of course.'

'We haven't looked back since.'

'And now you're my neighbour?'

'About ten miles away.'

'The world, as they say, is surprisingly small.'

FIVE

I had no friendship for Pollard. I never have had, nor ever will have. I have known him introduce me to strangers as 'my closest friend' and, at first, the description surprised me. How can a man who uses you quite shamelessly be called a close friend? And, most assuredly, I used him.

But I think that's what he thought, and I let him live with his illusion.

For myself, and after that first reunion, Pollard was merely a man with whom I spent one evening in each week. Usually it was on a Monday. Monday, it seemed, was generally a quiet day at the gallery. We'd meet, early evening, have a quiet dinner somewhere, then go on the town a little. A strip club, perhaps. An occasional skin flick. A gentle booze-up. Whores usually found their way into things. The Swinging Sixties were taking off, and just about anything was permitted.

The year 1960 (in the February) saw me installed in the converted stables. The builders had done a good job. There was a moderately sized bedroom, complete with enough fitted wardrobes, an efficient enough bathroom and a kitchenette equipped to allow one person to rustle up makeshift meals. The main room, however (and as had been planned), was the 'studio'. Roughly, eight yards by six yards, one of the longer walls was almost entirely taken up by a window. Sealed double-glazing, of course. The floor was of thin oak strips, sanded then beeswaxed. There was a Baxi open fire set in the wall opposite the window, with sufficient slim-line night storage heaters to provide background warmth.

A sprinkling of decent rugs, a settee, a couple of decent

chairs, a fair-sized bookcase, a stereo record-player and a couple of well-made side-tables. The result was quite spectacular. A large, light and airy room which was, at the same time, very cosy.

As required, the architect called at the site every day, and it became my habit to invite him into the studio for a drink (sometimes tea, sometimes something stronger) while we discussed the progress of the conversion and, at times, aired ideas about making even more comfortable what was already going to be comfortable.

One day he said: 'The contents of the gun-room? I've made arrangements for the books in the library to be taken from the shelves, packed in polythene and stored in a container, pending the slight alterations and redecorating of the room. But the guns are a different matter.'

'Your place,' I suggested.

'What?'

'You'll have a strongroom. Something of that nature.'

'No.' He shook his head. 'We couldn't accept the responsibility.'

'What, then?'

'There's a retired gunsmith,' he said slowly. 'Frisch. Karl Frisch. We did some work for him a few years ago. Strongroom. Workshop. That sort of thing. He might store them for you.'

'Do you have his number?'

'Sorry. He's ex-directory.'

'Very secret.'

I know we were drinking canned lager at the time. That, combined with this gunsmith's name, brought out the childish humour. I made the remark in a mock-German accent.

The man had the shoulders of an ox, arms as muscular as any weight-lifter, yet his hands and fingers were as elegant as those of a Burmese temple dancer. That was the immediate contradiction when first you met him. Dozens of other contradictions followed as you grew to know him.

36

'Guns', he once said, 'are used to kill men who *use* guns. I therefore encourage their use whenever possible.'

But that remark was made years after our first meeting. When we'd entered what might be called a 'working relationship'. At that first meeting I started by thinking he was an out-and-out crank.

It was the time of year when the crocuses had taken over from the snowdrops. When the daffodils were forcing the first hint of yellow through the green envelopes of their heads. The tattered tag-end of another winter still brought an occasional night frost but, during the day, the sun was gathering its warmth.

Frisch lived in the country. Far enough in the country to need his own generator to provide electricity with which to make his farmhouse home habitable. He was on the telephone but (as I later learned) the link-up had cost him the price of poles and cable for a distance of almost two miles across open moorland. The house, which had once been the heart of an isolated hill farm, was more than two hundred years old. Its thick, tiny-windowed walls had shrugged off more storms than the mind could encompass and, moreover, looked well able to shrug off as many more.

My road-map showed the Pennine Way some few miles to the west, but the Pennine Way takes in some of the wildest countryside in the United Kingdom – and none more wild than this. It was a place of falcons and merlins. Of curlews and plovers. Over the years, I've seen many a V of honking geese heading for some secret destination. And many a fox hugging the shelter of some broken dry-stone wall.

But that first visit. . . .

I stood in the shelter of the stone porch, hammered the heavy doorknocker and waited.

I heard a key turn, then the door opened and the girl said: 'Who is it?'

She wore jeans and a heavy woollen shirt – the sort of shirt lumberjacks are reputed to wear – and her hair was fastened in a loose pigtail. She wore no make-up and, with that complexion, she needed none. She was quite blind. She hadn't even eyes. Where the eyes should have been, the lids were sunken and permanently closed.

At that moment, I estimated her age at sixteen years. Nor was it a whimsical thought. A passing, and unimportant, thought. Some people have a look – and immediate manner – absolutely compatible with a certain age group. They 'represent' perfectly. *She* 'represented'. I was never mawkish but, at that moment, she personified the expression 'sweet sixteen'.

In fact (as I later learned) I was a year out. She was only fifteen. Perhaps the empty eye-sockets were responsible for my miscalculation.

I said: 'I'm afraid you don't know me, miss.'

'No. I've never heard your voice before.'

The simple certainty of that remark was the first hint of her fine-tuned hearing.

I remember, I moved my foot. Just a little. I had no intention of even stepping closer to the threshold. I merely moved my foot slightly . . . and she heard the movement.

'Sheba,' she said gently.

The Irish wolfhound joined her, and stood staring at me. In shoulder-height it reached her waist and, although it made no noise, nor even showed its fangs, its presence was enough.

In as steady a voice as I could command, I said: 'I wish to see Mr Frisch, please.'

'What about?'

'I understand he's a gunsmith.'

'Why do you want to see him?'

'I have some guns. At the moment, they're safely under lock and key. But I'm having alterations done to my property, and it's been suggested Mr Frisch might be able to keep them safe, pending the completion of those alterations.'

'Who told you about us? Who sent you here?'

The questioning went on for a full ten minutes, and I answered every question as fully as possible. I had the impression she was listening to more than the words. She

38

was also listening to the tone. Even the pauses and the hesitations.

Eventually, she gave a slow smile of belief, opened the door wider and stepped aside for me to enter. I followed her, and the dog followed me . . . and I had no doubts about what would happen if I made a wrong move.

There was an uncanny certainty with which she moved between the heavy, old-fashioned pieces which furnished the main room of the farmhouse. Into, and through, the modernised kitchen, then into the extension at the rear. A magnificently equipped workshop.

Frisch turned from the bench as we entered and, for the first time, I saw the man who was to become a vital part of my life.

The eyes and the hands. Those were the first things you noticed. Then the head and the arms. The eyes were those of a master-craftsman. Even of an *artist*. They were clear enough, keen enough, intense enough to see flaws where less perceptive vision might only see perfection. And it was there. It was *obvious*. The watchmaker's eyeglass which was clamped to his forehead seemed superfluous; what those eyes couldn't detect without it would not be visible *with* it. And the hands complemented the eyes. What the eyes could see, the hands could manipulate. Slim-fingered. Elegant. Beautifully manicured. Again, the hands and fingers of an *artist*. The arms I've already mentioned. A blacksmith's arms, sprouting from a blacksmith's shoulders. Arms which were utterly wrong for such hands.

The head was round. Quite spherical and as bald as a billiard ball. (I later learned that Frisch had suffered alopecia in his youth.) The neck was almost nonexistent, and the body was broad and a little square, but without giving the impression of deformity.

'Power' was the word that immediately sprang to mind. But a very concentrated power. A very controlled power. The power of immense energy pared down to a pencil-thin laser beam.

Later in life, I was to meet other men whose charisma

reached out and took you by the throat the moment you saw them . . . but nobody quite as immediate as Karl Frisch.

As the girl introduced me Frisch seemed to strip me mother naked then, for good measure, take the flesh from my bones. I had the feeling that this man knew me – knew me better than I even knew myself – before he spoke a word.

And yet when the girl had told him who I was, and the reason for my visit, his voice was friendly enough. A beautiful voice. Deep. Resonant, and with perfect diction. The voice of a man who might have been trained as an operatic baritone.

'I once met your uncle,' he said, but made no movement to shake hands. 'Years ago, I used to lecture at some of the better-known gun clubs. I met him at one. I even bought a gun from him.'

'Really?'

'A Springfield, fifty-eight-calibre rifle-musket. One used at Seminary Ridge in 1863.'

'Oh?'

'It helped to stop Pickett's Charge.'

'I'm sorry, I don't know much about —'

'About what interested your uncle?' He smiled, and the smile was slightly condescending. 'About what interests me? That is obvious. I'm talking about the American Civil War, my friend. I'm talking about the first authorised use of a rifled firearm. Ten thousand enemy casualties within an hour. What we now call "the rifle" proved itself on that particular day.'

'Very interesting.'

'Don't lie to me.' It wasn't an accusation. It was a simple, politely spoken request. 'Your uncle might have been interested. He *was* interested. You're not.'

'Will you take custody of the guns, pending the completion of the alterations?' I asked.

'Yes.' He nodded.

'I'll pay, of course.'

'Why "of course"?'

'I don't do favours, Mr Frisch. I don't *ask* them.'

40

'As you wish.' He unclipped the watchmaker's eyeglass from his ears and placed it carefully on the workbench. He continued speaking in a slow and very measured voice. 'I met your uncle twice. No ... three times. About the Springfield. That's all. Each time, he mentioned his nephew. You. You were important to him. I think his possessions should be important to *you*.'

'I'm sorry. I don't see what you're getting at.'

'Some men are connoisseurs of food. Some of wine.' I might never have spoken for what difference it made to the flow of his deliberate speech. 'Your uncle was a connoisseur of firearms. More than a mere enthusiast. A connoisseur. I liked him for that. I'm sorry he's dead. You are not very sorry.'

'I'm not very emotional,' I admitted.

'Nevertheless. . . .' The smile came, and went. 'I won't take money. Instead, a favour *for* a favour. A fair exchange. Four weeks from today, bring the guns. A standard target, at twenty yards. Whichever of his rifles or handguns you wish. One bull, in five shots. Plus the correct answer to one of three questions. Questions he would have thought ridiculously easy. That's my price. Take it or leave it.'

'Why?' The man fascinated me. Perhaps because he was a fanatic, but a very special breed of fanatic. 'Why this deviousness? Why not just simple cash?'

'A gun', he said solemnly, 'is the most perfect piece of machinery ever invented. What it can do, coupled with the speed with which it can do it, has never been equalled. Moon-rockets are cumbersome things by comparison. Motor cars, aeroplanes are mere extensions of the wheel. Put a good bullet into the breech of a good gun, exert less pressure than that required to turn a key in a lock and, faster than sound, you can bring death to any creature alive. For one split second of eternity, you become God.'

'You love guns,' I said gently.

'For the sake of your uncle, I would like you to *appreciate* them.'

* * *

It must not be assumed that Frisch (or, indeed, anybody) turned me into what I became. I was my own man. I always had been and I always will be. Merely that guns interested me no more than any other subject. I knew the difference between a revolver and a pistol. Between a rifle and a smooth-bore. I knew the rudiments of sighting. I knew what most men knew about guns . . . but no more and no less.

I think Frisch's challenge had triggered it off. I could, of course, have found another gunsmith. One willing to store the guns in exchange for cash payment. But that would have been a cop-out. In a back-to-front sort of way, Frisch would have outfaced me. He might have had a quiet chuckle to himself when I'd left.

That evening, I took all the literature about guns from the shelves of the study, carried them across to the studio and started a one-man crash course on the subject.

SIX

'Prone,' I said.

Frisch grunted some sort of approval and nodded.

I lowered myself on to the groundsheet, spread my legs wide, settled my elbows, then fed the first round into the Fashingbauer.

He'd met me at the door of the farmhouse, as I'd braked the car to a halt. I think he'd heard my approach on the loose gravel of the lane. If he hadn't, the Irish wolfhound would certainly have heard.

He'd walked the few yards towards the car and, as I'd opened the car door, he'd asked: 'Which, first?'

'Is the target ready?'

'It's ready.'

'Fine. If I can't hit a bull, we won't waste time on the questions.'

His expression had registered mild surprise when I'd opened the boot of the car and chosen the Fashingbauer. I thought I knew why. It was a custom-built rifle which, in the shooting world, meant it had been tailor-made for my uncle. The weight, the length of the stock, the angle of the stock to the barrel, the balance, the trigger-pull. A man goes to a master-tailor and orders a bespoke suit. It is made to fit *him*, and nobody else. It sits on *his* shoulders, it reaches *his* wrists, it wraps itself comfortably, but firmly, around *his* waist, it moulds *his* hips, and the turn-ups of the trousers swing at a perfect level around *his* ankles. On anybody else, the suit is less than perfect. Sometimes very *im*perfect. As with a suit, so with a rifle. To the man it was made for, a custom-built rifle 'fits' with the same perfection.

But, just as some off-the-peg suits leave little room for improvement, so I'd found the Fashingbauer a comfortable gun to handle.

I'd dropped the rounds into my jacket pocket, then followed him to the rear of the farmhouse.

There was a square of hard-packed sandbags, large enough to take a man lying on his stomach, and with enough room for movement. It raised the shooting position slightly above the height of the surrounding heather. Twenty yards away a heavy brick wall had been built. It was about ten feet high. In front of it, more sandbags, to a depth of a yard. Beyond and around the sandbagged wall . . . nothing. Only the hazy horizon. The end of the world. And a biting wind from the north-west, which gusted and fell, and sent flurries of light rain in at an angle.

The target – such a tiny target, even though it was standard twenty-yard size – was already fastened to its steel frame in front of the wall.

'How do you fire?' he'd asked.

And I'd said: 'Prone.'

I nursed the stock to my cheek, then took a couple of deep breaths. I curled my finger around the trigger and my thumb around the narrow of the stock. I pulled the stock into my shoulder, then gripped firmly, but not tightly enough

43

to cause a tremble.

I lined up the sights. Fore-sight and rear-sight, in perfect alignment. Not on the target centre, but on the top edge of the target ... well above the bull. Then a deep breath – but not *too* deep – and a slow lowering of the aim, still keeping the sights aligned. A tensing of the thumb muscles. The release of my breath, until my lungs felt normal and comfortable. The feel of the gusts of breeze on my left cheek. And still the very gradual lowering of the aim. A gust of wind eased, the tip of the aligned fore-sight touched the bull and I squeezed ... the action being to pressure the thumb into meeting the trigger finger.

The explosion smacked at my right ear and the stock nudged into the muscle of my right shoulder.

Four more times I repeated the sequence. Each time as slowly and as deliberately as the first time. Then I cleared the breech, lay the Fashingbauer on the sandbags and pushed myself to my feet.

Without a word Frisch walked the twenty yards, unclipped the target from its frame and returned.

'An inner. A magpie. A bull. An inner. The last one was an outer – you timed the wind-gust badly.'

'But a bull,' I said quietly.

'More than I expected.' He bent and picked up the Fashingbauer. Perhaps it was a gesture. That *he* took possession of it, and didn't leave it for *me* to pick up. As we walked back towards the house, he said: 'You were firing over somebody else's sights. The weather was against you. With adjusted sights, and in good conditions, you'd have done better.'

'Thank you.'

'Unless, of course, the bull was a fluke.'

'Are you suggesting it was?'

'No.' He shook his head. 'I asked for one bull. You've given me what I asked for.'

'I might have had the sights adjusted,' I teased.

'No.' There was no hint of doubt in the word. 'I set those sights up for your uncle. They haven't been tampered with.'

44

That, I think, was the first time I realised the extent of Karl Frisch's skill as a gunsmith.

We ate cinnamon cakes and drank hot porter in front of an open log fire. We each sat in an armchair. Frisch on one side of the fire, the girl on the other and myself between them. Each armchair was different from its fellows; at a guess, each had been chosen for comfort rather than for looks, although each was a little old-fashioned and had been made before mass-produced furniture had become commonplace.

The dog was stretched out across the door of the living-room, with its snout resting on its forepaws. I could see it, if I moved my head. Periodically, it closed its eyes but, at the slightest movement, the lids opened . . . and, always, *I* was the first person it checked.

Outside, half a gale had blown up, but the room was warm and safe, and the logs in the fire-basket flared and crackled as the resin oozed from the burning wood and fed the flames.

We'd brought the guns inside, and Frisch was systematically examining them. Running his fingers along the exterior metalwork, removing each breech. Peering at each firing-pin. Testing the point of each pin with the ball of his thumb. Squinting up the barrel as he held the weapon up to the light from the window.

He reminded me of a dentist examining each tooth in a mouth for the first sign of decay.

When we'd first sat down – after we'd stacked the guns alongside his chair, and before the girl had brought in the cakes and porter – he'd said: 'The Armalite.'

'Also known as "The Widow-Maker"', I'd murmured, as I'd settled into the armchair indicated by Frisch.

'They *all* make widows, widowers . . . and orphans.' A quick cloud of annoyance had crossed his expression, before he'd added: 'The bullet from an Armalite rifle tumbles in flight. End over end. It tears into the target and produces a wound far in excess of its size.'

'That's not true,' I'd smiled.

'No?'

'Ballistically, that's not on.'

'The popular press have made great play with the so-called "tumbling bullet" in the past.'

'Look.' I'd leaned forward a little in the chair. I'd used my hands to emphasise and help me explain what he already knew. 'A bullet has to spin for accuracy. To *spin* ... not tumble. If it spins too much, the slight increase in accuracy is offset by the bullet passing *through* the target – like a drill – and wasting its energy beyond the target countering friction, air drag and gravity. Too much explosive charge will do just that.

'The 5.56 mm bullet fired from an Armalite is designed for an effective range of about three thousand feet. At that range, it's accurate. The spin is enough to keep it on an accurate course for its fighting range ... but no more. Any interference – even a leaf – and the spin drops, and the bullet's stability is knocked to hell. So just by striking the target the bullet stops spinning. Every ounce of its energy goes into knocking that target for six. It "tumbles" – *if* it "tumbles" – after it's hit what it was aimed at. It's made as a "man-stopper", and that's just what it is.'

SEVEN

The chief constable knew what he could do. More important, he knew what he *couldn't* do. His forte was 'man management'. A lifetime of soldiering in India and Palestine had taught him how to allocate and co-ordinate. As a colonel, with never enough men to do what was expected of him, he'd learned how to make full use of what manpower he *did* have.

Which, in turn – and now his army career was over – made him an above-average chief constable. Moreover, he looked

46

the part; he looked what a lot of 1963 chief constables *wished* they looked. Lean and parchment-skinned. Hard-eyed and with a voice which demanded obedience.

All this ... but he knew he wasn't a copper. He was a figurehead, and the type of man the city's watch committee listened to with respect. Which, in turn, *was* his job. But he wasn't a copper.

The man in whose office the chief constable now sat, on the other hand, *was* a copper. He, too, looked the part. OK, there was now fat where there'd once been muscle. The chins were multiplying and the jowls were heavy, but the weight – the *real* weight – remained. As a detective superintendent he'd terrified villains only fractionally more than he'd terrified his underlings, but his crime-detection record told its own tale. He'd deserved the leg up the ladder of promotion. He'd deserved to be made detective chief superintendent and head of the city's CID. Nobody could argue away *that* proposition.

But. . . .

'Have you settled in yet, Lewis?' asked the chief.

'When something happens', growled Lewis, 'they'll know they have a new head of CID.'

'Quite.'

'It takes more than three weeks, polishing the seat of his chair.'

'The mailbag robbery?' The chief made it sound rather more like an observation than a question.

'It should have put the Buckinghamshire mob on overtime,' grunted Lewis.

'Two and a half million,' murmured the chief. 'It should take some moving.'

'It was an inside job.' Lewis made the remark with the air of absolute certainty.

'You think so?'

'For God's sake! Used notes, on their way south to be pulped. That one train. Somebody knew ... somebody told.'

'It makes the whole police service look foolish,' sighed the chief.

47

'It doesn't make *me* look foolish.' Lewis's podgy chin jutted. 'The man responsible for security should be strung up by the balls. That, for sure. But, take it from me, if any of that cabbage moves into *this* police area, we'll know. *I'll* know.'

'You have men out, asking questions?' Then hurriedly: 'Of course you have. I shouldn't have asked.'

'Listening,' said Lewis grimly. 'Listening and watching. Every snout in the city. I can wait till Doom cracks. If any of those notes ends up in *my* area, I'll know.'

'Good. Good.' The chief unfolded himself from the chair. 'I just thought I'd call in. See how things were settling.'

'I'm not worrying myself about nicked milk-bottles, Chief Constable.' Lewis made no attempt to soften the sarcasm. 'Nor, at the moment, am I too concerned about mail trains. When something big breaks, I'll take over.'

Two days later, Lewis took over his first murder enquiry, as head of the city's CID.

'How long?' asked Lewis.

The police surgeon scratched his chin pensively with the nail of his left thumb. It was always the same. The same question. The poor devil was dead. The top half of his face and most of his forehead blown out. Sprawled out in the awkward posture of death, in a forgotten corner of this scrapyard. And, already, this damn policeman was asking for miracles.

'He was dragged here.' The police surgeon fenced for time.

'I may be dumb, but even *I* didn't think he'd hauled himself, feet-first backwards, with half his bloody head blown off.'

'It's August,' said the police surgeon patiently. 'We've had a spell of very hot weather.'

'So?'

'Chief Superintendent, the temperature can play the very devil with calculations concerning time of death.'

'I'll pass the word,' said Lewis nastily. 'No more murders

in August. It upsets the medical fraternity.'

'Dammit, man!' The police surgeon allowed his temper to surface for a moment. 'Four days, to a week. Take your pick.'

'Between four days and a week?' sneered Lewis. 'You're sure it was *this* August . . . not last?'

'Lewis, I'm not here to —'

'To be honest, I don't know why you *are* here,' interrupted Lewis. "Life extinct"? We can all see that. We didn't have to waste years of our life going through medical college to work *that* one out.'

'Get him on a slab, open him up, check his stomach contents. Then we might be able to give you something more substantial than guesswork.'

'Promises, promises,' growled Lewis.

'Lewis.' The police surgeon lowered his voice until the handful of officers standing a few yards away couldn't hear. 'If ever I get *you* on a slab, opening you up won't interfere with my sleep one little bit.'

'No.' Lewis grinned wickedly. 'And I'll be in no condition to worry . . . will I?'

People who didn't know Lewis – people who could never fully understand Lewis – described him as 'a man-hunting machine'. He was that, but he was more. He was far more complex than that.

Oddly enough, he would have made a superb criminal. A supreme criminal. He had the concentrated fury of a charging rhino. Not for him the subtleties and patience of prolonged interviews. Not for him the quiet piecing together of the various parts of the jigsaw. By joining the police service he'd tacitly declared war on the criminal world and, to him, it was an all-out war. A war of noisy aggression, because that was the only form of war he acknowledged. The rest was skirmishing. Fannying around. 'Sissy' – to use his own expression.

To Lewis the Law was merely an armoury of weapons at his disposal. He chose which weapons might do most damage, and ignored the rest. The Law, to him, was not a whole. It had a variety of parts, some of which were a hindrance. Those that hindered he threw aside; they didn't apply, because they were useless and only softened the pain of those that did apply.

At a pinch, and had he had *his* way, thumb-screws would have been re-oiled.

Every man in the room knew Lewis. Knew his beliefs and knew his fury. Knew, also, that this was Lewis's first murder enquiry. Not the first he'd been involved in – not that, by a long way – but the first in which he, personally, carried the final can.

Some of them wanted him to fail. Lewis had far too many enemies not to have *some* men almost praying he'd fall flat on his arse. But the majority, while not members of his fan club, saw the additional lines on his heavy features and the ashen complexion which comes only with prolonged lack of sleep. They'd worked hard during the last six weeks – Lewis had made damn sure of that – but none had worked harder than Lewis himself.

More than forty men were crowded in the room. All of them city detectives. They ranged from detective constable, up through the ranks to Lewis's 'field commander', Detective Inspector Raff. Raff stood to one side, and a little behind Lewis. A worried man. He looked as tired as Lewis, and not a little dejected. Of them all, he'd taken most of the detective chief superintendent's rage during the last six weeks.

Lewis moved his head. Slowly. Deliberately. He seemed to pause as he caught the men's eyes, in order to share the loathing and contempt equally between all the officers present.

'A fine body of bloody men,' he sneered. 'Six weeks, and we don't even know who the bastard is.'

Somebody murmured: 'We've tried hard enough.'

'Who said that?' snarled Lewis.

One of the detective constables half-raised a hand and moved a step forward from the group of which he was a part.

'Detective Constable Hoyle.' Lewis's lip curled in an ugly sneer. 'Tell us all how hard *you've* tried.'

'As hard as possible.' Hoyle flushed, but held his ground. 'We all have.'

'Such as what?'

Lewis had a specific target. He hadn't needed one; he'd been prepared to share his black mood with every man present. But, now he had one, the concentration of his attention would have frightened most men.

'Every snout I know.' Hoyle's voice was steady, but it was a deliberate steadiness. It didn't quaver, because Hoyle refused to allow it to quaver. 'I've been round them all, at least twice. Some of them three times.'

'A wasted journey?'

'Yes, sir,' agreed Hoyle.

'And that's the best you can do?'

'I'm open to suggestions, sir.'

'Are you being bloody impudent, Hoyle?'

'No, sir.' Hoyle sighed. 'I've done my best. I know so little.'

'You know *something*, then?' pounced Lewis. 'Are we allowed to know? Or is it a state secret?'

Hoyle hesitated, then plunged in.

'I've seen the corpse, sir. I think he was left-handed – he wore his wrist-watch on his right wrist. He wasn't circumcised – therefore, he wasn't a Jew.'

'That narrows the field,' sneered Lewis. 'A left-handed Gentile ... perhaps. Good God, man! If that's the sum total—'

'I think it was more of an execution than a killing, sir.'

'To the best of my knowledge, he's *dead*.'

'He wasn't robbed, sir,'

'He was murdered, sonny,' snarled Lewis. 'To you there may be a difference between a murder and an execution, but not to me. The hound was killed in this police area. I want the bastard who killed him to see the inside of a hanging-shed.'

'The motive, sir.' Hoyle had gone too far for retreat.

'That's what I'm getting at.'

'More Holmesian deductions?'

'Sir, the bullet went in at the back of his head. The nape of his neck. Short-range. That's an *execution*, sir. Presumably, for something he'd done. Or, if not that, because of who he was.'

'In hell's name. . . .' Lewis turned on Raff. 'In hell's name, Raff, who put this dream-laden lunatic in plain clothes? Who was conned into believing he was an ounce of good in CID?'

'He's a good detective, sir,' said Raff heavily. 'He works hard.'

'Does he? Does he, indeed? He reads a damn sight too many Agatha Christie novels ... that's *my* opinion.' He switched his attention to the other occupants of the room. 'Now, let's forget left-handed Gentiles, shall we? Let's not piss around differentiating between executions and murders. There's a stiff in the morgue, and we don't yet know who the hell he is. Now, I don't give a damn if your loving wives and families don't clap eyes on you – any of you – till pension time. You think you've worked? You haven't even warmed up yet. I want the name of that stiff. I want that name, because I want the germ who stiffened him. It's that simple.

'Damnation, we don't know who he is. We don't even know *where* he was killed. Two people – the killer and the victim. Two places – where he was killed and where he was found. For those of you without the deductive ability of friend Hoyle, there *has* to be a vehicle involved. A corpse can't be carried around in your back pocket. It's heavy. Bloody heavy. It's either floppy or stiff as a board. Chances are, therefore, two men – at least two men – to lug it from point A to point B. There's a mess somewhere ... or *was* a mess. We've given whoever we're after six weeks to clean that mess up. But, hopefully, he *can't* – at least that's what the test-tube experts claim. If it's there, they'll find traces.'

He paused then, in an explosive outburst of disgust, ended: 'Jesus Christ! They're not invisible. Whoever killed him. The vehicle. They were *seen*. Somebody *saw* them.

Nothing impossible – nothing too difficult – I'm not asking anybody to walk on water. Just find somebody, and make 'em talk. Make 'em admit something – anything.... I'll do the rest.' He favoured the detectives with a last glare of indignation. 'Just *do* something. Earn your corn, for a change.' As he turned to leave the room, and in a quieter tone, he spoke to Raff. 'That Hoyle character. Chop the stupid sod down to size. Impress certain facts of life on the young lunatic. Detecting crime does *not* include contemplating the navel, then coming up with half-baked opinions.'

'He's impossible to please,' complained DC Hoyle.

'He's difficult to please,' Raff corrected him. 'He wouldn't be where he is if he was a soft number.'

The meeting had broken up and, acting upon the instructions of his boss, Raff was 'impressing certain facts of life' on the young detective constable. Raff had chosen Force Headquarters canteen, and had eased his task by buying beakers of tea and chocolate biscuits. They helped, but only a little. Hoyle felt badly done by, and did nothing to hide the fact.

'We do our best,' he grumbled. 'Christ Almighty, it's more than a week since I had a bath. Since I had a proper meal.'

'You're not alone,' murmured Raff.

'So why doesn't he give credit?'

'He's not the sort of man to hand out lollipops,' said Raff patiently.

'I'll tell you what he is.' Hoyle sipped the near-cold tea. 'He's an ungracious sod.'

'He's also a chief superintendent.' Raff's tone hardened. 'My instructions were to bollock you, Hoyle. Personally, I don't think you deserve a bollocking. But that doesn't mean I'm prepared to take sides with you against a man who outranks us both.'

Hoyle grunted.

'It's the job, son.' Raff relaxed the rank a little. 'We're all tired ... Lewis, too. We're all too knackered to see straight.'

'I still think it was an execution,' muttered Hoyle.

'I'm inclined to agree.' Quite smoothly, they moved into the status of two dedicated coppers exchanging opinions. Again, the differences in rank didn't mean much. 'All that left-handed-Gentile crap. You could be right. You could be wrong. But I'd agree it's more than a straight up-and-down murder. But *where*? That's what's getting up the chief superintendent's nose. *Where!* There's one hell of a mess somewhere. Or there *was* a hell of a mess. We haven't even found *that* yet.'

'I've been thinking. Maybe. . . .' Hoyle closed his mouth. There was a certain petulance in his expression.

'What?' asked Raff.

'Somebody would immediately call me a smart-arse,' said Hoyle glumly.

'Not me,' promised Raff. 'We'd better start getting smart, otherwise we've an undetected killing on the books.'

'Blood,' mumbled Hoyle. 'Y'know – blood and mess . . . where blood and mess *is*.'

'Sorry?' Raff raised an eyebrow.

'Look. . . .' Hoyle's tone gained confidence. He moved his hands a little to emphasise his argument. 'An assassination. Let's assume an assassination, for the moment. That means, y'know, somebody out to do the job. Deliberately. Not an argument. Not even revenge. At least not revenge on the part of the killer. Let's assume that . . . *right*?'

Raff nodded.

'A. . . .' Hoyle swallowed. 'Somebody paid.'

'A professional?'

'That's not from a book, Inspector.' Hoyle was on the defensive again. 'I know it sounds a bit far-fetched, but. . . .'

'Hoyle,' said Raff gently, 'you don't have to tell *me*. I'll tell *you* something. Documented. Not once, but dozens of times. In the 1920s – before the IRA trained its own killers – every ship from the USA carried gunmen. Contract killers. The standard price for a copper or a Black and Tan was four hundred dollars. For somebody in public office – somebody under guard – the price was a thousand dollars. That is *not*

54

from a book. That's from court records, and authenticated statements, taken by the police. The heirs to those killers are still around. Only the price has changed.'

'Thank you, sir.' Hoyle sounded relieved. 'Well, a contract killer . . . let's assume a contract killer. If he knows his job, he knows there's going to be a mess. He also knows he hasn't time to clean things up. So why not kill where killing takes place? Somewhere where more blood won't be noticed?'

'A slaughterhouse.' Raff nodded slowly. 'The city abattoir.'

'It seems possible.'

'It seems', said Raff, 'a damn good idea.'

EIGHT

It struck Raff as odd that he and Hoyle, respective pawns in an intricate engine of law enforcement, should have worked themselves to near-collapse because of the violent death of one human being whereas here, at the city's main abattoir, violent death was the reason for it all. The same stench was present. A mix of sweetness and decay, which penetrated the heavier smell of disinfectant. There was cleanliness, but it was the cleanliness of the mortuary. Dead flesh. Somehow having no connection with the joints of meat tastefully displayed in a butcher's shop. Nothing to do with Sunday dinners, crackling or mint sauce.

'God knows how people work here,' he muttered.

They crossed the concrete yard, tapped on a door and entered the office of the man in charge. An appointment had been made, they were punctual and the man was waiting.

He rose from a chair, held out his hand, smiled and said: 'Gubbins. You'll be Inspector Raff . . . am I right?'

'Yes.' Raff shook hands, as he added: 'And this is Constable Hoyle. One of our detectives.'

'Pleased to meet you, Mr Hoyle.'

Gubbins swung his smile towards Hoyle, and kept his hand outstretched. He was obviously a man given to shaking hands at every opportunity. A gushing man, with a mouthful of off-white teeth. Slim. Moderately well dressed, but with dark stains on the front of his trouser thighs. Raff guessed the stains were dried blood, and the thought sickened him a little.

'To what do we owe this pleasure?'

'Just . . . enquiries,' said Raff carefully.

Hoyle asked: 'Can you give us some idea of the workings of this place, Mr Gubbins?'

'Just a general outline,' added Raff.

'Well, it's a slaughterhouse.' Gubbins moved his arms expansively, as if he personally had created the set-up from scratch. Had he been introducing a hit West End musical – written, scored and directed by himself – he couldn't have sounded more satisfied. 'We kill every day, but Monday's the day we drop most beasts.'

'Monday?' repeated Hoyle.

'Rushed off our feet, Monday.'

'Where – where you kill . . . ,' began Raff hesitantly.

'We slaughter in three places,' beamed Gubbins.

'Clean, of course?'

'*Very* clean.'

'How clean?'

'Well, now, this meat's for human consumption. We have the inspectors here, all the time. We have certain standards, Inspector. Legally required standards. We can't afford to be lax in the —'

'After the day's killing?' interrupted Hoyle. 'Is the place washed down? All three places?'

'Every day.'

'Thoroughly?' insisted Raff.

'It's hosed down. It's scrubbed down. It's squeegeed. All three slaughterhouses. Very thoroughly. Everywhere else,

56

too, of course. But especially the slaughterhouses. We can't afford to take risks.'

'That's what I suspected,' sighed Raff.

'You're not complaining ... surely?' Gubbins sounded almost offended.

'Not the way you think,' said Raff.

'Can we see these slaughterhouses?' asked Hoyle.

'Certainly, Mr Hoyle. Anywhere at all. We'll go now, if you like.'

It was a charnel-house, but it was a clean charnel-house. The walls of the three slaughterhouses were tiled, ceiling-high. The floors were of smooth concrete, with deep runnels converging on a massive grate.

Gubbins kept up a running conversation throughout the tour, but the two officers remained silent.

'As you can see, very humane. No cruelty. No suffering. Pity we can't all go like that. They don't even know what's happening, until it's too late. Until it's all over.'

Overhead, oiled rails and chains provided a soft background of smooth whir. Carcasses, still twitching from muscle-spasm, were hoisted from where they'd fallen and conveyed through tall openings in the walls.

'They have to be bled, then skinned and gutted, you see. That's the *skilled* job. The edible portions for the markets, of course. The parts *we* don't eat cleaned and used in pet food. Not much gets wasted.'

There was a great surfeit of water. They seemed to be walking through water an inch deep, wherever they went. Hoses snaked across the concrete floor surface, and they all sent a weep of water from their nozzles. Some of the water was hot, and the steam caused more water to run down the wall tiles.

'Scrupulously clean, you see. We have to be. The law requires it – but you'll know that, of course. Not like the old days. Blood and shit coagulating in every corner.'

'Shall we go back to your office?' suggested Raff.

'Of course, Inspector. I'm at your disposal.'

Back at the office, they sat on chairs and drank hot, sweet

tea. Raff smoked a cigarette, and the two detectives steadied themselves after what had been something of an ordeal.

Gubbins exposed his teeth, then asked: 'Am I – y'know – am I allowed to know why you're here, Inspector?'

'Why not?' said Raff heavily. 'It's about the murder. The man found in the scrapyard. He wasn't *killed* there, We're trying to find out *where* he was killed.'

'Oh!'

Hoyle said: 'This place is locked up at night, of course?'

'Of course.'

'But, presumably, somebody could get in. If he really wanted to?'

'No.' Gubbins sounded very sure.

'Oh, come *on*,' said Raff. 'It's not Fort Knox.'

'I, personally, lock the gates every evening. I open them every morning. They're very substantial gates, Inspector. They have to be. There's a lot of expensive equipment here.'

'Granted,' agreed Raff, 'but there's a perimeter fence. That's not —'

'Concrete posts, Inspector,' intoned Gubbins. 'Steel wire link-fencing, eight foot high, with a triple barbed-wire topping on angle-iron brackets, set at an angle outwards. It's checked every day. I check it.'

'It's an electric fence, of course,' murmured Raff sarcastically.

'No. Of course not. Why should—?'

'Who else has a key?' interrupted Hoyle.

'Nobody.'

'Every lock is issued with two keys. At least two keys.'

'Two. I have them both. One on my key-ring. The other I keep locked away in my desk, at home.'

'Six weeks ago,' said Raff wearily. 'Let's say between six weeks and seven weeks – thereabouts – anything unusual?'

'Unusual?' Gubbins frowned.

'The gate – the fence – tampered with. Anything?'

'No.' Gubbins shook his head.

'No interference with the gate? With the fence?'

'No. Why should there be?'

58

'You'd have noticed?'

'Of course I'd have noticed. Look, I don't know why you're here, but —'

'*That's* why we're here.' Hoyle took a photograph from his inside pocket and handed it to Gubbins. 'That's why we're asking questions.'

'Know him?' Raff screwed what was left of his cigarette into a tin ashtray.

'No. I don't know him.' Gubbins stared at the photograph and said, 'He's – he's. . . .'

'He's dead,' confirmed Raff in a flat voice. 'That's a head-and-shoulders morgue shot. What's left of his face . . . it's not much.'

'Christ!' breathed Gubbins.

'So how the hell do you know whether you know him or not?'

'It's – it's. . . .'

'Somebody knows him. Why not you?'

Gubbins became aware of a delicate change in the tone of the conversation. A brittleness. A slightly sharper snap to the words used by the two detectives, which matched the hardening of their eyes.

'A proposition,' said Hoyle calmly. 'Let's assume you wanted to kill a man. . . .'

'*Me?* Why should *I* want to . . . ?'

'Listen to the proposition,' said Raff.

Hoyle continued: 'To shoot him in the back of the neck. Blast his face away. Very messy. Lots of gore. Where better than a place like this? It's made to handle blood and guts. It's made to shift it. Dispose of it. Where better?'

'For God's sake! You can't seriously think *I*. . . .'

'We don't know,' said Raff. 'Somebody . . . but we don't yet know who. We don't even know where.'

'This,' added Hoyle. 'The ideal place.'

'I – I – yes . . . I suppose so.' Gubbins took a deep breath. 'But not here. I'm the only key-holder. Nobody else could. . . .' His voice trailed off. 'Oh my God!'

'Start telling us why it shouldn't be you,' suggested Raff.

59

'Start explaining why it *couldn't* be you.'

To the man-in-the-street there could have been no excuse, but the man in the street would never have understood. It was a combination of bone-weariness, self-disgust at the complete lack of progress and, perhaps, the sickening sights witnessed on the tour of the abattoir. That, plus a certain desperation. Of course it was unfair, but the whole damn thing was unfair. The job was unfair. Lewis was perpetually and monumentally unfair. The lack of any semblance of social life was unfair. Therefore, what happened to Gubbins was unfair – grossly unfair, in that neither Raff nor Hoyle thought for a moment that Gubbins knew anything at all about the shooting.

Nevertheless, and for almost fifteen minutes, they threaded him through the type of interrogation used against principal suspects.

'We don't know where he was killed. He *could* have been killed here. . . .'

'If he *was* killed here, it wouldn't be during working hours. Not with all the slaughtermen watching. . . .'

'During the night. When nobody could get in. Except *you* of course. . . .'

'Gubbins, you're holding the crappy end of a very dirty stick. You'd better start working out a way of convincing us it isn't *your* stick. . . .'

'You say you don't know him. *Nobody* knows him, from that photograph. So how do you *know* you don't know him?'

'Six weeks ago – seven weeks ago – come on. Where were you? What were you doing? Who was with you? Who can *prove* you're not the character we're looking for?'

'Start giving us some facts, Gubbins. Something we can work on. Something we can check. . . .'

It was what, in police parlance, is known as 'a going-over', and it left Gubbins both sweating and trembling. Gone was the toothy smile. The *bonhomie* had gone down the plug hole within the first sixty seconds.

'*I didn't kill him!*' He almost screamed the words as the terrible possibility of a police frame-up brought on panic.

They knew they had him. They knew that, on the million-to-one chance they'd accidentally stumbled across the man they were after, he'd have cracked. Therefore, they eased the pressure. Just a little ... but enough.

Raff lit another cigarette, allowed the atmosphere time to become less electric, then drawled: 'You've got to admit, there's a hell of a case against you Gubbins.'

'No. I'm innocent. How can there be a case against—?'

'Nobody admits to murder, Gubbins. Nobody! There's a noose at the end of that particular lane.'

'I didn't kill him.' This time, the plea to be believed seemed a prelude to tears.

'He could have been killed here,' insisted Hoyle quietly. 'He could have been killed here ... and no sign of blood.'

'A dozen places,' moaned Gubbins. 'More. This isn't the only place.'

'Name them,' challenged Hoyle.

'Private slaughterhouses. Most of the butchers come here to kill ... but not all. Some have their own small slaughterhouse, usually at the back of the shop. Licensed. *Those*, for example. The knackers' yards. There's two main ones. That's not counting the unofficial dropping. A pig here, a sheep there. It happens.' He turned to Raff, and repeated: 'It *happens*, Inspector. On my oath. It's wrong – it's against the law – but it *happens*.'

'You'd better be right, Gubbins,' warned Raff as he stood up. 'You had better be *very* right. At the moment, this place tops the list ... if only because it's big enough. And, while it tops the list, the hook's still there, and you're on it.'

It happens. It's not supposed to happen but, nevertheless, it happens. Take the aggro, as much as you're able. Take it, and digest it. It's part of the job. But, if the aggro comes too hard and too heavy, spread it around a little. Share the load. Find somebody like Gubbins – somebody who, by stretching the imagination to near breaking-point, just *might* be Jack the Lad – and slap a percentage of the aggro across his shoulders.

61

As they walked back to the car, Raff rubbed the back of his neck, gave a twisted grin, and said: 'I feel better for that.'

'*I* feel an absolute shit,' muttered Hoyle.

'Easy, son,' advised Raff. 'He'll have a couple of sleepless nights, then he'll forget it.'

'Dammit, it seemed a reasonable possibility.'

'It *was* a reasonable possibility. It still is.'

'Inspector, don't be patronising.'

'It was a *possibility*,' insisted Raff. 'And as sure as hell it was some sort of execution . . . not straight murder.'

Lewis was waiting in the murder room at City Police Headquarters, and Lewis was as happy as a man like Lewis could ever hope to be. It was a happiness based on satisfaction and, in turn, the satisfaction was rooted in the fact that he could, justifiably, rocket somebody into outer space.

'Where the hell have you two little beauties been?' he demanded.

Raff told him, and Lewis was not impressed.

'Abattoirs!' he mocked.

'It seemed reasonable,' said Raff quietly. 'We've done everything *but*.'

'You will be delighted to know', rumbled Lewis, 'that our half-baked country cousins in the County Constabulary have found a burned-out car. Six weeks – more – and they've actually found the bloody thing. Out in that wilderness they call the Tops.'

'It's very isolated up there, sir,' murmured Hoyle.

'Not half as isolated as the space between the ears of the yokels responsible for policing that area.'

'Is – er. . . .' Raff cleared his throat. 'Is there a definite connection, sir?'

'The timing fits. We can assume a car was used. It sounds a damn sight more promising than abattoirs.'

'Yes, sir,' sighed Raff.

'We're taking Carr with us,' said Lewis. He allowed himself a wicked, self-satisfied grin. 'I was just going to rope in some other clown to hew the wood and carry the water. You two will do. You've timed it badly, Inspector.'

NINE

The man Lewis had called 'Carr'. Lewis's tone had been similar to that of the ordinary person's remarks when suggesting, 'We'll take the dog with us', or 'We'll pop our raincoats in the back of the car'. But Joseph Carr, MSc, PhD, director of the Area Forensic Science Laboratory, deserved far more than Lewis's throwaway mention. In his own down-to-earth way, he dealt with facts. Not theories. Not hypotheses. Not even possibilities. Carr was a power to be reckoned with, as more than one defending barrister had discovered to his discomfort.

He strolled round the burned-out car. Slowly. Pausing, periodically, to peer closer and, occasionally, to lift some tiny piece of potential evidence, sometimes with tweezers, sometimes with his fingers, and drop it carefully into a tiny plastic envelope held ready by his assistant. There was no hurry. There was no need for hurry. And Carr carefully circled the razed vehicle three times before he joined the group of police officers standing some distance away, alongside the cars.

'Well?' demanded Lewis.

'There's been a shot fired,' said Carr. He took one of the envelopes from his assistant and held it for Lewis to see through the transparent plastic. 'Part of the windscreen. The slight curve gives the game away. That shattering, at one corner. Typical bullet-hole shattering and, from its position in the concave shape of the glass, fired from inside the vehicle. Other pieces of windscreen glass, with slight stains. It could be blood. Punched clear of the vehicle, therefore unaffected by the fire.'

'Human blood?'

'It seems likely.'

'For Christ's sake. . . .'

'Lewis, be thankful for small mercies. I'll tell you whether it's human blood after tests. If it is, I'll even tell you the blood group.'

A uniformed superintendent from the county constabulary said: 'Before you search the interior, Doctor. We'll get the scene thoroughly photographed.'

Carr nodded friendly agreement.

'Oh, for God's sake, photograph it, Ripley. *Photograph* the damn thing.' Lewis turned on the uniformed superintendent. 'Having left the sodding thing here to rust for more than a month, by all means *photograph* it.'

The uniformed superintendent smiled. It was a slow smile. Almost a grin. But not a *friendly* grin. 'A quiet word with you, please, Chief Superintendent,' he murmured.

'Eh?'

'Alone . . . if you don't mind.'

'What about?'

'Something rather important. Something you ought to know.' Then, to the two officers from County Constabulary Photographic Section: 'Get cracking, please, As many as you like. External and interior. But don't disturb anything. Inspector Raff will make necessary suggestions. The detective constable from the city force will help, if necessary.'

Ripley strolled to a point well beyond earshot of any of the others and, reluctantly, Lewis followed.

'Now,' demanded, Lewis, 'what the hell is it you want to—?'

'Very important, Lewis.' Ripley fished a battered pipe from the side-pocket of his tunic. Then a pouch and matches. As he spoke, he concentrated upon charging the pipe with tobacco. The charging of the pipe seemed to demand all his attention, nevertheless the quietly spoken words carried an absolute warning. 'Beechwood Brook ... *my* division. Criticise, if you must, and I'll happily answer your criticisms.

But you're well out of your own hunting-ground, Lewis. Remember that. Remember this, too. Use that tone of voice to me again – just *once* – and I'll have your tripes on a plate for breakfast. Your chief constable. *My* chief constable. The Home Secretary, if necessary.' He zipped up the pouch and raised his eyes until his cold stare met the angry glare of the detective chief superintendent. 'I'll chop you off at the knee-caps, Lewis . . . bet on it.'

'You're soon offended,' sneered Lewis.

'Aren't I?' Ripley closed his teeth around the stem of the pipe, struck a match into flame, then seemed to forget the existence of Detective Chief Superintendent Lewis as he teased the tobacco into a steady glow.

Two hours later, Carr and the photographers were finished. Pieces of cloth from the upholstery – strips which had escaped the fire, by reason of their being tucked into folds of the seats – had been collected then stored. Flakes of scorched paint, larger pieces of twisted metal, blobs of molten goo, which had once been plastic-based material. It had all been carefully collected and packed into the boot of Carr's vehicle. The engine number and the chassis number had been located, cleaned up and noted.

'You'll let me know.' Ripley made the remark to Dr Carr.

'As soon as possible.'

'About what?' demanded Lewis.

'Whether your body was shot in this car,' said Ripley.

'I think', said Carr carefully, 'we can save a certain amount of time by assuming it was. Pending final examination, and proof, of course.'

'I'm obliged,' smiled Ripley. Then to Lewis: 'I'll expect photostats of statements – all the paperwork relating to the case – as soon as possible, Chief Superintendent.'

'Why the devil should we . . . ?'

'If he was shot here, it's *our* pigeon,' said Ripley innocently.

'Eh?'

'Liaison, of course. I suggest Inspector Raff . . . if you can

65

spare him. And this other officer. What's his name?'

'Hoyle,' choked Lewis.

'Raff and Hoyle?'

'Look, Ripley, if you think we've spent six weeks —'

'Oh, I'm obliged,' interrupted Ripley. 'I'm very much obliged. I'll see you're kept informed of the progress we make.'

It was *fait accompli* played to perfection. Lewis, the human steam-roller had had every ounce of steam extracted from his engine without Ripley even having to raise his voice. Carr's eyes twinkled with secret delight, but the lower-ranked officers had sense enough to keep very straight-faced.

Ripley turned to Raff, and his tone carried neither satisfaction nor triumph.

'Inspector, if you're agreeable – and if Mr Lewis doesn't object – I'd like you to dovetail what's already been done with what yet needs to be done. Detective Constable Hoyle can be your right-hand man, of course. Contact me for whatever you need – however many men you need – I'll see you get them.'

'Yokels?' growled Lewis.

'Maybe,' smiled Ripley. 'But city slickers don't often find needles in haystacks. Yokels do it all the time.'

This time, they didn't. They moved some hay. A monumental amount of hay ... but no needle! Nor was it the fault of either Raff or Hoyle. It certainly wasn't the fault of Ripley or the men under Ripley's command. They worked. Like the city boys, they worked round the clock. They worked until they felt they'd drop from sheer fatigue, but what little headway they made didn't amount to much.

From the engine and chassis numbers they traced the car. It had been stolen in Darlington some two months before. The owner was a man of some repute, and well beyond suspicion. Nor did he jump for joy when he learned what had happened to his beloved Vauxhall.

They even found the bullet.

Raff made the suggesion: 'It went through the head. It went through the windscreen. It must have lost a hell of a lot of its initial velocity. It's *possible*.'

'How many men?' Ripley didn't argue. 'Fifty men? More, if you think you need them?'

Thereafter, a small army of uniformed constables, augmented by as many 'specials' as they could rope in, crawled on their hands and knees. Virtually inch at a time they crept forward conducting a finger-search. They started two hundred yards from the vehicle and moved at a snail's pace. Five days later, they found the bullet. Carr performed his scientific wizardry and came up with a half-answer.

'A thirty-eight, soft-nose. From a revolver – so don't waste time searching for the cartridge case. We think a Colt. That doesn't help much, I'm afraid. Colt make at least half a dozen revolvers, all with thirty-eight calibre.'

'Availability?' Raff's quesion carried little hope.

'Thousands of 'em,' grunted the scientist. 'Legally held. Illegally held. They're popular handguns.'

'If we find the gun, can you match it up?'

'If you find the gun.' Carr nodded. 'But, if you find the gun, you've almost reached journey's end.'

Thereafter, more legwork. Certificate-holders both in the city and in the county area were visited. Test rounds were fired into sandbags, then retrieved and sent to the forensic science lab. Nor did Raff interest himself only in Colts. Every logged thirty-eight-calibre revolver was systematically tracked down and fired. Known and suspected GBH men were visited and leaned on by experts. Some of them broke, and more than twenty illegally held firearms were collected in.

'All negative,' said Raff bitterly. 'Like marking time. A lot of energy, it looks good, but you're getting nowhere. Dammit, we still haven't identified the victim.'

'Can a man move from the face of the earth without being missed . . . by *anybody*?' mused Ripley.

'This one did.'

They were in Ripley's office at Beechwood Brook DHQ.

Ripley, Raff and Detective Constable Hoyle. Hoyle had become an accepted part of the trio, and deservedly so. His filing and cross-referencing were immaculate. Despite his rank as mere DC it was recognised that he knew more about the enquiry than any of them. He'd read all the statements, studied all the reports, compiled all the summaries. The crime was six months old and, for those six months, Hoyle had quietly occupied the centre of the whirlpool. More than once he'd come up with some new and promising line of enquiry ... and Raff had sent men out to trudge down one more dead-end.

'Hoyle?' Ripley smiled at the youngest of the trio. 'We're open to suggesions.'

'Well, sir.' Hoyle hesitated. Had it been Lewis, he'd have kept his opinions to himself, but this man Ripley had proved himself more than reasonable. A man you could talk to. A man who tried to understand. Hoyle continued: 'I think – y'know – I think we're more or less agreed it was some sort of an execution. Not a simple bang-bang shooting job.'

'We can assume it was some sort of an execution,' agreed Ripley. 'We may be wrong ... but it's a fair assumption.'

'The – er – the man "executed"....' Hoyle seemed to gather courage. He leaned forward a little in his chair as he went on: 'Look, sir, everybody's *somebody*. That's a silly way of putting it, but. ...'

'We know what you mean, Hoyle.'

'To become "nobody" – a *real* "nobody" – isn't easy. It's almost impossible. No documentation. No letters, no cheque-book, no driving licence. But more than that. The body ... *our* body. The shoes are hand-made. They *have* to be hand-made. They don't carry a brand name, and it hasn't been removed. It was never there. Hand-made ... but no maker's name. That *has* to be deliberate. The same with the suit. The same with the shirt ... even the tie. The socks, the underclothes ... everything! No keys. Not even keys to the car. A wallet – a cheap plastic wallet, and *that* doesn't go with hand-made shoes – with almost a hundred quid in notes. A cheap buy-them-anywhere wrist-watch. Presumably he

68

had to know the time, but didn't want tracing via an expensive watch.

'Sir, that man has no identity. No rings. No recorded fingerprints. Nothing! And whoever killed him hadn't time to do all that. *He* did it. He didn't *want* to be known.'

'A lot of that's guesswork, Hoyle,' said Raff, but it was an observation and not a criticism.

'But *good* guesswork,' added Ripley. Then to Hoyle: 'Any more?'

'Just that. . . .' Hoyle moved his shoulders. 'Somebody who goes to all that trouble. Not to be known, I mean. Not to risk identification . . . under any circumstances. If, for example, he's arrested.'

'Ah,' murmured Raff.

'Finish your train of thought, Constable,' encouraged Ripley.

'Well, sir. . . .' Hoyle moistened his lips. 'Ordinary crooks don't go to all that trouble. In the first place, they don't expect to be caught. They rarely take *that* into consideration. And if they *are* caught . . . identifying themselves isn't an admission. Therefore, somebody special. *Very* special. And very professional. Unlikely to be caught, but if he is . . . who is he? He keeps his mouth shut, and there's no means of knowing. No means of moving from him to somebody else. Somebody *employing* him.'

'A contract killer.' Raff spoke the three words in little more than a whisper.

'If so, top-drawer.' Hoyle nodded. 'Somebody prepared to go to extraordinary lengths to preserve the anonymity of his client. And somebody who's never been in police custody before. His dabs aren't on file.'

'I like it.' Ripley nodded gently. The ghost of a grin touched his lips. 'The execution of an *executioner*. Nice thinking, Hoyle. Excellent thinking. Bricks, with very little straw . . . but very strong bricks. Very logical bricks.'

'Thank you, sir.'

'We close the file.' Ripley didn't mince words. The decision had to be made, and he made it. 'Unofficially, of

69

course. A killer gets killed ... one less to worry about. Give my compliments to Mr Lewis, Inspector. Put him in the picture.' Then to Hoyle: 'I'll put a room here, at DHQ, at your disposal, Constable. Store the murder records. Keep them in order. Feel free to visit, at any time ... if that very logical brain of yours moves a few more steps forward. Meanwhile, I'll personally see your chief constable hands down a recommendation.'

TEN

I repeat, nobody made me what I am. It happened gradually, I knew it was happening and, in a perverse sort of way, I rather *liked* what was happening.

Karl Frisch had been so right. The modern firearm was (still is) the ultimate in the marriage of scientific and mechanical engineering. Slowly the realisation dawned. The perfection became apparent.

The man with the gun – the man capable of *handling* the gun – is master. King or commoner – he can die. Bulk and muscle mean nothing. Authority melts away; the only authority worth a damn rests in the muscle of the trigger-finger. Brains? Intelligence? The flight of a bullet outpaces the practical speed of any thought.

Given the right circumstances, a man with a gun can hold the world to ransom!

In retrospect, I suspect it started that day in 1960. When I sent my first bullet into a bull. When I explained the fallacy of the 'tumbling bullet'. When I gave the true name of the 'Brown Bess' as the Long Land Service Musket, barrel-length forty-six inches, weight eleven and three-quarter pounds, effective fighting range two hundred yards. That the quickest way to distinguish a Kalashnikov AKM from a

Kalashnikov AK47 is to look for the gas-relief cut-out above the barrel, and that the AK47 can fire at a rate of six hundred rounds a minute.

Those were the questions, and I answered them.

Simple stuff now, but *then* I kidded myself into believing I was already something of an expert.

For the rest of that year, and well into 1961, I learned how little I *really* knew. Frisch fascinated me as (to a lesser degree) did the sightless girl. Even the dog, Sheba, came to accept me as a frequent visitor.

Yet, at the beginning, I didn't visit as a friend. As an acquaintance, with a growing interest in a skill which Frisch had elevated into an art form. Eventually, I suppose, as an eager pupil seeking expertise from a master.

Early in 1961 he took me into his workshop and introduced me to his own adaptation of the 'Halger' rifle.

'The barrel has a gradually diminishing calibre,' he explained. 'It needs a special bullet, of course. It fits into the breech, but is capable of being squeezed as it travels along the barrel. This, of course, increases the gas pressure at the base area of the bullet and boosts the muzzle velocity considerably. Perfect accuracy, at a much greater range. Each bullet is virtually precision-built. The jacket is swelled out – slightly convexed at the wall – therefore, it can be compressed without deforming the core of the bullet.'

'Special rifle. Special bullet,' I observed.

'Gerlich thought of the idea . . . years ago.'

'And it worked?'

'A handful of sniping rifles were made. And bullets, of course. But it was costly.'

'The perfect assassin's rifle,' I said quietly.

'A few refinements.' He smiled. 'This. . . .' He stroked the rifle lovingly. 'A good telescopic sight, the right propellant and a skilled marksman. More than a match for any normal "security" arrangements . . . I guarantee.'

It was the first intimation. The first hint, and such a tiny hint I didn't even notice it.

Meanwhile. . . .

I find it difficult to explain. This three-cornered relationship. Frisch was, basically, as much a loner as I was, yet we were comfortable in each other's company. The blind girl (her name was Anne) merely made up the number. She obviously adored Frisch, and was prepared to accept me because Frisch accepted me. But no depth of real friendship from either of them, as far as I was concerned. Nor, it must be admitted, on my part.

At home, the conversion had long been completed. I'd moved into the central maisonette, with a completely soundproof luxury flat above my second-floor ceiling. I'd spent money. (Via my stepfather, I'd spent a *lot* of money.) I lived a life that suited me. Most meals were taken out. I visited London on an average of once a month, stayed at good hotels and attended whichever first nights took my fancy.

My love life (for want of a better expression) was adequate. It was the so-called Swinging Sixties, promiscuity was becoming the 'done' thing, and I made no claim to stud-like qualities. If I felt like a bed-companion I had a reasonably varied choice. But no strings. No 'affairs'. And certainly no distant sound of wedding bells.

The furnishing of the maisonette occupied my interest. I was determined to make it elegant *and* comfortable. The library (I'd come to call it the library, whereas my uncle had called it the study) – the library became the warm heart of the place. I rearranged the books, cataloguing them to suit my own purpose. I had a top-quality hi-fi system installed and, almost to my own surprise, became a music buff. Symphonic, opera and concert-platform music suited my various moods to perfection, and I was almost sad when, in March, Sir Thomas Beecham died. Why? Emotion – that brand of emotion – had never touched me before. I didn't know the man. I hadn't even seen him conduct. But, already, I had many of his recordings . . . and it was as if some lout had deliberately destroyed part of what was becoming a good record collection.

The architect had not exaggerated. . . .

I contacted a leading firm of house agents, and left the leasing of the flat and the other two maisonettes in their hands. With, of course, the proviso that *I* had the final say. They leased on a monthly basis, and at an exorbitant rent. But they were all three occupied within as many weeks. Above me was a well-known ITV executive. On my right was a notably flamboyant QC, with a slightly overpainted lady he claimed to be his wife. On my left was one of the top fashion designers of the North, with his male lover. An oddball collection, but all with loot and to spare. A moderate percentage of that loot found its way into my bank account.

It was May 1962 when my world tottered slightly.

'Your father has gone quite mad.'

'My *step*father.'

'You know what I mean . . . he's gone quite mad.'

She'd called unexpectedly. Not that that was unusual. She *always* called unexpectedly. She merely 'arrived' and flicked away any suggestion that her arrival might be in any way inconvenient. That was Mother. It was also why, at first, I refused to take her outburst too seriously.

Probably her husband had disagreed with her choice of hats. Cancelled some visit to one more of her boring soirées. That's all it needed. Had he done that, he would have been pronounced 'mad' in the same tone of voice.

I said: 'Sit down, Mother. Have a sherry.'

'I couldn't. I'm too upset.'

'Have a sherry, Mother. Don't exaggerate.'

'Exaggerate!' The outraged glare looked almost genuine.

'Sit down.' I guided her across the library, and eased her into one of the high-backed wing-chairs. I could feel her trembling a little but that, too, could be a deliberate put-on. With a little coaching, she could have made a fortune as an actress – assuming she concentrated on the more hammy roles. 'Good sherry has a soothing effect. It puts things into perspective.'

The moistness around the eyes looked genuine enough, too. But (as I say) it was a part she'd learned to play with consummate ease.

As I walked to the booze cabinet, she said: 'The little bitch. She's young enough to be his daughter.'

'He has his flings.' I unstoppered the decanter and chose two glasses. 'It's happened before.'

'He hasn't wanted to marry any of them before.'

I smiled to myself, and said: 'She must be rather special.'

'Special! My dear boy, she's a raving nymphomaniac, from what I hear. She'll kill the poor man within a year.'

'So don't give him a divorce.'

'You don't understand. *He's* going to divorce *me*.'

'He's. . . .' I muttered, 'Damn,' as the decanter shook slightly and spilled sherry on to the glass counter. Then, 'How on earth can he divorce *you*, Mother? He's the one who regularly takes part in the Sex Olympics.'

'Last Christmas. . . .' She had the grace to mumble a little. To pause before she continued: 'There was this rather dishy man. A perfect gentleman. One of the most charming men I've ever —'

'Get on with it, Mother.' I handed her one of the glasses.

'St Tropez.' She sipped the sherry. Her damp eyes took on a dreamy look. 'We had a *wonderful* time.'

'Both in and out of bed,' I murmured as I settled in the other wing-chair.

'Please don't be crude, dear.'

'Get on with it,' I said impatiently.

'Your father – '

'*Step*father.'

' – saw fit to engage this disgusting little man to spy on us.'

'A private detective.'

'That's what he called himself.' She tipped more sherry into her mouth. 'A snooper. He took photographs. Copies of the hotel register. Statements from some of the maids.'

'In other words, he *has* you.'

'That's a very sordid way of putting it.'

'It's a sordid business,' I countered. 'At your age, it's more

74

than a little ridiculous.'

'I'm not yet in my dotage,' she snapped. 'Some men find me attractive.'

'You . . . or your money.'

'Your father – your *step*father – has stopped my allowance.' Her voice was that of a spoiled and sulky child. 'He's being very unpleasant about things.'

'I don't blame him.'

'Whose side are you on?' she flared.

'I'm on the side of common sense. He's a randy old devil . . . of course he is. But you're as bad. Traipsing off to St Tropez for a dirty weekend with a complete stranger. You deserve each other.'

'He *wasn't* a complete stranger. He was a charming—'

'Anyway, you can take your husband to court, and force him to pay you an allowance. Bed-hopping on his part has to be paid for, too.'

'It will take money,' she said in a little-girl-lost voice.

'What?'

'Taking him to court.'

'So what?' You're not destitute. You have enough money of your own to—'

'I am,' she interrupted.

'What?'

'Destitute . . . almost.'

'Let's have it,' I breathed.

'I've had bad advice. Stocks. Shares. Investments. That sort of thing.'

'Some other "charming man"?' I sneered.

'He convinced me he knew what he was doing.'

'But of course. They all do.'

'I've – I've lost it all . . . almost.'

There was a silence. It wasn't a very warm or comfortable silence. This stupid bitch had obviously lost her marbles, along with the comfortable living my real father had provided for her. Her brains had slipped. They'd ended up somewhere in the region of her crotch – and at *her* age!

Frankly, I didn't give too much of a damn about *her*. My

75

own life-style was also on the Cresta Run – and that's what concerned me most. I could live, of course. Rent from the flat and the maisonettes would keep the wolf well away from the door, but I'd also become accustomed to a full quota of cherries on top of each knickerbocker glory. Those cherries had been provided by a steady stream of three- and four-figure cheques. And those cheques had originated from the man who had now turned off the fiscal tap.

I finished the sherry, stood up and returned to the booze-bottles. I needed something stronger than sherry.

As I poured myself a stiff whisky, I said: 'You're telling me you're broke. That it?'

'Put bluntly, I'm afraid I am, dear.'

'Mother,' I said quietly, but very calmly, 'you're a stupid cow. I always knew you were dumb. I've always accepted the fact that you were dizzy. But this! Sweet Jesus, for the sake of a piece of hole-in-the-corner tail, you've dumped yourself in the gutter.' I tipped whisky down my throat, then ended: 'Go get yourself washed down the drain, Mother. Just don't think you're taking me with you.'

It was nice to get her out of my way. To get her off my back. We'd neither of us gone in for apron strings but, nevertheless, she'd always been *there*. Something of an embarrassment. Something of a pain. But necessary if the pot was to remain filled. Now the pot could only empty.

I had enough, for the moment, but I needed more. I needed much more. Indeed, I needed as much as I could get.

I am, you must understand, honest. I have faults galore, but dishonesty isn't one of them. Screw compassion. Screw tolerance. Screw every aspect of the love-thy-neighbour gag. I'm as big a bastard as the next man. The difference – the *only* difference – is that I don't pretend. I don't waste time play-acting. I have one life, and I intend to live it. Not waste bloody great chunks of it tooling around making 'brotherly love' gestures.

Which, I suppose, is one reason why I mentioned things to Frisch.

We were on the range. I was practising with a .38 Mark IV Webley revolver against a moving target. It wasn't easy, and Frisch had dismissed the suggestion of ear-muffs with open contempt.

'It is only noise. At first, noise makes you blink, and spoils the aim. Eventually, you will become accustomed to the noise and you will no longer blink.'

I'd reloaded five times and, so far, I hadn't hit a damn thing. The targets were cheap, unglazed side-plates. The sort of thing you throw wooden balls at at fairgrounds. They rolled down a slotted rail, in front of the sandbags, dipped, then climbed up a slight incline before they gathered speed again down another slope. They came from left to right, and Frisch released them, one at a time, by pressing a bell-push button fixed to a low table at one side of the firing-point. It had looked easy. Even at twenty yards, it had looked easy.

The hell it was easy!

I growled: 'It's costing us a fortune, in ammunition.'

'Two things wrong.' His deep voice showed no impatience. 'You're deliberately *aiming*. And when you squeeze the trigger you're stopping the swing of the revolver.' He held out a hand. 'Here. Give it to me. Then release two targets, one after the other.'

He reloaded, nodded, and I pressed the button, then pressed it a second time. Two shots were fired, and two plates were shattered.

'So bloody easy!'

'It *is* easy.' The smile that wasn't quite a smile touched his lips. 'Like riding a bicycle. Once you can do it, you can *do* it ... every time. The two-handed grip. Firm, but not tense. Point, like you might point a finger. Like you might point a torch beam. Forget the sights. Point at the leading edge of the plate, and a little low. The slight kick will bring you in line. And keep the barrel moving in time with the target.'

Ten shots later, I broke a plate. Five shots later, a second plate. Thereafter, I could more or less guarantee two plates with each six-shot reload.

It started to rain. Gusts of fine moisture blown across the open moorland.

As we hurried towards the house, he said: 'You're hooked, my friend.'

'Hooked?'

'Like your uncle. Like me. A little gun-happy.'

'It's a hobby,' I admitted.

'More than a hobby.'

'OK.' We ducked into the porch and he opened the door, then stood aside to let me enter first. I asked: 'How much do I owe you for the rounds?'

He told me, and my lips puckered into a silent whistle.

'You don't agree?' he queried.

'No argument,' I assured him. 'Just that, in future, I'd better not waste too many bullets.'

That's how I told him. Not because I wanted sympathy. Not because I wanted cut-price ammunition. I was getting top-class tuition, and knew it. It was just that trigger-squeezing had to be tailored to a lower income.

In his workshop, he disassembled the Webley, cleaned the various parts and oiled them as I watched. He wore the watchmaker's eyeglass as he worked. No firearm was ever cleaned better, or with such loving care.

The conversation was desultory. At least, it was *supposed* to be desultory, but it wasn't as desultory as it sounded.

'Too much oil. The wrong type of oil. Oil which is too thick. Just "oiling" a gun isn't enough.'

'So I see.'

'You work the oil – the *correct* oil – into the metal. Then you wipe it off, with cheesecloth. It doesn't *all* come off. Not at one wipe. Not without a good oil dissolvent. What's left within the atomic structure of the metal is *about* the correct amount.'

'Only "about"?'

'You're not a poor man, of course. Despite your mother's indiscretion – despite the coming divorce – you won't be a poor man.'

'I've grown accustomed to money.'

'You can sell one of your guns. The right buyer, the right gun . . . you'd get a good price.' He squinted up the barrel of the Webley. 'A mistake most people make. They don't *clean* the barrel. They only oil it. The lands and the grooves need far more than a pull-through. They need a brush.'

He took a copper-wire brush from its place on the rack above the bench. I think it was one of the many tools he'd made for himself. The head of the brush fitted snugly into the bore of the revolver. He smeared a touch of silversmith's paste on to the bristles then, as we talked, he worked the brush up and down the revolver's barrel.

'The edges of the lands must cut. Cleanly and without any interruption. *Then* you get a near-perfect spin . . . and accuracy.'

'Doesn't anything satisfy you?'

'Perfection isn't possible.' He squinted up the barrel, and seemed satisfied. 'Your mother will need financial assistance, I presume.'

'She may expect . . . she won't *get*.'

'Not an abundance of affection?'

'What affection I had – I have *ever* had – I keep strictly for myself.'

His unique smile came and went. He threaded a clean piece of four-by-two through the eye of a short cleaning rod and began to polish the paste from the inside of the barrel.

'I have no intention of selling a gun,' I said gently.

'Merely a suggestion.'

'Of course. I'll find other means of making money.'

'Something.'

Having once more examined the interior of the revolver barrel, he replaced the piece of four-by-two with a new piece, then dropped a single spot of oil on to the tiny oblong of flannelette and returned to working on the barrel.

'Work, of some sort,' he murmured.

'That depends what is meant by the word "work".'

He finished with the barrel, then started on the cylinder. He worked on the cylinder for about five minutes, spent a few more minutes on the firing mechanism and the striking pin, then began to reassemble the revolver.

As if he'd just heard my last remark, he asked: 'What do *you* mean by the word "work"?'

'Minimum exertion. Maximum reward.'

'Something for nothing?'

'No. I don't gamble. But somewhere in this world there must be somebody who wants what I've got ... and is prepared to pay for it.'

'What *have* you got?'

There seemed to be a certain emphasis on that question. A very light emphasis, which had to be recognised ... but it was there. I answered both honestly and carefully.

'No ties. No conscience. A belief in myself, but a complete trust of nobody else.' I smiled, and added: 'I'm also young and healthy.'

He returned the assembled Webley to its holster, then placed the holster in its position behind the steel-wire-mesh doors of a wall cabinet. He locked the doors, and I guessed (more than guessed) that the revolver, along with the other collection of handguns which decorated the rear wall of the cabinet, was quite safe. Frisch was the sort of man to have very sophisticated alarm signals around the house.

As we left the workshop, he said: 'Tea and crumpets? Very English. If you can stay.'

'I'd like that.'

'Anne will prepare them, while we talk.'

He left me to call in at the kitchen, then joined me in the armchairs. Oddly enough, one of the armchairs had, by silent agreement, already become 'my' chair. It was the one I always used, and while I sat in it Sheba seemed to be more at ease than if I wandered around the room.

When he returned, he sat silently for a few moments, then asked: 'How well can you drive?'

'Better than I can shoot,' I fenced.

'That's not saying much.'

'I can drive,' I said quietly.

Again, that feeling. That faint tingling of the nape hairs. He was asking simple questions. Innocent questions. But, as

I already knew, he wasn't the sort of man to waste time on empty talk. Therefore, my answers were truthful, but careful. It was as if we didn't *quite* trust each other ... but, given a chance, were prepared to take that extra risk.

'At speed?' he asked.

'As fast as the next man.'

'Land-Rovers? Four-wheel drives?'

'I've driven them.'

'Often?'

'Often enough to be able to handle one.'

'Well?'

'You're getting at something.' I smiled as I made the mild accusation. 'You know damn well I can drive. I drive out here. I can drive a Land-Rover as well as I can drive my own car. If that's what you're asking, that's the answer. But why the question?'

It tipped the tilt-button. It was meant to. I had the impression that my show of impatience rather pleased him.

He rubbed a hand across the skin of his hairless skull, then said: 'Tea and crumpets. Then you can show me.'

The Land-Rover was in top nick. The 'feel' of it left no doubt. A touch on the pedal, and the engine responded as if it was part of my own brain. Not a hint of slack in the steering-wheel. The tyres were almost new and all at exactly the right pressure.

'Yours?' I'd asked as he'd opened the garage doors.

He'd nodded and handed me the keys.

A few miles down the moorland track I'd remarked: 'She drives well.'

'I like what I own to work.' He'd pointed across me and to the right. 'Four miles ... thereabouts. There's a pine forest. Forestry Commission. Make for it, across country. Keep it at about sixty.'

Few other vehicles of its size could have taken it. Springs would have gone. Back axles would have snapped. The steering mechanism would have wonked out. The Land-Rover bucked and slewed, and the impression was that, half the time, the wheels weren't in contact with the ground. By this time, the rain was pouring and the ground was like wet rubber, but each time I pulled her out of a skid and the four-wheel drive kept her going and drove us forward. *And* the needle stayed around the sixty mark.

It was his vehicle. If he wanted to knacker it up, that was his prerogative. All I did was drive.

I slowed as we reached the trees.

'Into the forest,' he ordered. 'Zig-zag. Double back. Stay off the tracks. Enjoy yourself. Let's see how well you *can* handle a car.'

For more than half an hour I had a ball. We smashed through undergrowth. We controlled skids in order to nip between trees with inches to spare. I think I tried to drive that Land-Rover to destruction, without actually hitting any of the trunks. In short, I had a feeling it was what he wanted . . . and, in the circumstances, at suicidal speed.

All Frisch did was hang on to his grab-handle and say nothing. Occasionally – when I'd a few yards to spare – I shot a glance at him. He remained stone-faced, but I had the impression he was, if not impressed, *satisfied*.

At last, he pointed and said: 'Fine. Out, that way. A straight course for home.'

'You can drive.'

Frisch made the observation when we'd settled back in our chairs. We were all three there. Four, including the dog. Frisch and I nursed a warming rum-and-pep. We needed it. Spring comes late on the high moors, and we'd been tear-arsing around like lunatics in the Land-Rover. Nor was the log fire yet superfluous.

The girl listened to our conversation. Turning her head as each of us spoke. As if she could see. As if her world was not of a darkness beyond comprehension of those with sight.

I sipped my drink and said: 'I enjoy driving.'

'And this stuff?' He moved his glass.

'It warms the cockles.'

'No . . . I don't mean just *this*.'

82

'Booze?'

He nodded.

'A little social drinking,' I hedged.

'That's what they all say. Including drunks.'

'Ah, but I'm not a very social type. I drink – I don't drink.' I moved one shoulder. 'Wine at a well-organised meal. Nice . . . but not essential.'

It was part of the same pattern. The pattern that had included the gentle questioning in the workshop. The driving of the Land-Rover. But now we both knew and didn't make pretence. I gave honest answers, without excuses attached to their tails.

'Cigarettes?' he said.

'No more than five a day. One to end a good meal. One at bedtime. I'm not hooked . . . and I don't merely *think* I'm not hooked.'

'Women?'

'I'm not married.'

'That signifies very little these days.'

'I've had women,' I said gently. 'At my age, who hasn't? But what they have to offer doesn't drive me crazy.'

'Men?' he asked pointedly.

'Do me a favour!' I glared a little, and tipped some of the drink down my throat. 'I have the equipment. I just don't want to wear it out before middle age.'

He chuckled. He had the voice for chuckling. Deep, fruity and infectious. I found myself grinning on the rebound.

He tasted rum-and-pep, then said: 'You have a mother. You don't like her too much. No sisters, no brothers . . . I've already checked that out.'

'That could be called "invasion of privacy".'

'What about uncles? Aunts?'

'Forget them. I never see them. I don't even send Christmas cards.'

'Friends?'

'Frisch, I'm a loner.' My patience was getting thin. 'It takes one to know one . . . and *you're* one. Screw the world. *I'm* the world. The only part of the world that matters. Start from that basis, then say what you want to say.'

'Five thousand?' he murmured.

'Five thousand what?'

'Notes. Pound notes.'

'A nice round figure. Now tell me about the catch.'

'Just to drive. A Land-Rover. The Land-Rover you drove today. Through a forest . . . again, like today.'

'And the *real* catch?'

'It won't be legal,' he said calmly.

'Tell me what I haven't already guessed, Frisch.'

'Oh, no.' He shook his head. 'An affirmative or a negative. That's your choice. One answer brings you five thousand pounds. The other answer? Everything's on a "need to know" basis. You now know as much as you *need* to know, before you decide.'

'An affirmative,' I smiled. 'Five thousand affirmatives, in fact.'

'Good.' He nodded slow satisfaction. 'From now on, no booze, no women and keep it to five cigarettes a day.'

'And, of course, silence?'

'What can you tell anybody?' This time it was his special smile that came and went. 'That you've driven a Land-Rover. That you're going to drive the same Land-Rover again. Somewhere. At some time in the future. For the moment, you *know* what you "need to know".'

Without suggesting I was a mastermind or even, at that stage, was aware of the world I was stepping into, I knew I'd crossed a line. In effect I'd agreed to an illegality. An obviously very large illegality. The friendly neighbourhood copper who motioned a silent greeting whenever we passed in the street would no longer be the friendly neighbourhood copper. He would be one of Them. The enemy . . . even though (hopefully) he would be unaware of being the enemy.

Self-preservation insisted that I try to keep it that way.

The idea of what can only be termed a cut-out came to me

84

one night, just before I fell asleep. A gap, between myself and whatever it was I had become involved in. A missing link in a chain – put it that way.

The next day I worked on a few half-cock ideas then, quite suddenly, the perfect answer slipped into place.

It was mid-to-late afternoon when I strolled into the gallery and asked to see Pollard. Five minutes later I was in that tiny office of his, and we were shaking hands and making great play with the glad-to-see-you-again routine. It was all crap, of course – we'd seen each other regularly – but this was the first time I'd visited his gallery since Mother had blackmailed me there, some considerable time ago. The coffee was soon out, and we were talking. The reason for his exaggerated delight was obvious. I'd seen the light. I was actually *interested* in the meaningless garbage hanging on the walls.

'I knew you would,' he gushed. 'Dammit, I *knew*. It grows on you. Suddenly, you understand. You can *see*.'

'I've tried my hand,' I lied.

'What?'

'Y'know. Cubism. Impressionism. I – er – I haven't mentioned it before, but. . . .' I fluttered my hands in what I hoped looked like embarrassment.

'You must let me *see*,' he enthused.

'No!' I shook my head. 'Not yet. It isn't finished yet. But I – y'know – I think I'm on the right lines. I think I've *got* something.'

'Good. Good.'

'Pollard.' I leaned forward a little. Tried to put pleading into my tone. 'If I *have* got something – if I've the knack – if it *does* come out right – will you hang it?'

'What?' He stared.

'Here. In the gallery. Please.'

'Look, old man, I can't make any promises. Sight unseen . . . that sort of thing.'

'Just for a week,' I said gently. 'No more. One week. To see the reaction.'

'It's asking a lot. We've a whole queue of —'

'In a corner, somewhere,' I insisted. 'Anywhere.'

'All right,' he agreed reluctantly. 'For the sake of friendship.' Then, as an after-thought; 'I'll have to see it first, of course.'

'Of course. When it's finished.'

'What's it called?' he asked.

'Oh!' The question caught me flat-footed. I hadn't even started painting the damn thing, much less given it a name. I treated him to a shy smile, then said: 'Just a number, at the moment.'

'A number?'

'Six-nine-eight.'

'Why six-nine-eight?' he frowned.

'Well, y'see *I* know what it represents.' I was pushing things to the limit, but there was no other way. I continued: 'But that's not good enough, is it? It's what the viewer sees that really matters. Six-nine-eight – it's just a number. A lucky number. When you see it – when I've finished it – *you* tell me the immediate reaction. What *you* think it represents. Then I'll know whether I've got it right.'

There was more of the same. Empty pseudo-artistic gunge with which to spoil moderately decent coffee but, before I left, I'd convinced Pollard of the novelty of putting up an unknown ... who just *might* take the fancy of a clique of patrons as crazy as *he* was.

On my way home I called to buy the canvas, the paint and the brushes.

I set up shop in the studio that evening and, in less than an hour, I ruined a perfectly good canvas. I didn't even *try* to make sense; to make sense would have defeated the whole object. I daubed solid black squares, broken and overlapped by scarlet oblongs and linked by squiggles of white against a dark green background. I filled the whole canvas with colour, and I used as much skill as I'd have used painting a garden fence.

Then, on an impish impulse, I signed it with a flourish at the bottom right-hand corner. 'L. Lados.' It wasn't my name, of course. It wasn't even a pseudonym. It was a piece of off-beat humour which Pollard would never see. He wasn't the sort of man to read a name backwards!

'A week on Friday. June the ninth.' Frisch used a manicured finger to point the locations on the open road-map on the bench. 'North on the B6320 to just south of Bellingham. Left on the unclassified road towards Hesleyside. Then stop. Park and wait. Be there at half-past noon. A blue VW will join you. It will come up behind you. Stay behind the wheel, and keep the engine running. Three men will load what there is to load into the Land-Rover, then they'll climb in with you. Then, away ... through Hesleyside, west. Along that unclassified road until you have Kielder Reservoir on your right. Not before. Anybody following will have a choice of six turnings you *might* have taken. The reservoir on your right. You'll be on the northern fringe of the bulk of Kielder Forest. *Then* turn left. Through Kielder Forest, across open countryside, through Kershope Forest – south-west – cross the B6318, and make for Haggbeck.' He rested his finger on the two spots which located the hamlet on the map. He continued: 'One of the men will leave you just beyond Haggbeck. Then south-west – unclassified roads – to Longtown. A second man will leave you at Longtown. South along the A7 to the M6 motorway. The service station south of junction 43. The third man will leave you there. After that, you're on your own. Any sign of police activity, leave the motorway. Make your way back here. I'll be waiting.'

He raised his balloon-like head and waited for questions.

'Trouble?' I asked.

'There shouldn't be any. It's well planned.'

'But if there is?'

'You're a man of some initiative.'

I nodded slowly, then said: 'Once they're in the Land-Rover – whoever "they" are – any trouble, any difficulties, and *I* give the orders.'

'You're the new boy,' he said flatly.

'*I'm* behind the wheel.' My voice was as flat and as

unemotional as his. 'Let's assume the worst – let's *assume* trouble – there may not be time for a secret ballot.'

'Point taken.' Again, the slow nod. 'The others might not like it. . . .'

'I'll take orders from you. Now. I don't take orders from some stranger.'

'All right.' He'd made his decision and I knew he'd stick to it. 'I'll pass the word. Any slip-ups, *once they've reached the Land-Rover*, you're the boss.' A pause, then: 'Don't *you* make any slip-ups.'

As he folded the road-map, I murmured: 'The money. The five thousand pounds.'

'You'll get it,' he grunted.

'Ah, yes. But *my* way.'

'You seem to be taking over.' He picked up the folded map, and we walked from the workshop. He warned: 'Don't make too many qualifications. Other people can drive Land-Rovers.'

It was a bluff, and we both knew it. Other people *could* drive Land-Rovers, but he knew how well *I* could drive one, and it was too late to take chances. I took my wallet from my inside pocket, slipped out a pasteboard card and handed it to him.

'It's a picture gallery,' I explained. 'There'll be a painting. It will be numbered. Six-nine-eight. They're all numbered. This one . . . six-nine-eight. Send somebody to buy it. Some "innocent" somebody. Five thousand. That's its price. No haggling. Just buy the painting.'

He frowned at the card, and said: 'Do these people know?'

'They can't even *guess*,' I smiled. 'They haven't even seen the painting yet.'

'You are', he murmured, 'a very suspicious man.'

'Careful,' I corrected him. 'I can make calculated guesses. In fancy language, I like to determine my own destiny.'

He chuckled. It amused him. Great. Now we were *both* happy.

* * *

88

Pollard was an even bigger fool than I'd taken him for. I'd leaned the daubed canvas against the wall of his office, and he'd solemnly eyed it for all of two minutes, with his head slightly on one side.

'Yes,' he'd said slowly. 'Quite startling, really.'

'Startling?'

'Startlingly *good* . . . actually.'

And now I was waiting. Watching him walk towards the artistic lunacy, then back away from it. Squinting his eyes and pursing his lips.

'It's – er – it's supposed to have an emotional impact,' I said, without much hope.

'Of course. Of course. A whirlpool . . . that's obvious.'

'A. . . .' I swallowed, then cleared my throat. 'A whirlpool. Actually, I was thinking of calling it *Maelstrom*.'

'*Maelstrom*. Of course . . . of course!'

I made noises of modest satisfaction and, silently, wondered when the hell he'd last seen a square whirlpool.

'The black of the unknown,' he enthused. 'The red signifying danger. Those carefully positioned greens and whites. The sea and the foam. Oh, yes. *Definitely*. *Maelstrom*.'

'You'll show it?'

'Certainly, old boy. What was it? A week? I'll do more than that. A month with pleasure.'

'Do you think it might sell?'

I couldn't resist the question. Pollard's crass stupidity forced it from me. This immaculate gag had to be played all the way.

'Well, now. . . .' Quite suddenly, much of the enthusiasm dissipated. Business was business, and nitty-gritty didn't mix too well with smooth con-talk. He cupped his chin in the V of a thumb and forefinger, then said: 'You're unknown, of course. That name – what is it . . .?' He leaned forward a little.

'"Lados,"' I said, '"L. Lados."'

'Why "Lados"?'

'I just. . . .' I moved a hand in a vague gesture. 'In case it

89

was laughed at, I suppose.'

'You won't be *laughed* at, old boy.'

'Anyway, leave it,' I insisted. 'And – as a favour – give it number six-nine-eight.'

'Your lucky number?' he smiled.

'Don't let's take any risks.' I bowed my lips into a return smile, then said: 'You think it *might* sell?'

'It's possible . . . for a modest price, of course.'

'Of course.'

And that is how I left it. Pollard was being used . . . but didn't know it. As a bonus, the whole thing was a private giggle, and proof of what I'd long suspected: that the ingots of the art world were made of gilded lead. Nevertheless, I wasn't complaining. Pollard was the innocent 'cut-out'. Whatever happened on Friday, 9 June – whatever fun and games Frisch had arranged – the chain between Frisch and myself had a link missing.

The rest is criminal history. That June Friday in 1962, and the half-million wage-snatch. It wasn't *quite* half a million, but the media people like round figures. The security guard who earned himself a few days of fame, and a limp for the rest of his life, by mixing it with a man carrying a pump-action twelve-bore.

I was waiting, near Hesleyside, and they arrived in a rush. The Volkswagen slewed to a halt and, before it had quite stopped, the front passenger was out and racing towards the Land-Rover.

He screamed: 'Move it! They're on to us.'

Behind him, I saw his buddy struggling to haul the injured man from the rear of the car. Something had gone badly wrong, and the frightened man clawing his way into the back of the Land-Rover wasn't helping.

I pulled the keys from the ignition and, ignoring the shouted curses, ran to help the guy struggling with his mauled pal.

I took the legs, and snapped. 'What happened?'

'They're behind us. Not far behind us.'

'Who? The police?'

'A copper . . . but not a squad car. Some bloody have-a-go civilian.'

We were both panting as we hoisted the injured man aboard the Land-Rover, but now *I* was the one giving orders. The creep who'd been concentrating on his own skin was still shouting the place down, but I ignored him. The man we were carrying seemed to have had half his side shot away, therefore all *he* could do was moan a little. I snapped questions, then orders, at the man carrying the shoulders.

'How far behind?'

'I don't know. They were on to us on the B-class.'

'Radio link?'

'I shouldn't think so. Maybe walkie-talkie.'

'The policeman?'

'A glory merchant. He commandeered the bloody car . . . *and* the driver. He picked lucky. The sod can drive.'

'Chances are they missed this turning,' I mused.

'They'll back-track. They're too bloody —'

'With squad cars,' I agreed. Then I bawled at the terrified man in the Land-Rover: 'Will you make less blasted noise! Make your pal as comfortable as possible.' Then, in a quieter tone, to the third man: 'What's still in the car?'

'The money.' And almost as an afterthought: 'The pump-gun.'

'Get the money loaded into the Land-Rover.'

'Look, we haven't —'

'Do it!'

I raced to the VW and opened the door. A Winchester twelve-bore pump-action shotgun was on the rear seat.

As I ducked inside the car to grab it, I asked: 'How many shells still left in the magazine?'

'Four.' He had the boot of the car open and was already hauling canvas bags on to the road.

'Load up,' I snapped. 'You're going nowhere till everything's on board.'

'Sure. Sure.'

He was a reliable man, therefore I took time to explain my

91

own line of thought.

'Assumptions. The police will know. That means squad cars. They'll be on the B-class. They'll each take a turning. If one takes *this* turning before we're ready, I'll stop him.'

'Check.' He dumped bags from the road into the rear of the Land-Rover.

'The car following you – what colour?'

'Red. A Fiesta.'

'Get your pal ready for a rough ride. Then yell.'

I sprinted down the lane, in the direction from which the VW had come. I stood at a bend, half-hidden behind the bole of a strategically placed oak; a position from where I could see both the Land-Rover and the lane as it snaked towards the B6320. I heard the man shout, glanced and saw him wave and, at the same time, heard the approach of the car.

Later Frisch asked me, and I told no less than the truth. That car had to be stopped. Squad car, Ford Fiesta – whatever car it was going to be – it *had* to be stopped, and those in it prevented from seeing the Land-Rover and passing on information. If, by 'thinking' what is meant is weighing pros against cons and reaching a decision, I didn't 'think'. I instinctively *knew*.

It just happened to be a police squad car.

I 'stopped' it by sending the first blast full-face through the oncoming windscreen. I even had to step aside to allow the car to swing out of control and smash, bonnet first, into the oak I'd been standing alongside. Nobody had time to lift a microphone.

After that, it was easy. I merely walked to the wrecked car, pushed the snout of the Winchester twelve-bore through the shattered window and took off the tops of the heads of the two coppers.

It was all so very obvious. Any following car would stop, the driver would see the wreck, then the carnage and (whoever they were) the shock would give us extra time and extra distance.

ELEVEN

Some portraitists return to the same model time after time; they redrape the model and repose the model, but it is always the same model. As with artists and photographers, so with musicians. Some have a wide span, while others, no less gifted, concentrate upon two, perhaps three, great composers; they dedicate their life to reaching beyond the notation, and even beyond the notes, in an effort to understand the man and the mind responsible for the composition.

What is not often realised is that policemen – especially great policemen – occasionally have this 'one-person' determination which builds up to a near-religion. Daniel Barenboim is a pianist of immense stature, whose interpretation of any composition must be listened to with wonder but, over and above that, he is recognised as a world expert on Beethoven; he 'knows' Beethoven – especially Beethoven's piano music – better than any other man alive. Equally, with Superintendent Leonard 'Nipper' Read. He was a superb detective who solved more than his fair share of crimes but his reason for living – the rank he carried at New Scotland Yard – was the destruction of the Kray firm; and only when he'd smashed *that* outfit was he prepared to contemplate possible retirement.

They are good men, these dedicated coppers, but not necessarily good husbands. They have a mistress whose name is Law Enforcement, and their wives must learn to live alongside that mistress . . . wondering whether she or they take first place.

David Hoyle didn't realise it but he, too, was becoming one of these one-track-mind manhunters.

Nor, come to that, did his newly-acquired wife realise it. But what she *did* realise was that, for some of the time, his thoughts were straying along paths which, in the circumstances, were rather strange.

'Hey, boyo,' she said, with some asperity, 'we're on our honeymoon . . . remember?'

'What!' Hoyle jerked his head from where he'd been gazing from the hotel bedroom window. He gave a half-embarrassed smile, then added: 'Sorry.'

'"Sorry," he says.' Alva Hoyle's indignation was almost wholly genuine. The Welsh lilt gave the words a delightful sing-song quality, but the dark eyes glinted and there was enough anger there to give warning. 'David, my pet, I never mistook you for a raving sex maniac – '

'Good.'

' – but, two days after marrying you, I didn't expect to see you gaping out to sea, looking for inspiration. Or are you bored with me already, perhaps?'

Hoyle blushed slightly, then snapped: 'Don't be so bloody stupid.'

'Oh, so it's swearing already, is it?'

'I'm not swearing.'

'"Bloody" is swearing, where I come from.'

'Oh, for Christ's sake.'

'So is *that.*'

'Are you asking me to make love to you?' he said heavily.

'My God, no.' And now the outrage was genuine. 'Asking? You think I'm going to *ask*?'

'In that case, what the hell are you on about?' And now *he* was becoming angry.

The exchange demonstrated their newly wed naïveté. They had yet to learn that a blazing row can be, and often is, the prelude to an immaculate, no-holds-barred coupling. That passion of one kind can so easily slip into the passion of another. They thought they were quarrelling; that this was the first quarrel of their married life. She having come from the shower and exchanged bathing costume for panties and bra. He still in swimming-trunks, prior to taking his turn

94

under the needle-spray. Sexually, they were innocents ...
but they were learning.

He glared at her – saw a woman he loved apparently
goading him, like some experienced coquette – and struggled
to control what was happening. She lowered her eyes from
his face, saw his unwilling arousal and, woman-like, smiled
as her outrage melted.

As he strode past her, on his way to the bathroom, she
caught his arm.

'David, boy....' She looked up into his face again. 'All
right, boy. I'm asking.'

'You....' The words came from the back of his throat.
'You little Welsh witch.'

He stooped, lifted her effortlessly and, with her arms
around his neck and their lips bruising each other's, carried
her to the bed.

The Clifton Arms Hotel at Lytham St Annes deserved its
four-star rating. Thus the opinion of David and Alva Hoyle
as, later that same evening, they sat in the hotel dining-room
and enjoyed a first-class dinner. Not that either of them had
had experience of other four-star hotels, but it *was* their
honeymoon ... and Hoyle had been newly promoted to
detective sergeant.

The waitress skilfully boned the Dover sole and placed the
twin fillets on David's plate. She'd already done the same for
Alva.

'The roe, sir?' she asked.

'No, thank you.'

A waiter and a second waitress moved between them,
serving the trimmings. The button mushrooms, the baby
sprouts, the potatoes. Here, at the Clifton Arms, a meal was
far more than a meal. It was the gastronomic equivalent to a
West End production.

Having filled the plates, the waitresses left.

The waiter murmured: 'Everything satisfactory, sir?'

'Fine, thanks.'

Then the waiter, too, left.

Alva raised her glass of wine a few inches from the spotless tablecloth, grinned across at her husband and said: 'How the other half live.'

'Make the most of it. You're lumbered with fish and chips, and washing-up, when we get back.'

'You're going to be a brute of a husband.' Then, having sipped the wine, and in a more serious tone: 'What's worrying you David, my love?'

'Who says I'm worried?'

'Before we. . . .' She ran the tip of her tongue across her lips.

'Conjugal rights?' he teased.

'You were miles away.'

'I know,' he sighed. 'Back at Lessford. Bobbying.'

'Something wrong?' And now all the banter had left her voice.

'Not wrong.' He frowned. 'Not exactly *wrong*. Just worrying.'

'Can't you share it?' she asked gently.

Thus, they talked, while they ate a fine meal. They ate slowly and talked softly, and Alva learned of one more burden required to be carried by a policeman's wife.

'Ripley's wrong,' he began.

'Ripley?' She raised quizzical eyebrows. 'I thought you liked Ripley.'

'He's a good man. A fine copper.'

'He was responsible for your promotion . . . wasn't he?'

'That he was, and I'm grateful.' A quick chuckle as he raised a forkful of fish to his mouth. 'Lewis blew a gasket when the chief took more notice of Ripley's recommendation than he did of *his* assessment.'

'In that case. . . .'

'But he's still *wrong*. "A killer gets killed. One less to worry about." That's how he put it, but you can't dismiss murder like that.'

'Ripley can . . . apparently.'

'Oh, I understand him.' He waved the empty fork a little. 'But he's *wrong*.'

96

'David, my pet, it's not even in your police area.'

'I know more about that murder than anybody,' he insisted. 'I've visited Beechwood Brook DHQ at least once a week since the file was "unofficially" closed. I know the statements. I know the reports. I can damn near quote them verbatim.'

'And that's *worrying* you?'

'Dammit, darling. . . .' He loaded the fork with vegetables. 'A murder shouldn't be "forgotten". If we can't detect a murder. . . .'

'But, as I understand it, you're pretty sure the *victim* was a killer. A professional killer.'

'It seems likely.'

'In that case. . . .'

'A *murder*, Alva. . . .' He chewed as he talked. It wasn't the best of manners, but that wasn't important. 'What a man is isn't the issue. If he's killed, deliberately – without a proper trial and sentence – that's murder. A whore can be raped – it's the same thing. The man *was* murdered.'

The theme continued throughout the meal. In fairness, Alva Hoyle tried to understand . . . but failed. Eventually, she *would* understand; she'd become the complete wife of a man to whom law enforcement wasn't merely a job – was more, even, than a vocation. To Hoyle it amounted almost to a sacred trust. The practicality of perfection was something he refused to acknowledge. To Hoyle no crime was 'undetectable'. It simply hadn't *been* detected and, as such, it was an affront to the ability of both himself and his colleagues.

Later, in the lounge and as they sipped their way through coffee, Hoyle expanded the theme; expanded it but, at the same time, brought the exchange to a concentration upon one man. The man whom (although Hoyle didn't know it at the time) Hoyle's whole police service would pivot upon.

'Y'see,' he said, 'we haven't just *one* unknown. We've *two*. It's as if the victim went out of his way to make himself utterly unidentifiable.'

'You've said,' she reminded him. 'The victim was a

97

contract killer – *if* he was a contract killer – that explains things. If he *was* a contract killer – if he *was* engaged in his work – that's it.'

'No.' He shook his head. 'OK, if he was a contract killer, who was he supposed to kill?'

'Whoever killed *him*.'

'No, no.' The headshake was more vigorous. 'It *takes* a contract killer to *kill* a contract killer. And, according to Raff – who seems to know more about these things than me – the rule is for *two* contract men to be detailed for the job. It's not easy, pet. You're not killing a run-of-the-mill bloke. You're after a professional.'

'So . . . you're after two men?' She looked slightly dazed. 'I mean, till now. . . .'

'I don't know.' The sigh was deep and worried. Then: 'No – dammit – not *three*. Three hit men – icemen, mechanics, what the hell the present slang calls them . . . not *three*.'

'You've just said. . . .'

'They aren't so thick on the ground, pet. In America, maybe. A legacy of the Syndicate crowd. But here – in the UK – it's not like in films. On television. Not the real *professionals*.'

A waiter approached to refill the cups with coffee and, for a moment, their talk stopped. They were in the lounge of a class hotel, and the conversation was of assassins and assassination. It was all wrong. They were on their honeymoon – the first days of their honeymoon – and their thoughts were concentrated upon men who kill for a living. That, too, was all wrong. Priorities had gone to pot. They should have been happy – indeed, they *were* happy – but their happiness was clouded by some unknown man (or men) whose profession was destruction of life. There was a ghost there; a spectre which, although they didn't yet know it, would haunt Hoyle and, via Hoyle, his wife for years.

The waiter left, and Hoyle spooned sugar into his coffee and mused: 'They can't, y'know . . . "not be".'

Alva's expression was of complete non-understanding.

'They can't "not be",' insisted Hoyle. 'Two men. The

98

victim and the murderer. Two grown men . . . and, as far as we're concerned, they never existed. We can't put a name to either of them.'

'Tramps do it, my pet,' she said quietly. 'They do it all the time.'

'But – don't you see – they're not tramps. They haven't "opted out". The dead man. He was well dressed. He wasn't a tramp. He lived somewhere. He must have used a bank. He must have bought his clothes somewhere. His watch. His shoes. Everything. He must have *lived* somewhere. Eaten somewhere. Known somebody. Dammit, if he *was* a killer, he must have had something with which to kill. Where's that? Alva, my pet, you can't just arrive, adult and fully clothed, on this planet. You have to leave some ordinary, normal signs of living. You can't *not*.'

'*He* did,' she reminded him gently.

'No!' She was to grow to recognise the grim, determined growl. 'We haven't yet found them . . . that's all.' He tasted the coffee. It was a punctuative gesture, and something to do with his hand. 'Then there's whoever killed him. Whoever moved him from Beechwood Brook to the scrapyard. Lewis is right. More than one. Some sort of vehicle. And they weren't invisible. Somebody must have *seen* something – *heard* something – *know* something. Somebody!' The chin jutted slightly. The nostrils widened a fraction. 'I'll find him. However long it takes . . . I'll find him.'

'Yes, my love.' Her voice was more gentle, but just as determined. 'However long it takes, you'll find him.'

TWELVE

I suspect friendship is not in my nature but, had it been, I think Frisch and I would have become good friends. Age apart, we were of a kind. We could plan then, if the plan went wrong, we could (to use an expression) 'think on our feet'. With me, it came naturally, and I demonstrated it on that Friday in 1962.

The hell with the dropping-off spots. The immediate problem was to get clear, while the police net still had holes. For more then ten miles I stayed with the forest; clear of tracks and weaving the Land-Rover between trees and over streams. At first we left clear proof of our passing, but that was unavoidable; our first priority was distance. Then, gradually, I sought firmer ground, less undergrowth and fewer tyre-marks, then tracks, then little-known roads and, finally, B-class roads and eventually on to the motorway.

Frisch needed no lengthy explanation. The injured man had died on us, and the frightened man wasn't far from hysterics.

'You.' He snapped orders at the man who'd kept his nerve. 'Into the house. Anne will show you. Into the bathroom, scrub down, then clean clothes from the skin out. Tell Anne. She knows where things are.'

As the man hurried indoors, I said: 'What about *that* apology for a man?' I motioned towards the frightened man, as he crouched alongside the corpse. 'What do we do with *him*?'

'Get him out here.'

I vaulted into the rear of the vehicle and rained kicks at the coward's ribs until, eventually, he scrambled to the ground.

'Don't!' rapped Frisch as the man made as if to run. 'You won't get twenty yards.' The dog had joined us, and Frisch pointed and murmured: 'Guard him, Sheba.'

That *really* terrified him. He froze and, other than the uncontrollable trembling, remained motionless.

'Be advised. Don't try anything,' warned Frisch. 'She won't go for your leg. She'll go for your throat.' Then to me: 'Let's get the money inside.'

In the workshop – under the bench – there was a false wall. As with all things to do with Frisch, it was a minor work of art. The shelves and racks above the bench masked the difference in the wall and ceiling lengths and, anyway, the false wall didn't merely *look* solid, it *was* solid. Solid enough to give the lie to any 'tapping' nonsense.

By the time we'd stacked the bags into the foot-wide cavity and returned the false wall to its place, the other man had bathed and changed. He looked a different person; smart almost to the point of spruceness. The clothes fitted him quite well.

'Let him use your car,' said Frisch.

'Of course,' I agreed.

'Harrogate.' Frisch didn't seem to have to think. He gave orders to the man without hesitation. 'Leave the car in the station car park. Leave the keys in the glove compartment. Here. . . .' He held out a thin wad of notes. 'A meal, then a train. You'll have plenty of time. Don't rush things.'

The man took the money, smiled and nodded, then caught the keys as I tossed them towards him.

We waited until the car was out of sight then, without a word Frisch walked briskly to the side of the house, and returned carrying a spade and two shovels. He threw them into the back of the Land-Rover.

He turned to the frightened man, and said: 'It's time you did some work. Climb up.'

'The – the dog. . . .'

'She's going with us. Move slowly – carefully – she'll only attack if I tell her. Or if you do anything foolish.'

* * *

I don't know where the grave was. I know it was out on the moors; four – maybe five – miles from any footpath. I know the ground was peaty and easy to dig; that the frightened man worked like crazy in an attempt (I think) to keep his mind off the dog; that, in less than an hour, we had a rough-sided grave, six feet deep.

'Bring the body,' ordered Frisch, and the frightened man and I hoiked the dead man from the Land-Rover, carried him to the lip of the hole, then swung him outwards and inwards and let go. He landed in a boneless heap, face downward, in the hole.

The frightened man stood on the lip and gazed down at the corpse. It was almost possible to watch the terror taking over again.

Frisch and I exchanged glances, and we both knew what had to be done.

I soft-footed back to the Land-Rover and picked up the Winchester repeating twelve-bore. I strolled back to where we'd been digging, pumped the last shot into the chamber and took the frightened man in the small of the back, from a range of less than a yard. He was dead before he landed on the corpse of his buddy.

'You have quite a flair,' murmured Frisch. He bent forward to reach for a shovel. 'Throw the gun with them. And the ejected case. We'll fill in.'

'Quite a flair,' he repeated musingly.

'That or prison.' It was a pleasant evening, and the Land-Rover handled beautifully, despite the absence of road surface. 'Prison for a long time.'

'Nevertheless. . . .'

We were silent until we reached the track and turned for Frisch's place.

'Will they be found?' I asked. It was something to say. I could have guessed the answer.

'Eventually.' He smiled. 'Some as-yet-unborn archaeologist might make a name for himself . . . by mistake. These moors. . . .' He turned his head and slowly gazed at the great

102

expanse. 'God knows how many graves. Most of it's bog-moss. Give it a month – less – nobody will be able to find it.' He tilted his head slightly, and looked at the sky-colouring in the west. 'Such a small thing,' he mused. 'One body.'

'Two bodies,' I corrected him.

'A thousand bodies. Who would miss them in a place like this?'

'Who would miss them . . . period.'

The remark seemed both to please and amuse him, but he kept his thoughts to himself until we reached the farmhouse.

At the farmhouse, we cleaned ourselves up, then enjoyed a good meal. What people in the northern counties call a 'fry-up': eggs, bacon, sausages, liver, tomatoes and fried bread. I hadn't realised how hungry I'd become. Anne had prepared it, and I think Frisch recognised my wonder at her sightless ability.

'Her sense of touch, her sense of hearing and her sense of distance,' he explained. 'She knows where everything is. Exactly! She can feel the heat from the rings. Hear the sound of it frying. Smell the aroma.' A pause, then a little sadly: 'The eyes are important . . . but not vital.'

'Obviously.'

I forget what else our talk touched upon. It wasn't important. It was mere empty conversation, used to fill the gaps between chewing and swallowing.

Then, after the meal, Frisch backed his own Cortina from the garage, and we set off to Harrogate, to pick up my own car. And there, in the privacy of the sweet-running Ford, he first touched upon what was eventually to be my profession.

'You kill easily,' he observed gently.

'A few ounces of pressure on a trigger.' I stared ahead, and down the headlight beams. 'Anybody can do it.'

'That's not true.'

'A basic truth.'

'Quite. But few people are so "basic".'

'I'm one of the lucky ones, then.'

'Lucky?'

103

'I don't think about it.'

'Not even afterwards?'

'Would it bring them back?' I allowed myself a gentle smile. 'Thoughts? Regrets? If that's all resurrection required, we'd live in a very crowded world.'

'Nevertheless. . . .' He paused, then in a lower voice said: 'Three men in one day. It must add up to something.'

'Five thousand pounds,' I said calmly.

'You'll get that. And more . . . much more.'

'Really?'

'At the moment I'm interested in your mental reactions. A triple murderer. What does it feel like?'

'I feel', I said, 'as if I'm a passenger, in a Ford Cortina, being driven towards Harrogate. That's what I feel, and that's *all* I feel. If you're worried about me having nightmares, don't be. I won't have any.'

'So sure!'

'I know myself, Frisch. This thing everybody calls "love". This "conscience" I hear mentioned. This "compassion". It isn't there. Once upon a time. . . .' I chuckled quietly. 'It isn't something new, Frisch. Years ago, I knew I lacked something. A void, somewhere. An emotional vacuum. I wasn't like other people. They were happy; I was unmoved. Sorrow made them cry; I wondered what the devil they were crying *about*. "Sorrow?" What the hell *is* "sorrow", anyway? I've never known . . . and I don't think I've missed much.

'I've killed three men today, Frisch. Two coppers, one coward. Until you mentioned it, I'd forgotten. It had slipped my memory. I didn't know them. Why should I mourn for them? Why should I *pretend* to mourn? When I go, I don't want anybody to mourn *my* death. I'll look after myself while I'm alive. The rest? Who cares? Who do I *expect* to care?'

We drove for about a hundred yards, before he murmured: 'Ice instead of blood.'

'No,' I argued quietly. 'I bleed. I feel pain . . . physical pain. But not *emotional* pain. Emotional ice, perhaps. But not even that. I don't feel *anything*. Not hot, not cold. Not *anything.*' Then in a slightly piqued tone: 'Dammit, Frisch, I thought you'd understand. You . . . of all people.'

'I understand.'

'You press the brake pedal, and the car slows. You don't feel sorry for the bloody car. You'll sleep soundly tonight, even if you *have* turned the ignition key and stopped the engine.'

'I understand,' he repeated. Then in words which were little more than a whisper: 'I understand perfectly . . . and I'm very glad.'

We spoke no more until we reached the car park at the entrance to Harrogate railway station. I was annoyed – slightly annoyed – and he lived with whatever thoughts were filling his mind. It was a nice night, and a good drive, and the mood had left me long before we reached our destination.

He parked the car, and I made a movement to open the door on my side.

'Wait.' He touched my knee as he spoke. Then: 'Today we earned ourselves a large cake.'

'That's obvious.' I relaxed back into my seat. 'All the "need to know" business. Wasted . . . don't you think?'

'Some of it,' he agreed. 'What you don't yet know you'll read about in tomorrow's newspapers.'

'We carried a fair amount of cash into the workshop,' I said.

'A large cake,' he agreed. 'Without you, we could have gone hungry.'

'Lots and lots of porridge.'

'I don't like porridge.'

'Nor do I. That's why I took over.'

'Two slices of the cake unclaimed,' he said flatly.

'No claimants to press their claims.'

'Therefore, the other slices become fatter. Much fatter.'

'Am *I* at the party?' I tried to keep non-interest in my tone. Even with Frisch, I wanted to retain as much privacy as possible. I added: 'I was engaged as stand-in chauffeur . . . surely?'

'I think we should stop fencing,' he said bluntly. 'You can

be trusted. You've proved that.'

'I'm told crime doesn't pay,' I smiled.

'Stealing apples . . . *that* doesn't pay.'

'The hiding-place, under your bench, was no apple-loft.'

'My friend,' he growled, 'no more fencing. You've killed three men, today. 'You're "safe". If I wasn't sure of that, you'd be in the grave, up on the moors.'

'I had the gun,' I reminded him.

'I, too, had a gun. I also had Sheba.'

I waited. The sparring was over, and Frisch would say what he intended to say.

'Your talent could make you a rich man,' he said at last.

'Immediately?'

'A *very* rich man . . . eventually.'

I moved cautiously, and asked, in an innocent-sounding voice: 'There'll be more than the five thousand?'

'Considerably more.'

'The first five thousand through the picture gallery, as arranged.' Now we were talking business, therefore I adopted a business-like tone. 'The rest . . . let me know. There'll be other paintings to buy.'

'Still suspicious?' he smiled.

I'd given thought to the matter. The truth is I'd contemplated the possibility of earning money by breaking the law. It hadn't needed much imagination to reach certain conclusions, as far as Frisch was concerned. I therefore put my cards on the table face upwards.

I said: 'Capone became rich. "Considerably" rich, to use your own phrase. But he was a fool. He dodged the police, but forgot about the taxman. I'll pay my taxes. I'm an honest man, Frisch. An honourable man. I want no tax haven. No Swiss numbered account. A good accountant, perhaps . . . but no more than that. I'll pay my tax.' I chuckled quietly. 'I – er – sell my paintings, Frisch. *That's* my talent. Painting. A man called Pollard. He handles them. He sells them . . . on my behalf. He takes his cut – his ten per cent – and *I* pay tax, like the good citizen I am, on the remaining ninety per cent. The trick, as I see it. You don't trip up over St Paul's

106

Cathedral; it's the unseen – unnoticed – kerb that brings you down.'

'There is logic there,' he murmured. 'It makes a pleasant change from greed.'

'My present concern', I said, 'centres around gunsmiths.'

'Gunsmiths.' He dropped the word like a pebble on ice. Then: 'Do you know many gunsmiths?'

'You.'

'And?'

As calmly as possible, I said: 'Gunsmiths equate with guns. They deal in guns. They deal in ammunition.'

'Obviously.'

'The law is very touchy on that subject. Policemen like to know what's going on. They visit. At a guess, they visit very often. Today I killed two policemen. You see my point?'

'Quite invalid.' The tone was warmer and more friendly. The impression was that he almost chuckled. 'You know little about the police mind, my friend. On the face of things, to get a gunsmith's licence isn't easy . . . on the face of things. Enquiries are made. Documentation is required. But produce that documentation and you become a trusted man. Completely trusted.'

'And, of couse, you produced that "documentation".'

'Of course. I'm a licensed gunsmith.'

'Neat,' I smiled.

'My friend, I am Persil-white. I can *prove* that. I am a very responsible person . . . otherwise, I wouldn't be a licensed gunsmith. To visit me – other than when the licence needs renewal – would be a waste of valuable police time. And policemen are very busy people.'

On the Monday, Pollard telephoned. I'd been expecting the call. I'd even been expecting – probably *half-* expecting – to hear what he said.

'I've sold the picture.'

'Really! Already?'

'It needed pushing a little.'

'Of course.'

107

'But I did it.'

'Good for you.'

'A good price, too.'

'How much?'

'Five hundred.'

'Five hundred?' I put surprise, but no real enthusiasm, into the words.

'More than I expected.'

'Of course.'

'But I pushed to the absolute limit.'

'Naturally.' Then off-handedly I asked: 'Who bought it?'

'A chap called Jones.'

'Jones?'

'A Welshman, I think. With a name like that, chances are he's a Welshman.'

'All the way from Wales, eh?'

'No. Not from Wales.' He gave me an address – which was what I was fishing for.

'When do I collect?' I asked.

'This afternoon, if you like.'

'Fine. I'll be round.'

'Cash . . . if that's what you want.'

'I'd prefer a cheque.'

'Of course. Of course.'

'Minus your ten per cent, of course.'

'I've worked for it, old boy.' The quiet chuckle came over the wire quite distinctly.

'I'll bet.'

'See you this afternoon, then?'

'About three?'

'I'll be waiting. I'll have the cheque ready.'

It really was like coaxing a lamb into the slaughter-shed. It was as easy as that. There was no such address, of course. I checked that before I went on to the gallery; the house-numbers stopped long before the number Pollard had given me. But I played it along, and gave him his few moments of glory.

108

We toasted the 'deal' in sherry, then he passed me the cheque, along with the official paperwork, with the gallery's heading. The cheque was for £450; a Barclay's cheque, with Pollard's signature.

As I slipped the cheque and the documents into my pocket, I said: 'Quite a coup for a junior partner.'

'They'll be pleased,' he smiled.

'Will they?'

'They – er – they still have doubts. About *me*, I mean.'

'But not now?'

'Not now,' he agreed.

'Now that you've robbed me – or them – of more than four thousand pounds.'

The blood left his face. It was meant to.

'Five thousand, Pollard. Not five hundred.'

'How – how . . . ?'

'Let's say I asked the "Jones" character.'

'You. . . .'

'You have sticky fingers, Pollard. You've just given me documentary proof. Sticky fingers . . . but no brains.'

'Oh, my God!'

'Sit down, Pollard. Listen to me. Listen well – because, if you *don't*, you have more trouble than you can handle this side of hell.'

He sat down. He lowered himself very shakily, and very gingerly, on to a chair. The wonder was he didn't *fall* down. I tasted my sherry – it was rather good sherry – then took time to light one of my occasional cigarettes. I wanted to give Pollard time for it to sink in; to give him time to sweat. Equally, I wanted to impress upon him that it was going to be *my* way . . . or not at all.

I chose a very conversational tone of voice.

'A call at the nearest police station,' I said. 'A talk with some detective sergeant. What you've given me, plus a few statements. Plus an examination of your personal bank account. It's called "obtaining money be means of false pretences". Oh yes, there's also a blood-stained school cap. I still have it. I've treasured it for years. Somewhere, deep in

109

the police files, they'll have a record of the gamekeeper's blood group. They may still have the – er – "murder weapon".' I drew deeply on the cigarette before I continued: 'You're walking across cobwebs, Pollard. One wrong step – one wrong word – and your neck goes. There's an unclaimed noose waiting. Keep *that* firmly in mind.'

'What – what . . .?'

'Don't pass out on me, Pollard. Concentrate. We don't want any more mistakes.'

'What do you want?' he breathed.

'In a nutshell . . . *you*.'

'I – I. . . .'

'First, the full five thousand pounds. All of it. This time we'll skip the ten per cent. That, plus the cheque you've already given me. Let's call *that* payment for a very important lesson.'

'Yes. Yes . . . of course.' His head nodded wildly.

'You're my man, Pollard.' There was no need to threaten. No need for melodramatics. A gently spoken reminder sufficed. 'When I need more money. I'll paint another picture. I'll bring it in, and you'll find hanging-space for it. It will be sold. It *will* be sold – have no doubts on that score. I will know how much it is sold for – how much it is *bought* for – and you'll deduct your ten per cent. No questions. You'll *do* that. "L. Lados." That's the signature they'll carry. Always. They'll always be numbered six-nine-eight. You will know who "L. Lados" is – nobody else. The cheques will be made out to me, of course. Cheques from the gallery. Not from your own account.

'You're a staging post, Pollard.' I smiled down at him. 'You're that, or you're an accused murderer and an accused thief. No questions. No explanations. No . . . anything. Is that understood?'

He nodded.

What else could he do?'

Thereafter things went a little mad.

My cut from the wages snatch added up to more than

110

triple what I'd already been paid. It was therefore necessary that I daub three more canvases. They each sold for five thousand pounds . . . and 'L. Lados' started to be known and talked about.

Within the lunatic world of modern art the gallery became quite famous. Only at *that* gallery could a new 'Lados' be bought and, within a year, these meaningless smudges were actually being sought after.

'I can't help it,' complained Pollard. 'I'm being offered more than you expected. And by *genuine* clients.'

I sought advice from Frisch.

'Become "Lados",' he said. He laughed aloud at the joke, and I joined him. 'Why not? Suckers are born to be taken. Ride the merry-go-round while you can.'

'I could be astride a tiger,' I smiled.

'No, no. Play your cards right.' He was greatly amused as, indeed, was I. 'A public figure. A respected figure. In private be yourself. In public be this "Lados" character.'

'How the hell . . .?'

'Played carefully, it could be a bonus.' Some of the mirth left him, as possibilities became apparent. 'Dark glasses. Large dark glasses. You don't wear a hat . . . let "Lados" wear a wide-brimmed hat. Indoors and out. That, and the glasses. Different clothes-style. Flamboyant. Eye-catching.' He nodded gently. 'It could be a good thing, friend. A real *bonus*. Build up the "Lados" front. Hard-to-get, but somebody real. It's what *you* hide behind – the real you. It's perfect.'

It was, as I say, a little mad.

Of necessity, I had to bring Pollard into the scheme. He hummed and hawed a little, but had no choice.

'They'll recognise you,' he whined.

'They'll recognise who?'

'You.'

'Oh, no. They'll recognise "Lados". I'm nobody. I'll remain a nobody.'

'The – the money?' He almost wrung his hands as he asked the question.

'"Lados" has a sponsor.' I'd worked it all out. I wanted no tax dodge. 'An anonymous sponsor ... who insists upon *remaining* anonymous. He pays you. Cash. Used notes. You put it through your bank, deduct your ten per cent, then pay me by cheque.'

'It's possible,' he said slowly.

'It's easy.'

'The – er – the used notes. It – y'know – sounds illegal.'

'Don't ask questions, Pollard.'

'Look, if it *is* illegal, I want no —'

'Since when was killing gamekeepers *not* illegal, Pollard? When did twisting this gallery become OK? Don't start scrubbing around looking for a conscience, friend. You lost it years ago.'

That (if you recall) was 'The Year of Lados'. The culture pages in all the nationals tagged it as such. When 1963 staggered through the door, as tight as a tic, and garlanded with paper streamers and fancy hats, the art pundits all agreed that 1962 had been 'The Year of Lados'.

I, personally, wandered around my own private meadow, knee-deep in clover. I became moderately rich, but I remained very careful. I wanted no stupid slip-ups. The taxman, a tight-lipped accountant, Frisch and Pollard. *They* knew who this new-found genius was ... but nobody else.

That Christmas (Christmas 1962) I took my recently divorced mother to London for a long weekend. It had nothing to do with affection. She was still a pain; she'd *always* been a pain and always *would* be a pain. But – what the hell? – some of the money had to be spent on something.

We stayed at one of those lush hotels that don't horse around with AA or RAC ratings. One of the handful capable of telling Egon Ronay to go jump in the nearest lake. You put your shoes outside the bedroom door each night, and next morning they look as if they've been coated with glass. Your newspaper comes with all the folds ironed out. Leave your cash on the dressing-table and, when you wake up, it's all been switched for crisp new notes and shining new

112

coinage. If they could *breathe* for you, that, too, would be part of the service.

Mother (of course) took it in her stride.

On the last evening, she sipped her third Pimms and said: 'Rather a presentable place, dear.'

'Fair,' I agreed.

'I must mention it to Florenz.'

'Who's she?'

'He, dear. *He.*' Her eyes glazed with that dreamy faraway look I recognised from past twitterings. 'A dear little man. So sweet. So shy. I think he's screwing up courage to ask me to marry him.'

'You will, of course.'

'I need companionship, dear.'

'You need money.'

'You seem to be rather well off, these days.'

'Mine, Mother dear,' I assured her. 'No misconceptions. It's all mine . . . and not to be shared.'

'I never thought I'd give birth to a *mean* child,' she sighed.

'Mother,' I advised, 'marry your sweet little Florenz. Get your hooks in *his* money. Don't look upon this little jaunt as the hors-d'œuvre to what comes later. It's a one-off job.'

'You must be filthy rich,' she pouted.

'If I am, I intend to stay that way.'

'Where does it come from?'

'Investment of talent,' I smiled.

'You? *Talent?*'

'Periodically,' I said sweetly, 'a dung-heap produces a prize-winning rose.'

'Somebody', she snapped, 'must be even more stupid than *you* are.'

'So many people,' I murmured. 'So very many people . . . fortunately.'

If she heard me, she made no comment, but it was no less than the truth.

The year 1963 also saw gullibility stretched to near breaking-point. The television people invited me to take part in one of

113

those monumentally boring 'culture slots' with which the viewing public are encouraged to become art-conscious. Half the programme – the second half – was devoted to an examination of the works of 'L. Lados', followed by an interview, conducted by the current connoisseur of dilettantism.

'You can't do it!' Pollard was terrified of the idea. 'I mean, what do you *know*?'

'As I recall,' I reminded him, '*you* went slightly gaga about that first painting.'

'It – it had promise,' he dithered. 'I said —'

'You said a lot of things,' I interrupted.

'I – I didn't know what I know now.'

'What, exactly, do you know *now*?' I inserted a warning note into my tone.

'Just that – that. . . .' He floundered.

'What?'

'I – I don't think you're altogether honest,' he breathed.

'Is that all?' I raised an eyebrow, and added: 'And from *you*?'

'I – I was jockeyed into an impossible situation. I couldn't help myself. I didn't *mean* to be —'

'Cut it out, Pollard,' I snapped. 'You're as bent as a country lane. You're sweating because, if I don't pull this thing it will make *you* look stupid.' I paused, then played what I knew was the trump card with Pollard. 'Concentrate on what's going to happen when I *have* pulled it. You'll be able to take a mortgage out on the Bank of England.'

It quietened him. His pores still leaked, but I think he crossed everything until after the transmission.

Frisch had no doubts. Since I'd delivered the money from the wages-snatch, Frisch had had no doubts. Our relationship had developed. We were both solitary men – born loners – but, as far as such men allow 'friendship' to impose itself on their lives, we were friends. We had our own unspoken rules. The trust was complete, yet we each had secrets.

For example, I knew he was a criminal of no small stature. He had no 'firm'. His personality was such that he couldn't head any sort of gang. That didn't matter. He knew people: men who accepted his temporary leadership without question. I suppose I was one of them. It was the safest way. A gang – a 'firm' – carried with it the weakness of possible infiltration. Frisch's way eliminated that possibility. I found myself scanning newspapers, looking for some major crime – some above-average theft – and, when one was reported, toying with the idea that Frisch was the man behind the planning of that crime. I never asked. To have asked would have broken our self-imposed rules. I trusted him and I, in turn, was trusted – and, strangely, to be trusted by Frisch was of great importance.

Frisch was quite certain.

'They're crappy programmes, anyway,' he said. 'Be controversial. Be outrageous. It will build up the image and make the façade that much stronger.'

In the event, I enjoyed myself. The goon doing the interviewing was in a mild panic. *His* image, too, had to be preserved and, as he waffled on opinionating about what few 'Lados' paintings were around, he left himself balancing on a very precarious limb.

I'd 'read up' a little. I wore baggy trousers, a velvet jacket, a cravat and a wide-brimmed hat. I also wore dark glasses, with the largest eye-pieces I could find. I looked a typical artistic goofball and, when it came to interview-time, I acted the part like crazy. The first question set the pace.

'Tell me Monsieur Lados, which school of painting do you follow?'

'Where do you get the "Monsieur" from? I'm English.'

'Oh! I rather thought. . . .'

'Why should you think I'm French?'

'The – er – the name.'

'Originally, it was "Lodder". Down the centuries it became twisted into "Lados". "Lodder" is an old English name.'

'I – er – I didn't. . . .'

'Meaning "dweller at a lode". A lode was a footpath.'

'I see. Now, can we . . . ?'

'My name doesn't even *sound* French.'

'Our researchers must have. . . .'

'What researchers? I haven't been approached by researchers.'

'I'm sorry, *Mister* Lados. Can we . . . ?'

'Originally, it was a Dorset name. You can't get much more English that *that*.'

'Quite.' He swallowed. 'As I was saying, which particular school of painting do you follow?'

'I lead.' I fitted a cigarette into a three-inch holder.

The sign read 'No Smoking', but I pointedly ignored it. This part of the programme was going out live, and the interviewer wasn't going to screw things up by having a free-for-all about cigarette-smoking. The floor manager scowled displeasure, but he was off camera, so who cared?

The interviewer gave a sickly smile, and tried again. 'I would have thought that the Dada period might have had some bearing.'

'*Dada!*' I glared.

'It seems to me that —'

'The Duchamp crowd. The *Mona Lisa* with a moustache and a dirty caption.'

'I – I really didn't —'

'An exhibition in a café lavatory.'

'I wasn't thinking of —'

'I did not come here to be insulted. I assumed this to be a serious programme about modern art. Not a discussion about the merits of toilet-door graffiti.'

'Surrealism?' he suggested desperately. 'The – er – the juxtaposition of unexpected forms and colours. That, perhaps?'

'Names,' I said airily. 'Surrealism, constructivistic cubism, suprematism, automatism. You could, I suppose, call my work "Ladosism" but, unless you're prepared to *look* at it, it wouldn't help you understand it.'

'I – er – I see.'

'The essence', I explained with a theatrical sigh, 'is

similarity and opposition. The analogy alongside the simile. The contrast carries the message and the message constitutes the picture. I'm not in competition with a camera. I catch the "impact" and translate it into an image.'

'For example?' he said warily.

'Take *Storm in the Atlantic* . . . my latest painting.' I waved the holdered cigarette around. 'A storm. A storm does damage, therefore you have broken lines. Wind – gale-force wind – wind comes in gusts. Great gobs of moving air. Therefore curved and rounded shapes. Crimson, because of their destructive power. Green background, denoting the sea. A storm-tossed sea, therefore whorls of purple and irregular triangles of black. The green of the sea. A mid-green, because it's the Atlantic. Had I been painting the Pacific, it would have been a much deeper – much richer – green.' I glared at his face, with its stunned expression, and snapped: 'It shouldn't have to be *explained*. It's so damned *obvious*.'

He nodded and muttered: 'Well, yes – of course – I agree . . . it's so *obvious*. The – er – impact. The *image*.'

As of that moment, I had him. I talked gobbledegook for most of the next fifteen minutes, and this idiot hung on to my every word. Had I mentioned it, he would have been prepared to believe that the most accurate likeness to a full moon was a black square. Anything! We were talking 'modern art', therefore nothing was too outrageous. Even the floor manager smiled his approval.

Such is the power of television.

The asking price of a 'Lados' masterpiece almost doubled overnight. The television critics were split down the middle. Those with brains called me a boorish fool, and found a dozen ways of saying it. Those without brains labelled me an instant television personality and the top expert on twentieth-century art in the country.

Pollard's grin threatened to split his face.

Frisch nodded contented approval and said: 'The perfect façade, my friend. Like a wall. They can't see you. They'll *never* see the real you.'

117

THIRTEEN

It was a Sunday; a cold, bleak January Sunday. The news had made a bleak day bleaker, and everybody knew that an era had ended.

Ripley raised his glass in a tiny token toast and muttered: 'We won't see his like again.'

'A great man,' agreed Hoyle.

The two officers were off duty and in plain clothes. They lounged on the padded bench of a country pub, on the outskirts of Beechwood Brook. Ripley had telephoned and Hoyle had driven out to meet the county superintendent and, as suggested, they'd met as equals – as two working coppers – at the pub and well away from official externals.

Over the past couple of years they'd grown to be friends. It hadn't been difficult. A superintendentship in the county constabulary hadn't stood in the way of friendship with a detective sergeant in the neighbouring city police force. Nor had the few years' age gap been an encumbrance. They liked the same things, had the same interests, and each respected the other as a hard-working, thoroughly honest policeman.

And now on this Sunday evening, on 24 January 1965, they drank together and, like most other men and women in the Western world, felt a little heartbroken.

Churchill had died and, with his passing, lesser men's futures seemed less secure. Laughter would have been out of place and a joke would have seemed like a blasphemy.

'It's bloody awful.'

Ripley muttered the meaningless words which, on that day, tens of thousands of other ordinary men mouthed to themselves in an empty attempt to express their feelings.

They finished the round, then Hoyle took the empty

118

glasses to the bar and returned with fresh drinks. The sad silence lasted long enough for the two men to take two tastes of bitter, then Ripley fished pipe and pouch from his jacket pocket and spoke.

'We're getting short on space, David.' He fingered shredded tobacco into the bowl of the pipe. 'The room where you keep the murder file. It's been earmarked as an extra stationery store.'

'From on high?' Hoyle smiled.

'The County Architect's office. At a guess, pushed by the Standing Joint Committee.'

'The case isn't yet closed.' Hoyle knew he couldn't win, but a mild protest seemed called for.

Ripley scratched a match into flame, held it to the surface of the tobacco and used his middle finger to tamp the glowing, curling tobacco into a more solid draw. He spoke between puffs.

'Sorry, David. Written instructions. It has to go into the archives, pending further information coming to light.'

'I'm sorry, too,' sighed Hoyle.

'You've done all you can. More than most men.'

'You see. . . .' Hoyle compressed his lips, shook his head slowly, before he continued: 'My only murder case, and nowhere. Nowhere!'

'It plays hell with the ego.' Ripley waved out the match and dropped it into a nearby ashtray. 'It won't be your only murder.'

'But *mine*.' Hoyle's quick grin was twisted, and without humour. 'It sounds daft. We shouldn't get involved.'

'We're always involved. We have feelings ... we're involved.'

'It's just that. . . .' Hoyle tended to flounder. *His* feelings were difficult to put into words. The damn murder had become part of his life, both on duty and off. Other crimes could be (and were) dealt with; detected or tabbed as 'undetectable'. But this one crime – this one murder – was there, under his skin. Deep inside his brain. It had grown to be an obsession. He said: 'Two contract killers, both in this

119

district at the same time. That's what it boils down to. It *has* to be that. *Two* of them. And they're in and out like ghosts.'

'Maybe more than two,' agreed Ripley heavily.

'You can't move for 'em,' said Hoyle sardonically.

'What?'

'Killers. Hit men. You can't swing a cat for 'em . . . but *we* can't put a name to even *one* of 'em.'

'I can,' said Ripley softly.

'Roaming around my patch – your patch – and —' Hoyle closed his mouth, then opened it again, then closed it, then said: '*What was that?*'

'David,' warned Ripley, 'there is such a thing as becoming *too* involved.'

'You said something,' accused Hoyle quietly.

'I say lots of things.' Ripley lowered his pipe and tasted his beer.

'You said you knew a name.'

'Not the man you're after.' The glass was lowered to the table. The pipe was replaced between the teeth.

'Superintendent Ripley.' Hoyle's voice was low and hard. The words were deliberate enough to be slow-spoken. 'I've worked my arse off on this case.'

'I know.'

'As many off-duty hours as on-duty hours.'

'I know that, too.'

'And now you tell me you have a name.'

'He didn't do it,' said Ripley.

'He didn't?' Hoyle wasn't convinced.

'I've checked. Thoroughly. He wasn't involved.'

'Who's "he"?'

'It isn't important.'

'We differ in our opinions, Superintendent. I think it's *bloody* important.'

'David. You know me by this time. I wouldn't —'

'I *thought* I knew you. Now I'm not sure.'

'Oh my God!' Ripley allowed himself an exaggerated sigh. 'When a sergeant gets the bit between his teeth, there's no—'

120

'I need to know.'

'It's not necessary. He's not involved.'

'Superintendent Ripley, I need to know. Dammit, I'm *going* to know. If you've —'

'Cool off, David.' There was, perhaps, a hint of steel in Ripley's tone. The eyes may have had a touch of flint in their depths. Nevertheless, the county superintendent's expression remained friendly enough as he waved the pipe in a tiny gesture of silence. Ripley continued: 'For Christ's sake don't build a wall of rank between us. That won't help. You're not unique in having something of a temper. Drink your beer . . . and listen.'

Ripley, too, tasted his drink before he started. 'He lives in these parts. He carries the same first name as you. David.' The tone took on a slight dreamy quality. As if Ripley was remembering and, at the same time, giving reluctant admiration. 'A very honest man. A killer of men. A killer of less honest men than himself. Less honourable men than himself. We've touched gloves a couple of times in the past. No more than that. Never more than that. If it *had* been more. . . .'

Ripley paused to draw on the pipe. His lips curled into a half-smile.

'You mean he's a *killer*?' Hoyle's look of shocked surprise had a certain comic quality. 'He's – what is it – a hit man? And you *know*?'

'Oh, yes, I know.' Ripley nodded. It was a pleasant, cheerful nod. 'I know . . . but I can't *prove*. We're talking about a certain type of man, old son. One of the élite. Not a "criminal" . . . not as you and I understand that word.

'Once – not too many years ago – he climbed mountains. He was well known . . . as a mountaineer. He's licked the Eiger. The North Face. That, of itself, makes him very special.' There was a quick, but quiet, chuckle. 'Then he had an accident. A domestic accident. He fell down some steps and smashed his spine. He's been in a wheelchair ever since.'

'In that case. . . .'

'He doesn't like being reminded of that. He tells people it

121

was the Eiger. That he fell from that North Face. It's not true . . . but he has his pride.'

'Pride?' Hoyle's face registered mocking disbelief.

'Oh, they have pride, David. Make no mistake. They have a price . . . agreed. But they also have a pride, and that pride is well beyond price.' Ripley tilted his head, very slightly, and smiled at the younger man. 'You'll learn, old son. It's not all black and white. And I'm not talking about gun-carrying hooligans. Gangsters. Syndicate killers. I'm talking about men – even women –*governments* use. The CIA. Our own people. Their allegiance can be bought. It *can* be bought and, when it *is* bought, it's absolute. It's paid for by the day – by the week – however long it takes – but for that period of time, an acceptance of their own death is included in the deal . . . if that becomes necessary.'

'You – er. . . .' Hoyle took a deep breath. 'You sound as if you *approve*.'

'Not approve. Understand.'

'I'm damned if *I* —'

'David, we're coppers, but we live in the real world. Look at it this way. Cancer is part of that world. It's lousy, but it's a *part*. Accept it . . . and give thanks we have surgeons.'

'You're equating surgeons with murderers?' The question was heavy with reprehension.

'The victim,' said Ripley wearily. 'The victim of the murder you've tried so hard to solve. He was one of the men I'm talking about. That, to my mind, without a doubt. Maybe he was killed by the man he was being paid to kill. Maybe the man who killed him was himself being paid. Maybe . . . anything. But the victim *was* somebody from Gawne's world. Nothing surer.'

'Gawne?'

'The man I know. The professional killer.'

'The man you admire? The man you approve of?'

'Damnation, no!' The explosion was soft, but no less angry for its lack of noise. Then Ripley caught his flying temper, and said: 'I don't approve, David. Don't deliberately misunderstand me. I don't approve. I *condemn*. But I'm

122

helpless – helpless as you are – and I've learned to live with that helplessness.'

'David,' mused Hoyle. 'David. Gawne. David Gawne. At least I know his name.'

'It won't get you anywhere,' said Ripley softly. 'The file's closed. Accept that.'

'The file is *not* closed. There's only one way to close a murder file.'

There was an apparent impasse. The impasse of two strong-willed men, each equally sure of his own stance and neither prepared to give way. Subdued anger was there, but it didn't weaken the friendship. Mutual respect ensured that the anger was controlled and without disgust.

The room had filled up a little since they'd entered. It was a pub, not a road-house, therefore the customers, even on a Sunday evening, tended to be quiet drinkers rather than rowdy tipplers. It was also mid-winter, and the evening bite had kept all but the regulars in front of their own hearths. Added to which, Churchill had died.

The two officers sipped their drinks in silence. Nor was it a sulky silence; their disagreement was just that. A disagreement between complete men, who remained friends.

Ripley stood up and went to the bar for two more half-pints. As he resumed his seat, he spoke.

'I'll take you to him,' he said in a low voice.

Hoyle nodded his satisfaction.

'Just don't expect anything.'

'I'll know him.'

'He already knows *you*.' Then as the younger man's expression showed surprise: 'It's his business, David. He has a mind like a filing system. Coppers worth a damn – especially coppers in his own area – he knows them all.'

Having made up his mind, Ripley wasted no time. This was the nature of the man. They finished their drinks, left the pub and, in Ripley's car, set off for the Tops.

It was a moderately long evening ride – almost twenty miles – and it took them through villages and past isolated

123

hamlets, until the moors and the heather of the Tops surrounded them, like a black sea, and touched the slightly less dark sky, miles away on every side. They left the roads and drove along tracks: tracks which snaked and branched until Hoyle was completely lost.

'Old pack-horse trails,' explained Ripley. 'Pre-Industrial Revolution. Smugglers used them sometimes. You won't find them on maps.'

Hoyle grunted easy belief.

The car heater was on full blast, but the view from the windows removed all doubts about the outside temperature. The utter silence augmented the absolute blackness, and it was an obvious wild and killing world in which even the night creatures sought what little shelter they could find.

'Before the snows come,' said Ripley. 'It can be isolated for three months at a stretch.'

'Not much – er. . . .' Hoyle hesitated, then added, 'killing.'

'They come to him,' said Ripley sombrely.

'To be murdered?'

'They don't know it, of course. Until it's too late.'

'Quite a bogey-man,' observed Hoyle with a hint of sarcasm.

'David.' There was real warning in Ripley's tone. 'He's out of our league. Never forget that. Special Branch. MI5. Sometimes MI6. Even *they* tread very carefully. David Gawne.* He can't *be* caught. The powers-that-be – the *real* powers-that-be – wouldn't allow it. Push too hard . . . you'll be out of a job.'

'For God's sake. . . .'

'During the war he worked alongside Lieutenant-Colonel Sir Claude Dansey.'

'Never heard of him.'

'Of course not . . . but he *was* around. He carried more clout than the monarch.'

Hoyle's eyes widened.

---

* For details of David Gawne, see the author's *Freeze Thy Blood Less Coldly* (Macmillan, 1970) and *The Hard Hit* (Macmillan, 1974).

'Gawne was in the Army,' amplified Ripley. 'During the war – even more so after the war, while the occupied powers squabbled over the spoils – odd units were around.'

'Odd units?'

'Groups. "Unofficial" groups.'

'Doing what?'

'Look, old son. . . .' Ripley sighed. 'Berlin. The whole of defeated Germany. If you weren't there – if you weren't *there*, at the time – it's impossible fully to understand. Hundreds of thousands of men. Trained fighters, trained scavengers, trained killers. There was no "law" – not as we understand that word. Black-marketeering was a way of life. Millions of pounds were there, under the counter. Anything and everything. Europe was going crazy and, somehow, somebody had to slam on the brakes. These units – these groups – dealt with the Mr Bigs.'

'Killed them?'

'Killed them,' agreed Ripley flatly.

'You're telling me this Gawne's a government killer?'

'Was.'

'But he isn't any more?'

'If it's needed,' said Ripley heavily. 'If it's needed, he's engaged.'

'And when it's not needed?'

'He . . . kills.' Ripley spoke the two words in little more than a whisper. He added: 'It's his job. His profession. And he's a professional to his fingertips.

'Judas Christ! And you've known this all along.'

'He's not involved.'

'How the hell do *I* know that?'

'Because *I've* told you,' snapped Ripley.

'And how the hell do *you* know?'

'Because *he's* told *me*.'

'Just that . . . eh? Some psychopathic lunatic, who apparently kills for a living, tells you that, this time, he *hasn't*—'

'Leave it!' Ripley almost shouted the words. Then in a harsh, but more controlled, voice: 'Leave it, Sergeant

Hoyle. Don't pass judgement on me – on anybody – until you *know* what you're passing judgement on. I have tried. Believe that or not ... I don't give a damn. Nevertheless, I'm *telling* you. In the past I've worked my breeches' seat out, gunning for David Gawne. Like you. You're not the first mad bastard to join the police service, Sergeant. Me, too. I could tame tigers. I could sandpaper elephants down to greyhounds. But I couldn't reach Gawne. I couldn't get within a million miles of Gawne.

'You think it's easy, knowing there's a paid killer living on *your* patch? You think that's *easy*? I have lived with it, Sergeant. Lived with it, and had to *like* it. When I learned – learned what *you* know now – God, I went mad. I said all the things you've said. Thought all the thoughts you're thinking. That Special Branch man who told me – came up from London, specially, to tell me – I wouldn't accept it. "They have to live *somewhere*." That's what he said, and my reaction was what yours is. "Not on *my* bloody patch." *And* I meant it. *And* I tried to make it stick.' Ripley gave a wry grin. His tone became softer and less harsh. 'You have to accept things, old son. Things you don't want. Things you hate. You *have* to accept them. The murder – *your* murder – it's finished and done with. It's never *going* to be detected. That's one reason why we're visiting Gawne. To convince you. To prove something. To round off your education – let's put it that way.'

The building was both monstrous and a monstrosity; a huge 'folly' of a place, built by some Victorian eccentric, and set miles from any other habitation. Around it, the moors went on for ever, and the heather touched the walls of the weed-infested gardens.

And yet the house, and its size, complemented its owner.

The room was large – Hoyle guessed that it was three rooms knocked into one – but Gawne dominated it. He *needed* a room of that size. He was anchored to an invalid's chair but, even so, his sheer size dominated the room. Upright, and in his prime, he must have topped the six and a half foot mark, and been correspondingly broad across the shoulder.

'A Happy New Year to you, Charlie.' Gawne's voice went with his body; went with everything about him. It wasn't loud, but it was full of power. Like the roar of a distant hurricane. 'A bit belated, but never mind.'

'And you.' Ripley nodded, then lowered himself into one of the oversized armchairs which scattered the room.

'And this – lemme see – this is Hoyle . . . right? Not from your mob, though.'

'From Lessford.'

'The gilded city.' Gawne chuckled, and it was a little like padded sticks playing a gentle roll on a kettle-drum. He waved a hand. 'Sit down, Sergeant Hoyle. If Charlie Ripley vouches for you, that's good enough for me.'

Hoyle, too, sat down and, already, Hoyle was learning things. Things about this Gawne character. A chair-bound cripple . . . but the chair meant less than nothing. The man – the charisma of the man – overwhelmed the invalid's chair. There was a unique, but magnificent, 'Englishness' about him. A Dickensian quality. Like – like . . . Pickwick. No – dammit – not at all like Pickwick. But, nevertheless, *Dickensian*. Like . . . the Ghost of Christmas Present. That was it. Exactly! Larger than life – much larger than life – but with a chuckling, joyful menace. An extrovert . . . but take care, lest this extrovert squash you into pulp as he roars with laughter. Noisy and boisterous . . . but that belly-laugh could well be the last sound you hear on this earth.

Ripley said: 'Sergeant Hoyle wants to ask you some questions, Gawne.'

'Does he?' That question, too, was a joke. Some subtle joke, shared between Ripley and Gawne. Gawne rumbled: 'Very important questions, are they, Sergeant? Very *pointed* questions?'

'They. . . .' Hoyle cleared his throat. 'They might be.'

'Pointed questions, Charlie.' Gawne turned his head, but Ripley remained straight-faced. Gawne returned his attention to Hoyle and growled: 'Don't make 'em *too* pointed, young 'un.'

127

Hoyle knew he was being deliberately intimidated. He paused to take a couple of deep breaths before he spoke . . . but he *still* felt intimidated. But, my God, why not? Ripley was remaining strictly neutral and he (Hoyle) was rowing his own boat . . . *and* against King Neptune. That's what it boiled down to. That damned wheelchair was a throne, and the giant occupying it was, indeed, a king and absolute monarch within his own realm.

Again, Hoyle cleared his throat, then moistened his lips.

He said: 'It's about murder.'

Gawne remained silent.

'You might call it an "execution",' added Hoyle.

Still Gawne waited.

'It happened a couple of years ago.' Hoyle's voice grew stronger. 'It happened in 1963. A man was shot in the county area. His body was dumped at Lessford.'

'Why come here?' grunted Gawne.

'We thought you might be able to help.'

'"We"?'

'*I* thought you might be able to help . . . after Superintendent Ripley told me you existed.'

'I exist, boy.' The warning was like a boulder, creaking softly before it crashed and took all in its path.

'You're a big man, Gawne.' Hoyle tried to match tone for tone.

Gawne nodded.

Hoyle took a deep breath, then said: 'So was Churchill. Another giant. Like him, you're mortal.'

Gawne's eyes blazed. Just for a moment, the naked power of the man hit Hoyle like a physical blow.

From behind the wheelchair, Ripley said: 'He's right, Gawne. Even you can't last for ever. Remember Dansey?'

'Leave Dansey out of. . . .'

'Dansey was Churchill's man.' Ripley refused to be silenced. 'Churchill died today. We're still all on the same side, Gawne.'

'Like hell we're on the —'

'*We're still on the same side.*'

Quite suddenly, Hoyle realised his own status in the over-sized room. He was little more than an open-mouthed spectator. These two men – Gawne and Ripley – matched each other perfectly. The immovable object had met the irresistible force, and God only knew what was about to happen.

'Charlie,' growled Gawne, 'I don't want to —'

'Don't put too much strain on it, Gawne,' snarled Ripley. 'Don't put *too* much strain on what masquerades as "friendship". I don't have to remind you. I can be as big a bastard as you. I *can* be. I *will* be.'

'If you think you can —'

'Anything! *Any* bloody thing. I can fix you. I know enough. I can have you tied up in pink ribbon and delivered to the nearest dock before anybody can do a string-pulling act. You'd better believe that, Gawne. You had better *believe* that.'

'You'd be finished.'

'You'd be *dead*,' countered Ripley. 'Those hole-in-the-corner buddies of yours. They'd have to be sure. They'd have to be *damn* sure. You wouldn't reach a crown court . . . and you know it. They'd blow this bloody place sky-high, and you with it, rather than risk that.'

'You think I don't know that?' Gawne's contempt was absolute.

'Mr Gawne.' Hoyle pulled his wallet from a breast pocket. He slipped a cellophane-covered photograph from one of its compartments and held it out. 'This man. Who is he? He's dead. He was killed two years ago. That's all I'm asking. Who is he? Not who killed him. Just . . . *who is he*?'

Gawne took the photograph without moving his eyes from Ripley's face.

Ripley rasped: 'Tell him, Gawne. If that's all he wants to know, tell him.'

'Charlie, you can't —'

'Don't bluff, Gawne. I'm not bluffing.'

'We're on the same side, Charlie.'

'Prove it.'

It was neither a capitulation nor a victory. A truce perhaps. An offer and an acceptance. But, whatever it was, the tension eased a little. Gawne flicked a glance at the photograph, then returned his gaze to Ripley's face.

Very quietly, he said: 'Jacopo Davanzati.'

'Italian?' asked Hoyle gently.

Gawne nodded.

On an impish impulse, Hoyle asked: 'Left-handed?'

'If that's of any use to you.' Again, Gawne nodded. 'But that's as far as I go.'

'Thank you, Mr Gawne.' Hoyle took back the photograph and returned it to his wallet. 'He died two years ago.'

'I know that.'

'He was shot through the back of the head.'

'I know that, too.'

'I – er – *you* didn't shoot him?'

'Charlie.' The man in the wheelchair allowed a crooked smile to touch his lips. 'Tell this high-spirited protégé of yours.'

'Gawne didn't shoot him,' said Ripley flatly. 'And, if he knows who did, he won't tell us.'

'Thank you, Charlie.'

Hoyle said: 'Thank *you*, Mr Gawne.'

FOURTEEN

'Quite a man, your Superintendent Ripley.' Alva Hoyle raised an eyebrow in mock-suspicion. 'Sunday night – your day off – and he keeps you out until the small hours. Meanwhile, your innocent little wife sits up, waiting and wondering.'

'I'm sorry, my pet. I should have —'

'You're sure this "superintendent" wears trousers . . . not a skirt?'

'For God's sake!' Hoyle's jaw dropped.

'Cool it, lover-man.' Alva stopped teasing. 'You couldn't lie without me knowing.'

'Look, I'm not —'

'I *know*.' She uncurled herself from the armchair, stood up, placed her book on the arm of the chair and tightened the cord of her dressing-gown. She smiled her affection, and said: 'David, boy, I *would* know. We Welsh ... we have a sixth sense. You *couldn't* two-time me, my sweet. I'd *know*.' She stood on tiptoe and touched his cheek with her lips, then asked: 'Coffee or tea?'

'Tea, please.'

'Tea it is. Tell me all about this super-superintendent while I get it ready.'

It was a small flat – their first home – and they could hold a conversation with ease while she was in the tiny kitchen and while he unwound himself in front of the two-bar electric fire.

'A hell of a man. If ever I reach that rank, I hope I'm as good.'

'You will be.'

He slipped his jacket from his shoulders and draped it carefully over the back of a small chair. He heard her filling the electric kettle from the tap.

'This Gawne character. God ... I thought they only lived in spy novels.'

'Why?' she called.

'Why what?'

'Why *not* "government killers"?'

'I just didn't. . . .' He unknotted his tie. Then reluctantly: 'I suppose you're right.'

'You were so sure.'

'Eh?'

'That it was an execution.' Then: 'Biscuits or scones?'

'Scones, please.' He flopped in the chair she'd vacated and began to untie his shoe-laces. 'True enough. It *was* an execution . . . not a simple murder.'

'So you were right?'

'Yeah.' He sighed. 'I think I wish I *hadn't* been right.'

'Why? That's it surely? Finished. Wrapped up.'

'Like hell.' He eased his feet from his shoes and wriggled his toes. 'I've learned the name of the corpse. That's a step in the right direction.'

'You'll be stopped, boy.' He heard a cake-tin being opened and closed. Then the fridge. 'If they stopped your Superintendent Ripley.'

'They won't stop *me*,' he muttered, and picked up the book his wife had been reading.

'What's that?'

The book was Peter Madison's *Freud's Concept of Repression and Defence* and a frown of mild annoyance touched Hoyle's expression as he read the title.

He murmured: 'Good God!'

'What's that?'

'Nothing.'

But it wasn't 'nothing'. It was the one minor hiccup in their married life. Their respective intellectual levels. Alva was a PhD and, although she never pushed her born gift to soak up knowledge on even the more obscure topics, Hoyle couldn't rid himself of the nagging realisation that *he* hadn't even made grammar school. It was the one thing he couldn't come to terms with. He knew he loved his wife. Equally, he knew she loved *him*. But, to Hoyle, that wasn't quite enough. He was (and he readily accepted the charge) ridiculously chauvinistic, in his own quiet way. He was quite happy to discuss problems with his wife, and to take full notice of her opinions, but when the time came *he* made the decisions. He earned the money via which they lived a comfortable life, and no wife of his was going out to work ... whatever her qualifications. On the other hand, he was quite pleased at her recently acquired post as general, and unpaid, dogsbody at the local hospital; it gave her an outside interest, without impinging upon his right to be sole breadwinner.

All of which was OK, until it came to things like this damned book she'd been reading. Not light stuff, and well beyond his immediate understanding. The sort of thing calculated to make Detective Sergeant David Hoyle feel a mite insecure.

Which was why he was sprawling in the chair, frowning into the middle distance, when Alva returned from the kitchen carrying a tray holding two mugs of piping-hot tea and a plate of buttered scones.

'Pooped?' she asked brightly.

'This thing.' He tapped the still-opened book with a forefinger. 'You can understand it, can you?'

'No.' She placed the tray on the hearthrug, by the fire, and helped herself to one of the mugs.

'In that case. . . .'

'Nobody can understand Freud.'

'I think you can.' He bent forward and took the second mug and one of the scones. Then, as she squatted on the rug and leaned back on to his shins, he added: 'Don't pretend, sweetheart. That hurts even more.'

'Hurts?' She made believe not to follow his reasoning.

'Every time I see you with one of these things – a book like this – it makes me wonder *why*. Dammit, you're wasted as a copper's wife.'

'That depends on the copper . . . surely?'

'I'm talking about *me*.'

'I know. *I'm* talking about you.'

'Alva, my pet, please don't be —'

'Hank Janson, perhaps?' She reached for one of the scones, bit into it, and talked as she chewed. 'Would *that* please you? Or a steady diet of cheap romantic paperbacks.'

'It's not that.' He blew out his cheeks. 'God, it's not *that*. I'm – I'm holding you back. I'm a bloody brake. I can't. . . .'

'Freud.' She waved the bitten-into scone airily as she interrupted. 'Now, supposing I said something like this to you. "A raindrop is wet. It's wet, because it's a raindrop. By the nature of its *being* a raindrop, it *has* to be wet." Now, does that make sense?'

'Well . . . does it?' he countered warily.

'Only to Sigmund Freud.' She bit into the scone again.

133

'Oh, he doesn't – *didn't* – say that exactly. Raindrops didn't interest him. But it's *his* sort of argument. Squirrel-cage. It chases its own tail for ever. But. . . .' She waved what was left of the scone. 'He was a great man. He "understood" things. To ordinary people – like you, like me – he was a complete nutter.'

'You mean that?' He was still suspicious.

'Honey' – she tilted her head, and smiled up at him – 'tomorrow, start reading *Uses and Abuses of Psychology.* Eysenck's book. It's easier reading than *The Spy Who Came In from the Cold.* I swear. A hell of a lot easier than *The Ipcress File.* And you enjoyed both those yarns.'

'I just want to understand. That's all,' he muttered.

'Eysenck,' she said.

'Have we a copy?'

'Somewhere. I'll find it for you. Meanwhile . . . what about this Italian hit man?'

'Jacopo Davanzati?'

'Tell me about him. Tell me how you're going to get to know something about him.'

FIFTEEN

'Jacopo Davanzati.'

I waited, and watched Frisch's face. I sought some sign of emotion, but saw none. He was in his chair, alongside the unlit fire. It was late July 1963 and, if you recall, we were enjoying one of those so-called 'heatwave' spells which in England we mistakenly call 'summer'. It was a meteorological con trick; it wouldn't last and when, in a few days' time, it turned to thunder and downpour the mugs would turn on sickly smiles and make a quick grab for raincoats and umbrellas. Meanwhile both Frisch and I wore short-sleeved shirts and sipped iced lemonade.

He'd telephoned me and asked me to come. It had sounded urgent – or, should I say, as urgent as Frisch allowed *anything* to sound?

He was alone.

'The weather's nice. Anne has taken Sheba for a walk across the moors.'

I hadn't made any observation. A blind teenage girl, wandering those open moors might, in normal circumstances, have raised questioning eyebrows, but the Irish wolfhound made all the difference. Who was taking *who* for a walk might have been open for debate, but while Sheba was around the girl was quite safe.

I'd looked for some signs of disquiet and, perhaps because I *had* looked, had noticed the hint of jerkiness about Frisch's movements. The smooth – almost slow – cat-like motion of his limbs and fingers wasn't there. The surface of the drinks had magnified the barely noticeable tremble, and now his crossed leg swung, ever so slightly, as he hunted for words and explanations with uncharacteristic hesitation.

'You don't know him, of course,' he said.

'Jacopo Davanzati? No.' I shook my head. 'The name doesn't ring a bell.'

'He kills for a living.'

I rather think he expected the remark to shock me. At least, to surprise me – even if it was make-believe surprise. It neither shocked nor surprised, and I saw no reason to make pretence.

I murmured: 'It's one way of earning a crust.'

'He's an Italian.'

'The Mob?' I asked with a smile. 'The Mafia?'

'He has,' he said sombrely. 'But only when they've not wanted to be connected with the killing. More often than not, they use their own men. Enthusiastic amateurs. Allowed to make it obvious who's behind the death.'

'But not – what's his name?'

'Davanzati?'

'Not Davanzati?'

'Davanzati kills for money.'

'Is there a better reason?'

'He kills for whoever pays him.'

'Frisch,' I said gently, 'stop paddling in the shallows. Take a deep breath and dive.'

He gave a single nod of agreement, then said: 'I want Davanzati killed.'

'You have the equipment.' I glanced at the door leading to the workshop.

'I want *you* to kill him.'

His voice was quite steady. The way he said it, it sounded a reasonable and very ordinary request. A sort of good-neighbourly suggestion.

I smiled and waited.

He said: 'He killed Anne's parents.'

This time, my eyes rounded a little in surprise, but I masked it by raising the tumbler and sipping the cold lemonade.

'I was his bodyguard,' he continued musingly. 'Anne's father's bodyguard. He needed one. He was. . . .' He closed his mouth, compressed his lips for a moment, then said: 'What he was isn't important. He needed a bodyguard, and I was his bodyguard. For three years. Three very good years.

'We grew to know each other well. Became more than employer and employee. I respected his wife and grew to love his child. His only child. Then. . . .'

Once more he closed his mouth. He closed it very tightly and, for a moment, self-disgust flickered at the back of his eyes.

'Davanzati killed him. Then killed his wife as an insurance. She shouldn't have been there, but she was. He didn't kill the child. She was blind. She wasn't dangerous. *I've* looked after her ever since.' Again, something approaching emotion touched his expression. In a soft, barely audible voice he said: 'She can't see me. She's never seen me. It has its compensations. I sometimes wonder what she thinks I look like. Just the voice . . . that's all. The hands. The rest is imagination.'

136

He lapsed into silence. For him, a strangely sad and brooding silence.

'So . . . kill Davanzati,' I said softly.

He nodded slowly.

'It's what you want. Retribution.'

'And Anne?' He raised his head and stared directly into my eyes as he asked the question. 'Davanzati's a professional. I think I could take him. I *think*. But if I'm mistaken? If I'm not quite good enough?'

'That's why you want *me* to kill him?'

'Two hundred thousand,' he murmured.

'That's a nice round figure.'

'For one trigger-squeeze – but he has to *know*. He has to know why and who.'

'I've no doubt you can arrange it.'

'The groundwork has already been done.'

'Fine.' I enjoyed another sip of the lemonade.

'I've been waiting for a man. Somebody like you. Somebody who won't hesitate. Who won't give him that split second to shoot first.'

He didn't look too tough. He didn't look like a professional killer. On the other hand, what *does* a professional killer look like?

He was medium height, middle-aged, medium build. Medium everything. He didn't even look *Italian*. His complexion wasn't swarthy, nor was his hair black. Dark hair, suntanned complexion. When you'd said that, you'd said everything.

He could speak English. Not good English – not the flowing, natural manner in which a man speaks his native tongue – but, nevertheless, not broken English. He spoke slowly, very grammatically correct and as if the thought of what he was going to say was a deliberate prelude to each word spoken.

Frisch had warned me.

'He's a pleasant man. He smiles a great deal. He'll smile as he's blowing your head apart.'

137

I'd been briefed well.

'No names. Names are never used. Somebody might slip up, and use the wrong name ... the *correct* name. Therefore, no names.'

Frisch had been right. I'd booked in at the Midlands hotel. The only time I'd used a name, and that name not my own. At breakfast, I'd ordered kippers, then toast, then marmalade. Specifically *mandarin* marmalade. I'd given the order deliberately, but not in too loud a voice. But loud enough for anybody listening to hear.

I'd eaten the breakfast, then smoked an unaccustomed cigarette until ten o'clock. Ten o'clock – punctually. Then I'd stubbed out the cigarette, dabbed my mouth with the napkin and strolled from the dining-room.

I'd been joined in the lift by a stranger. By the man I now knew to be Jacopo Davanzati. He'd allowed me to operate the lift. He'd followed me to my room; about two yards behind me and slightly to my left. As I'd opened the door, he'd wheeled inside, closed the door ... and smiled.

'He's careful. He takes *no* chances.'

I, too, had been careful. *Very* careful. I'd returned the smile, spread my legs and raised my arms. The frisking had been quick, but professional.

And now he said: 'You have the money?'

'Two hundred thousand.'

'Please?'

I turned my back on him and walked to the bed; to the deep suitcase which (supposedly) held my belongings but which, in reality, held a shaving kit, a toothbrush ... and two hundred thousand pounds, in used five-, ten- and twenty-pound notes.

'With caution, please,' he warned.

I glanced back and saw he was still smiling. The levelled Colt semi-automatic hadn't teeth, therefore it *couldn't* smile.

It was quite a moment. For the first time in my life I was within a trigger-pull of stopping a .38 bullet. I didn't faint, or anything like that. I was (I reminded myself) quite safe. The man holding the gun was on my side ... or so he thought. He was an expert, and a cool-headed gentleman, therefore the likelihood of an accident was remote.

Nevertheless. . . .

'Of course.' Again, I returned the smile. 'With *extreme* caution.'

I folded back the lid of the suitcase and stood aside.

He stepped to the bed and, still keeping the Colt steady, pushed a hand in amongst the notes. I remained very still and very friendly.

'Count it?' I suggested amiably.

'I trust you.'

'Good.'

'I trust the person you received it from.'

'Good,' I repeated – and, for a moment, wondered who he thought that unnamed benefactor was.

'We will now leave.'

'My bibs and bobs.' I motioned with my head at the communicating door. 'In the bathroom.'

'With care.' The permission was given with the same, smiling proviso . . . plus a gentle movement of the Colt's barrel.

We left, I handed in my key and paid my bill, then we strolled to the underground garage. Not alongside each other but, as before, with Davanzati a couple of paces behind me, and slightly to my left. He kept his hand in the pocket of his lightweight jacket, and now I knew why.

It was, of course, a stolen vehicle. Carefully stolen, in that the owner lived in the north-east and was known to be away on a month's holiday in some Spanish resort or other. He'd left his car tucked away in its garage and, having stolen it, one of Frisch's minions had carefully relocked the garage. Thereafter, duplicate keys and, although it *was* a stolen car, it was not yet *known* to have been stolen.

'The keys, please.' Davanzati held out his left hand.

He kept his right hand in the jacket pocket while he unlocked all four doors and the boot of the car. Then the search of the car's interior was remarkably thorough. Had there been anything easily get-at-able, he'd have found it.

Finally, he raised the bonnet and gave the engine a quick but complete going-over.

The smile was switched on again, and he said: 'I must take care, of course.'

'Naturally.'

'You will drive.'

'If that's what you want.'

I threw the suitcase on to the back seat and slid behind the wheel.

Thereafter we headed for the M1. I drove carefully. Quickly, but not too quickly. I had a schedule but, at the same time, I had to drive as if I hadn't a schedule. At least, not a *tight* schedule. I kept to the middle lane and was content to allow the needle to hover around the sixty mark. It was a nice day; a nice July day, with the sun keeping the temperature cosy, but with the slipstream from the partly opened window stopping the interior of the car from becoming stuffy.

North, passing Mansfield on our left then Chesterfield on our left. As we approached junction 30 I glanced at the fuel gauge. It was just about right. Frisch didn't make many mistakes.

I said: 'We need petrol. We'll call in at the next service area.'

Davanzati seemed to consider the suggestion for a moment, before he nodded agreement.

'We're well ahead of time.' I made it a conversational remark. Meaningless, and merely an observation. I glanced into the rear-view mirror, then pulled into the overtaking lane to pass a heavy-goods vehicle, as I added: 'We could have more than an hour to wait.'

'Wait?'

'When we get there.' I moved left, in front of the lorry. 'I'm told he's very punctual.'

'I do not like waiting.'

I moved my shoulders and played the part. He'd taken the bait. It only required him to bite on to the hook.

'These service areas. They provide food, do they not?'

140

'Of a sort.'

'When we have bought petrol, we will eat a small meal.'

'It's not cordon bleu.'

'We will eat a small meal,' he repeated.

'Sure. You're the boss.'

And now the hook was bedded well into his flesh . . . but he didn't know it. Hopefully, he *wouldn't* know it, until it was too late.

The next part was painful. Painful but necessary and, for two hundred thousand, necessity elbowed a little pain into second place.

Did I say a *little* pain?

The Mini was there in the car park, a scarlet Mini, and I checked the number before I found a space to ease our own car into. I timed it well, and placed it well. So, be it understood, did the man driving the Mini.

Davanzati was carrying the suitcase. He was on the footpath leading to the café, when I walked between the Mini and its neighbour to join him. I obligingly put out my left foot a little and, equally obligingly (as arranged), the driver of the Mini reversed his car over it.

Both Frisch and I had agreed that it was necessary. Acting performances, however good, are dangerous substitutes when put on for the benefit of men like Davanzati. That, however, was poor consolation, and did nothing to counter the sudden pain. A Mini is a small vehicle but, when reversed over the foot, it feels like a steel-wheeled traction-engine.

My howl of pain was not make-believe.

The driver of the Mini stopped and (as arranged) hurried to me, and claimed to be a doctor. A small crowd milled around, my shoe was removed and my foot was examined. It was swelling visibly.

The 'doctor' made great play at gently moving the bruised toes.

'I think you should have an ambulance,' he suggested.

'No ambulance. I'm in a hurry.'

141

'You can't possibly drive with this foot.'

'It's OK.' I waved the 'doctor' and the onlookers aside, tested my weight, winced, then gasped: 'I'll manage ... somehow.'

'You can't *possibly....*'

'Leave it. Put the sock back on. And the shoe. Just don't lace it up.'

Davanzati watched, from a distance.

It took all of five minutes to shoo everybody away, then I hobbled painfully towards the café, and Davanzati followed at a discreet distance.

At the table, I took a few deep breaths, while Davanzati queued at the counter, then joined me with coffee.

I lit my second cigarette of the day, and was grateful to taste even service-area coffee.

'That's screwed things up a little,' I sighed, and gave a watery grin.

'I can drive.' Again, the impression was that he'd given the matter some thought before making the suggestion.

'You don't know the way.'

'You can direct me.'

I made believe to consider the suggestion, then said: 'It might be better if we postponed things.'

'I have a reputation.' Quite suddenly, and although the tone remained the same, the eyes seemed to film with ice. 'My reputation is far more important than a clumsy injury to your foot.'

'OK, OK ... I'm sorry.' I half-raised a hand in surrender. 'You drive. I'll guide you.'

He nodded, and the smile came back.

'They'll sell aspirins at the counter,' I said. 'It might quieten the pain a little.'

'Buy some on the way out.'

'I also need to empty my bladder.'

'That, too, on the way out.'

And *that* (although he didn't know it) sewed Davanzati up.

In the toilet, I entered the correct cubicle. The Colt

142

'Agent', with its stubby two-inch barrel, was where it should be, wrapped in oiled silk in a corner of the cistern. With it was the ankle-holster. It took less than two minutes – less time than it might have taken me to pee – to check that everything was dry and well oiled, then strap the holster to my right ankle, before limping into the foyer to join Davanzati.

Frisch, I decided, was a superb organiser.

In the car, I occupied the rear seat. Directly behind Davanzati, with my injured foot stretched out along the upholstery. The suitcase rode on the front passenger seat, with the semi-automatic tucked under it, but with the grip within easy reach. The interior mirror was angled to give him an instant view of myself, and he used the external mirror for driving purposes.

A smart boy . . . just not quite smart *enough*.

It was a beautiful summer evening and, had the *hoi polloi* known the spot, it would have been like Blackpool sands in Wakes Week. But they didn't know, and it wasn't easy to find; metalled roads didn't come within ten miles, and some of the cart tracks weren't even shown on maps. The impression was that it was a hundred miles from nowhere and, again, Frisch had planned wisely.

The Land-Rover was parked where it was meant to be parked, and Davanzati braked to a halt about ten yards from its bonnet.

'You change vehicles here,' I lied . . . but knew it wasn't *quite* a lie.

The Land-Rover looked empty and I felt, rather than saw, the suspicion gather. As he eased a hand towards the semi-automatic, I pulled the Colt revolver from its ankle-holster and, in a single movement, pressed its snout firmly into the nape of his neck.

'Don't even change the rhythm of your breathing, Davanzati,' I warned, and to emphasise the point I thumbed the hammer back, held it in place and took up full pressure

143

on the trigger.

I didn't even have to squeeze. An easing of the pressure of my thumb, and the driving-seat of the car would be occupied by a corpse.

In fairness, the man had guts. In the mirror, I saw the smile come back to his mouth and, very carefully, he returned his left hand to the rim of the steering-wheel.

Frisch strolled from behind the Land-Rover and stared at Davanzati through the open car window.

'We pay for our stupidities, Jacopo,' he murmured.

'Always,' agreed Davanzati.

There was, of course, hatred there, but it was a strange hatred. A very pure, very concentrated hatred, which needed no sound effects. A very quiet, 'conversational' hatred and, strangely, a hatred without contempt. Indeed, it seemed to have shadings of mutual respect. Even admiration.

Frisch said: 'You've lived too long, Jacopo.'

Davanzati's smile widened.

Frisch glanced at me and gave a tiny nod. I released the pressure of my thumb on the hammer. Beyond Davanzati the windscreen blossomed into scarlet as a hole centred the webbed glass and the car seemed to expand and contract with the explosion from the revolver.

As much as I was able, with my injured foot, I helped Frisch carry the dead man and dump him in the rear of the Land-Rover. Then I collected the suitcase of notes before, once more, helping Frisch empty two jerry-cans of petrol over the car.

Frisch took the two guns and the ankle-holster, then dribbled a trail of petrol away from the death car. He dropped a match, and as we drove away and gathered speed, the car flowered into flame; then, as we topped a slight rise and before it left our view, the tank exploded.

On our way back to Frisch's farm, I asked: 'Why not leave him in the car?'

'People should know,' he replied shortly.

'People?'

'Like yourself.' He paused, then: 'People who kill for a living. A select band, my friend. He won't be identified. *He'll* have seen to that. But those who *should* know *will* know.'

SIXTEEN

Two hundred thousand is a lot of money. It can cushion a lot of bad thoughts and, if you have it, a lot of guilt. I had neither, therefore I was able to lean back, allow my foot to heal and, in effect, realise my good fortune.

I was what life had made me, and what the sixties boiled down to. Macmillan was Prime Minister and, because he was a statesman as well as a politician, the old country was moving up the gears and ready for overdrive. Beeching had slashed the dead wood from the railway system, Gaitskell was dead (some said his death had black question marks attached), Wilson was the new Great White Hope of the Labour Party, a poor guy called Profumo was publicly crucified for what a lot of his buddies were doing on the quiet, some hare-brained creep did the first solo climb of the north wall of the Eiger, and the greatest mail-snatch of all time was pulled on the Glasgow-to-London line.

That's the sort of world it was. Somebody coined the word 'swinging', and that just about described it. I was in there, scooping up my spoonful, and who could blame me?

So I was a contract killer?

The realisation didn't worry me. Twenty years before there'd been a few million 'contract killers'. The only difference was that they'd worn uniform, their killing hadn't been illegal and, when they killed with genuine flash, they'd been given medals. But, unlike me, they'd killed for peanuts.

145

In those days the world had bulged with contract killers. Now they were thinner on the ground ... and they cost more.

My immediate problem, which, I allow, was not worth describing as a 'worry' was the uncommon amount of cash I had to process through the 'Lados' machine.

I had a heart-to-heart talk with Pollard.

'Two hundred thousand!'

We were in the pokey office and, while his mouth drooped and his eyes widened, he lowered himself into a chair in order to take the force of the shock from his legs.

'My anonymous "benefactor" will take care of half of it,' I explained. 'The other hundred thousand? I think a couple of "Lados" masterpieces are called for.'

'Look, I don't know where you're getting all this cash from. But. . . .'

'I killed a man.'

I made it a quietly spoken remark and, for a moment, he thought it was some sort of off-beat joke. His mouth corners began to lift, then he realised it wasn't a joke and a hand went to the collar of his shirt, as if he wanted to loosen it for air.

I was still limping a little, and I used my walking-stick to tap the side of his leg to ensure I had his undivided attention.

'Two "Lados" paintings,' I said. 'Twins, Two that go together. *Night* and *Day*, shall we say? *Male* and *Female*. Something idiotic like that. Each worth, say, forty thousand. As a pair they should bring a hundred. The mugs are still around, Pollard. You can still find enough suckers to convince.'

'I. . . .' He seemed to choke on the words. 'I want no part of it. I want no *part*.'

'Pollard, you already *are*.'

'No! I didn't know you. . . .'

'You'll plead Ignorance, will you?' I said sweetly. 'When we share the dock, you'll waste breath trying to convince a jury that you didn't *know* the daubing amounted to so much crap? That when you tried to pocket five thousand, and give

146

me only five hundred, you were acting in the cause of art? That all the loot you've joyfully laundered for me so far crept through the books without you noticing it?' I paused, then said: 'Take a few deep breaths, Pollard. Get some oxygen to your brain. You're part of it. Since you killed that gamekeeper, you've been part of anything I've wanted you to be part of. Till they lower you into a coffin, Pollard. Then! But, till then, your mind and your body belong to *me*.'

'You're – you're a bastard,' he breathed.

'Keep that in mind,' I advised. 'That I'm a bastard, and that *you're* terrified of me . . . and with cause. You'll live. You might even live in luxury.'

Over the next few years I learned many things. Universal truths, which most men never appreciate within the span of their whole life. For example, that there is a hell of a lot of money slopping around in this old world, and that much of it is controlled by fools. Fools who weave themselves into cat's-cradle scrapes, and are prepared to pay through the nose for somebody to remove that which is causing them sleepless nights. Fools who profess to know about art; men and women prepared to bust a gut, and dig deep into their pockets rather than risk the possibility of missing out on the latest fad.

On a personal side, I learned a little about music and a lot about guns. My record collection grew, until it embraced just about everything composed by Mozart and Beethoven. All Tchaikovsky's symphonies and ballet music. The complete piano works of Brahms. And enough of the other old masters to keep me listening for weeks, without repeating any of the magic worthy of the name 'music'. Of the so-called 'Moderns' . . . nothing! To me they were the audible equivalent to the 'Lados' crap. Garbage, wrapped in the cheap tinsel of meaningless explanation.

But as for guns – as for shooting. . . .

From a .22 target rifle to a .500 Express, capable of dropping an elephant. Eventually, I could guarantee eight bulls out of ten, with the other two inners, and at virtually any range. If I could see it, I could hit it. I grew to know rifles. The Hammerli, the Stoeger, the Holland & Holland, the Rigby, the Krieghoff, the Mauser, the Mannlicher-Schoenauer, the Marlin. And, of course, the better-known makes: the Savage, the Winchester, the Browning, the BSA and the Husqvarna. Frisch produced them, and I practised on them, and grew to know the 'feel' of them. Like a concert pianist, who can distinguish between a Steinway and a Bechstein, I grew to know and master the tiny idiosyncrasies of each model and each make.

I became what the Americans might have called a 'gun nut'. But secretly. I allowed the 'Lados' character to grow; gradually to take over centre stage. But the other man – the *real* me – remained in control and, above all else, remained hidden.

Equally, I grew to know handguns, and how to use handguns with the same expertise. But, in the main, the handgun was always a back-up weapon. Something I carried on an assignment, but used only when necessary.

Frisch guided me, as he continued to guide me in most things.

'When you need a handgun, they're too close. They can see you – they can recognise you – and if you miss. . . .'

As with revolvers and semi-automatic pistols.

'With a revolver, you carry the spent cartridge case away in its chamber. The pistol ejects the case, and if you can't find it before you leave. . . .' And: 'The semi-automatic has more moving parts. More things to go wrong. The gas from the cartridge is a vital part of the mechanism, therefore you're relying on the weapon *and* the round. . . .'

It was not all killing, of course. In fact, most of it was *not* killing. Most of it was a sombre, but necessary, last warning.

In February of 1964 I took a trip to Monaco. Not to Monte Carlo, but to the more industrialised port of Fontvieille. A would-be jet-setter was hitting the gossip columns, in company with the teenage daughter of exiled royalty, and refused to be warned off.

It was a neat shot. I used a Norrahammar, Husqvarna action, 243, and without a telescopic sight. It was a quiet evening; no wind and a mere street-width away. The window of his upstairs apartment was open and he was dressing for one more night on the town with his blue-blooded sleeping partner. He was from American stock, therefore I presume he would describe his early-evening drink as bourbon. I do not doubt that it was expensive. Nor do I doubt that the receptacle he'd poured it into had not come from Woolworth's glass-counter.

He'd just fingered the finishing touches to his bow tie, and was taking a drink. I shattered the glass in his fingers, when it was no more than an inch from his lips. It was quite a magnificent aim.

I could have chosen a lesser bore, but the 234 did what I intended it to do. It drove broken glass into his hand, it sent a shard into his eye and others into the lower half of his face, and it convinced him that he'd been very lucky. He will go to his grave believing that he should have died.

I was in a power-boat, heading towards Nice, before the ambulance arrived.

For that small service, I received five thousand pounds.

Frisch also taught me about bullets.

To the uninitiated, a bullet is merely a bullet; it fits (or it does not fit) into the chamber of a firearm – and that, in effect, is the only point of difference.

Not so.

Discounting the cartridge, and the endless permutations of the charge, the bullet, too, has a specific job to do. It may be a simple lead bullet. It may be lead, but copper-tubed; the tiny copper tube in the nose producing an expanding effect when it penetrates. It may be lead, but hollow-nosed, metal-covered, but soft-nosed, split-nosed or (again) hollow-nosed – each giving a different degree of expansion after penetration. It may be solid, metal-covered, metal-covered and copper-pointed, or metal-covered and pointed and capped – each giving a different degree of air-resistance, less energy-loss and more penetration.

These (and others) are readily available on the open market. Frisch, as a registered gunsmith, obtained any of them merely for the purchasing. Thereafter, he adapted both charge and bullet for whatever target I was aiming at.

He imparted knowledge concerning aiming-points.

'The heart. Forget the fallacy that the heart is on the left. It is merely tilted to the left. Aim too far to the left and you miss vital organs. The centre of the chest. An area about the size of the average saucer. Tear *that* apart with an expanding bullet, and he's dead before he hits the ground.'

Or. . . .

'The so-called "bullet-proof" vest. It is possible to use it as a means of killing. A good magnum charge, combined with a soft-nosed round. It is on a par with hitting the victim over the heart with a trip-hammer. He'll die.'

I accepted the wisdom of this man. He had learned the skills of assassination, and was eager to pass them on.

And when I was bored, or needed more ready cash, I produced another 'Lados'. It took less than a day and the buyers were waiting in line to outbid each other.

On 3 November that year (1964) Johnson beat Goldwater for the Presidency of the United States of America. Nobody told me who 'John Doe' voted for and nobody had to tell me that 'John Doe' wasn't his real name.

From his photograph I knew he was a big man. Fleshy, with more than his fair share of bulk. The killing had to be made in the penthouse suite of a top-class New York hotel. In his bedroom with, it was thought, at least one muscle-man (presumably armed) in the next room.

'You're not expected either to shoot your way in or shoot your way out,' explained Frisch. 'Just kill him.'

I waited. Already, I'd grown to trust the planning of this man, and to know that reasons would be given.

'A silencer,' he mused. 'Revolvers are out. The small leak of explosive gases at the barrel's joint with the cylinder makes the noise, and that *can't* be silenced.'

'Despite what they say on films?' I smiled.

'Despite *what* they say on films.' Then: 'The only thing a silencer – *any* silencer – does is reduce speed. The speed of the escaping gases or the speed of the bullet. Subsonic, and you don't have noise. Supersonic, and you *do*. A .45 US automatic pistol cartridge – that's *sub*sonic. We work from there.'

How many palms were greased I don't know, but some must have been. I merely walked through the production and did what I was being paid to do.

I was a make-believe waiter. At 7.45 a.m. on that November Tuesday I walked into the foyer of that hotel. Under my belted mac I wore the uniform of a waiter; the same uniform worn by every other waiter employed there. It was quiet at that hour, but nobody stopped me. Nobody seemed even to notice me.

I caught the lift to the fifth floor, then found the unlocked linen-cupboard exactly where it should be. That's where I left my mac. Next, the service lift to the tenth floor and there (again, waiting for me) was the food trolley, complete with hot coffee, plates, cups and cutlery. And, of course, the lidded serving-dish.

The service lift took me, and the trolley, to the penthouse and, after knocking on the door of the suite, I smiled a pleasant greeting to the man who opened the door. A pale-eyed hoodlum, still without jacket and carrying a holstered revolver at the rear of his right hip.

'Hold it, sonny.'

I paused, and he stretched a hand towards the convex lid of the dish – when, as planned, the telephone bell shrilled sudden urgency.

Thank God for split-second timing. Equally, thank God for minions taught to obey without question, and immediately and without being required to reach a personal decision.

He will never know how near he was to getting the toe of my shoe in his balls. Had he even touched that lid, it would have been necessary and things might have become ugly. As it was, the quick look of indecision, almost amounting to panic, was something to be marvelled at.

He withdrew his hand and, as he turned to answer the phone, he grunted: 'OK, sonny. Take it through.'

The character I was being paid to kill was easing a bleary-eyed way from sleep as I quietly back-heeled the door closed. He waved a ham-thick arm, before starting to scratch the thicket of hair on his chest.

'OK, kid. Just leave it. I'll—'

The gun was under the lid, and I lifted the lid with my left hand and gripped the gun with my right. Despite Frisch's skill, it was an awkward weapon. A modified and cut-down De Lisle Carbine, with the silencer giving it a ridiculously thick-barrelled look, But it worked. Not even the near-obligatory 'Phut!' of the make-believe silencers of fiction. Just the faint click of the firing-pin hitting the base of the cartridge. It took him in the neck, blew his voice-box to hell and made sure he wouldn't yell. The second round went in behind the ear – and I was replacing the weapon under the lid before the blood dripped from the bedclothes onto the carpet.

Then, out of the bedroom, a cheery wave to the goon still using the telephone and down the lift to pick up my mac. As I read things in the evening edition, I was in a cab I'd flagged, two blocks from the hotel, before the telephone conversation ended.

Not 'John Doe'. Some Syndicate would-be big-shot who'd stepped out of line; who had to be removed, without starting a full-scale street war.

I took a few days' vacation, and tasted the Big Apple. I found it plastic-flavoured, with more than a few maggots. The impression was that a lot of the bar-talk had been invented by writers like McBain; the slobs who mouthed it obviously hadn't the wit to *invent* it. On a couple of nights I purchased a woman and they, too, counted themselves unique ... and weren't. Any moderately priced Soho slag could have given them a furlong start and romped home streets ahead.

It taught me a small lesson. From now on, 'Buy British'.

In little more than a week I'd grown bored, and was glad to take a plane and fly back to my own nest. Thereafter, a couple of quick 'Lados' masterpieces to launder the seven thousand I'd earned for squeezing a trigger a couple of times.

That was when Pollard said: 'The old man's thinking of retiring.'

'The old man?'

'The man who holds most of the shares in the gallery. He's contemplating putting them on the market.'

'Buy him out,' I suggested.

'Me?' The one-word question, and the facial expression, told its own tale. Friend Pollard was spending it as fast as it came in.

I contemplated things for a few seconds, then said: 'Find how much he's asking. If it's reasonable, *I'll* buy.'

'You?'

'I like the idea of being your boss, Pollard,' I smiled. 'Y'know . . . *really* being your boss.'

SEVENTEEN

David Hoyle huddled himself in the warmth of old-fashioned flannelette pyjamas under the thick woollen dressing-gown and stared across the hearth of the blazing fire at his wife. She looked as tired as *he* felt. Tired, shocked but in a back-to-front way content. Two days ago, they'd heard the news on the radio and, almost without conscious thought – certainly without saying much – they'd packed bare essentials and driven south-west.

At the neat little semi, in the outskirts of Merthyr Tydfil, they'd learned that Alva's father was already at the scene.

153

After a quick snack they'd joined him and, along with scores of other volunteers, they'd worked like galley-slaves ever since.

'Tired, my love?' Alva smiled across at him as she asked the question.

'Tired. Sad. But happy.'

'I'm proud of you, boy.'

Proud? He'd done little to deserve pride. No more than the rest of them. With others he'd gone in, under the still-shifting muck, and fought to free children. He hadn't been alone. Other coppers – Welsh coppers – had worked alongside him. Miners, too. They'd needed the miners; men who knew from terrible experience what creaks and groans made by the suffering earth around them meant. Which to ignore and which to take as a warning. Welsh miners and Welsh coppers – volunteers who, like himself, had been shocked into rushing to help – a handful of students from Cardiff University.

All of them filthy-black, with tear-stains marking their cheeks. Passing kids, from hand to hand, towards the daylight. Terrified kids. Injured kids. Far too often, *dead* kids.

She, too, could have kids. The thought startled him. Frightened him. Scrubbed clean, without make-up, her still-damp hair combed back from her forehead. Wearing one of her mother's nighties. That, too, made of flannelette. And the spare dressing-gown. Everything a few sizes too big . . . or perhaps she was a few sizes too small. The light from a single stand-lamp, augmented by the glow from the piled-high coal fire.

Coal. . . .

The cause of it all. The comfort of this room, but also the horror of less than eight miles away. God had given coal, but He'd asked a terrible price in return.

'No kids.' Hoyle spoke the words gruffly, and in little more than a whisper. His tongue touched his dry lips, and he added: 'If one of them had been *mine*. . . .'

'Ours,' she said gently.

'Ours,' he corrected himself. Then, as they heard the sound of water gushing from the unplugged bath, he glanced at the ceiling, and said: 'Your da's a bloody hero.'

'You're both heroes.'

'Ah, but he *knew*. It didn't stop him. It didn't even slow him down.'

Thereafter, silence. A long, slow silence, thick with affection and heavy with unspoken grief. They were young. They'd get over it ... or, at least, most of it. At that moment, they'd have scorned the idea. Forget 1966? Forget Friday, 21 October? Never! But they would. They'd remember when they thought to remember. When some incident, or some remark, sparked off the memory of what had happened. *Then* David Hoyle would remember being entombed, with other men; of working a way through slurry-filled debris to reach screaming children; of wanting to tear a passage to them, but only being able to scoop the deadly muck up, virtually handful at a time; of walking an invisible tightrope, between getting at the trapped kids or bringing more of the damned stuff down on everybody. *Then* Alva Hoyle would remember carrying children to waiting ambulances; of trying to comfort women who would never again be comforted; of carrying trays loaded with bowls of soup and mugs of tea, till her arms ached; of forcing herself *not* to think of her man, and of what might be happening to him.

Like the rest, they'd forget – or, at least, half-forget – but very soon remember.

Almost 150 dead – 116 of them kids – buried under a shifting coal-tip. Aberfan had earned itself an immortality as black as the choking filth responsible for the deaths.

'Where's your mam?'

The father-in-law joined them. He, too, was in pyjamas and dressing-gown and, as he walked to a spare chair, he towelled his still-damp hair.

'She's out, comforting some of the women.'

'They won't be easily comforted.' He settled in the chair

155

and continued to rub idly at his iron-grey hair. There was disgust in his tone as he added: 'The damned gaffers. Any miner could have told them. That tip was unstable. Dammit, there was a stream running into it. This thing *had* to happen, sometime.'

'Why *weren't* they told?' Hoyle's question carried an innocence only to be found beyond a mining community.

'They were told, David.' It was a flat, uncompromising answer. As if it was the obvious answer to a question which needn't have been asked. 'The buggers were always being told . . . but they didn't listen. They never listen. They always know best, boy. They always have their priorities carefully listed, see? Well, the buggers know *now*, don't they?'

'Da, don't be bitter,' murmured Alva gently.

'Look, girl. . . .' Then, in a quieter, sadder tone: 'All right. It's nobody's fault. Not really. Nobody set out to kill those bairns. They're as sorry as we are – I'm not saying they're not – but, good God, they should have *listened*.'

There was more silence. A sad and helpless silence; a silence beyond words, and a silence striated with unspoken anger. Gradually, the silence changed. The father-in-law lowered the towel to his lap and, for a moment, sat motionless, with out-of-focus eyes.

Then he seemed to make a great effort to pull himself from the black mood, and said: 'There's whisky in the side-cupboard, pet. I reckon we all deserve a good nip.'

Alva left her chair and walked towards the side-cupboard. As she fixed the drinks, the father-in-law spoke to Hoyle.

'We did our best, boy.'

'For what good it did.'

'We did our best,' repeated the elder man. 'Not like those ghoulish buggers from the media.'

'They have a job to do.'

'Aaah!' The father-in-law made a disgusted swatting motion with his hand. 'From all over the world, they were. Aberfan . . . suddenly the centre of the universe. America, France, Italy, Germany. Everywhere. And for why? Dead kiddies, that's why. Shoving their televison cameras into

156

every corner. Wanting to interview everybody. It's a sick world, boy. Top viewing, see? Watching pictures of people whose kids have been killed.'

'Da.' Alva carried the drinks across and handed them round. 'It's done, Da. It can't be undone.' She returned to her chair. 'There'll be blame enough, when things have settled. And people want to know. They *should* know.'

Part-mollified, the elder man grunted and tasted his whisky.

Then he said: 'Good of you to come down, David. We all appreciate it.'

'What else?' smiled Hoyle. 'A good job the annual leave fell when it did. I didn't have to ask favours.'

Alva said: 'We go back tomorrow, Da. David's back on duty the day after.'

Hoyle frowned at the surface of his drink, as he murmured: 'I'll go back to the scene, first thing tomorrow. Before we set off. Have a last look round.'

EIGHTEEN

By 1965 I was getting rich. As 'Lados' I was quite a power in the art world. There was a vociferous 'anti-Lados' lobby. Of course there was, and who could blame them? Even in art, *everybody* isn't crazy. But, fortunately for me, there seems to be some sort of natural law which applies to creeps anxious to buy paintings: the less you know, the more money you have with which to buy.

I hammed like hell on television, which, in turn, gave me more exposure time. And, the more outrageous my declarations, the more the various 'presenters' sought to have me on their programmes. And, of course, the highter the fee.

My accountant began to worry a little.

'I think it might be wise if you. . . .' He paused, eyed the ceiling of his somewhat flash office, then ended: 'There comes a point when the United Kingdom tax burden seems ridiculous. Wouldn't you agree?'

'Are you suggesting a tax haven?'

'It might be worth considering. A sunny climate. To be allowed to keep a larger percentage of your earnings.'

'I like the weather here,' I said flatly.

'If not the climate, then. . . .'

'I also like to keep an eye on my own interests.'

'That's no problem. We could do that for you. It might. . . .'

'It *would*,' I assured him.

'What?' The ceiling lost some of its interest.

'Mean paying you a hell of a lot more.'

'You'd save far more than that in tax relief.'

'No tax haven.' I left no room for doubt in my voice. 'I'm an Englishman. I pay English taxes.'

It sounded good, and in part it was true. But most of the truth revolved around mistrust of other people. I had to be around to check things didn't go wrong. I trusted Pollard about as far as I could see him with one eye closed. I owned the gallery, which, in effect, meant I owned *him*, but the gallery made big money only through the 'Lados' trash. Much of that money, in turn, came from my real profession, and *that* depended upon Frisch. Frisch was the contact man between what I had to offer and people who wanted my services. He was a planner – the best planner I've ever known – and I needed him both as a cut-out between the buyer and myself and as a reliable back-up. We were a pair. A team. We understood each other perfectly; therefore, without him, I'd be a lot less than perfect.

More than that, I'd grown to like where I lived.

Above and on both sides of me were people beyond reproach. My own home couldn't be faulted. My library and record collection had become a vital part of my life. Things moved comfortably and without so much as the hint of a hitch. The tax men were happy and, on paper, I was the

158

immaculate, law-abiding citizen.

What was left more than kept me in a rut made comfortable by all the silks and satins I required.

Other than the 'Lados' gimmick, I had no intention of attracting publicity.

1965 also saw the double-hander. Thursday, 1 April ... a very appropriate day. The snarl-up almost spoiled my reputation.

To this day, I don't know the name of the creep I was paid to chop. I knew the car, I knew the registered number and I knew that between 3 p.m. and 3.15 p.m. it would be travelling north, at some speed, on a straight stretch of motorway. That's all I knew. That's all I needed to know.

The object was to make it look like an accident. To take a tyre, spin the car off the road and, if he was lucky, let him crawl from the wreckage.

I chose a Keith Stegall rifle – manufactured for a 7 mm magnum, but adapted by Frisch to take a long .22 cartridge – fitted with a Bausch & Lomb telescopic sight.

At first, I was doubtful about the long .22, and I expressed my doubts to Frisch.

'It loses itself,' explained Frisch. 'If you can hit the tyre –'

'I can hit the tyre.'

' – a .22 will cause as big a blow-out as a .45 and, if things go as expected, the flattened .22 will lose itself in whatever metal is left of the car. The police aren't fools. They might notice a larger piece.' Then: 'A long .22, to give it slightly more propulsion. A hit in the right place, and the round will go into the tyre, ricochet, then come *out* of the tyre immediately before the car goes completely out of control.'

'In which case. . . .'

'I know. But we've no control of the ricochet. We build from a basis of Kelly's Law: if a thing *can* go wrong, it *will*.'

Unfortunately, our version of Kelly's Law did not take into account a dumb-bell called David Fleischer, who preferred to be called David *Fletcher*.

I'd spent a fortnight – on an average, four hours each day –

out on Frisch's range. Figuring distances, getting the feel of the rifle, checking the absolute accuracy of the scope and aiming at a target travelling at an angle, towards me, at anything up to eighty miles an hour. With all the skill in the world, it was a cow of a shot, and I wasn't stupid enough to think otherwise.

Frisch gave continuous advice, and it was good advice.

'Move with it, move ahead of it, keep moving, then fire.'

'Forget the speed of the target. Estimate the swing of the rifle.'

'Get the target in the cross-wires. Then move the cross-wires to where the target's *going*. Then fire.'

'Dammit, man! The rifle's not moving when you fire. You're hitting where the target's *been*.'

It made circus trick-shooting look like falling off a log, but within two weeks I was scoring three hits from every five shots and, by any yardstick, that was *good*.

It wasn't good enough and, three days before the shot that mattered was due to be squeezed off, Frisch introduced Fletcher.*

He was at the farm when I arrived for my stint on the target, and that, of itself, made me eye the man with some surprise, not unmixed with suspicion. Until that moment it had only been Frisch, Anne and the dog. No strangers. No spectators. No hangers-on. Nor was I impressed.

He was a very medium guy. Medium height, medium build, medium brown hair. Maybe he was medium tough. If so, and in my immediate opinion, he wasn't tough enough.

In a very flat, deadpan voice, Frisch said: 'This is Fleischer. David Fleischer.'

'*Fletcher*,' corrected the stranger.

'Fletcher,' agreed Frisch. 'He landed in this country from America yesterday.'

'So?' Neither Fletcher nor I made any movement to shake hands.

---

* For further adventures and misadventures of Fletcher, see the author's *The Hard Hit* (Macmillan, 1974)

'He's – er – he's going with you.'

'Where?' I played deadpan for deadpan.

'You need a back-up,' said Frisch gently.

'Doing what?'

'He's in our line of business,' insisted Frisch patiently. 'In America, he's well known. Respected.'

'For doing what?' I demanded quietly.

Frisch hesitated, then said: 'Killing people.'

'You kill people?' I asked the question of Fletcher.

'It's been known,' said Fletcher carefully.

'*Boring* them to death, perhaps?'

'Boring holes in them.' A corner of his mouth lifted in a quick half-smile.

'Smart-arse with it,' I grunted. 'What do you do? A comic turn, then hope they die laughing?'

The man was a rank amateur. He'd made no attempt to hide the butt of the Smith & Wesson, snugged away in its hip-holster. The sure sign of an amateur, in that it was like a placard informing the world that when, and if, he moved it was going to be a waist-level cross-draw.

It was like taking candy from a child. He disliked what I'd said. His right hand moved across the front of his body. I stepped to my left – to *his* right – took a quick pace forward and brought my right fist down in a hammer-blow across the bridge of his nose.

The blood gushed, the tears streamed, and I'd continued the movement of my hand downwards to twist the revolver from his fingers almost before it was clear of the holster. I stepped behind him, hooked my left arm around his neck and rammed the muzzle of his own gun into his ribs.

'Don't play kids' games with a man, friend,' I warned.

Frisch smiled. It was a smile filled with meaning. It carried quiet satisfaction, but it also carried gentle determination.

'He's still going with you,' he insisted. 'Hate each other as much as you like – just don't *kill* each other until after the job. You *can* miss. *If* you miss, he blasts away at the wind-screen – at the car, generally – and we hope for the best.'

* * *

It was a nice day. A nice afternoon; one of those peculiarly March/April afternoons. The sky hadn't a stitch of cloud to its name, but the blue was softened by a gossamer haze that seemed to melt long before it reached the earth. The sun was up there, slightly to our right; light in plenty, but without sticky heat. Not a hint of wind. Not a hint of distance-shimmer. It was as if somebody had processed the required conditions through some celestial computer, and what was needed was what we had.

We were on a bridge which spanned the motorway. One of those private bridges linking one part of a farm to another. Some dumb civil engineer had originally planned the motorway slap through a damn great farm, then (because cows can't fly) had had to arrange a cow-path bridge high above six lanes of traffic.

We were on that bridge. Frisch, as always, had planned meticulously. We were suspended in a very private world. Maybe the farmer knew, but my money said he didn't; that he knew only as much as he needed to know, and that a bundle of notes had made sure he made no effort to find out any more. The parapet was a nice height for an elbow-rest and the getaway car was little more than fifty yards away, at the point where the bridge changed into a cart-track and made for an unclassified road.

Almost a full mile of arrow-straight motorway aimed south, and with the binoculars we were going to spot the target car well before it came within range. The round was in the chamber, the scope-sight was set and the rifle was leaning against the parapet, ready.

In my considered opinion, the jerk on my left was superfluous but, like a wart, he was an inconvenience I was required to suffer. He already had the Smith & Wesson out and in his hand hanging by his side. He'd cocked it – which meant it was on hair-trigger – but that was his business. If he yearned to shoot one of his toes off, that was OK by me.

I glanced at my watch, then raised the binoculars to my eyes and watched the triple line of vehicles hammering north. It was busy. *Very* busy. This was going to be no range-shot, whatever the make-believe target.

I took a couple of deep, oxygen-giving breaths in order to keep my body on top peak and ready. Like a class violinist, picking one note from the opening movement of Tchaikovsky's 'unplayable' concerto and hitting it, smack on the button, I had to pick one tyre, of one car, in this oncoming spray of assembly-line speed – and hit *that*.

Jesus!

I can say it now. For a moment, or two, I just *wondered*.

Then I saw the car.

'It's here,' I said and, at the same time, lowered the binoculars and reached for the rifle.

The scope replaced the binoculars, and I lined in the oncoming car. I settled myself; feet comfortably placed, knees unstiffened; elbows solid and chest just touching the rim of the parapet; cheek nestled against the stock. I watched the target approach; then, as it swung into the overtaking lane, I saw the lorry in the scope's aperture.

My mind worked on oiled bearings. What happened was planned. Despite subsequent remarks – despite what happened – what happened was *planned* . . . and it worked.

It was a damn great lorry, with foot-wide tyres. High-cabbed with its load roped and sheeted half as high again as the roof of the cab. It was in the middle lane, hammering along like the clappers and, for a moment, it shielded the target car on the overtaking lane.

The distance was perfect. The front offside tyre of the lorry was a larger target, and if, at the right moment, *that* went. . . .

That's what happened. I reached a decision, cross-wired the lorry's tyre and squeezed off the shot. For a shard of a second the driver fought to counter the blow-out, then the monster slewed, seemed to dive-bomb the target car, then the two of them jumped the central reservation, locked like lovers at the moment of climax.

As I lowered the rifle, Fletcher yelled: 'Dammit, you've missed: You've —'

As he hoiked the Smith & Wesson for unnecessary

blasting, I swung on my heel and smacked him across the side of the head with the ba rel of the rifle.

The revolver's hair-trigger mechanism did the rest.

I took the .35 slug low in the flesh of my left shoulder, and the impact threw me back against the parapet.

'You crass pillock!' I reached for the revolver which had left his fingers, and pointed it. I snarled: 'It was perfect. *Perfect.* You – you mad bastard – you aren't fit to be let loose with a water-pistol.' Then the pain started to hit me, and I rasped: 'Get to the car, dumb-bell. Drive.' He half-opened his mouth, as if to speak, and I almost screamed: '*Drive.* That's all. Don't talk. Don't even break wind . . . otherwise, you're crow pickings.'

It took more than an hour to get back to Frisch's place, and it was an hour I don't want to repeat. Like the gradual wind-up scream of a jet engine the pain grew to be almost unbearable. Every jolt, every roll of the car touched like white-hot metal. I sat in the rear seat, immediately behind Fletcher, and a hundred times I could have sent a slug into him – into the lower half of his body – and watched him die in agony as a price for giving me this pain.

The shoulder and sleeve of my jacket – the shoulder and sleeve of my shirt – were soaked in blood. As was one side of the waist of my trousers. Sticky gooey stuff that seeped into the upholstery of the car. I kept things as still as possible. I'd that much sense. Maybe I should have applied pressure. A folded handkerchief. Something like that. But I wanted my right hand free; I wanted to keep as firm a grip as possible on the Smith & Wesson. If I was going to flake out, that dumb bastard Fletcher was going with me . . . and he *wouldn't* wake up!

In as objective a way as possible, I periodically glanced down at the mess. The colour was dark; not brilliant enough to suggest recently oxygenated blood. No artery – which was something of a relief. Nevertheless, the red stuff leaked out of me at an alarming rate for the first fifteen minutes or so. Then, very gradually – and as the pain built up – the flow eased from a stream to a trickle.

I'd live. I'd reach Frisch's place ... and we could take things from there.

NINETEEN

David Hoyle – Detective Inspector David Hoyle – almost staggered into the living-room of his home, flopped into one of the twin armchairs and allowed his arms to dangle, loosely, alongside the sides of the chair. In no way breathless, nevertheless, he gave the impression of a man having just pushed himself to his absolute limit.

The faint rattle of crockery, coming from the kitchen, stopped.

'You home for the night, David?'

Hoyle nodded. He seemed not to have energy enough to speak.

'David!'

Hoyle took a deep breath, then called: 'For the night, pet.'

'Fish fingers?'

'Oh my God!'

'What's that, pet?'

'Fish fingers', said Hoyle, 'will round off the day beautifully.'

'Good. I'll pop them into the frying-pan.'

Hoyle nodded, then closed his eyes. There was an air about him of utter defeat. His eyes remained closed. Nor did he move until Alva wheeled the dumb waiter from the kitchen and positioned it between the two armchairs.

'Convenience foods, boy,' said Alva cheerfully. 'I sometimes think the man who invented them had policemen in mind.'

'Could be,' sighed Hoyle.

He roused himself and slowly reached for the tray upon

which the evening snack was neatly laid out. He bent forward a second time and lifted the sauce-bottle from the dumb waiter.

'Don't drown it in that stuff,' complained Alva. 'It's tasty enough, as it is.'

'My pet,' said Hoyle, heavily, 'don't *you* start.'

'What?'

'This day. This date.' Hoyle sloshed sauce on to the side of his plate. 'The year of Our Lord, One Thousand, Nine Hundred and Seventy-Six. The year some bloody fool mistook "big" for "beautiful".'

'I'm sorry, my love. I don't. . . .'

'Amalgamation!'

'Oh!'

'The day. The Big Day.' Hoyle attacked the fish fingers as if they, personally, were responsible for his outraged feelings. 'The day we aren't a force any more. The day we became an oversized *nothing*.' *

'David, it's not as bad as that. It *can't* be.'

'Look.' Hoyle waved his fork to lend emphasis. 'I joined a force, see? Lessford City Police Force. *That's* the force I joined. A good force. Very efficient. Bigger than Bordfield. Not as sprawling as the county. *My* force. With its own ways, and its own way of doing things. Not too many passengers. Not too many bastards. Not too many stabbers-in-the-back. And *now* look what's happened.

'Lessford *and* Bordfield *and* the damned county area. One great – what do they call it? – one great Metropolitan Police District. Not for any real reason. Not because it's going to make things easier. Or more efficient. Some bloody fool in Whitehall, see? Some clown who shouldn't be allowed to clean the bogs. He gets an Esso road-map and draws lines. And *that's* the "Metropolitan Police District". He should have his balls skewered and roasted over a slow fire.'

'Look, David, I think you're —'

* For one result of this amalgamation, see the author's *Who Goes Next?* (Macmillan, 1976).

166

'Gilliant.' Hoyle talked and chewed at the same time.

'I thought you liked Gilliant.'

'Sure I like Gilliant. What's wrong with Gilliant?'

'Nothing. It's just that you —'

'Gilliant,' repeated Hoyle. 'He's had us in today. A sort of get-together. Telling us who's who and what's what. The figures . . . astronomical! A million and a half acres, no less. A population topping the three million mark. Who the hell can police *that*, with any sense?'

'You've always said Gilliant could do —'

'Gilliant isn't God!' exploded Hoyle. 'Gilliant and two assistant chiefs. Deputies, really. Sullivan and a chap called Bear. Sullivan's as good as a second chief constable, and thank God for that. Bear' – he moved his shoulders – 'seems all right. From up north, somewhere.'

'Scotland?'

'No. Geordie country.'

He seemed to have quietened down, and for more than five minutes they ate in silence. Alva Hoyle watched her man, without giving the impression that she was watching him. She saw anger, deep inside him. A strange, exhaustive anger which seemed to have no real cause. This husband of hers was not a devious man; not a man given to secret moods or unexplained bouts of ill-temper. He was emotional – perhaps too emotional to be quite the complete policeman he might wish himself to be – perhaps even emotional enough to deserve the description of 'Romantic', in its widest sense; but, if so, she wasn't complaining. He was exactly what she wanted him to be, and that he was also a very dedicated copper was merely an unimportant spin-off.

Very gently, she said: 'Promotions?'

'All round,' grunted Hoyle. 'That was expected.'

'But not you?'

'Oh, for God's sake!' The implied suggestion genuinely shocked him.

'Something's disappointed you,' she observed.

'Nothing I can do about it,' he growled.

'Nevertheless. . . .' She waited.

167

Hoyle finished the last of the fish fingers, then sipped at a beaker of tea before he spoke.

'Rucker,' he said shortly.

'Chief Inspector Rucker?'

'Detective Chief *Superintendent* Rucker,' he muttered grimly. 'Gilliant pulled a real blinder. Quite a few had their eyes on Lessford Region Head of CID. He bypassed 'em all. Upped Rucker two pegs and gave *him* the job.'

'They'll hate Rucker,' gasped Alva.

'Of course.' Hoyle's lips twisted into a quick grin. 'I hate Rucker. *Everybody* hates Rucker. It's mother's milk to him. He thrives on it. And now the bastard's my gaffer.'

'Something about a rape,' murmured Rucker.

'What!' Hoyle jerked his head up and his attention from the inch-thick file in which the intricacies of an involved credit-by-fraud had demanded his concentration. 'A long-firm fraud job.' He touched the open file with a knuckle. Then, as an afterthought, added: 'Sir.'

'Something about a rape,' repeated Rucker flatly.

Hoyle wondered how Rucker had entered the office so completely unobserved. The Rucker way, of course. Unlike other men, Rucker didn't 'arrive'. He 'materialised'. One moment he wasn't ... then he *was*! One more of his countless, less charming tricks.

'It's a rather involved case, sir,' said Hoyle patiently. 'Not just one accommodation address. Three. Three bogus firms, and each firm —'

'I know what a long-firm fraud is, Hoyle.'

'Yes, sir.'

'I also have a passing knowledge concerning the ingredients of rape.'

'Yes, sir,' sighed Hoyle. 'Detective Sergeant Simpson's handling it. With one of the policewomen, of course.'

'While you – a detective inspector – wrestle with the uncertainties of the Debtors Act.'

'Sir, I try to get my priorities right.'

'Inspector Hoyle.' Another knack perfected by Rucker.

To keep his voice at little more than a murmur – albeit always a sarcastic or a sardonic murmur – and yet to ensure that every word reached, and was heard by, the person at whom he was aiming his everlasting contempt. He continued: 'Yesterday – I think you were present – the chief constable lumbered me with no small responsibility. Top Jack, in Lessford Region.'

'Yes, sir,' muttered Hoyle.

'*I* set the priorities. *I* set the pace. I neither seek advice nor take it. Nor do I *give* advice. I give orders. That way, the crime detection rate remains normally healthy – and, if a few weaklings fall by the wayside, that's a price I'm quite happy to pay.'

'Yes, sir,' breathed Hoyle.

'When you're ready, Inspector. We'll see what this woman who alleges she's been raped has to say for herself.'

As Hoyle followed the newly promoted Detective Chief Superintendent Rucker along the corridor towards the interview rooms, he (Hoyle) felt badly done by. The seas had been stormy enough when Lewis had occupied the Golden Throne; Lewis the wild bull of crime detection; the runaway tank of a man to whom noise and destruction had been a way (and, as far as he was concerned, the *only* way) to enforce the law.

Lewis had gone. Lewis had pushed things too far, once too often and, for a period, comparative sanity had reigned.

But now Rucker.

Rucker was much more dangerous than Lewis had ever been. There was no noise – no bombast – in Rucker's personality. Only universal loathing. He was a cavern-eyed, hollow-cheeked man; a creature of angles and sharp corners, spindle-shanked and knuckle-fingered. The impression was that to touch him would be to risk laceration. He had a terrible contempt for the whole human race; a contempt which almost amounted to a disease and which, over the years, seemed to have flensed the flesh from his bones and all humanity from his soul.

He was a terrible man ... and yet, even as he hated him, Hoyle found himself reluctantly admitting that Rucker was one hell of a detective.

Rucker opened the door of number three interview room and before he'd stepped into the room was speaking.

'Leave it, Sergeant.'

'Sir!' The DS straightened from the chair at the plain deal table, as if he'd received a sudden electric shock.

'Leave this case to your betters.'

'Sir, the statement's already been taken. All it needs is —'

'*A* statement. Not necessarily *the* statement. I'm not asking for a show of hands, Simpson. Go to Inspector Hoyle's office. There's a fraud file on his desk. Read it. Digest it. Summarise the contents on one sheet of foolscap, in language even a jury might understand.'

'Do it, Sergeant,' sighed Hoyle.

'Er – yes, sir.'

'You, Constable.' Rucker spoke to the policewoman. 'You know your reason for being here?'

'Yes, sir,' said the bewildered WPC. 'To see that —'

'To ensure that nobody commits indecent assault – or whatever – on the complainant. Had she merely been driving a motor car dangerously, had her home burgled or her handbag snatched – in such circumstances your presence wouldn't be necessary. But she says she's been *raped*. Therefore, somebody with a mind like a cesspit obviously thinks she might have enjoyed the experience and has ordained that a member of her own sex be present while she's being inverviewed by hairy-chested policemen.'

'Sir, I hardly think —'

'You're not here to *think*, Constable,' purred Rucker. 'You're here to sit on that chair and concentrate upon being a silent witness.'

It was a gambit calculated to make any Civil Liberties person have an immediate heart attack; a destruction of all previously built-up rapport. It was all wrong, in that it smashed the rules to hell and sneered at common courtesy.

And yet. . . .

The detective sergeant left the interview room, closing the door very quietly behind him. The WPC sat, goggle-eyed and speechless. Rucker picked the quarto-sized sheets from the table and began to read them. Hoyle lowered himself on to a spare chair and looked at the woman.

Maybe there was fear there, at the back of the eyes. The wrong *sort* of fear. Not, perhaps, a fear edged with outrage, nor a fear coloured with disgust. A rape victim showed signs of fear . . . of course! The most disgusting, the most humiliating offence any woman could suffer. Only one short step below murder. Therefore, fear – even terror – was part of the pattern.

'Mrs May.' Rucker murmured the name, while still reading the statement.

The woman gave a tiny nod.

'Olive May.' Rucker flipped a sheet, and continued reading. In little more than a whisper, he added: 'On the other hand, Olive may *not*.'

The woman compressed her lips a little, but kept silent.

The WPC made as if to say something, but Hoyle quietened her with a glance.

The silence stretched out, like a piano-wire being gradually subjected to an impossible strain and, when Rucker dropped the quarto sheets back on to the table, it was as if the wire had suddenly snapped. Hoyle felt his nerves give a tiny jerk.

Rucker stood over the woman, and drawled: 'Rape. A very traumatic experience . . . they tell me.'

'Yes,' breathed the woman.

'*I* wouldn't know, of course.'

'No.'

'Eleven o'clock, last night . . . right?'

'Eleven o'clock.' The woman's agreement had a certain throaty quality.

'You'd just left the Bunch of Grapes?'

'I'd – I'd been for a quiet drink.'

'At the Bunch of Grapes?'

'Yes.'

'A very palatial pub, the Bunch of Grapes. They even provide spittoons.'

'Look, it's not as bad as —'

'It is *not*', interrupted Rucker, 'the most obvious place in the world in which to have a "quiet" drink.'

'*I* like it,' she muttered defiantly.

'Obviously . . . otherwise you wouldn't have gone there.'

'I was *raped*!' The woman's fury surfaced for a moment.

'Of course,' smiled Rucker.

'That's why —'

'That's why you've waited almost twelve hours before allowing the world to share your joy.'

'I was – I was too upset.'

'Naturally.'

'I was – I was. . . .'

'Pissed?'

'No! I was *not* pissed.'

'Not that it would make any difference,' drawled Rucker. 'Drunk, sober – conscious or unconscious – rape is still rape.'

'Oh!'

'As Albert Dexter should know.'

'He's a dirty devil.' Her lips curled.

'Of course. Nor is he one of nature's gentlemen.'

'And that's a fact.'

'Was *he* drunk?' Then, before she could answer: 'Not that that makes any difference, either.'

'He'd had a few.'

'Nasty with it,' murmured Rucker.

'A real nasty sod,' she agreed.

'And, of course, you fought for your – er – virtue.'

'Eh?'

'You struggled. You didn't lie back and think of England.'

'Of course I struggled. You don't think. . . .'

'This woman.' Rucker moved his head and spoke to Hoyle. There was no change of tone in his voice. 'This creature who complains that somebody's violated her body. Do you know her?'

'No, sir,' breathed Hoyle.

The soft, but absolute, derision in Rucker's words charged the whole room and made Hoyle's nape hairs tingle.

'You *should* know her, Inspector Hoyle. You should know them all. Complainants as well as crooks. How in hell can you recognise the goats, if you don't know the sheep?'

'I. . . .' Hoyle swallowed. 'I'm sorry, sir.'

'She's a whore,' said Rucker flatly. Then, as the woman made to say something: 'Not even a professional whore. Merely a wildly enthusiastic one.

'This is her third complaint of rape – that, to my certain knowledge,' he continued mockingly. 'I accepted the first, when I was a detective constable. Before I learned more sense. I accepted it and it was laughed out of court, and I've kept an eye on her ever since. She complained in the county area once. I sat back and watched. Nothing to do with me. Some county detective was the mug that time. Again, it was laughed out of court.'

He turned his head with slow deliberation and stared at the white-faced woman for a full three seconds before he returned his attention to Hoyle.

'She rapes with remarkable ease, Inspector. Rather like Pavlov's dogs. Ring the right bell, and she's on her back, waiting. Her husband's in the merchant navy. God knows what he thinks she gets up to while he's away. The chances are he doesn't know about her propensity towards being raped. If he does, he's either an idiot or monumentally broad-minded.'

There was a pause – a very carefully timed pause – then Rucker mused: 'The scene last night. At the Bunch of Grapes. Something of a booze-up. There always is . . . *every* night. This female, need I say, is enjoying herself. Dirty stories. Naughty suggestions. Hubby, of course, is way and gone to hell over the foaming main. Everything quite safe. William Hickey isn't likely to concern himself with the fornicatory antics of non-socialites like Mrs Olive May. Therefore, safe . . . "drunk" safe.'

Again, the immaculately timed pause, before Rucker

continued: 'Come the dawn, of course, she's sober. Little things are remembered. Little things that might mean a lot. Did she, or did she not, take the Pill? The great lover of a few hours before – Albert Dexter – *did* he use a condom? Worrying questions, Inspector. Because even hubby can count up to nine.' Suddenly, the tone changed. Not the volume – the words were as soft-spoken as ever – but the blistering contempt gave ugliness to every syllable. 'She's a cow, Inspector Hoyle. I know, the textbooks say even cows can be raped – but not by men like Dexter, and not without having marks to prove it. She didn't resist. She'd be a hospital case if she had. I know *him*, too. Damn near twelve hours before she makes a complaint. Why? Embarrassment? With that one you *have* to be joking. She – her kind – *she's* the reason genuine rape victims don't like complaining. They're going to be questioned. With bags like this around, ready to sling the accusation in case there's an unwanted pudding in the pot, of *course* they'll be questioned. Hard!'

Then the silence. A silence which seemed not to affect Rucker but which, to the other three occupants of the room, seemed to bound and rebound from every wall louder than any scream.

At last, and in a low, hoarse voice, Hoyle spoke to the woman.

'Well?'

'He's a bad bastard.' The words came from behind dry lips, tight with hatred. 'He's no bloody right to. . . .'

'You know what I mean.' Hoyle was no 'Rucker'. Hoyle lashed out with all the fury of a man just been made to look a simpleton. 'Make your damned complaint if you want to. If you must. If it's true. But understand this. It had better *be* true. I'll have statements from everybody you were with last night. Everybody who even *saw* you. Detailed statements. I'll hold the case, pending your husband getting back to port, then have a statement from *him*. What *he* thinks about your morals. How *he* rates you as a loving and faithful wife. I'll have statements. Statements enough to send this Dexter character inside for life . . . or to sink *you*, without trace.'

174

'You buggers never believe, do you?'

It was as near complete capitulation as she was ever likely to get. Not complete surrender, although the truth was there in the manner in which she mouthed the words. She pushed herself to her feet and walked a little unsteadily towards the door.

The fury and disgust were all-pervading, as she repeated: 'You buggers *never* believe!'

'I'll go with her.'

The policewoman stood up and followed the older woman from the interview room.

The emotional impact of the episode seemed not to have touched Rucker. He stood there, gaunt and sardonic, toying with the statement the woman had given to the detective sergeant.

'And what if she has?' An ashen-faced Hoyle croaked the question as he looked up at the newly appointed Head of CID. 'What if she *has* been raped?'

'You think she *has*?' mocked Rucker gently.

'I don't know. *You* don't know. I don't *think* she was raped. But, unlike you, Chief Superintendent Rucker, *sir*, I don't claim to have a hot-line to God. I could be wrong.'

'The essence of good policing', said Rucker calmly, 'is never to *admit* to being wrong. No waffling, Inspector Hoyle. I want no nebulous wafflers holding positions of authority under *me*. You give an order. It is the correct order – merely by reason of *you* having given it. You make a decision. It's the *correct* decision, and for the same reason. In colloquial language, it's known as "holding your own water". It makes for respect from the underlings. Not love ... but if you want *love* you're in the wrong job. They know you mean it. They know you won't budge. They won't waste time – your time or their time – in trivial arguments.'

'Pavlov's dogs!' muttered Hoyle.

'Quite.' The half-smile held no humour. 'The trick, Inspector, is to be "Pavlov". Not one of the dogs.'

TWENTY

Frisch and the creep Fletcher had helped me from the car. They'd half-carried me into the farmhouse and up the stairs; into the bedroom and on to the bed. They'd stripped off my jacket and shirt and agreed that this was more than a first-aid job.

'There is a quack,' Frisch had said.

'If he's safe, get him.' The swing of the pain and the gentle in and out of focus of my eyes had encouraged a certain laxity of caution. 'The damn slug's still inside.'

'He's safe.' Frisch had sounded very certain.

'OK . . . get him.'

That was more than two hours ago, and now the slug was out, I'd had antibiotics pumped into me and my shoulder was cotton-woolled and bandaged into a more or less comfortable position.

The medic was a thin, solemn-looking individual. When he stood alongside Frisch they reminded me of those old *Chips* characters, Weary Willie and Tired Tim. But the guy knew his job, and I was grateful for the release from pain.

'How long?' I asked

He lifted a questioning eyebrow.

'Up and about,' I amplified.

'The dressing needs changing every twelve hours,' he fenced.

'You will stay here a while,' said Frisch.

'How *long*?' I insisted.

'Assuming the wound remains clean, assuming you have flesh with a normal healing time – '

'Let's take the assumptions for granted.'

' – the bandages should be off within a fortnight but, for a few months, the shoulder will be stiff. The muscle's been torn. There's bound to be a certain amount of scar tissue. That has to be loosened.'

'Two months. Three months,' I murmured.

'About that.' Then he added: 'You're right-handed. You'll be able to use a brush long before that.'

I let the remark slide past without comment, but later, when the medic had left and Frisch had rejoined me in the bedroom, it seemed sensible to straighten things out.

'What's the quack's name?' I asked.

'It doesn't matter.' Frisch poured three-star brandy into two glasses and handed me one. 'Here. I know you don't drink too much, but this might counter delayed shock.'

'No delayed shock.' Nevertheless, I took the glass, sipped and said: 'The quack's name, Frisch. I want to know.'

'He can be trusted.'

'He knows who *I* am.'

'No. In this situation nobody asks —'

'Frisch! That remark about me holding a brush. He doesn't think I'm a bloody house-painter. He's recognised me as "Lados".' Then as Frisch frowned sudden worry: '"Lados", Frisch. And he's just excavated a thirty-eight slug from my shoulder. He's not an idiot.'

This time Frisch tasted the brandy, and it was rather more than a sip.

'He can be trusted,' he repeated. 'We've used him four times in the past. We've never had trouble. We won't this time.'

'Tell me about him, Frisch,' I insisted.

'He's. . . .' He moved the hand holding the glass. 'He's a doctor. A good doctor. He hasn't been struck off the register. Nothing like that. He has a practice. A private practice . . . but a practice. He's —'

'Tell me *about* him.'

'His name's Arnold,' said Frisch heavily. 'He's ex-Army. He carried the rank of major in the Medical Corps —'

'So he'll know all about bullets.'

177

'He's from Lessford. He's married. Has two grown daughters —'

'Three women. Three! That doesn't please me, Frisch.'

'Dammit, he doesn't talk.' Frisch was becoming worried, and the worry made him impatient. 'We've used him before. He does *not* talk.'

'Who are you trying to convince, Frisch?'

'He doesn't talk.' This, the third time, it was a muttered remark as he lowered himself on to a chair. He tasted more brandy, took a deep breath; then, almost pleadingly, said: 'The bullet had to come out. What else? No do-it-yourself surgery on the kitchen table. That's for cheap Westerns. A multiple pile-up on a motorway. Somebody with a slug in his shoulder. Where's the connection? He knows I'm a gunsmith. He accepts that there's been an accident.'

'Accepts?'

'He doesn't *question* it.'

'He knows "Lados".'

'Half the country knows "Lados". You've had enough television exposure. You've been in enough Sunday supplements. *Not* to have known "Lados" would have made him almost unique.'

There was more talk along the same lines. I played devil's advocate, while Frisch worried a little and worked to convince me that logic and past experience were both on his side.

The logic sounded fine ... other than that the profession of paid killer doesn't admit of too much logic. There was (and still is) a double façade to keep in position. The unknown butcher; the man from the shadows of whom nobody knew anything. And the extrovert and eccentric modern painter, about whom there was continual controversy. The logic of one could never be the logic of the other. Equally 'past experience' didn't mean a thing. As far as I knew I was the only man ever to 'hide' behind a blatantly public exhibition.

The talk was inconclusive, in that I was not *quite*

convinced. But what else? Dr Arnold had to be either trusted or removed – and, as we both knew, unplanned, spur-of-the-moment killing was *not* within the rules of our own particular game.

'Which, in turn, edged the conversation towards Fletcher.

'Where is the dumb bastard?' I growled.

'On his way back to Uncle Sam Land.'

'Now, that one I *could* remove from Mother Earth,' I said. 'Nor would it be any great loss.'

'He's not in the same league,' said Frisch soothingly. 'I grossly underestimated you. It was a beauty . . . and it was an "accident".'

'How many?' I asked.

'Three dead – including the target – and one woman in intensive care. She might not survive.'

'Three . . . possibly four.' I allowed my satisfaction to show itself in a gentle smile. 'One shot. One .22 round. That's what I call economy, Frisch.'

'That's what *I* call "professionalism".'

And, coming from Frisch, that was real praise.

Anne looked after me. Anne of the eyeless sockets; of the certainty of movement in a world of complete blackness; of the gentle touch and the sure, cool-fingered positioning of fresh dressings.

She was a witch. I guided her hand to my elbow and, after that, I relaxed and allowed her to clean and re-dress the wound. There was never a hesitation. Never unnecessary pain caused by clumsiness. Never any doubt about what came next or where the proud flesh needing balm was situated. And it became a practice, after each gentle re-bandaging, for her to drape the pyjama jacket over the injured shoulder then slide her hand down my arm and give my fingers a quick squeeze of friendship.

On the third day there was a short exchange.

I said: 'I think you should wear sunglasses.'

'Why?' She was truly puzzled.

'To cover your eyes.'

'I have no eyes,' she said bluntly.

'To cover *that*, then.'

'Does it offend you?'

'It would make you look a little more attractive,' I insisted. 'It would take away that pinched appearance.'

'I'm pinched? I'm too thin?'

'Not too thin. Just. . . .' I couldn't find the right words, and ended: 'It would make you *look* better.'

The next day, she wore dark glasses. Large, round eye-pieces, dark enough to hide the empty sockets. She no longer *looked* blind. She looked quite attractive.

Within the week I was up and moving around. Watching Frisch in his workshop; marvelling at the certainty with which he tooled new trigger-movements for near-antiques, seeing the apparent ease with which he sleeved a barrel and reduced a chamber to take a lesser bore.

'You're rather more than a craftsman, Frisch,' I remarked.

'There are very few of us left.' There wasn't a hint of brag in the words. A simple statement of fact. 'To hand-make a gun. Decide the barrel-length, decide the bore; then, if necessary, hand-make the ammunition. We're a dying race.'

'A "killing" race,' I smiled.

'That, too.'

'All in the same line of – er – "business"?' I slipped real meaning into the question, but didn't expect an answer.

Nevertheless, I got an answer.

'A killing tool,' he said quietly. 'Specifically made for one job. Not mass-murder – not warfare – but a one-time, specialised occasion. Where else to get it? Therefore. . . .'

He stopped talking, but he'd answered the question.

During that convalescing period we got as close to each other as either of us would ever allow. In the evenings we talked guns, and I was even allowed to argue with him . . . almost as an equal.

It was not home. I missed my books and I missed my music. But it was a pleasant break – a holiday of a sort – and Anne and I took to walking across the surrounding moors. My arm was slinged, but that didn't stop us covering anything up to six or seven miles in an afternoon. Nor was it all talk, or all silence. The mix was both steady and comfortable. She knew the birdsong and, what was more surprising, she knew the wind signs. The direction, the force and the 'feel' of the temperature. And, as if by magic, she could estimate the cloud cover and forecast the weather for the next few hours. And with mind-boggling accuracy.

'We'd better start for home, otherwise we'll be caught in a storm.'

And, above, the sky was duck-egg blue with clouds on the far horizon looking no more menacing than distant hills. But she was right and, virtually, as we reached the shelter of the farmhouse drops as big as ten-pence pieces heralded one of those early-summer torrents.

Then one day she said: 'I've been listening to *Jane Eyre*.'

'Listening?' For the moment I'd truly forgotten her lack of sight.

'The Talking Books,' she explained. 'Karl keeps me well supplied. I usually listen for half an hour or so before I go to sleep.'

I'd heard of the Talking Books project; the arrangement whereby novels are read aloud by actors or actresses, and recorded for use by the blind. One hell of a good idea. To read aloud takes far more skill than does merely mouthing the words from the page.

'A fine novel,' I said. 'One of the classics.'

'I don't understand the woman,' she said solemnly. 'This is my third time of listening ... and I *still* don't understand her.'

'Jane?'

'No. Charlotte Brontë. This character, Rochester. He's all *wrong*. Whoever he married, he'd be a terrible husband. But he was created, as a hero, by a *woman*.'

'A romantic woman,' I corrected her. 'A very passionate woman, who was forced to keep her nature in check.'

'He'd have frightened her to death. Jane, I mean ... even Charlotte.'

'Some women like being dominated,' I said.

'You speak from experience?' Her mouth corners lifted a little as she asked the question.

'I've never known a woman long enough – or intimately enough – to dominate her,' I countered.

'Don't sell yourself short,' she said softly.

'Short-changing myself is *not* one of my faults,' I assured her. Then, when the purport of what she'd said and how she'd said it registered: 'Hey, honey. Turn down the gas. I'm only good for myself.'

We walked, perhaps fifty yards, in silence; then, in a little-girl innocent voice, she said: 'That makes me a tart.'

'Christ, no! I'm just – y'know. . . .'

'Queer?'

'No. Not that, either.' And, strangely, the suggestion, coming from her, annoyed me.

'It's *me*, then?'

'No.'

'Poor little blind girl. That sort of thing.'

'Hey, look, child. Nobody's —'

'*I'm not a child.*' I'd asked for it, and I got it. She almost screamed the words. Then, hardly less harshly: 'The eyes. That's all. All the rest of me works fine. Because I can't see doesn't mean I can't feel. Haven't grown up. That's the way people think, and they're crazy. Karl, too. . . .'

'Karl's been father and mother to you, kid. Don't you knock—'

'He *watches* me.' The accusation fed spiders on to my spine. The accusation and the tone of the accusation. 'Do you know that? All the time. He watches me. I know he's there. He never says a word – never makes a movement – but I know he's there. Watching! In the bathroom. When I'm undressing. When I'm in bed. One day, he'll find the courage.'

'In hell's name, what are you saying?' I croaked.

'You don't know?' she sneered. 'You can't *guess*?' Then the bitterness left her, her shoulders quivered and tears slipped from behind the dark lenses of the spectacles. In

182

little more than a trembling-lipped sigh, she repeated: 'You can't *guess*?'

That was all. Nothing more was said, and we walked back to the house. A couple of other times we went for a walk, but the conversation never again moved on to similar lines. Nor, to be honest, did I push it.

I moved back to my own place and returned to my normal way of living. The 'Lados' way. It was nice, it was cosy, and I shouldn't have given a damn.

The truth is I didn't give *much* of a damn ... about anything.

The year 1965 was a very easy-going year. That was the year they closed the hanging-sheds. The profession – *my* profession – opened its doors to anybody. No sweat. Get caught, and things became a little uncomfortable for a few years, but the universe didn't go out. I visited Frisch, often enough to keep a keen edge on my shooting, and occasionally we talked.

'They blast away, and hope for the best,' he sighed.

(That was well into 1965 and moving fast towards another year.)

I smiled and said: 'There's a difference between a butcher and a surgeon.'

'Not when the only thing you want is a carcass.'

He was right. The killings kept pace, but the convictions mounted. Nobody planned. Nobody had enough pride to *take* pride.

The year 1966 saw me give the thumbs-down to a job for the first time.

August – a nice August, as those who can remember will verify – and Pollard had arranged for a London exhibition. Fifty 'Lados' masterpieces – almost half of them loaned from private suckers – and the culture clowns were putting on their own circus. I was housed at the Savoy, and for five days I was as busy as a dog with a surfeit of fleas. Television, radio, art magazines – the lot. I spent hours explaining why circles meant squares, squares meant triangles and triangles meant straight lines. The patter, by this time, was kiss-easy; the deeper the garbage, the readier the dumb bastards were to accept it. The Flat Earthers had talked simple logic by comparison. But such was (such still is) the eagerness of fools to masquerade their foolishness as wisdom that I was listened to, 'understood' and even 'explained'.

As a byproduct of the London trip, I learned things which worried me. The studios and canteens of both radio and television organisations are the places in which to hear the hottest gossip around and, at that time, the names 'Kray' and 'Richardson' were tossed around like balls in a bingo machine. 'The Richardson gang.' 'The Kray firm.' Talk of torture, talk of wide-ranging protection rackets, talk of evil for its own sake. Stupid talk. Worrying talk. The coppers were no longer as easy-going as they should be. Three names – John du Rose, Leonard Read and Henry Mooney – matched the names of the bad bastards and, as anybody with enough grey matter to fill a needle's eye could have worked out, those three had for ever and all the money and manpower they needed. London was due a clean-up, and the vacuum team had already plugged in the machine.

I was glad to get out of the place. Glad to get north, and back to my own safe corner.

Then, less than a week after I'd got back, Frisch propositioned me.

'South Africa,' he said off-handedly.

'I understand it has a pleasant climate.'

We were on the range, target-practising with handguns. Mine was a Bergmann-Bayard 9 mm automatic, Frisch's was a 9 mm Mars automatic. We were wagering, a pound a time, on every five shots fired.

Frisch sighted the Mars, squeezed off, then said: 'A close-quarter job.'

'How close?' I raised the Bergmann-Bayard and squinted along the sights.

'Within touching distance . . . if possible.'

'Would you say "easy"? Or would you say "not easy"?'

'That's never troubled you before.'

'Oh, I can *do* it,' I assured him. 'I'm interested in my freedom of movement *after* I've done it.'

'Can't say.' We strolled towards the targets. 'I haven't been asked to do the planning.'

'Somebody I don't know?' I'd nicked the bull twice. Frisch had only touched it once. He peeled a note from a wad he took from his hip pocket and handed it to me. I said: 'I don't work with strangers. The Fletcher clown taught me *that* lesson.'

'It's political.'

'I don't give a damn if it's religious. Without you, they don't get me.'

'The money's exceptional.' He'd been told to say it, therefore he said it.

'My compliments,' I said. 'But, without you, they don't mine enough diamonds.'

I recall the smile he gave. The gentle nod of appreciation. We understood each other, and nothing more remained to be said.

The next month – 6 September – Verwoerd was assassinated. A close–quarter job. Bodged up, and suicidal. The trigger-man hadn't the whisker of a chance – but, with Frisch, and if *I'd* picked up the contract, things would have been very different.

That refused offer came in August. As the year ended I refused another offer. This time for a different reason.

Sunday, 11 December. We'd strolled the surrounding moors on a rough-shoot. Moving targets and twelve-bores. Again, our own version. We'd carried double-barrelled shotguns, but only loaded one of the barrels. It made for a higher degree of concentration. More than that, a 'runner' was counted as a miss. We'd taken some grouse, some partridge and a couple of rabbits, and we were in the Land-Rover, driving quietly back to the farmhouse. I was behind the wheel.

Again, in the throwaway manner to which I'd become accustomed, Frisch said: 'Newcastle . . . know it?'

185

'Some hick Geordie city.' I kept what concentration I needed on the road.

'It's expanding. Nightclubs. That sort of thing.'

'The Las Vegas of the North-East,' I murmured.

'Something like that. Somebody's been found with his hand in the till. Name of Angus Sibbet.'

'Slam the drawer,' I suggested. 'Chop his fingers off.'

'Fruit machines,' said Frisch softly.

'Jesus Christ!'

'A *lot* of fruit machines.'

'They're still only —'

'Enough fruit machines to allow Sibbet to fiddle the pay-out mechanism, and cream off up to a thousand a day.'

'Jesus Christ!' I used the same words, but the surprise was of a different kind.

'Ten grand to bury Sibbet,' said Frisch.

'Cheap at the price,' I smiled.

'You could be home, in your own bed, before the body was found.' Frisch seemed mildly enthusiastic. 'I'll fix the details. The background and the getaway. The police don't like Sibbet too much. At best, only a half-hearted enquiry.'

I drove in meditative silence for a mile or thereabouts. I couldn't then (and still can't) put a name to the niggling doubts. Maybe the approach was wrong; the name of the victim, the location of the hit and the reason for the contract, all named too easily. Too early. It wasn't Frisch's fault. Frisch was telling me as much as *he* knew; but, at that stage, it was more than he *should* have known. Somebody, somewhere, had too large a mouth. Maybe *that* was one of the reasons for my hesitation.

'Do we know who pays?' I asked at last.

'A London crowd. The Kray brothers. They're —'

'I know what they are,' I interrupted. 'London. So why Newcastle?'

'Fingers in pies. An expanding empire.'

'Leave it, Frisch,' I advised. 'Don't touch it. Don't even go near the thing.'

He looked surprised.

186

'All muscle, no brains,' I amplified. 'In the Big City it's an open secret. The cops – the *real* cops – have them lined up in their sights, but the Krays are too dumb to know when they're targets in a shooting gallery. They'll tumble. They'll bring the whole house down with them.'

The rest is criminal history. Sibbet was taken care of on the night of Wednesday, 4 January 1967. His corpse was found in an abandoned Jag at a dump called South Hetton.

He was dead. Other than that, it was like a Christmas pantomime. Two amateurs called Dennis Stafford and Michael Luvaglio had done the stiffening and, instead of a straight in-and-out job, they'd scattered red herrings left, right and sideways. They left enough pointers to 'prove' that they didn't, the local Law merely sat back, peeled the skins from the onion and allowed a jury to call them both liars. Even books were written, screaming 'frame-up' – and the authors looked pretty damn silly when, having worked his stretch, Stafford left HM Prison, smiled cheekily and openly admitted the Sibbet corpsing.

That was 1967 and, after the verdict, Frisch raised the subject.

'We could have done it better.'

'Nobody could have done it *worse*.'

He chuckled, then said: 'The house didn't tumble. The Kray firm is still in business.'

'Give it five years,' I assured him. 'Five years from now, they'll be inside.'

Less than five years, in fact. . . .

July 1969 had Reginald, Charles and Ronald waltzing around various appeal courts, but the glory boys of Scotland Yard had done a water tight welding job.

Frisch mentioned it just once more.

'Not the average trigger-man,' he mused.

'Who? Me?'

'A man whose opinion should be taken very seriously. We could have been in trouble, my friend. We aren't – and for that I thank you.'

187

TWENTY-ONE

Ripley died in 1975. Rucker died in 1978. They both died violent deaths; the former via his own hand,* the latter in the course of his duty and because, to the last, he counted himself fire-proof.†

Hoyle truly mourned the former; attended his funeral and, with Alva at his side, swapped police talk with some of the many officers from not a few forces who had come to pay genuine respect to the memory of one of their number who, within the timespan of a shortened police career, had become both a legend and a yardstick.

As they drove home from the funeral Hoyle was in a black and near-desperate mood.

'God, there'll never be another one like him.'

He made it a savage, muttered indictment aimed at whichever dark angel had the unenviable task of ordering the lives of policemen.

'From what you've told me, he was a good man,' agreed Alva.

'He was a great *copper* . . . that, too.'

'The same thing, surely?'

'Not by a million light-years.'

'David, you mustn't. . . .'

'They come once in a lifetime.' The words were wrapped in muttered disgust. They emphasised far more than a loss to the organisations of law enforcement. There was a personal loss, also. 'Not the bloody rank. Not the guff they spout

* See the author's *Death of a Big Man* (Macmillan, 1975)
† See the author's *A Ripple of Murders* (Macmillan, 1978)

about man-management. Others have that – Rucker has it – but Ripley had something extra. Dammit, he was *human*. He had weaknesses, but he knew those weaknesses and never tried to hide them. He accepted all the weaknesses other men had. Fellow-coppers, crooks ... everybody. He accepted them, understood them, even excused them ... and *still* remained a great copper.'

'Hey, boy – you're a great copper, too. Don't —'

'Forget it!' The suppressed anger in the interruption startled her. 'I'm good. I don't kid myself. I'm good – well above average – but there's a hell of a lot of *good* coppers around. Then there's a gap. A bloody great gap nobody can bridge without that extra something. I don't know what it is. Nobody knows. It can't be taught, it can't be learned. It doesn't even come with experience. It's just there. The difference between "good" and "great". Ripley had it. He had it by the ton.' The sigh seemed to come all the way from the soles of his feet. It raised and lowered his shoulders; expanded and deflated his chest. Then, with great sadness, he muttered: 'Ripley was a *great* copper from the day he joined.'

Alva Hoyle worried for a time. For some days and, perhaps, for some weeks. This man of hers was being beaten into the ground and he, himself, was doing much of the beating. Ambition? Sure ... ambition was part of it. But running neck and neck with the ambition was a feeling of frustration. A growing sureness of inadequacy.

He slowly built a shell around himself and sometimes, in the silence of late evenings, he retreated into that shell and refused even the simple comfort of communication. His was an ambition, not merely to better himself but to become *better*. To become more knowledgeable ... about everything.

Not for Hoyle the fiction of Chandler, or Christie, or Conan Doyle. Not even the writings of Hemingway, or Greene. He wanted to 'know'. He sought information and learning from textbooks and treatise and, because he tried too hard – stretched himself well beyond his own capabilities

189

– only a small percentage of what he read registered and remained.

Philosophy, psychology, art, history, political science, theoretic economics – the more obscure the subject-matter, the harder he tried.

'Minority interest' radio and television programmes constituted his main diet of listening and watching. He sat, hunched forward with a frown of concentration on his face, and listened and watched, only half-understanding and, because he couldn't fully understand, mentally cursing himself for being a dunderhead.

A typical episode occurred one evening in the autumn of 1976. Hoyle and his wife had driven to Bordfield – to the nearest 'art cinema' – to see a showing of the French film *Le Jour se lève*. On their return journey, Alva spoke her mind, but said the wrong thing.

'Well,' she said heavily, 'that's one way to ruin a perfectly good evening.'

'Didn't you like it?' In honesty, Hoyle's surprise wasn't a put-on.

'Did *you*?' countered Alva.

'It's looked upon as a classic.'

'The hell it is!' Alva lighted a cigarette.

'Marcel Carné is one of the great French directors.'

'Give me Sammy Goldwyn every time.'

'Alva, you can't argue with —'

'David, boy, that was crap, done up smart.' And now *her* impatience showed itself. 'You can't speak French – I'm not too hot on it myself – and they didn't even show the version with subtitles. Culture vultures and raving lunatics – that's what they cater for. And I'm neither.'

'Well, thank *you*.'

'For God's sake!' She drew on the cigarette, and saw no reason to quieten her Welsh outrage. 'The acting was pure ham. That tarty flower-seller. That working-class lounge-lizard – the conjuror's assistant – and that idiot conjuror. No wonder the poor sod committed suicide. A pity he didn't take the other three with him.'

'There was. . . .' Hoyle hunted for the right word. 'There was an "atmosphere".'

'It was a mock-up,' complained Alva. 'It wasn't even a *good* mock-up. Some sleazy industrial dump . . . supposedly. Damn, you could almost see the brush-marks on the stage sets.'

'Look, you can't have —'

'Jesus Christ, you've been conned.' She didn't shout the accusation. She didn't even *speak* it. She mumbled it, from behind clenched teeth. As if the pressure of her indignation was such that she had to keep it tightly held inside; as if to give it the freedom it demanded would have entailed screaming at the top of her voice. Therefore, she muttered: 'You. All of you. Every fool making pretence that they've seen some sort of unique picture-making. Conned rotten. The old put-on: it's French, so it must be a classic. It didn't come from Hollywood or Pinewood, therefore it's better than anything Hollywood or Pinewood could *ever* produce.'

'*I* liked it.' Like his wife, Hoyle kept his anger low-key and softly savage. He glared down the cone of the headlights, and added: 'I could *see* things in it.'

'There's perception for you,' she mocked.

It was the sort of argument that, at that moment, had no ending. A typical man-and-wife argument, indulged in by people sure enough of their marriage to know that the odd insult or two isn't going to be a home-wrecker.

Which was why they rode in silence until they reached Lessford. Until they were within half a mile of their home.

Then, in a low voice, Hoyle made an admission.

'All right . . . it wasn't as good as I expected.'

'It stank,' she said abruptly.

'I – er – I wouldn't put it as bad as that.'

'Well. . . .' She qualified her bluntness with a qualification, and met him halfway. 'To *me* it stank.'

'Those. . . .' He raised his hands a few inches from the rim of the steering-wheel, then let them fall back into place again. 'Those who know say it's a classic . . . that's all.'

'Those who *claim* to know.'

191

'You have to take notice.' It was almost an apology.

'David, my pet,' she said sadly, 'you take too *much* notice. Art, music, cinema. If it's "different", some fool will claim it's unique. Some fool who claims to be an expert ... and draws a damn good salary on the strength of that claim. More often than not, a spurious claim.'

'No more,' sighed Hoyle. 'I won't drag you to some art cinema again.' Then, as if an explanation was necessary: 'It's just that – y'know ... I want to *know* about things.'

'About everything, my love.' The smile was, perhaps, sadly maternal. 'You want to know about *everything*.'

Two years later, Rucker died.

There was much hypocrisy. The mode of Rucker's death was such that headlines, both local and national, suggested that he'd been a much-loved, much-respected Head of CID. Nor, and for the sake of police–public relations, could there be an official denial of this suggestion. Unlike Ripley, he'd died on duty; therefore, again unlike Ripley, he was accorded the panoply of an official funeral; officers in 'best blue' carrying the coffin, the uniformed chief constable, along with other high-ranking officers, escorting the body to the church.

'Hell's teeth, you'd think he was a hero.' Hoyle removed the jacket of his best suit and carefully positioned it over a coat-hanger. He it was who had been chosen to represent the plain-clothes branch at the funeral. 'The garbage that parson spouted. Talk about boning the truth.'

'He's dead, my pet.'

'I could say "Good riddance".'

'But you won't.' Alva reached for an envelope on the sideboard, and added: 'Who do we know in Italy?'

'Nobody that I know of.'

'This arrived with the midday post.' She handed him the envelope, with its Italian stamp, then said: 'A couple of hours at the hospital this evening. I'll rustle up a quick meal first. Do you mind.'

'Not at all.' Hoyle slit the envelope open. 'I've a few bits and pieces to see to at the office before I've finished.' He unfolded the sheet of paper he'd taken from the envelope, started reading, then exclaimed: 'Good God!'

'What is it?'

'Italian television.' He continued reading as he talked. 'It's from one of the reporters.'

'What, about the—?'

'Remember when we were at Merthyr? The disaster?'

'Yes. But —'

'The day we came home. That morning. I went back to Aberfan?'

'To have a last look at the —'

'Yes. That, too. But part of it was because of what your dad said.'

'I can't remember him. . . .'

'Television crews. Remember? From all over the world.'

'David, I don't see what —'

'The Italian crowd. I had a word with one of the reporters. I asked him to snoop around when he got back. Find out what he could about Jacopo Davanzati.'

'Jacopo. . . .' Alva frowned for a moment, then said: 'Oh, you mean. . . .'

'The murdered killer. Remember? The man Gawne identified.'

'David, that's going back *years*!'

'Undetected murder, my sweet. Still undetected.' Hoyle grinned his delight. 'This chap – this reporter – he's something of a digger. His job, I suppose.'

'Don't tell me he knows who killed him?'

'No, not quite that. But there's a name. Davanzati was a paid assassin – we know *that* – but he's got wind of somebody he once worked with. Years ago. Before he was murdered—'

'Good grief, that's—'

' – a character called Fleischer. Likes to be called Fletcher. English, he thinks.'

' – a lifetime ago. You can't chase the same criminal for ever.'

'Alva, my pet.' Hoyle refolded the letter and returned it to its envelope. There was quiet determination in his voice, as he explained his own philosophy of policing. 'It's so easy. It's *too* easy. That's the trouble. Davanzati was a bad sod. Agreed. And Charlie Ripley – rest his soul – he had the same idea you have. Davanzati deserved to die. But he didn't! That was one of Ripley's weaknesses. Murder stays murder, whoever the victim is.'

'*Your* murder,' said Alva gently

'That, too,' he admitted. 'Fifteen years, undetected ... but the file isn't closed. They never close.'

'He could be dead,' Alva reminded him. 'The murderer, I mean. He could be dead and buried.'

'It's possible.' Hoyle pulled a face as he dropped the letter back on the sideboard. 'That's a fifty-fifty chance. If he is. . . .'

Later that night, when Alva had returned from her stint at the local hospital, and Hoyle had returned home after checking the last crime file and pausing for a short exchange of the latest gags with the 'night catcher' on duty at the CID office, they touched upon the subject which had been at the back of their minds since Rucker had been killed. They'd bathed and changed into night clothes and dressing-gowns. They relaxed in armchairs and sipped drinking chocolate and smoked cigarettes.

Alva asked the question which touched off the exchange.

'Who'll take over?'

'Rucker's job? I don't think it's been decided yet. It was too sudden.'

'There must be some front runners.'

'I think Lennox can handle both regions, for a time.'

'Lennox.' She smiled. A pleasant, reflective smile. 'He's Head of CID in the Bordfield district ... isn't he?'

'Lenny can do it.' Hoyle's quiet chuckle complemented his wife's smile. 'It wouldn't be a bad thing if they gave him both regions ... permanently.'

'That's a big responsibility.'

'Lenny could do it,' repeated Hoyle. 'But there's the

"authorised strength" angle to consider.' He tasted the drinking chocolate. 'The old chase-me-Charlie game. "Authorised strength" and "actual strength". Every year the chief increases the demand for "authorised strength". That gives him elbow-room. He can push the "actual strength" up to meet the job.'

'Chinese mathematics,' smiled Alva.

'It's a game, played to fixed rules. He always asks for more than he expects ... but there's always *some* increase. Men and equipment. The "authorised strength".'

'And,'

'That's it.' Hoyle waved his cigarette. 'He has enough cash to bring the "actual strength" up, towards the "authorised strength", then next year he ups his demand for "authorised strength" ... so, on paper, he's always in a strong position to demand more.'

'And that's why Lennox won't get the job?' Alva looked puzzled.

'"Authorised strength." One Head of CID in charge of Lessford Region and one head of CID in charge of Bordfield Region. If the chief gives the impression of being satisfied with one gaffer taking on both regions, that will make the Police Authority suspicious. Why demand two, when one is enough?'

'But, surely, it depends on the *man*. If Lennox is good enough to —'

'They count heads, my sweet,' said Hoyle heavily. 'They're only interested in numbers. Men, cars, typewriters. It wouldn't surprise me if they counted the pencils.' The quick grin, followed by a draw on the cigarette. 'That's why a good chief constable isn't necessarily a good *copper*. If he can bamboozle the Police Authority a little bit more than the next guy, he's a good chief constable.'

There was a silence. One of those warm and comfortable silences which are far more than a mere absence of sound or talk. The gas-fire hissed, gently, as it pushed sleepy warmth into the room. The slight up-draught of the heated air carried the scarves of smoke from the cigarettes towards the ceiling. It was, perhaps, a slightly boring, long-time-happily-married scene but, if so, it suited Hoyle and his wife. They were both cosily tired, after a fairly full day. Bed beckoned, but they were perfectly content in the quiet of each other's company.

Alva squashed what was left of her cigarette into an ashtray and said: 'No chance of you, I suppose?'

'Eh?'

'Rucker did a double shuffle into the job.'

'Alva, my love, I'd have to do a *triple* shuffle. Don't even think about it.'

'Oh, I can *think* about it,' she smiled. 'Everybody's allowed a quota of dreams.'

'Chances are they'll end up by shoving an advert in *Police Review*. Something like that. That's the normal way of things.'

'It wasn't last time.'

'Ah, but that was *amalgamation*. Jobs for the boys – that sort of thing. There was a pool of senior officers to dip into.'

'So a stranger?'

'Who cares? Nobody can be worse than Rucker.'

'And, for the moment, Hoyle was happily satisfied. His wife – despite her PhD – remained a babe in arms in so far as police politics was concerned. You had to be in there, up to the neck in it, to understand the moves and counter-moves. It was part of the job – part of the swindle – and ever would be.

In fact, it wasn't *quite* as simple as Hoyle had made it out to be. Lennox held the two seats for a time, then he moved over to Lessford, while one of his underlings, Preston, tried the Bordfield chair for size. Preston's backside wasn't big enough and, again, Lennox took over the two jobs.

Then, in 1981, Blayde took over, and for a period there was stability. Blayde was a 'copper's copper' but, nevertheless, he had his faults. He was the loner to end all loners and that, in turn, earned him an unwarranted reputation of being unfriendly. He had no family and, perhaps because of this, he seemed to lack the humility of Ripley – and Ripley was still Hoyle's measure of excellence.

Added to this, Blayde's career had, in the main, been in the uniformed branch.

'He's a damned woodentop!'

It had been a day of minor frustrations, and Hoyle was ready to seek fault in things which in other circumstances he'd have accepted as insignificant irritations.

It was bad manners, and Hoyle had enough sense to realise that, but the guests were Chris Tallboy and his wife, Susan. Tallboy was a fellow-officer, and Susan was Ripley's daughter. The evening meal was drawing to a close – the cheese and biscuits were being nibbled, and the last of the dinner's wine had been poured – and, as always seemed to happen, 'bobby talk' had edged its way into the conversation and taken over.

Blayde was being picked over, like the skeleton of an after-Christmas turkey.

Very mildly, Tallboy said: 'There's supposed to be no difference, David. CID, uniformed branch – theoretically, they're equal.'

'Equal, my foot.' Hoyle tended to glare. 'A man moves into plain clothes. The powers-that-be go through the pantomime of explaining that it's not a leg-up. But, if he's no damn good as a detective, he's "demoted" back to trying doorknobs. How the hell can a man be *de*moted unless he's first been *pro*moted?'

'Hey, lover-boy.' Alva reached across and speared a cube of cheese from the board. 'Put your staff and handcuffs away. You're boring the ears off Susan.'

'They're all the same.' Susan Tallboy sighed a very theatrical sigh. 'Chris . . . all of them. One day somebody will arrange for hardship allowance to be paid to policemen's wives.'

'You wouldn't have us otherwise,' grinned Tallboy. Then, to Hoyle: 'A vast improvement on the late-lamented Rucker, though?'

'Anybody.' Hoyle returned the grin, and his mood

197

mellowed. 'After Rucker, there's only one way left.'

Thereafter, the talk moved to less contentious subjects and, as is the custom at evening parties, the Tallboys and the Hoyles duly put the rest of the world to rights, argued about television programmes, expressed their disgust at the activities of the (then) young and decided that the 'royals' were very nice people lumbered with the worst job in the world.

In short, it was one of their usual pleasant get-togethers.

Nevertheless, and despite his misgivings, Hoyle was content to work under Blayde until, in 1982, the post of Head of CID Lessford Region once more became vacant.

Until it *was* advertised in *Police Review*, and a man who was eventually to become his closest friend took over.

TWENTY-TWO

Somebody (I forget who) once made one of those witty remarks that hold a grain of wisdom. That a man knows he's rich when he can afford a new blade in his razor every time he shaves. (This, of course, before the age of throwaway razors!) It's one measurement. On the other hand, Paul Getty was renowned for his personal tight-fistedness; I doubt if *he* treated himself to a new blade every time he attacked his whiskers.

So what's 'rich'?

I suppose *I* was – 'Lados' was – but I didn't sling it around like tomorrow was one more false promise.

I spoiled myself, but why not? I had the old hi-fi system ripped out and a new one installed. A beaut! I brought in the experts and had it custom built. Not merely stereo. Quadrophonic, if required, with each speaker the best of its kind on the market, and each bedded firmly in a cabinet of firmly packed sand; to kill even the hint of a 'shake'. The console was a dream: radio, double turntable and double tape-deck. Having gathered all the bits and pieces, it took the experts more than a week to install it. As much of it as was possible was remote-controlled, therefore I sat in my wing-chair and organised my listening at ease. They even fixed the sound-output to concealed lighting – coloured lighting – and, if I *really* wanted to play footsie with the music, I pressed a switch and the base and treble were augmented with coloured shadows flickering and dancing as first one section then another section of the orchestra eased its decibel rate a little higher. Not spooky. Not garish. Neat, and sweet, and there to remind the listener which part to concentrate on. You have my word: to hear a Mozart symphony or a Bach fugue with coloured accompaniment is really *something*.

That little lot – with the hand-made teak cabinets and the hidden wiring – left little change from £3000 – and that was in the early seventies. But I signed the cheque on the day I received the account, and didn't count myself extravagant.

Then came the records. The collection had mounted into the two-thousand bracket and, with the new equipment, I wanted every rerecording which had originally been mono switched for stereo. At the same time, I arranged with the main record shop in Lessford to notify me of every new classical record to hit the market – and, if the music had been written before 1900, I usually bought a copy.

I suppose I became an expert – dammit, I *did* become an expert – but I kept my expertise to myself. I was a big enough trickster in the art world. I wanted nobody telling me what I *should* like in the world of music; I required nobody to take *me* for a mug.

Not that I had cause to grumble about the art boys.

'Lados' was, by this time, firmly established. Almost old hat. Some of the American whiz-kids were showing the crap I turned out a clean pair of heels. They 'painted' with everything except brushes. Bicycle wheels, bare feet, women's tits. One enterprising type simply poured a mix of colours on to a canvas, spread on the studio floor, dropped his pants and skidded around the mess on his bare arse . . . *and* it sold for a small fortune!

It was a lunatic world, and I was part of it; therefore, I hung my sanity out to dry on fine music. It was a very firm peg, and it was necessary.

If, at any time, I thought of myself as a 'criminal', my feeling of criminality was linked only with the barefaced trickery of the paintings. I was being paid – and well paid – for trash; for daubings which never took more than two hours to create. Daubings which bore no relationship to their various titles. Indeed, I often spoiled a canvas with paint, stood back . . . *then* decided what to call it. And, the more outrageous the title, the higher the price. Remember *The Love Child*? Remember *The Burning Gats*? Remember *Thesaurus of Pain*? All told, they took less than two hours to paint, yet each was rapturised over and, together, they brought me in enough money to live in moderate comfort while I was likely to continue as a denizen of this earth.

That from only three paintings – and by the late 1960s I'd produced more than a hundred.

I was rich. Without risking the accusation of exaggerating, I could add an adjective, and claim to have been *very* rich. I had built up a reputation: that of semi-recluse cum outrageous eccentric.

As to what I still considered my true vocation, I was almost childishly proud of it. I might not be able to paint, but I could certainly kill. I had nine corpses to prove the point: the gamekeeper, two policemen, the injured robber, Davanzati, the American mobster, the motorway driver and the two unknown people who had died in the pile-up. Nine people – all strangers – were languishing in hell, thanks to my expertise and yet, on the face of it, I was no shadowy 'hit man'. I was known nationally: indeed, without being immodest, I was known *inter*nationally.

And yet I was not a murderer!

Let that be clearly understood. I was not even a *criminal*.

200

Or, to be precise, if I *was* a criminal, my crimes related to the 'Lados' paintings.

I had not wished any of those nine people dead. They were dead because, for various reasons, they had been required to die. I had merely been the conduit via which their deaths had been brought about. Looked at logically, I was as blameless as the garden-centre proprietor who sells the paraquat-based weedkiller with which the poisoner despatches his victim. I was one of the means to a certain end.

Not, be it understood, that I had any illusions. Had the police been aware of my existence, as *myself*, they would not have equated me with a garden-centre proprietor. To them, I would have *been* a murderer; but, unfortunately, *their* view of the realities of life was, and always will be, bounded by the narrow limits of man-made laws.

And yet. . . .

The mild feeling of guilt I felt for my genuine wrongdoing – the confidence trick of the 'Lados' paintings – would not, to the police, have been in any way reprehensible. I was, therefore, able to quieten what few misgivings I had with very little difficulty, settle back, listen to my music and read my books.

Mother died in 1971. Monday, 15 February; the day the country went 'decimal'. I was neither shocked nor sad. She'd lived a good, expensive and comparatively long life – and done damn all to deserve it.

I didn't go to the funeral. All the expected rigmarole attendant upon such functions doesn't merely leave me cold. It annoys me. Instead, I arranged for a small wreath to be delivered and, instead, sought solace in the experienced arms of a particularly expensive whore. In retrospect, I think it was something Mother might have appreciated.

She left me a mere £7000, which, considering the way she'd squandered other men's fortunes was, while not much, something of a surprise. I never did get to meet her 'dear little Florenz' but, if he'd any sense, he would have followed my example. Taking things all round – even being charitable – Mother had never been a particularly indispensable person.

I kept up my practice on the range, visiting Frisch's place at least once every week. Without being immodest, I think I grew to be one of the most accurate all-round marksmen in the country. Rifles, handguns, smooth-bores – I even taught myself how to handle a crossbow – I could guarantee a dead-centre bull far more often than not. Even Frisch stopped wagering his own ability against mine.

But enquiries for my services petered out. There was a very simple reason. The best doesn't come cheap. That, plus the fact that I insisted that all aspects of planning – before and after – *had* to be left solely to Frisch. The hoods, the hoodlums, the tearaways were available. They were there virtually for the asking. Give them a gun, give them a razor, give them a cosh and they'd oblige. They would also be caught and, having been caught, they would talk.

What *I* offered was something far in excess of something with which to fill a coffin.

The year 1971 trundled by. A sad year: Louis Armstrong died in the July, the Attica prison riots were dealt with via forty corpses and, in the Oval Office, Nixon continued to lie in his teeth.

Nor did 1972 start with much joyfulness. On the first day of the year Maurice Chevalier died. Lunatics worked like hell to tread the surface of the moon, while other lunatics blew fellow-Irishmen to kingdom come, merely to see blood stain the pavements. There was no sense in it. Nobody was getting paid.

Some time towards the end of April, Frisch said: 'You should know. I've been approached, and I've refused.'

'I'll survive.' As usual, we were on the range and I'd ended my stint of practice. I asked: 'Am I allowed to know anything?'

'Yankee,' he said shortly. 'Mid-May. It should make the newpapers.'

It did. On Monday, 15 May some goon made a botched-up

assassination attempt on the Alabama governor, George Wallace. It should have been easy. Had Frisch and I picked up the contract it *would* have been easy. And successful. Maybe the money wasn't good enough. Maybe they wouldn't let Frisch handle things. I didn't ask. I had not yet been reduced to hawking my talents – my 'non-talent' more than paid the rent.

They were empty months. Strictly speaking, not *boring* – I could buy pleasure enough to keep boredom well beyond reach – but I was wasting a slice of my life, painting crap and talking more crap.

June, of course, saw the lighting of the Watergate fuse; the throwing to the lions of various big cats in a long-winded attempt to keep Nixon pure. From the side-lines it was a big laugh. The till at Washington is too big and too deep not to have *some* sticky fingers groping around inside. It always was and always will be. This time it was big – too big – and, before it even started moving up the gears, I warned Frisch.

'No "Jack Kennedy" job. I'm no Lee Harvey Oswald. If those Washington snakes are looking for another patsy ... no *way*.'

He chuckled quietly and said: 'Sleep easily, friend. 'I've already let it be known.'

You will see why I had such faith in Frisch. He had a mind like a chess grand master; he could see all possible ends to any game before the first move.

As for Anne, I kept her very much at arm's length. Her relationship with Frisch was no concern of mine, nor did I wish it to be. Not for me emotional entanglements. I was the cat that walked alone, and wanted it to stay that way. Maybe Frisch had moved beyond the point of merely watching. That was *their* worry.

That Christmas (Christmas 1972) I decided to spoil myself a little. Move away from the promise of slush and snow. I booked myself in for a month at the Myrtle Bank Hotel, Montego Bay. One of those watering-places frequented by 'the sunshine people'. It was (still is) a great hotel; one of the name hotels of the world.

Great . . . but every man to his own poison.

I couldn't equate conch shells and beach barbecues with Christmas. Nor was the company to my taste. The females were too conscious of their tits and the males figured a perpetual hard was a sure sign of masculinity. They bored the hell out of me with their high-pitched yammer, their pawing and groping and, at night, their cross-screwing. This was their idea of a good time. The hell it was mine!

I tolerated it for less than a week (for five days, to be precise) then I settled my bill and caught a plane. I hired a cab from London north, and was in my own bed by the twenty-third. I saw Christmas in, alone with my music and the comfort of my own home around me, and was far better pleased than I would have been whoring and roaring in Jamaica.

It turned out to be a better, albeit quieter Christmas than I'd hoped, but, after the holiday period, the 'British Disease' set in with a vengeance. The Irish lunatics bombed and shot their way into the headlines and the various unions demanded the impossible, then resorted to industrial blackmail in an attempt to *get* it. Banknotes cushioned me from any real hardship, but the inconvenience was there and, given a certain life-style, inconvenience itself can be mistaken for hardship.

In 1973 I worried a little. My aim was as good as ever, and each session on the range added to my skill. My hand was steady and my eye was clear . . . but what about my attitude?

It concerned me that good music and good books might be turning me soft. Not physically, but mentally. The great composers – the composers I loved – had minds and feelings to which I was not attuned. They spoke a mystical language which, while reaching me, I could not understand. The weep of the strings. The heroic challenge of the brass. The gentle sweetness of the woodwind.

The books, too. Not as much as the music, perhaps, but, nevertheless, the weave of words with which the masters told their tales.

I needed to know whether I could still perform my

function, without hesitation. Without it affecting me. Almost automatically, and without thought other than what I had to do.

I hinted my concern to Frisch.

'You come once a lifetime,' he smiled knowingly. 'Not a rogue. Far too honest to be a rogue. You accept birth, life and death as equals, and none of them important.'

'The death of other people,' I suggested.

'And your own,' he said with confidence. 'When it comes – however it comes – it will be accepted, without complaint, without surprise. Figuratively speaking, it will be one more squeeze of the trigger. No more important than that.'

It was meant to quieten what few misgivings I had and, indeed, it did, but only in part. That I *had* the misgivings continued to worry me a little.

Meanwhile, that much talked-about and ill-remembered 'winter of discontent' began to wind itself up, as autumn deepened towards the end of the year. First the firemen, then the ambulance-drivers. Then came the general 50 m.p.h. speed limit in an attempt to conserve fuel. After that, things went mad. The three-day working week greeted 1974, hand in hand with power cuts. The railway workers, the miners – everybody! – jumped on the strike wagon, and Wilson took on the job of sorting out the shambles little more than a fortnight after some goon tried to kidnap Princess Anne.

'The amateurs give us a bad name,' chuckled Frisch.

'The amateur', I said, 'was the fool who issued the bodyguard with a suspect handgun. The damn thing jammed . . . twice.'

He looked a little surprised, and said: 'You don't find it too amusing?'

'The self-styled "experts" responsible for the safety of the royal family.' The disgust was there, and I made no attempt to hide it. 'The wrong gun. That's more than carelessness.'

'Are you a royalist, then?'

'This is my country,' I growled. 'The royals are part of it. I find them important . . . *very* important.'

Then he changed the subject. Nor was I displeased. I

called myself a fool, but couldn't help the feelings I had. At that moment I would, personally, have shot the clown responsible for the issue of that semi-automatic to the bodyguard. It might have made the others take more care.

Then slowly – almost creakingly – the garbage was cleared from the streets, the sick were taken care of, the dead were duly buried, the lights came on and the gallery I'd bought looked less like a fairground grotto.

In truth, it had all made little difference to *my* life-style. Other than a light breakfast and, sometimes, a before-bed snack, I ate out, and the expensive restaurants had skill enough to provide good food, regardless of who was on strike. But, as the gloom lifted and spring moved up the gears, life grew a little less dreary and my regular visits to Frisch's place showed me the change of season out on the moors.

That May – Friday, the twenty-fifth, the day after Duke Ellington died – Frisch came up with the long-overdue offer.

'A killing, made to look like an accident.'

It was the recognisable throwaway tone. The tone I'd come to identify as the lead-in to something already part-arranged.

'They can *all* be made to look like an accident,' I smiled.

'A gas explosion. This North Sea gas can be very unstable.'

As always, we were on the range. It was the most private place in the world. He was testing a rebuilt 1906 7.63 Mauser Military Model: the 'rapier' of handguns, with a range, an accuracy and a penetrating power almost beyond belief. He squeezed off the last shot from the ten-round magazine and lowered the weapon before he spoke again.

'Glasgow,' he said gently.

'I've never been there.'

'Just up the coast from Stranraer.'

'Is this a geography lesson?'

'Not far from Kelvingrove there are a lot of flats. They used to be tenement blocks.'

'In Stranraer?' I played it a little dumb.

'In Glasgow,' he corrected me mildly. 'Within easy distance of the M8 . . . then away.'

'Motorways', I reminded him, 'can be closed off. Then whoever's on them is caught.'

'For an accident?' he smiled.

I returned the smile. Mine was as enigmatic as his.

He said: 'Special Branch – probably MI5 – have had a tip-off.'

'Special Branch.' I lowered myself on to the low platform of sandbags. 'Originally called "The Special *Irish* Branch".'

'Why is it', he asked as he squatted down alongside me, 'that you can always move beyond what I'm saying? And in the right direction.'

'Stranraer – Larne. There's a regular ferry service. It links Scotland with Ireland. The Special Branch, and it's original name. MI5 – the outfit responsible for internal security in the UK. It's not *difficult*, Frisch.'

'And?'

'The IRA connection falls snugly into place.'

'My friend. Cards on the table, face upwards.' He took a packet of cigarettes and a lighter from the pocket of his windcheater. It was a sign. That he was carrying them was unusual enough to make it near-unique. He rarely smoked, and only when he was troubled. He opened the packet, held it out, and I took one. As he closed the flap of the packet, he said: 'I have been approached.'

'And?'

'I have given a provisional affirmative. *Very* provisional. Provisional upon your complete agreement.'

'You do all the planning?' I held the tip of my cigarette in the lighter's flame. '*All* the planning?'

'That is already understood, and agreed upon.' He lighted his own cigarette. 'I wouldn't be mentioning the matter had I not already planned every detail.'

'So?'

'They claim they don't know you. They claim they don't *want* to know you.'

'"They"?'

207

'They *are* part of the "Establishment".'

'Special Branch?'

'Or MI5. One or the other . . . I'm no closer than that.'

'And the price?'

'A quarter of a million.'

I pursed my lips into a silent whistle.

'They pay for more than the death of one man,' he said sombrely.

'They aren't skinflints.'

'If this comes out, *you'll* be the whipping-boy.'

'There is always the implied acceptance of that, in the trade,' I reminded him.

'They'll laugh at any suggestion of prior knowledge.'

'As always, they don't know who I am,' I said gently.

'Officially.'

'And . . . *un*officially?'

'This, my friend, is a little different.' He drew on the cigarette and chose his words with care. 'Unlike other contractors, this one really *has* a bottomless purse.'

I waited. He sighed, inhaled cigarette smoke and allowed a frown of disquiet to touch his expression before he continued.

'They don't know me. At least, I *hope* they don't know me. We have to start with some sort of presumption. They don't know *me* – they don't even know the man who approached me – but they know somebody. However many cut-outs, there has to be a link, somewhere. I know the way they work. Not from experience . . . but I *know*. At this moment, they'll be digging away. Paying money. Making threats. They'll not rest till they've bridged the cut-outs and traced *me*. Not to do anything. Merely to be fully informed. And from me the next step is *you*.'

'Meaning you'll talk?' I asked the question quietly, but with a certain coolness.

'That question isn't worthy of you.' It was equally quietly spoken, but it carried a mild reprimand. 'I won't *have* to talk.' Again, he drew on the cigarette, and spoke with care. 'The police are blind blunderers, compared with these people. The police are ninnies. Who knows . . .?' He moved a shoulder resignedly. 'They may *already* know me. It's possible. They may have identified me, prior to putting up a smokescreen of false cut-outs. These people!' He drew on the cigarette. 'It's possible they already even know *you*. Unlikely . . . but possible.'

It was a strange conversation, and there was much of it, along the same lines. The voicing of doubts, the airing of possibilities, the arguing and counter-arguing of theoretical propositions. It gradually dawned on me that, in effect, Frisch was talking to himself. Thinking aloud, perhaps. He was (supposedly) explaining things to me but in fact – even though he might not have realised it – he was working like the clappers to convince *himself*. He was trying to remove a doubt which stubbornly refused to be moved.

He was scared!

I allowed him freedom, without interruption, until we'd almost finished our cigarettes.

Then I screwed what was left of my cigarette on to the surface of the sandbag platform and said: 'If it worries you at all, forget it.'

'We can't forget it,' he muttered.

'In hell's name, why not?'

'*They* won't forget it. Nor will they allow us to forget it.'

'I don't see how the devil. . . .'

'Look! It's a. . . .' He hesitated, then said: 'Call it a "Government contract".'

'All right. They'll pay. They may take their time, but that's —'

'Governments don't enter into blind contracts.' His voice was low and hard. 'Not this sort of contract. I've – I've let you down. Not deliberately, but that's of no importance. I didn't know it was them until it was too late. Until I'd been approached. Until I'd provisionally accepted the offer.'

'Only a provisional acceptance,' I reminded him.

'This is not a contract to build a hospital. To repair a stretch of motorway. This is a different *sort* of contract, my friend.'

'It's been done before . . . surely?'

'Yes.' He nodded slowly. 'Not through me. But I've known other men.' Another pause – another hesitation – then: 'As from that moment, they've ceased to be freelancers. Any choice they've had has been a choice with a veto attached. Any stepping out of line . . . a quiet word with the local police. An anonymous but very informative telephone call. Something like that.'

'They don't know *me* yet?' I said softly.

'It's very unlikely.'

'But they might know *you*?'

'That's not impossible.'

'Therefore,' I said quietly, 'if *I* kill *you*. . . .'

'I wouldn't blame you too much.' There wasn't even surprise in his voice. Only sadness and, perhaps, regret. Then he smiled and said: 'You'd have to kill Anne, of course. And the medic, Arnold. To be really sure, you'd have to kill the man who runs the gallery – Pollard. I can't think of any more. Perhaps you can. Quite a massacre. And I won't be around to plan things.'

'You've knackered things up beautifully, Frisch,' I choked.

'Guilty.' That half-smile came and went. 'I can't even plead ignorance.'

'A choice, you said,' I raged. 'A "provisional affirmative". What bloody choice? They have us. If we pick up the offer, they have us. If we turn down the offer, and another offer comes up, they still have us. What blasted "choice"?'

'Retire,' he said solemnly. 'Stop being a contract killer. Eight men – from what I know, you've killed eight men. You can earn a good living as an artist. As "Lados". *That's* the "provisional affirmative". It wasn't spelled out to me. It didn't have to be spelled out. I have a brain. I use it, sometimes. That's the choice – the only choice – and it's *your* choice.'

Men are mad. *All* men. I can't talk about women – I don't know enough about women – but, rest assured, every man who ever walked the face of this earth, and every man who ever will, suffers moments of sheer insanity. It stems from an arrogance. A refusal to accept unpalatable facts. A certainty that *he* is the sole guide to his own future.

Retire? The hell I was going to retire! I was one of the top men, if not *the* top man, in my own line of business. I'd outwitted Davanzati – and Davanzati had been as dangerous as a cornered wild cat. I'd strolled into the guarded bedroom of a Crime Syndicate boss, shot him, then strolled to freedom. I'd taken one vehicle – one man – from a surge of motorway traffic, and sent *him* to his grave.

Dammit, that's how good I was!

And now, if Frisch was to be believed, I had to move from top spot to nothing. That, or allow some Whitehall clown to work me like some pipsqueak marionette.

No way! No way at *all*.

And, of course, there was the business of proving myself *to* myself. That, too, had some bearing on my decision.

Frisch had given me forty-eight hours in which to reach a decision. It took less than twenty-four.

'We pick up the contract,' I said, and Frisch neither questioned my decision nor enquired about reasons.

He said: 'You need a partner.'

'Not Fletcher.'

'Just somebody to turn a tap – nothing more involved than that.'

'Pollard.'

'Is he reliable?' Frisch wasn't quite sure.

'If I tell Pollard to put his hand in a furnace,' I said grimly, 'he'll do just that. *And* keep it there till I tell him to pull it away.'

TWENTY-THREE

'A quiet guy,' opined Hoyle with some certainty. 'A sort of "Blayde", but without a chip on his shoulder. I like him.'

'He *should* have a chip on his shoulder.' They were walking hand in hand, and Alva's fingers squeezed a little tighter. 'He has a wife. She's confined to an iron lung for the rest of her life. Some sort of accident.'

'Oh Christ!'

'She seems a nice person. I've seen her a couple of times. They've given her a side-ward. That, my pet, would make most men bitter.'

'I don't *think* he's bitter,' mused Hoyle. 'It would show, wouldn't it? I mean. . . .'

They should have been happy. Indeed, and basically, they *were* happy. It was a beautiful summer's evening and the Lessford Gilbert and Sullivan Society's production of *The Yeomen of the Guard* hadn't fallen too far short of a D'Oyly Carte presentation. Maybe that was one reason for their slight melancholy. Jack Point, the most tragic character in the whole series of Savoy Operas – and the part had been performed to near-perfection, and by a young man not long out of his teens. The spell of his performance had bridged the footlights and, for a time, the audience had believed that a good man can truly die of a broken heart.

The Hoyles had intended topping the evening off with a late evening meal at one of the better restaurants and had, originally, planned to take a taxi from the theatre. Instead, they were walking. Strolling pavements which at noon were thick with jostling pedestrians, but which were now pleasant to walk along. Almost unfamiliar in their quietness. The pubs hadn't yet disgorged their customers, the traffic was easy and the only other walkers were people like themselves; twos and threes who were making their way from theatres or cinemas.

They strolled with their thoughts for a few moments, then Hoyle said: 'He got it wrong, you know.'

'Who?'

'Gilbert.'

'Got what wrong?'

'*The Yeomen of the Guard*.'

'How d'you mean, he got it wrong?'

'The Tower of London, see?' explained Hoyle. 'Yeomen Warders of the Tower. Yeomen *Warders*. Yeomen of *the Guard* are just that. The royal bodyguard. Nothing to do with the Tower of London.'

'Don't mess it up, boy,' she said peevishly. 'We've had a nice evening. Don't go messing it up. It's the same outfit. They wear the same uniform.'

'Ah, but they *don't*,' insisted Hoyle. 'Put the two uniforms side by side and you'll see a great difference. The breast emblem—'

'David, my pet,' interrupted Alva patiently. 'My sweet, my dear husband, my one-and-only lover-boy. Elsie Maynard has just jilted the poor guy who was crazy about her, and left him to peg out on Tower Green. Who cares which Yeomen they were? She doesn't. He doesn't. And *I* don't. You have no heart, boy. You have no *feelings*. Who cares for little things like uniforms at a time like that?'

'Point taken,' grinned Hoyle. 'I only hope his death hasn't affected your appetite.'

Two days later – Monday, 30 August 1982 – Flensing called in at Hoyle's office at Lessford Headquarters.

Ralph Flensing. Detective Chief Superintendent, departmental descendant of Lewis, of Rucker and of Blayde. The man upon whose lap every soiled nappy landed, where the detection of crime in that area was concerned – or, to be precise, the *non*-detection of crime. Unlike Lewis, he didn't bluster. Unlike Rucker, he didn't scorn the rest of the human race. Unlike Blayde, he hadn't built a hard and impregnable shell around himself.

And yet. . . .

A man whose voice was rarely raised; who conversed in what seemed to be a controlled drawl. A man who gave the impression of quiet certainty; who wouldn't panic, supposing he was within easy distance should some fool light the blue touch-paper to doom's final crack.

But without any 'salient features'. Big enough – broad enough – to be a bobby (obviously), but not *looking* like a bobby. Lacking the almost-required arrogance of the normal run of senior police officers. Fit and healthy, sure. Above average intelligence, naturally. Dedicated to his job, of course.

But he *could* have been Mr Average-next-door-neighbour and, if he was, *his* next-door neighbour would have no cause for complaint.

He closed the door of the office, smiled and said: 'Let me be the first to congratulate you . . . *Chief* Inspector Hoyle.'

For a moment, Hoyle didn't grasp the significance of the remark. A slight frown touched his forehead, he opened his mouth as if to say something . . . then closed it again, without speaking.

The fact was that David Hoyle (like so many other police officers) had subconsciously resigned himself to the completion of a service carrying the rank he held. Detective inspectorship had seemed the top branch of his particular tree. Not that he wasn't ambitious. Not that he didn't count himself able. Merely that he had no 'pull' – no friends in high places – and had enjoyed a good but, nevertheless, only primary education. The ranks – the *real* ranks – were there for the high-flyers, the whiz-kids, the forensic intelligentsia and, of course, the lick-spittlers, the crawlers and the nepotists.

Flensing held out his hand and continued: 'Official verification should land on your desk before the day's out, but I thought I should let you know the good news first.'

Hoyle stood up from behind the desk and shook hands.

They each had a firm grip; firm, but not bone-crushing.

Grinning, like something of a loon, Hoyle said: 'Thanks, sir. Thank you very much indeed.'

'*I* don't hire and fire.' Flensing lowered himself on to a spare chair and took cigarettes and a lighter from his pocket. 'You've a good enough track record. You deserve the rank.'

'God, wait while I tell Alva.'

'Alva?'

'My wife.' Hoyle took one of the proffered cigarettes. 'She's – y'know – she's a lot more in the attic than I have.'

Flensing raised questioning eyebrows as he held the lighter, first to Hoyle's cigarette, then to his own.

'She has a PhD,' said Hoyle. 'Had it before we were married. She'll be proud.'

'Nice.' Flensing nodded his head, slowly, in approval. 'Your wife, first. No immediate booze-up with the boys.'

'I don't drink much.' Hoyle drew on the cigarette, then said: 'I know – as you say – you don't "hire and fire". But you *can* veto.'

Flensing nodded.

'I'm grateful that you haven't exercised that power of veto.'

'Don't be *too* grateful.' Again, Flensing's smile came and went. It was a pleasant smile, but a little wry. 'As from tomorrow, you'll be field commander. I come up with the brainwaves. Your job is to make them work . . . or convince me they *won't* work.'

'The "impossible" may take a little longer,' countered Hoyle. 'It's still important enough to take Alva out for a celebratory meal.' Then, after a slight hesitation, and in something of a rush: 'Why don't you join us, sir – not that I'm crawling, just that I'd like you to meet my wife.'

'You're quite proud of her,' observed Flensing.

'You'd see why.'

'No.' Flensing shook his head gently.

'I'm – er – I'm sorry. It's just that —'

'Wednesday,' interrupted Flensing. 'September the first. That's our wedding anniversary. Bring your Alva, and make

215

it a foursome. Then I'll *know* you're not crawling.'

'Yes, sir. I'll. . . .' Hoyle hesitated. 'It's just that I understood. . . .'

'She's in hospital,' said Flensing quietly. 'She'll be in hospital for the rest of her life. But she's not sick. She's not *ill*.'

'Sir, I wasn't prying.'

'No, of course you weren't.' Very slowly, Flensing rolled a cylinder of ash from the cigarette into an ashtray on Hoyle's desk. It seemed important that he should not destroy the geometric perfection of the tiny cylinder. He stared at it . . . yet slightly beyond it. He talked softly – as if to himself – as if too much breath, upon which the words rode, might shatter the grey cylinder of ash. 'She's no less of a woman, Inspector. No less of a wife. It's an injury, not an illness. A smash-and-grab, in a stolen motor car. Some few years ago. It wasn't even much of a robbery. Botched up, really. Complete amateurs. On the getaway, they mounted a pavement, and dragged her – Helen, my wife – no small distance, trapped between the side of the car and a wall. She was out shopping. One of those ridiculous coincidences, Inspector. They can't happen . . . but they *do*.' He paused in his story, but Hoyle remained silent. Silence, not sympathy, was of importance. Flensing drew on the cigarette before he continued. 'I almost lost her. Like your – Alva, is it? – I almost lost her. But I was lucky. Very lucky. She stayed with me. In an iron lung . . . but still there. Still my wife. Still the only woman I've ever loved. Or ever will.'

Hoyle lowered his cigarette and wiped the dryness from his lips with the back of a hand.

Flensing sighed, then smiled, but there was no hint of mirth in the smile.

In a slightly stronger voice he said: 'That crime's still undetected, Hoyle. Those three bastards still walk the face of the earth. They don't deserve to, of course. And, God willing, one day. . . .'

He stood up, squashed what was left of the cigarette into the ashtray.

'Shall we say eight o'clock, at the hospital?' he said.

'We'll be there.' Hoyle also stood up, behind the desk. In a slightly hesitant voice he added: 'Black tie? Dinner jacket?'

'That', agreed Flensing musingly, 'would be rather nice. Not too formal . . . but a pleasant surprise for Helen.'

'We'll see you there, sir.'

'Good.' And as his hand reached for the doorknob: 'And what I've said about my wife, Hoyle. Just between us two, if you don't mind.'

TWENTY-FOUR

We (and by that I really mean Frisch) had planned it to the last punctuation mark. Less than a fortnight after I'd decided to take the government contract, the thing was done, and done to perfection.

In the early hours – just after 3.30 a.m. – on a Sunday morning. The streets of Kelvingrove were deserted. The combined booze and excitement of the previous evening ensured that all good Glaswegians were deep in the Land of Nod. The good and the not so good.

Pollard had arrived two days previously. Under some assumed name he'd moved into one of the flats of the block and, before he'd left Lessford, Frisch had given him an extra key.

I'd briefed him very carefully.

'Never mind soft-soled shoes. You let yourself into the other flat. Slowly and carefully. You open the door only far enough to give yourself space to enter. Then you stop until your eyes have accustomed themselves to night vision. Until you can see *every* piece of furniture. Watch out for crumpled

217

newspaper on the floor: it's an old trick, and it can awaken a light sleeper. Put your foot down *only* when you can see where you're stepping. *In your stockinged feet.* Don't forget that. Leave your shoes, your outside clothes and your suitcase ready, in your own flat.'

'I'm not a fool!' Pollard had protested, and Frisch had watched with a look of calm amusement on his face as I'd repeated his (Frisch's) instructions in cat-sat-on-the-mat language.

'You're a fool,' I'd contradicted. 'That's *exactly* what you are. A blind and groping fool, when it comes to this sort of thing. So listen. Every word.

'The flat is the twin to the one you're moving into. Exactly the same layout. Go through it. Not once, but a dozen times. When you get there, go through it till you're sick of it ... then go through it again. Practise. Rehearse. Rehearse in the dark. Above all, rehearse in the dark. The key you have will get you into the other flat. The diagram shows you where the furniture is. Memorise the diagram ... but don't trust it. Furniture can be moved around. Check. Check everything before you move an inch.'

'For God's sake! 'I'm not a —'

'You cretinous clown!' Maybe I'd been on edge a little. Maybe I'd been remembering Fletcher and the cock-up of my only previous double-hander. I'd been rough. I'd been angry. And I'd terrified Pollard by the tone of my voice. 'Listen, and don't argue. You're not belting some dumb gamekeeper over the head this time. This one has to go like clockwork.

'You have a good watch. Set it by the radio time-signal. At three in the morning – *exactly* at three – you leave the flat you're living in. Move into the other flat. Without a sound, right? Not so much as a rustle. You check the windows. Every window to be closed. Don't look at him. He'll be in bed. He'll be asleep. Don't do anything likely to awaken him. Then you turn on the gas-fire. Full on. *Almost* full on. Remember that. *Almost*. It lights automatically – but only when it's first turned to full. The switch is on the right-hand side of the fire as you look at it. Not *quite* full on. But as near as possible to the point where the automatic ignition lights it up. Then you leave the bedroom. Collect your things and leave the building. You walk along the street, towards Kelvingrove Park. . . .'

I'd hammered it home, repeated it, smashed every detail into Pollard's skull until even I was satisfied . . . more or less. And now I was driving the souped-up Austin van along the deserted street and peering ahead, looking for him.

He stepped from a doorway, and I drew the van alongside him, at the kerb.

As he climbed behind the wheel, I said: 'Thirty. No more, no less.'

He nodded as he flopped his suitcase on to the passenger's seat, and I clambered into the body of the van.

The Fabrique Nationale with its Mauser action was where I'd stored it under the hessian sacking. A single-shot 7 mm rifle, with the round already in its breech. Not an unusual rifle, but a slightly unusual bullet. Frisch had manufactured it by hand. An incendiary filling with an initial heat savage enough to destroy the lead sleeve. If things went as planned, one misshapen blob of lead mixed up in a few tons of debris.

I unclipped the false rear window and settled down before raising the rifle to my shoulder. As with most top-class executions, it was planned as a one-squeeze job, with a perfect cover; and if, over the years, I'd had doubts about my continued skill now was the moment of truth.

'Keep the van on a straight course,' I ordered quietly. 'Speed at a constant thirty.'

I reminded myself of the rules for firing from a moving platform. Use the imagination. The platform is 'stationary'. The target is 'moving'. Away from you, towards you, up or down. It's the *target* that's moving. Make the required allowances.

'It's coming up,' warned Pollard.

'Keep the van steady,' I muttered. 'Don't race away from the scene. Don't attract attention.'

Then the block moved into my vision. Third-floor windows.

Seventh window. The windows moved from my left to my right. The elevation was perfect. I closed an eye, tucked the stock comfortably into my neck and shoulder muscles and counted. One – two – three – four – five. . . . I was starting to swing the FN as the fifth window moved across the sight-line. On the sixth window I was arcing at the same speed as the windows. As the seventh window slid into line I was swinging slightly faster. Ever so slightly faster . . . but smoothly.

I squeezed, but didn't hear the charge of the bullet explode. Simultaneously – or so it seemed – the frontage of the block surrounding the seventh window spewed into the street and, with it, fire and noise.

The van jerked forward as Pollard's foot pressed down on the pedal.

'Thirty!' I shouted; then: 'Second turning right, third turning left. Don't start sweating and attracting attention.'

The van slowed to its previous speed, and I reclipped the false window, then replaced the rifle under the hessian covering.

We turned left, and I moved to the rear of Pollard's seat.

'A gas explosion,' I said softly.

I could almost feel the panic coming in waves from where he crouched behind the wheel.

'A gas explosion,' I repeated. 'Get your trafficator flashing. Just drive, Pollard. There's been a gas explosion . . . and we know damn all about it.'

By the time we'd reached the vehicle-switch he'd more or less recovered himself. He wasn't yet able to trust himself to speak, but he pulled up alongside the Cortina waiting in the public car park and, without having been told, transferred his suitcase then opened the boot for me to pack away the FN rifle. I took over the wheel and, instinctively, knew we'd done a top-class job. The van would be collected and disposed of within two hours. North Sea gas would carry the blame. And *nobody* could have lived through that explosion.

I pushed east along the M8, then turned south on the M74. Then, the A74 until we reached the M6, north of Carlisle.

After that it was a steady seventy, southbound motorway driving until we turned off for home.

And it had all been for nothing!

The damn security goons – MI6, Special Branch, who the hell they were – had been taken up the garden path. They'd been fed only what they'd been eager to eat.

A woman had died. Some unknown woman, who had had nothing to do with the IRA. Her teenage son had been crippled for life.

A few days later (on 17 June) people passing Westminster Hall paid the price demanded for the official cock-up. Eleven people took the blast from an IRA bomb that 'officially' shouldn't have been there.

I learned the truth, from Frisch, on Thursday, 18 June, the day after the Westminster Hall explosion, and I went quietly beserk.

'What the hell do they do?' I blazed. 'Stick a pin in a street-map?'

'Their information was that a commander of an IRA group was in the flat. The man responsible for organising yesterday's bombing.'

'A woman and her kid,' I stormed. 'Jesus Christ! Do they believe anything? Everything? Don't they even check?'

'They made a mistake, my friend. It happens.'

'*They* made a mistake! Up there, north of the border, I did not scrump apples, Frisch. I did what I was paid to do. I killed. I did it well. Better than any other man alive. You planned it, and it was a perfect plan. All *they* did was point us at the target – and they couldn't even find the right target. Any snarl-ups, and *I'd* have been the one with my neck on the block. Pollard and me, both. Somebody would have taken the key to mid-Atlantic and thrown it overboard. And for *what*?'

'They appreciate that.'

'The hell they appreciate it!' I snarled. 'They couldn't care less. One mistake – one hair-line out of true – and this whole set-up it's taken us years to build would have been blown sky-high. We'd have been nothing.'

'Pollard?' he asked in a sombre, but soothing, tone.

'What about Pollard?'

'How did he behave?'

'He did what *he* was told. He damn near crapped his underpants, but he did it.'

'He's safe?'

'He's either safe or dead,' I said coldly. 'He hasn't too many brains . . . but he understands *that*.'

'I'm to tell you they're sorry,' he murmured.

'You're to. . . .' I gaped at him. 'How, in hell's name, did they get through to *you*?'

'Like last time,' he smiled. 'Bridging the usual cut-outs. They want us to know they accept full responsibility.'

'Get word back to them,' I growled. 'Tell them – draw them detailed diagrams, if necessary – just make them understand. If I ever get the bastard responsible for this balls-up lined up in the sights of a gun, he won't have enough life left to draw another breath.'

That night, for the first and only time in my life, I got drunk. Wildly, gloriously, maudlinly drunk. I had sense enough to do it at home. I had sense enough to lock all the outside doors and close all the windows.

It was a very private booze-up. Very secret . . . but, at the same time, very complete. Gradually and systematically, I drank myself unconscious.

TWENTY-FIVE

Friendships can sometimes start at a specific moment in time and, thereafter, last for life. Not quite like the crack of a start-gun but, equally, not a gradual over-the-years thing. The over-the-years part merely cements and binds ever tighter that which began rather like a strip of time-lapse cinematography showing the blossoming of a flower. As smoothly, as naturally and as beautifully as that. And as quickly.

That's how it happened with David Hoyle and Ralph Flensing.

Without realising it, Hoyle had started the sequence. His tentative suggestion that the men wear dinner suits; that the occasion *be* an occasion; that the inconvenience of an iron lung should not be made an excuse for anything less than the complete works. That suggestion had placed Flensing and Hoyle on the same plane of simple, decent consideration.

The evening did the rest.

Having been given the news, Alva took it upon herself to visit the side-ward, introduce herself before she, too, made a parallel suggestion.

'Mrs Flensing, I know this is meant to be a surprise, but let's *pretend* it's a surprise, and turn the surprise back on *them*.'

'My name is Helen.'

'Look, don't think I'm doing this to —'

'I've no intention of going through life calling *you* "Mrs Hoyle".'

'Alva,' grinned Alva.

'Therefore, "Helen".'

And, on the evening of Wednesday, 1 September. A

whole box of surprises and make-believe surprises. All pleasant. All adding to a memorable anniversary.

As always seemed to happen on these occasions, Hoyle was kept ridiculously late at DHQ. So late, in fact, that he entered the hall and called: 'It's me, pet. Sorry I've cut things so fine, but I'll go straight upstairs for a bath, then get the glad rags on.'

From somewhere inside the house Alva's voice answered: 'Your duck-and-soup's on the bed. So is your shirt and bow tie. All the other things are in the tank cupboard, airing.'

About fifteen minutes later came the first surprise.

Hoyle walked into the living-room, then stopped and stared.

'Like it?' Alva twirled to show off the ankle-length evening dress. The simple lines showed off her figure to perfection, and the single *diamanté* brooch, high on the shoulder, seemed to have been created just for that gown.

'Where on earth . . .?' began Hoyle.

'Beans on toast, instead of caviare,' she laughed. 'Brisket, instead of sirloin. I've been twisting you, boy. I've been hoarding housekeeping money.' Then, still smiling but in a more serious tone: 'You don't really *mind*, my love? I'd intended buying it for *our* anniversary.'

'Alva, pet. . . .' His voice choked a little. He stepped nearer and placed a careful kiss on her forehead. The hint of perfume made him close his eyes for a moment as he took a deep breath in order to steady himself. Still with his lips almost touching her forehead, he whispered: 'I love you.'

It was quite a moment. One of those moments which come in all good marriages; which nullify and cancel out all quarrels and all bad-tempered moods; which are remembered long after even the wildest passions have been forgotten.

They stood for all of five seconds, then Alva pushed him gently away, and busied herself patting and primping his breast-pocket handkerchief for a moment.

'We should go,' she murmured. 'I think they're nice people. We mustn't be late.'

224

Flensing met them at the hospital entrance, and together they strolled the corridors until they reached the side-ward. Then, when they entered, the men had their second surprise.

The iron lung and its attendant paraphernalia took pride of place, but Helen Flensing was no whey-faced patient. Her hair was touched with grey but, nevertheless, shone with health. It had been carefully dressed into an uncomplicated, but very becoming, style. Her regular features had been enhanced with just enough make-up to accentuate the sparkling eyes, the fine bone structure and the full-lipped mouth. And the upper part of her body – the part not encased in the iron lung – wore a long-sleeved blouse of brushed nylon; crisp and white, with a jet-black miniature cravat at the high neck.

Forget the side-ward. Forget the bulk of the machine which was keeping her alive. Her personality, plus her happiness, eliminated all these things. She was a beautiful woman, dressed to kill and ready to have an evening on the town.

Flensing breathed: 'My word!'

She held out her arms and said: 'You look very handsome, darling.'

Without embarrassment Flensing kissed his wife on the lips, then straightened and said: 'Helen, let me introduce two new friends. This is Mrs —'

'Alva,' interrupted Helen. 'We've met. We're already friends. She's been with me most of the day, helping me to look attractive.' Then she switched her eyes and said: 'And you, of course, must be David.'

'David Hoyle,' smiled Flensing.

'Ma'am.' Hoyle stepped nearer.

'David Hoyle,' she said with mock severity, 'you make me feel like a middle-aged schoolmistress. Helen, if you please.'

'Helen,' grinned Hoyle.

'You're a lucky man.'

'*Especially* this evening.'

'And don't be too free with the compliments. Not yet. I might mistake it for flirting.'

'I wouldn't do that. I daren't. Your husband's around.'

'So is your wife.'

'Ah, but she's a Welsh witch. Didn't you know? A direct descendant of Morgan le Fay.'

'And that *could* make you Arthur.'

The exchange set the pace. Gentle banter, but without malice. Helen and Alva were already on first-name terms – as, indeed, were Helen and David. Flensing used Christian names whenever he spoke to either Alva or Hoyle and, without doubt, expected them to call *him* Ralph. That they didn't – that they both drew back from that final intimacy – was rooted in good manners, and nothing more, nevertheless it was easy enough talk, without the topping of Flensing's first name.

Two nurses, acting as makeshift waitresses, carried the table into the side-ward and placed it where Helen could, in effect, form one of a quartet of diners. A vase of flowers stood in the table's centre. Good wine was there, and one of the hospital porters hurried in with piping-hot take-away fare from a nearby but very excellent, restaurant.

'Good people,' observed Flensing. 'They volunteered. I think they each deserve some small "thank you" gift.'

'And, of course,' quipped Helen, 'being a brace of high-ranking policemen smooths the way a little.'

'It helps,' agreed Flensing cheerfully.

There was no make-believe. No façade of mock good-fellowship, but genuine good-fellowship was there, and to spare. The laughter was there. The talk. The jokes. The smilingly expressed opinions. And that one of their number was helpless, and would remain helpless all her life, was completely forgotten – and by her, too.

When it was over – when they'd eaten their fill, sipped the last of the wine and drained their cups of coffee – Flensing took a slim cigar-case from the inside pocket of his jacket.

'A good smoke, David?' he suggested. 'It might help the digestive juices to flow a little more freely.'

Hoyle glanced at the 'No Smoking' notice and hesitated.

'Oh, not here.' Flensing pushed his chair away from the

table. 'This is a hospital, and they've been *very* hospitable, but we don't want to stretch their patience too far. A spot of fresh air, and we'll leave the ladies to their own talk.'

'It makes a change,' chuckled Helen. 'It's usually the ladies who retire.'

'No more than half an hour, dear,' promised Flensing. 'I'm leaving you in excellent company.'

When the men had left, Alva eased her shoes off and hoisted her stockinged feet on to one of the empty chairs.

'You don't mind?' she smiled.

'I'm envious.'

'Lady, with a man like that you need envy no woman.'

'Alva, dear, you, too, have genuine taste.'

'I'm working on him,' said Alva, with make-believe solemnity. 'He gets better by the day.' Then, after a pause, and in a more sombre tone: 'And people call them "pigs".'

'Do they?' Helen matched the younger woman's tone. She glanced at the tiny television set, placed where she could see it from her lying position. 'That's all I see. A quite genuine "window on the world". But it's not the *real* world. It's only what some cameraman – some editor – wants to show me. On that glass screen I've heard men, and sometimes women, call them "pigs". But how often? And who?'

'Swine,' said Alva bluntly. 'Scum. The hooligans who hog the camera at football matches and demonstrations. The rent-a-crowd types. The loud-mouth would-be ungovernables. That subhuman one per cent that always makes ninety per cent of the noise.'

'Often?'

'As often as they can, and while they think somebody's listening.' Then, after a tension-easing laugh: 'Don't worry about it, Helen. Our men belong to the most exclusive club in the world.'

'And deservedly so.'

'Amen to that,' said Alva softly.

Meanwhile the two paragons of masculine excellence strolled side by side, and smoked cigars as they chatted. It was a fine late evening, with a clear sky, a fine scattering of

227

stars and the first hint of autumn nip in the air. The lighted rectangles of the hospital windows were on their left, and around them stretched the gardens and lawns of the well-kept grounds, with tarmac paths and roadways slicing the green into irregular shapes.

'Y'know, David. . . .' Flensing allowed the smoke to drift from between his lips. 'Coming up here – coming north – was one of the better decisions of my life.'

'Contrary to popular belief, we cook our meat,' smiled Hoyle. 'We no longer eat it raw.'

'That's what I mean. Drollery. Most of the great comedians come from up north.'

'And London, of course.'

'I wouldn't want the Met.' As always, when two or more policemen talked together, the subject slipped smoothly and naturally into 'bobby natter'. 'Too damn big. Too concentrated.' He paused, then added: 'Too many people ready to grease palms . . . *and* too many palms.'

'Some magnificent thief-takers, though,' argued Hoyle.

'Agreed. But some equally magnificent scoundrels.'

They walked and smoked in silence for about twenty yards, then Flensing said: 'I won't say I'm looking forward to it, but when it comes I'll know.'

'What?'

'The first big case. "Yorkshire Ripper" size. I'll know whether I've bitten off more than I can chew.'

'That one was a bloody shambles.'

'Sutcliffe?' Flensing seemed to gather what excuses he could find before continuing. 'It was allowed to snowball. Too much panic. They wanted a detection – of course they did – but nobody was able to keep a cool head. Evaluate all the evidence. Too many petty hatreds . . . that was part of it, too. Too much headline-chasing.'

'He should have been inside,' agreed Hoyle sadly. 'It should never have reached thirteen killings.'

'But difficult,' sighed Flensing. 'Murder *is* difficult. When you have to *detect* the damn thing you start from scratch. Every time. They're all different; therefore, there's no "past

228

experience" to draw from.'

'Fortunately – fortunately for us – most of them don't *have* to be detected.'

'I remember my first,' ruminated Flensing. 'A chap called Fletcher – he called himself Fletcher, but his real name was Fleischer – we'd traced him . . . virtually chased him. We had him cornered on Clifton Suspension Bridge, of all places. Away and gone to hell out of our own police area.' Flensing drew deeply on the cigar, and Hoyle waited. Flensing continued: 'He had a gun in his hand. *And* he'd used it. Killed some London gang hooligan – that, it seemed, was his forte. Killing people. What the horror comics like to call a "hit man". I was Joe Muggins. The senior officer at the scene, and we couldn't hold out for somebody with more weight. My job was to walk up to him and take the gun.'

'What happened?' breathed Hoyle.

'Nothing.' Flensing laughed gently. 'I was scared, of course. Scared witless . . . but couldn't show it. Fortunately, he was even more scared . . . or something. He came like a lamb. Threw the damn gun into the gorge.'

'And he was convicted?'

'Of course. He pleaded "Guilty".' Flensing slowed their stroll to a halt. 'We'd better get back. Alva and Helen won't want us to be away too long.'

'Why didn't you tell him?'

The yellow wash from the sodium street-lighting gave the bedroom a warm, saffron-coloured haze. Not harsh. At first glance, not immediately noticeable. But, with the curtains drawn back, and once the eyes had become accustomed to the gloom, the golden tinge touched all but the shadows.

The love-making had been special. Each would have argued that it was always special, but this time it had been *very* special. She had accepted him with an eagerness which had bordered upon greed; with a prolonged sigh which had not been too far short of a moan of suddenly fulfilled need. He, in turn, had matched her mood. Harsh and masterful, but without being brash; hard and deep, but without hurt.

They had made love scores of times – hundreds of times – but never more completely than this time.

And when it was over – when each had held back, until they could hold back no more – when the massive and simultaneous explosion of savage passion had, for one sublime moment, taken possession and fused them in a clinging, grasping unit – when it was over, and its shuddering close had quietened – she'd dropped her head on the pillow and closed her eyes.

She'd breathed: 'Oh God! Oh my God . . . that was *good*.'

Then, when he'd rolled away from her, and was staring into the golden darkness of the bedroom, she'd asked the question.

'Why didn't you tell him?'

'About Fletcher?'

'About Davanzati, and what the Italian TV man told you.'

'I don't know. Damned if I know.' He threw back the bedclothes, swung his feet on to the carpet and reached for his dressing-gown. Then he muttered: 'Years . . . eh? How many years? Too many years to let me share it with anybody.'

'Not even Ralph?'

'Coffee and a cigarette.' He changed the subject abruptly. 'Come downstairs with me, pet. A cigarette, and some hot, strong coffee.'

She stared up at him, through the dimness of the bedroom.

She said: 'I love you, boy. So pig-headed. So stiff-necked. I think they must have made you, then they must have smashed the templet.'

He padded out of the bedroom in his bare feet.

TWENTY-SIX

Despite the complete screw-up, they paid: £250,000! What they paid Frisch, what 'overheads' they took care of, how much Pollard received – I wasn't interested, therefore I can't tell you. But *I* was richer by a quarter of a million, and all I'd done was slaughter some unknown woman.

Whichever mob it was – whichever branch of secret muscle behind national security – it obviously had a direct line to whoever held the key to the national petty-cash box. The money had to be laundered, which, in turn, meant a sudden rash of 'Lados' paintings. That was the period when (among other daubs) I gave the gawp-mouthed public *Mother and Child*. It was sold from the gallery for £10,000. A few weeks ago it was sold for the second – perhaps the third – time, and the fetching price was £120,000. It took me less than an hour to dash off. It meant nothing, and still means nothing. The colours clash and run into each other, the shapes have no geometric pattern – it is, in fact, an insult to any thinking person's eyes – but the pundits saw tears and anguish, the torture of mother-love and the unintentional wickedness of a woman's child somewhere in the splurge.

Mother and Child – and its companions – saw a great surge of 'Lados'-inspired conversational crap in the art world.

Meanwhile, Pollard seemed to be enjoying himself.

I kept a very keen eye on Pollard. I saw him expand; blossom out until he became quite cocky in his attitude. Even in his attitude towards me.

Shortly after 1974 became history, he required quietening.

'You talk too much, Pollard,' I warned quietly.

'Who? Me?' He seemed genuinely surprised.

'You talk about things you should not talk about.'

'Only to *you*.' The grin was far too self-assured. 'You don't think I'm even going to *hint* to anybody else how we. . . .'

'"*We!*"' I have been told that, when required, I can hang icicles on my words. If so, this was one of the times. I stared my contempt directly into his face, and said: 'You drove a van, punk. That's all. Look out of any window, and you'll see scores of people doing the same thing. And not along deserted streets. What *I* did concerns you not at all. It must not be talked about. Not even to me. It must be forgotten – completely! And, be assured, Pollard, it *will* be forgotten. This. . . .' I'd come prepared. I took my hand from my jacket pocket, opened my palm and let him have a good, long look at the .25 Beretta lying flat on my hand. '*This*', I continued softly, 'can wipe out all memories and silence all tongues.'

'You – you wouldn't. . . .'

'Why not?' I allowed him to gaze at the semi-automatic, and fed him simple logic. 'I own the gallery. You can be replaced very easily. Even cheaply. In fact, it seems rather foolish to take the unnecessary risk of allowing you to live.'

'I won't – I won't. . . .'

'I don't want promises,' I warned. '*I* make the promises . . . and *I* keep them. Believe me. That's all you have to do. If I even *think* you've opened your mouth – to *anybody*, including me – you won't even know when it arrives. You'll die, Pollard. Not slowly, not painfully, but very quickly.'

Thereafter, Pollard posed no problem.

1974 was a rather 'unnatural' year. The first few months seemed to set the general tone. There was much unnecessary waffle about joining the EEC; Wilson filled No 10 with pipe smoke and platitudes. The lunatics in Ireland bombed and shot each other with gay abandon and the Vietnamese war continued to demonstrate that *my* profession was a comparatively clean way of life.

Across the Atlantic the Watergate production brought on more and more dancing girls and, by July, Superman himself couldn't have saved Nixon's head from the axe.

From some dark corner somebody tried to entice me into the action.

As always, we were on the range when Frisch raised the matter. As always, it was the same, giveaway tone. Like a meaningless, off-handed remark.

'There's an open cheque waiting to be picked up.'

'Open cheques?' I raised quizzical eyebrows. 'They don't come through the mail every morning.'

'You could retire.'

'I *can* retire,' I corrected him gently.

We stooped to collect the spent cartridge cases; then, after a pause, he said: 'You could be a *very* rich man.'

'The richest man in Death Row.' I straightened. Very bluntly, I said: 'Frisch, it stinks.'

'They covered the Kennedy assassination,' he murmured.

'No, Frisch.' I shook my head. 'It was an assassination ... *that* wasn't covered up. They found a patsy, then they manufactured a few smokescreens. But, already, there's a wind getting up. When it reaches gale force, that smoke will disappear.'

'There'll be another smokescreen.'

'Maybe.' I smiled. 'Let's say I'm careful. Let's say I need something more substantial than smoke.'

It is, I suppose, arguable that Nixon lived because I said 'No'. Equally, I might be taking too much for granted; maybe it *wasn't* Nixon 'they' wanted out of the way. Who knows? Certain it is that, in August, Nixon tumbled and I still think my decision to keep my fingers clear of that particular pie was a wise move.

Other than that, 1974 was a quiet year as, indeed, was 1975. I put myself on show as 'Lados' a few times; when, in September, Rembrandt's *The Night Watch* was slashed, I was hauled before cameras and microphones to make appropriate noises of disapproval.

'I do not like his style. He had great talent but, in my opinion, he fell well short of being a genius.'

That, I think, is my most oft-quoted remark. That I didn't know what the hell I was talking about I freely admit, but I never *have* known what I was talking about when it comes to art! But television and radio studios – journalists and chat-show hosts – screamed for controversy, and that's what I delivered.

In truth, I suppose, that was *my* 'smokescreen', but I made my own smoke and I made damn sure it remained thick and impenetrable.

Then, as 1976 took over – in the January, and at about the time when Concorde carried its first passengers – Anne hanged herself.

I think if Sheba had still been alive it would not have happened. I think. . . .

God knows what I think. I think so many things. I think – to be accurate, I think it *possible* – that she did *not* hang herself.

I know there was a hook. One of those hooks fixed firmly into the beams of farmhouses; hooks originally meant to hold slabs of bacon. I know there was a length of old-fashioned flex; the sort once used to hold light-fittings dangling from a ceiling rose. I know there was an overturned chair, an inquest, a verdict and a cremation.

That is the sum total of my *knowledge*.

But add to that my knowledge of Frisch and the words spoken one spring day, more than ten years before, when the girl and I had walked alone across the moors.

For obvious reasons, I stayed away from the farm, kept clear of the inquest and didn't attend the cremation. Various styles and types of policemen were required to attend to matters, and the last thing I wanted was the link between Frisch and myself to become public knowledge. Nevertheless, I kept myself updated on things . . . and I worried a little.

In February – Sunday, 10 February – I slipped on ice, twisted my ankle and needed a medic. On an impulse, I telephoned Arnold. I had the handy excuse that my own doctor was away on holiday, that I was a 'private' patient and that my need for medical attention did not require know-

234

ledge of what little previous medical history I had.

His initial reaction was what I'd expected.

'He'll be in some sort of group practice.'

'Yes,' I agreed.

'In that case, one of his partners. . . .'

'I have no confidence in any of his partners.'

'My dear man, it's not a —'

'From where you're sitting it's nothing. From where *I'm* sitting, it's very painful. There seems to be the possibility of a broken bone.'

'You're a complete stranger.'

'"Lados",' I said gently.

'I know. The painter. But —'

'Therefore, not *quite* a stranger.'

'Look. . . .' There was a second or two of silence, then: 'I'm Frisch's doctor. When I last saw you —'

'We can', I suggested, 'do things the convoluted way. I can hire a taxi to Frisch's place, then get *him* to call you out.'

'You seem determined that *I* play locum in the absence of your own doctor.' A quiet chuckle accompanied the remark.

'You could put it that way,' I agreed.

'I suppose I should take it as a compliment.'

'If that pleases you.'

'There are certain ethics. . . .' He was toppling, but not yet quite ready to commit himself.

'It's a long way to Frisch's place,' I teased. 'A long drive, on bad roads. If your ethics demand you do things the hard way, that's your decision.'

'If I have your assurance that you'll mention this to your own doctor.'

'Of course,' I lied.

'This evening, then?' he suggested. 'Shall we say about six o'clock?'

'Six o'clock,' I agreed. 'I'll be waiting . . . in some agony.'

Such an exaggeration, of course. I was suffering very little pain, much less in agony, and almost as soon as I'd replaced the receiver I almost wished I hadn't made the call.

I was aware that, in contacting Arnold, I was taking a risk.

235

Equally, I was aware of my own ignorance of exactly how great that risk was. He'd attended me at Frisch's place and (if Frisch was to be believed) had accepted some cock-and-bull story about an accident with a firearm. But *had* he accepted that story? Had he even been *told* that story? Was he, perhaps, fully in the picture as far as Frisch's homicidal activities were concerned? Or, if not fully in the picture, at least in a position to make an educated guess?

He was a general practitioner, an ex-Army man, therefore a person of *some* intelligence. Frisch had (or so he'd said) used Arnold before – presumably when other men had needed bullets digging from their flesh. Which, in turn, made Arnold very gullible, or Frisch a particularly accident-prone gunsmith . . . or the other thing!

The options were very limited.

I *was* taking an unnecessary risk.

Which, in turn, raised the 64,000-dollar question . . . *why*?

Not 'love'. Not unrequited love, or secret love, or suddenly realised love. Nothing mushy or pseudo-romantic. What the hell Anne felt – what the hell she had once felt – did not interest me. Throughout that Sunday afternoon I took the problem, twisted it, turned it, eyed it from a dozen different angles and, eventually, came up with some sort of cock-eyed part-solution.

I was a loner. Frisch was a loner. But – Christ! – compared with Anne, we were gregarious. No parents. No friends. No eyes. The dog – the one creature she'd been able to communicate with – no longer around. A world of everlasting blackness and, other than Frisch – who, unless she'd changed her mind over the years, she accepted, without liking – not another living soul. That made her the loner to end all loners. And perhaps not by choice.

Maybe I owed her something, if only because she'd represented *me* . . . multiplied a few thousand times. I remembered that first time we'd met. The porch, the dog, the slight shock at seeing those empty eye-sockets, and that first amazement at her poise and certainty, despite her blindness.

236

I pushed myself from the chair, hobbled across the room and put Schubert's Ninth – 'The Great' – on the turntable. Then I returned to the chair, hoisted my foot on to a stool, leaned back and closed my eyes.

This guy had worked it all out. All the answers. All the answers to *everything*. All you had to do was listen.

Arnold had aged. He was living proof that tempus fugits at an alarming rate of knots once a certain threshold has been passed. He'd lost weight. The military shoulders were bent. What little hair he had left was the colour of dirty linen, straggly and without life.

Nevertheless, he still knew his job and, at a guess, none of his wits had left him.

He straightened from his examination and said: 'Nothing broken. You've pulled a ligament badly. Rest it as much as possible. Try bathing it. Water as hot as you can bear; then into iced water; then, when it's numb, back into the hot water. Do that a couple of times a day.'

'No comfrey?' I smiled. 'No "Knitbone"?'

'It won't do harm.' He was quite serious. 'I could prescribe some expensive concoction, if that's what you want. It won't do the job any quicker.'

'Over there, in the cabinet.' I waved a hand. 'Pour yourself a whisky. Be generous.'

'I prefer gin.'

'Gin, then. Mix your own. I'll have a whisky . . . fifty-fifty water.'

I waited until he had his back to me, until he was juggling the glasses and bottles, then I opened the subject I wanted to talk about.

'Do you see Frisch these days?'

'Rarely. He's a very healthy man.'

'The death of Anne must have shocked him.'

'Frisch isn't the sort to dwell too much on grief.'

'*If* he grieved,' I murmured.

'In his own way.' He turned to carry the glasses across the room. 'Some people show it. Some don't.'

237

'But no tranquillisers? No sedatives?'

'Frisch is my patient, Mr Lados.' He smiled what was meant to be a forgiving smile. 'We don't discuss patients with strangers.'

'Very laudible.' I kept it very deadpan. Very polite. I took the whisky from him, motioned towards a nearby armchair, then moistened my lips before asking: 'Was Anne your patient?'

'Naturally.' He settled into the chair and sipped his drink.

'What was wrong with her?'

'My dear chap, I've already —'

'Was *anything* wrong with her?'

'She was healthy enough. Like her father. The usual run-of-the-mill bugs. A very healthy person . . . in view of her blindness.'

'He wasn't her father,' I said softly. 'He wasn't even related.'

'Oh!' The off-grey eyebrows lifted a little.

I allowed it time to ferment. A few seconds. I already had his measure; our telephone conversation had leaned the straw against *his* wind.

I tasted the whisky-and-water, then said: 'She's no longer your patient, of course.'

'She's dead,' he agreed.

'Can we at least discuss her blindness?'

'I don't see why.'

'Can you see why *not*?'

'If it's of any interest,' he sighed. 'She was blind. She was born blind – at least, that's what I was told.'

'That, at least, is true,' I agreed.

'In that case. . . .'

He tasted the gin. It was, I think, a way of using the glass as a means of half-hiding his expression.

'She knew her way around that farmhouse,' I said.

'Indeed.'

'Knew her way around all the rooms. Knew where every piece of furniture was. It was quite remarkable.'

'Remarkable.' He nodded. 'Almost uncanny.'

'The dog – before it died. Remember the dog?'

'Sheba?'

'I wonder why Frisch didn't buy her another dog?' I mused.

'People get fond of them. They can't *be* replaced.'

'She was a guard dog,' I reminded him. 'She wasn't a "seeing eye" dog. She guarded Anne ... and was Anne's constant companion.'

He hesitated a split second, then said, 'True,' as he once more raised the glass to his lips.

'As something of an expert.' I tried to keep all trace of mockery from my voice. 'Blind people. Are they normally as independent as Anne was? Knowing their way around every room of the house?'

'It varies. Some more than others. Some far more than others.'

'And the ceilings? Do they know their way around the *ceilings* of their homes?'

He stared.

'That hook,' I explained. 'The one she hanged herself on. It was beyond her reach. She had to use a chair.'

'Look, I don't see what —'

'Tell me, Doctor Arnold.' I lowered the temperature of my tone. 'How many "very healthy" people hang themselves?'

He tipped what remained of his drink down his throat and pushed himself from the chair.

In a voice with just a hint of a waver, he said: 'I think this conversation should end.'

'Get yourself another drink, doctor,' I said mildly.

'Lados, I've no intention of —'

'The conversation ends when *I* decide it should end.'

'Damn it, man, you're not a policeman. You can't —'

'We can,' I said smoothly, 'rectify that. If you'd prefer a policeman to be present, I'll arrange it. Conversely, I can explain the various inconsistencies *to* a policeman – and ask *him* to visit you. Forget that idiotic oath you once took. In the past you've broken it well beyond repair. You're going to answer questions. From me . . . from *somebody*.'

It was, of course, bluff versus counter-bluff, but Arnold couldn't win. I wouldn't have dragged coppers into the thing – I *daren't* have dragged coppers to within a thousand miles of the set-up I had with Frisch – but Arnold didn't *know* that. All Arnold could be sure about was that *he* had things to hide. Whether *I* had or not . . . well, that was the bluff he had to call.

He walked to the booze cabinet. He walked slowly and a little stiff-legged. As if he was gathering all that solid-gold discipline a commission in the armed services had injected into his frame. He poured himself another gin – a very large gin this time – then returned to the chair and very deliberately folded himself into its comfort.

'Well?' he asked at last.

'She didn't kill herself?' I made it part-statement and part-question.

'I don't know. I certainly wasn't treating her at the time.'

'Common gumption, Arnold,' I said. 'The circumstances – as we both know them – insist she did *not* kill herself.'

He slurped gin, and waited.

'Ten years ago,' I said. 'Thereabouts. At about the time you fished the slug from my shoulder. She confided in me. Out on the moors, one day. Frisch was playing Peeping Tom games.'

'How could she know that?'

'How did she know where a chair was? Where a table was? How *do* sightless people know things they shouldn't know?'

That was when I saw something in his face. A flash of expression. Annoyance, with an overlay of fear. A slight tightening of tiny muscles at the mouth corners. It came, and went, in no time at all, but I spotted it and knew I was talking to a man who was basically weak.

'Cough it,' I said bluntly.

'I don't know what —'

'Don't crawl back into the woodwork, Arnold. Your neck's too far out for that.'

He swigged a mouthful of gin, took a deep breath, then

blew out his cheeks as he exhaled.

'She was pregnant,' he said gruffly.

'The report of the inquest didn't mention —'

'Not when she died. A couple of years ago.'

'After Sheba died?'

'Yes.' He nodded.

'Sheba would have to be dead,' I muttered. 'He wouldn't have dared to do it with Sheba around.'

'I wouldn't know about that.'

'I would,' I growled.

'There was no mention of the father.'

'No . . . there wouldn't be.'

'Just a quiet abortion.'

'My Christ!'

'Don't raise your hands in horror, Lados.' He made some sort of a puny fight back. 'If, as you say, Frisch *wasn't* her father, it's not the first time. It won't be the last.'

'It will with her.'

'You know damn well what I mean.'

'No,' I sneered. 'I don't know what you mean. I know you fixed an abortion. I also know you *thought* Frisch was her father. The Medical Council would be proud of you, Arnold. The police might be interested too.'

'And the last time we met? I'm not a total fool, you—'

'*Don't!*' It stopped him. It stopped him as effectively as a brick wall. In a much quieter tone, I said: 'Don't make guesses, Arnold. Don't even remember. Get out of here. Be grateful that, when you leave, you cease to exist . . . as far as I'm concerned. Don't send a bill. Don't mention this visit, to *anybody*. You've answered a few questions. Don't put yourself in peril by *asking* any.'

TWENTY-SEVEN

'Why?' asked Flensing.

'I need authorisation.'

'Of course.'

'I don't carry the rank. You do. *You* arrested him.'

'You're being strangely coy,' smiled Flensing. 'You ask for authorisation to interview Fletcher. Fine. I'll arrange for that authorisation. But I have to have a *reason*.'

'A....' Hoyle swallowed, then muttered: 'A murder enquiry.'

'Shouldn't I know something about it?' asked Flensing gently. 'Where – and when – did this murder take place?'

'Here. Lessford.' Then, awkwardly: 'No, not *here*. The body was found here. The killing took place in the old county area. Beechwood Brook Division.'

'When?'

'Twenty years ago. Nineteen sixty-three,' mumbled Hoyle. 'It was my first murder enquiry. It was never detected.'

'And you have reason to think Fletcher's your man?'

'No, sir.' Hoyle squared his shoulders and became slightly more formal. 'I have certain information. If the information's correct – and I've every reason to think it is – Fletcher might be able to help.'

Flensing turned back the cuff of his jacket with the forefinger of his right hand. He glanced at his wrist-watch, then said: 'I think it's about time for lunch, David. Join me. I've found a nice little café. Plain food, but good. Above all, clean ... and very private.'

'Look, I....'

'Not here.' Flensing stood up from the desk chair. 'I have

the feeling you don't yet quite trust me.' Then, pleasantly, and before Hoyle could reply: 'I don't blame you. Nor is my office the ideal place for off-the-record conversations. The café will be neutral ground ... you won't feel obliged to say "sir" as often.'

'Are you from Staffordshire?' grinned Flensing.

'No.' Hoyle looked puzzled.

'They tell me a Staffordshire bull terrier never knows when it's licked. They say it will die, still thinking it's winning.'

'People say silly things,' growled Hoyle.

As promised by Flensing, it had been a nice meal. The lamb, new potatoes and broccoli had had the flavour of good cooking. The apple pie and cream had been meltingly good. And now the coffee – served in full-sized cups, and not thimble-sized fiddles – was clearing their palates.

They were smoking cigarettes and, unlike the exchange in Flensing's office, they were talking as friends.

'I know,' sighed Hoyle. 'I'm selfish. Damn it, it wasn't even my case.'

'If not yours, whose?'

'I was only a detective constable. Outside cheap paperbacks detective constables don't handle murder enquiries.'

'All right.' Flensing nodded his understanding. 'Lewis didn't want it. Raff didn't want it. Even Ripley didn't want it. They passed it down the line. You couldn't pass it to *anybody*. But at least you didn't bury it. You didn't conveniently "forget" it.'

'Selfishness,' insisted Hoyle. 'A killer gets killed. Who the hell cares, other than a raving maniac? What sort of idiot nurses a crime – keeps it to himself – all through his service? *One* crime!'

'David, all coppers are selfish,' said Flensing sombrely. 'All *good* coppers. It's not a "team effort". That's pure propaganda. That's bullshit.' He raised and lowered the cigarette, then blew a plume of smoke. 'It's an eyeball-to-eyeball thing. Always. Cornish nailed Robinson in the

Charing Cross Trunk Murder job. Morrison slapped a name – and a conviction – on the Black Panther. Joe Mounsey: too selfish – too pig-headed – to rest till Hindley and Brady were inside. These people – the *real* coppers – *use* the force. Everybody else *gathers* the information. Because they can't be everywhere at once – and, by God, they would be if they could – but, because they can't, they use other men's legs, other men's reports. But it stays *their* crime. They're too proud – too selfish – to share it. And, at the end, it becomes what it always *was*. A one-to-one thing. Two bastards slugging it out, and nobody else in the world being allowed to interfere.'

'Two *bastards*?' Hoyle raised slightly disapproving eyebrows.

'Well, aren't we?' Flensing smiled. 'When we're coppers – when we're *being* coppers – at our level. Sure, we're after a rogue but, to do the job properly, we're only allowed to *see* him as a rogue. He may be a good husband, a fine father – anything – but to us he's a rogue. We're blind to his wife, his kids, his family. We have a job to do. To rip him away from his family and slap him inside. It happens, David. We close our eyes to it, because we couldn't do what we have to do if we followed the ripples too far, but it *does* happen. This man you're after. Whoever killed Davanzati. Fletcher? OK, maybe Fletcher – maybe not Fletcher – but all he did was rid the world of a man who'd killed other men. Who knows? He may have saved lives.'

'You don't approve?' muttered Hoyle.

'We don't make judgements, David.' A quick, slightly sad smile. 'Bastards *don't* make judgements.'

'Therefore, *because* we don't make judgements, we're bastards?'

'Have you ever thought ... ? Flensing leaned forward a little. It was friend-to-friend talk. Sympathetic. Understanding. Consolatory. 'We're real-life, what the crime authors write about. The writers have a ball. They create villains. They *like* creating villains – because the heavies always get the best lines. But, however hard they try, they can't create

244

real villains. You know – I know – the genuine crook, the big-time mobster, wouldn't be accepted in a work of fiction. He'd be *too* bad. *Too* evil. So the cardboard hooligans fill the pages, and are chased by make-believe heroes. But the make-believe hero is never – never! – tougher than the hero. Oh, sure, the hero beats the villain in the end – the make-believe hero and the make-believe villain – because convention demands it. But he shouldn't. He should be left bleeding to death in some dark alley, before the novel reaches the halfway mark.'

Flensing tasted coffee and inhaled cigarette smoke before he continued his thesis. 'That's the make-believe villain. But the real-life villain – the brand of villain too dark, too outrageous for the novelist even to invent – he, too, has to be caught. That is the object of the exercise, David. To topple *that* sod. The animals who go over the edge and end up committing Sharon Tate carnage. The Mansons, the "Rippers", the "Stranglers". The gangland bosses. The God-fathers and the psychopaths.'

'Sweet Jesus! Could Bond, or Holmes, or Poirot have handled *them*?'

'And we have to,' said Hoyle softly. Sadly. 'Because we, too, are "real-life".'

'And', added Flensing, 'we can't afford to be left bleeding to death in some dark alley.'

'Therefore . . . bastards.'

'We have to be, David. Bigger than they are. We'd *better* be.'

Flensing allowed Hoyle time to digest the proposition. To accept the wingless butterfly, without throwing up. To come to terms with it, yet not completely discard all self-respect.

After a few moments, Hoyle said: 'Fletcher?'

'Can we get hold of the file covering the Davanzati killing?'

'I have it at home,' said Hoyle. Then, hurriedly: 'Not the original. Photocopies of the complete file.'

'I'll fix you up with authorisation to interview Fletcher. I'll find where he is.'

'Thanks.'

'Alone?' asked Flensing. Then: 'I'm not pushing. It's merely a suggestion. I arrested him, remember. I know him. He knows *me*. I think he might even respect me. It might just give you an edge.'

'I'd like that.' Hoyle allowed his lips to twist into a slightly rueful smile. 'It's quite a relief. To share it, I mean. Like getting rid of an albatross.'

TWENTY-EIGHT

It made a difference, although the difference would have been hard to see, and is even harder to explain. To a certain extent, Frisch and I needed each other. Whether or not he had a 'stable' of men (and, perhaps, even women) upon whom he could call for the commission of carefully planned acts of lawlessness I do not know. I never knew, and I was wise enough not to make it my business to know. But (assuming this to be the case) the fairy atop his criminal Christmas tree was, without doubt, me. I was honest enough with myself to know that; that I possessed some strange, inverted 'star quality' denied the vast majority of other people. I was something Frisch had once searched for, found and could now not allow to escape.

Equally, of course, I needed Frisch. I could not hawk my expertise in the open market. The go-between was as essential as the gun, if I was to remain even moderately safe. Added to which – and to keep myself keen-edged and ready – I needed the facilities of the range and the breadth of weaponry made available by Frisch.

Anne, and the death of Anne, could not be allowed to break the partnership.

Nevertheless, there *was* a difference.

The coolness – the difference, if you like – almost surfaced late that summer. Towards the end of August 1976. It was a Sunday, we'd spent a couple of hours on the range and we were sitting in folding chairs, taking the evening sun on the patio, alongside the farmhouse.

'Do you feel lonely?' I asked.

'What?' Whether or not my question, coming, as it did, after a long silence, startled him I don't know. But, for whatever reason, the single-word counter-question was almost barked at me.

'Lonely?' I repeated. 'Without Anne.'

'I don't need company,' he said in a more normal tone.

'I wasn't enquiring about your "needs".' I shielded my eyes and squinted into the sun. 'Strictly speaking, we don't "need" to wash . . . but basic comfort insists that we *do*.'

'Are you worried about me?' I thought I detected the hint of a sneer.

I lowered my hand, turned my head and looked him full in the face before I spoke.

I said: 'Frisch, the only creature on God's earth about whom I *worry* is myself. If, after all these years, you haven't realised that you're not as wise as I thought you were.'

'The question puzzled me,' he said gently.

'The question?'

'About Anne.'

'The question was about *you*,' I reminded him.

'But, indirectly, about Anne.'

'Anne hanged herself,' I said flatly.

'Do you have doubts?' he breathed.

'*Should* I have doubts?'

'My friend, I'm not a mind-reader.'

'Nor I,' I countered. 'Therefore, I don't know what strange thoughts are passing through *your* mind.'

It was a short exchange, followed by a longer silence. It might never have happened. The small-talk – the gun-talk and the range-talk – took over. And that was the only time the truth even *looked* like crawling from its dark corner.

Thereafter, life carried on as if Anne had never lived.

* * *

Throughout that year and into 1977 the 'Lados' daubs were produced on what amounted to an assembly-line basis. One every month or six weeks. That was the period when I presented the art world with another matching pair. *Fellatio* and *Cunnilingus*.

It was, I admit, sheer black humour on my part. An attempt to shock the general public and, at the same time, expose the lunacy of the Art World.

At first, it did neither. The general public seemed not even to understand the meaning of the twin titles, and it wasn't until the television programme (parts of which are still screened whenever it is felt that the viewing public need a slap in the face) that passions were roused.

The interviewer was uniquely honest.

'I can see neither an erect penis on one painting, nor an open vagina on the other.'

'Really?' I put full-bore scorn into the word, and matched the tone with my expression.

'Supposedly they represent the two variations of oral sex.'

'Not "supposedly".'

'To me, they *don't*.'

'In that case,' I drawled, 'you're either blind . . . or you've led an uncommonly sheltered life.'

That short game of conversational ping-pong was all that was needed. Of course the interviewer was right. Of course the scribblings of colour meant nothing. Less than nothing!

But, from that moment, they became either 'advanced works of art' or 'dirty pictures', dependent upon which side of the puritanical line you happened to be. The furore was quite ridiculous. Two words – that's all. The rubbish *above* those words was meaningless. Yet (if you recall) the Minister for Arts was asked to ban their exhibition in public.

They earned me a small fortune, which, in turn, added to a growing and much larger fortune.

Looking back, even from this short distance of time, I think this was the stage at which the strain began to tell. It must be understood that, for years, I'd lived a decidedly schizophrenic life. To the world. generally, I was on show. I was a one-man circus, flamboyant and garish enough to be forever newsworthy; an outrageous, neon-lit monstrosity forever claiming the spotlight. Conversely, as a genuine, flesh-and-blood person I didn't exist; I was an unknown, anonymous exterminator of unwanted men and women.

I needed the one, but I *was* the other and, other than in the secure privacy of the maisonette, I could never truly relax.

All my life I've been a healthy man. Coughs and sneezes – no more than that. But gradually – *very* gradually – I was smoking more. I kept to mild, and I kept to cork-tipped, but I ended up averaging twenty a day. The same with booze. More than a bottle of whisky a week. Not much to a tippler, but I was no tippler, and the neat bedtime double began to be very necessary if I was to enjoy a good night's sleep.

Understand me, it was not a backlash to the killings. They were unimportant. I'd ended the lives of strangers – so what? But the continuous, and very necessary, 'Lados' façade was beginning to wear me down. I'd started an avalanche, and I couldn't stop it. It was, I suppose, a little like dope. The hard stuff. And I was hooked.

I hinted my problem to Pollard.

'These creeps who paint – these artists – do they ever stop? Do they ever retire?'

'Why?' He seemed surprised at my question.

'You're the expert. I'm asking.'

'Rarely.' He scratched his cheek meditatively. 'No. The great ones paint until they're too old to see the canvas.'

'Nice thought,' I grunted.

'Are you' – Pollard waved a somewhat airy, and very arty, hand – 'running out of inspiration?'

'Are you', I said coldly, 'taking the piss?'

'Good Lord, no.' And, strange as it may seem, I think he meant the denial.

'The crap I splash on canvas. . . .'

'No! No!' He held his hand, palm forward, to silence me. 'Some people – you're one of them – need no apprenticeship. Need no training. You paint abstracts. *Beautiful* abstracts. You're a genius. You were *born* a genius.'

'You're out of your mind.'

'No. It happens,' he insisted. 'In art, in music, in literature. Not often . . . but it *does* happen. They explode on to the scene, and that's it. It's a shot in the arm. They have something new and exciting to say – to show – and they have a completely new way of saying it.'

I let him ramble on, without bothering to listen. Pollard had fallen for his own sell – sucked his own egg completely dry – and there was no hope for him. It didn't worry me too much. It was my decision . . . and *I* had to make it.

To retire, you see. To ease the strain a little. But it wouldn't be easy. This 'Lados' persona was no blushing violet. Not the kind to grow old gracefully, or even ease himself into the wings and stroll to centre-stage less and less often.

Nevertheless. . . .

For a few years I took to following the sun a little. Not the package-tour trail, nor even the jet-set path. Indeed, rarely for more than two or three weeks at a time. But I found places. Peaceful places – beautiful, unspoiled places – where the 'Lados' legend had not yet run. Where, hopefully, it would never run.

I concentrated on islands. People buy islands. They *buy* the damn things, then set up their own rules and regulations. That was the way my mind worked. It was crazy, but it grew less crazy the more I looked into it.

As sure as hell, people *did* buy islands.

The years 1978 and 1979 saw me 'island hunting'.

I moved around Scotland – the Western Isles – for starters. Islands galore! The Sound of Harris has more islands than a dog has fleas. South of Barra there is a necklace of them. Cold, inhospitable places. Storm-swept and primitive. Whether any of these pimples of rock poking from the sea could have been bought I'll never know. I liked them not at all, and followed my original plan . . . to seek the sun.

250

I tried the Mediterranean. East of Spain. West of Italy. Again, islands, and to spare. The Balearic Islands and specks of land south of Elba. But the shoe-box hotels of mass tourism were too handy. If I bought an island, I didn't want a Capri set-up; I was no 'Gracie Fields', nice-to-see-you-luv type.

That in 1978, 1979; and when I hinted things to my accountant he was delighted.

'Financially, you'll feel the difference.'

'And if I lived in a dog kennel,' I growled.

'What?' He couldn't follow simple logic.

'I wouldn't have to pay rates, water-rates, heating bills.'

'Oh!'

'What you have to do', I instructed, 'is keep things quiet. *Very* quiet. When I find it – *if* I find it – you will do the bargaining and the buying. Nobody knows. Nobody will get to know. If anybody finds out, *you* will be the one whose bill won't be paid.'

That was one side of me. The 'Lados' side. The other side – the *real* me – might have made history. I was asked to kill a king . . . and I agreed.

Mid-December is a cold, inhospitable month anywhere in the United Kingdom. The first flush of an approaching Christmas has faded, the boredom of waiting has caught up and the few days of that final dash have not yet arrived.

I'd arrived home from my latest 'island hunt' at the beginning of December 1978. Frisch telephoned me within twenty-four hours of my arrival and, for him, the tone was urgent.

It was equally urgent – equally insistent – when we talked, face to face, at the farm.

'They have to see you,' he said. 'They demand a face-to-face meeting.'

'No way!' I lighted a cigarette, and blew smoke at the high-banked open fire.

'They insist.'

'"They"?' I mocked. 'The crowd who snarled up the Glasgow job?'

'More or less,' he fenced.

'Frisch, they know *you* – am I right?'

'More or less,' he repeated, and it was said in a low, mumbling voice.

'For Christ's sake!'

'Yes . . . I think they know me.'

'Who contacted you?' I asked.

'He. . . .' Frisch moved his shoulders. 'He arrived. That's all.'

'Here?'

'Yes.'

'A stranger? Some sod you didn't know?'

'He knew about me,' muttered Frisch. 'He knew enough about me to justify me trusting *him*.'

'Trusting!' I didn't shout, but I think my voice trembled. I know the fury was there, inside me. I controlled myself, with something of an effort, then continued: 'Frisch, if "they" are the mad bastards responsible for the Glasgow set-up, I wouldn't trust them to snuff out this cigarette without setting the whole bloody house on fire. . . .'

'That wasn't. . . .'

'What is it?' I smashed into what he was going to say and silenced him. 'MI5? Special Branch? Some other poor cow, enjoying her night's rest? What the hell is it, Frisch? Have you taken leave of your senses?'

'My short-tempered friend.' Frisch was Frisch and, although I'd thrown him with my outburst, he now had control of himself and matched me, tone for tone. 'I can give them a negative answer. They will accept it. They *must* accept it.' The timing of the pause was perfect. 'It isn't *me* they'll be gunning for.'

'Explain that,' I said harshly. 'In single-syllable words, if possible.'

'Accept that they know me. There is every likelihood that, by this time, they also know *you*. What contacts have you? What *use* are you, other than a finger on a trigger? They desire to use both of us. Together, or independently. My friend, you are easier to replace than I am. Come down from

252

your proud little perch and face *that* truth. You're good – probably the best – but you're not unique.'

'Whereas you are?'

'No.' He shook his head, then added: 'Not unique – merely more rare than you are. More difficult to replace.'

'And I know too much?'

'We *both* know too much. We know far too much to be allowed any real choice.'

I think the long-term result of that talk was to make me search for my island with greater urgency; it certainly swept away any last doubts about needing some secure bolt-hole into which I might retire to await my dotage.

The short-term result was a lonely walk along the deserted promenade at a place called Little Bispham. December, with a half-gale belting in from the Irish Sea. The long-stalked street-lights on the upper walk merely emphasised the darkness of the lower walk. We were using the lower walk, it was almost midnight and, had we been rehearsing a day trip to the South Pole, I, for one, couldn't have felt more miserable. Coats, scarves and gloves were no match for the penetrating west wind.

'You get the picture?'

The question was almost shouted, but the rush of air shredded the North American twang almost before it reached me.

'To kill the Shah?' I bawled back.

'Yeah.'

'Then to get out alive?'

'Leave that to us, mac.'

'That', I yelled, 'is a damn sight more important than emptying the Peacock Throne.'

'Oh, sure.'

'To *me*.'

'Rest easy, mac. You can do it.'

I think, in the whole of criminal history, there was never a more bizarre briefing. From my first meeting with this Yankee lunatic outside the unlit telephone kiosk; to the

253

silent, side-by-side walk to a promenade cold enough, and windy enough, to do stand-in for Antarctica; to a throat-tearing conversation concerning topics sane men wouldn't even whisper.

And yet. . . .

It was the safest place on God's earth. Nobody could get to within eavesdropping distance. On the wild assumption that a directional microphone was pointing at us, all it would have picked up would have been the rush of the wind. The same with personal bugs; the weather would have swamped everything with white noise, and enough of it to kill all hope of needling out a single word of our exchange.

He was a short man. A stocky man, with the cockiness of so many small men carrying power and responsibility. In his own world – in his own estimation – he was a 'Napoleon'.

'We've liaised with them too long to be sure. We can't be sure which of our people they know. That's why we approached your government.'

'We' being the CIA. He didn't have to spell it out. 'Them' being the Pahlavian dynasty and, with it, the SAVAK. Without being given a choice I was part of another CIA 'Dirty Tricks' set-up.

'The way we read it, Khomeini can pull the peasants and a few of the religious extremists. The rest – the intelligentsia, the bazaaris, maybe even the Army – they're still deciding which way to jump. If Pahlavi gets assassinated, and it's made to look like Khomeini fixed it, with Iraqian backing, there'll be a swing of sympathy. Khomeini won't be able to hold them. By the time he climbs back into the saddle, *we'll* be in control. "Peace-keeping troops" ... that sort of set-up.'

Some cold-blooded bastard in Washington had worked out the moves like a chess-master. A few streets, ankle-deep in blood. A few thousand lynchings. Civil War, with its unimportant side-issues of rape, pillage and burning. All it needed was for me to kill a king. Whispering campaigns and professional rabble-rousers would do the rest.

The prize was big enough. The prize was oil, and a move

to the back door of the USSR.

Jesus Christ! And, by the world's yardstick, *I* was an evil man.

To kill a king, then. And, for killing a king, a king's ransom. Paid in advance, with no strings and deposited in a numbered account at a Swiss bank.

'Not your usual way, mac. Frisch explained it. How you launder the money. That's OK. It's *already* been laundered.'

That was it. That was the end of the eyeball-to-eyeball 'briefing'. Not once had he used my name. Not once had he used the 'Lados' tag. Nor, come to that, had he given *his* name.

He had, I suppose – and in naval jargon – 'inspected the cut of my jib'.

As I drove away from the west coast, I tried to empty my mind of the last few hours. The lunacy of it. The sheer size of it. OK, the *awfulness* of what I'd been jockeyed into. I was driving a car, on a bad night, and I needed all the concentration I could gather to do just that.

I drove directly to Frisch's place, and found him waiting up for me. At a guess he, too, was worried.

I drank whisky and hot water, smoked cigarettes, as we talked the thing out until well past dawn.

'I'm the fall guy,' I said in a harsh voice. 'One man? *Me?* This crowd doesn't give a shit about one man!'

'You could talk,' soothed Frisch. 'They must know that. You could save your life by opening your mouth.'

'Do you think I'm going to be allowed to *live* long enough to talk?'

Frisch tried to calm me a little. He showed me the gun to be used. A Russian-made Stechkin, with a fire-power of 725 rounds a minute. I wasn't too keen. It took a 9 mm Soviet cartridge, but it had a blowback action – and blowback actions depend upon the accuracy of the charge.

'I've checked the Stechkin.' Frisch worked hard to reassure me. 'I've had it to pieces, I've checked every millimetre of it, and it won't let you down. The same with the rounds. I've emptied and reloaded them. Be assured, the gun won't let you down.'

'It's still a "Four Feathers" exercise,' I countered. 'I end up with a gun that will work ... surrounded by a hundred times more screaming natives than I have bullets.'

'You'll be in an armoured car.'

'Of course,' I mocked. 'Courtesy of the Shah's own secret police. That makes me *very* happy!'

'It's a mock-up. An armoured car *supposedly* belonging to the SAVAK. In reality. . . .'

'In reality, what?' I snarled. I poured more whisky into the glass. 'In reality, CIA-paid killers. But what if I'm one of the people they're paid to kill? In reality, I drive into the Niavaran Palace to slaughter a monarch – but who keeps an eye on *my* back while I'm doing it? In reality, the streets are occupied by more CIA-hired goons, all the way to the outskirts of Tehran – but what if they're not?' I drank deep at the whisky. 'Frisch, it stinks. It stinks to high heaven. Some cockamalarky Yankee has concocted this glorified way of committing suicide, in the pious hope that Bakhtier just *might* take over from Khomeini. It hasn't a cat in hell's chance of working – and, whether it works or not, I haven't a cat in hell's chance of living through it.'

TWENTY-NINE

1982 was a busy year for Lessford CID. Specifically, and as far as Flensing and Hoyle were concerned, it was a 'proving' year. The Yorkshire Ripper case was of very recent memory; the monumental shambles of detectives besotted by their own filing system until the system became more important than the case it was there to solve. Thirteen women had died at the hands of Peter William Sutcliffe; a madman with an IQ of 110, who had been so sure of himself that he'd allowed his photograph to be used on the works calendar of the firm employing him; who was cornered, not because of good CID work, but because a uniformed copper from another force had become suspicious after a minor traffic offence. The Ripper and the Black Panther; Donald Neilson and a zig-zag of murders and robberies culminating in the foulness perpetrated upon Leslie Whittle. Not forgetting Myra Hindley and Ian Brady, the Moors Murderers.

Too much, and too near, and when Lessford seriously thought it might have a 'Copycat Ripper' within the force boundaries every stop on the manual was pulled out. Too many evil bastards were getting away with things, and Flensing and Hoyle breathed easier, and caught up with lost sleep, only when William Drever was convicted.*

By then it was too late.

'He ended his parole period early this year.'

'What?'

Flensing had joined Hoyle in the club room of Lessford Headquarters. It was mid-afternoon and, apart from three off-duty uniformed officers, who were bunched around the television set watching the horseracing, only Hoyle was in the room. Hoyle was playing bar billiards. To be accurate, playing *at* bar billiards. He was alone, knocking the balls around the stained baize while he killed time pending the end of his wife's stint at the hospital. He looked up from his half-concentration as Flensing joined him and spoke.

'Fletcher.' Flensing dropped a typed and headed sheet of notepaper on to the surface of the table. 'Last known address in the Bristol area. He left, after his parole period ended.'

'Rough.' Hoyle's rueful expression carried just the hint of bitterness. Then he grinned and added: 'That name – "Davanzati" – open me up, when I'm gone, you'll find it burned across my heart.'

* See the author's *The Distaff Factor* (Macmillan, 1982).

'Fortunately, no great loss.'

'Except to a certain detective chief inspector's ego.'

'I think you're mad,' said Alva cheerfully. 'Weather like this, and we could be comfy-cosy in front of a fire.'

'I think I'm mad,' agreed Hoyle.

'I also think we're lost.'

'No, I don't think so.' Hoyle peered through the streaming windscreen, and past the flicking wipers. He spun the steering-wheel and tried to give the tyre treads some forward traction on the mud-greasy surface. 'It's a long time ago, my pet, but when Ripley brought me here it was a very important journey. I know the way. I'm *sure* I know the way.'

'And when we get there – *if* we get there – what do you say to this . . . what's his name?'

'Gawne. David Gawne.'

'*David* Gawne?'

'I know.' Hoyle concentrated on the driving, and didn't move his head. 'You'll have two Davids. Don't forget which one to root for.'

'As good as that, is he?'

'He has – *had* – quite a personality. He matched Charlie Ripley.'

For five more minutes Hoyle pushed the car forward through the driving rain. He leaned forward over the wheel, his hands gripping its rim and ready to counter what seemed to be a never-ending combination of slides and minor skids. The gusting wind rocked the car and, in the headlights, the gale-shaking heather cramped the unmade road then disappeared into the overall blackness of the November night.

'What a bloody place!' muttered Alva.

'He's older.' Hoyle appeared to be arguing a proposition meant to convince himself. 'He's an old man, by this time. And *I'm* older. I'm a damn sight more experienced than I was last time we met.'

'Why on earth come at *night*?' pleaded Alva. 'Why not when we can *see* our way? And, for God's sake, why drag *me* into it?'

'Old men.' Hoyle answered the question in short, hard sentences. Biting off each sentence as he fought the car through the weather. 'They don't like the night. Late at night. What few wits they have left aren't functioning. They're dopey. They say things. Things they later regret.'

'And me?'

'You're good-looking.' His jaw jutted a fraction. 'You're attractive.'

'Eh?'

'Old men – *some* old men – they have memories. Certain memories. They're harmless, but they have. . . .' He paused then, in a whisper, ended, '*imaginations*.'

'You sod!' she breathed. 'You dirty-minded —'

'Not me. *Him*. Gawne. I'm hoping so. As I recall, he could be the type. I'm betting on it.'

They drove the rest of the way in savage silence. But it was all for nothing. They found the place, but it was no longer inhabited. It no longer had a roof and no longer had windows. A fire – a terrible fire – had gutted the place.

Hoyle earned a skin-deep soaking wandering round the ruins. He found a duo of shivering tramps, camping out for the night and, in exchange for a fiver, learned the recent history of the building and of its late owner. Gawne was dead – had died of a massive coronary less than two years before. Vandals and thieves had found the building and, between them, had gutted it, then set fire to it. It now belonged to nobody. Nature, the creatures of the wild and roadsters who strayed well away from beaten tracks had now claimed it.

Drenched, Hoyle returned to the car. He gripped the top of the steering-wheel in clenched fists and lowered his head on to the backs of his hands.

'Easy, my lovely.'

All anger had left Alva at the sight of the obvious dejection of her man.

'Always too late,' muttered Hoyle. 'Always that little bit too bloody *late*!'

THIRTY

When the Shah blew the Niavaran Palace, and took a plane for Egypt on 16 January, it was not too unlike some killer having a misfire when the snout of his weapon was touching the nape of my neck. He didn't know it, of course – very few people knew it – but I'd been due to board a plane on Saturday, 20 January, as the first step towards blasting him from the face of the earth. It had been planned as a zig-zag journey but, to me, it had still seemed a most decidedly one-way trip.

I heard the news on the radio, confirmed it with Frisch, checked that the whole crap-arsed scene had been abandoned and went back to sleeping nights.

Maybe in some story-book I would have changed my ways. Felt some regret for what I'd already done. Gone soft. Perhaps even gone religious. But I didn't – because my life had been a real life and not a story-book life.

Luck was still on my side. She'd been on my side all through life. I hadn't insulted her by taking her too much for granted and, in return, she smiled when necessary and allowed me to collect a fortune large enough to have widened even Mother's eyes.

So I stepped up the 'island hunting'.

Into 1980 – into 1981 – I dropped in on more islands than I'd previously thought possible.

I even took some positive steps towards disappearing into the sunset. I had the accountant contact a top-class removal firm and, while I was away, supervise the careful packing of some of the books, some of the records, some of the smaller and less-used items in the maisonette and put them in storage until further notice. I had a numbered bank account

– thanks to the CIA – so I began to use it. Gradually – not too obviously to attract attention – I moved parcels of my money into the same account, much to the glee of my accountant.

'Everything above-board,' I warned him. 'I'm not a tax exile.'

'That's understood, of course.' Then came the smile – a smile with just the hint of 'knowledge' at its core – and the gentle drumming of slim, well-manicured fingers on the desk-top. 'Let us say you're becoming financially wise.'

The 'Lados' crap kept the fiscal oil-well gushing, and still left me time to hunt around.

In January 1982 I thought I'd found it. The Hawaiian Islands and an outcrop north-west of Kauai and a few miles north of Niihau. That was when I found I belonged to a 'club' – people with enough folding stuff to scour out-of-the-way places seeking their own private paradise. I was pipped at the post.

There are islands south of New Zealand – South Island. South of Stewart Island. Uninhabited spots, a hundred miles by sea from Invercargill. Had I played the 'Lados' game it is possible I might have argued the New Zealand authorities into selling or, perhaps, leasing one of them. But that would have defeated one of the objects of my search. Anonymity.

Then, towards the end of the year – November 1982 – Frisch blew up on me. He had a stroke. A cerebral haemorrhage, which left him half paralysed.

Arnold was attending him. Arnold was showing his age; bent and peering from behind half-moon spectacles. He was a startling reminder that youth is a very temporary state of affairs, and that 'middle age' is an expression with only a certain amount of elasticity.

I'd arrived at the farm that morning – a Sunday morning, Sunday the fifteenth – for a stint on the range. A dull day, with a light fog. As if the stench of old bonfires was still around. The strange car warned me, and when I hammered at the knocker a hard-faced, starchy-looking woman

261

answered. Beyond her, I could see Arnold.

When I was inside – before I went to see Frisch – Arnold took me to one side and explained things.

'Yesterday,' he ended. 'He managed to get to the phone and, with some difficulty, I understood who was calling. I attended immediately.'

'Will he recover?'

'Hopefully.'

'Arnold,' I said, 'I'm not likely to have an attack of the vapours. I know the man – no more. There's no bond between us.'

'Friendship?' he asked gently.

'It's a luxury I deny myself.'

'If by "recover" you mean "live", the answer is yes.' He spoke slowly and carefully, as if trying to hurt a little with each word. He continued: 'He'll live . . . but he won't be the same man. One of two things has happened. A tiny clot of blood has bombarded part of his brain. That, or a tiny blood vessel, inside the brain, has ruptured. We don't know why these things happen, Lados. We can't prevent them. But we know the consequences.'

'And they are?'

'A subtle change in the personality. Of necessity, brain tissue has been destroyed, and can't be replaced. It makes a difference. However small that difference, it will be there.'

'He'll move again?' I pressed. 'He's not half-dead for the rest of his life?'

'My professional opinion?' he smiled.

'If that's the best you can offer.'

'He'll move again.' He nodded slowly. 'His movements won't be as certain as they once were. Nor will his concentration be as acute. His memory may suffer a little. He'll be changed . . . emotionally.'

'All that because of a tiny blood clot. A tiny blood vessel bursting.'

'We're talking about a very delicate piece of equipment.'

'The brain.' I moved a hand dismissively. 'Your colleagues – the scientists – they'd argue that the brain is merely an

262

above-average computer.'

'Not my *medical* colleagues. They know better.'

I took a cigarette from its packet and, as I held the flame of a lighter to its tip, I murmured: 'A pity about Anne.'

'What?' He looked startled.

'She could have looked after him. If she hadn't "hanged" herself, that is.'

'Don't upset him!' His concern was very obvious. Whether it was professional concern, or something stronger, I had no means of knowing. 'Don't upset him, Lados. Not if he means anything at all to you.'

'Another stroke?' I smiled. 'Lethal this time?'

'He needs rest. Tranquillity. He needs time for whatever caused it to clear or to heal.'

'I'll remember that.'

I left him, and climbed the stairs to see Frisch.

The right side of his face was quite immobile. Waxen and without expression. He tried to smile – the standard smile of the 'brave' invalid seeking sympathy – but it was a very cock-eyed smile. Nor could he mouth words well enough to make much sense.

'You are to relax, Frisch,' I said calmly. 'You are not to worry. I'm told you'll get better ... eventually. You should be in hospital, of course, but I understand why you're unwilling to leave this place.' I drew on the cigarette, then strolled to the window, opened it, flicked what was left of the cigarette outside, closed the window, then walked back to the bed. I said: 'Arnold seems to love you. That, at least, gives you the edge over me. He's arranged for nurses to attend to you. Good nurses, so he tells me. A very efficient one opened the door.' I smiled down at his slightly twisted face. 'I won't use the range until you're up and around. Telephone me, when you're able. When you can dispense with untrustworthy people. I'll start visiting you again. Not until.'

Too many people were beginning to know things – at best *suspect* things. At first, and after I'd blasted the two coppers, only Frisch. Maybe Anne but, *if* Anne, Anne didn't count any more. Only Frisch. Then, in order to tailor the money, Pollard. After Pollard, Arnold; and after Arnold ... God only knew who! Faceless men from the dark passages of Whitehall ... and their opposite numbers from America. How many? How many knew Frisch? How many knew *me*.

Figuratively speaking, too many unidentified people were breathing down the back of my neck. If I wasn't careful, I'd end up as the richest man behind bars.

It seemed wise, therefore, to absent myself from the United Kingdom as much as possible, pending Frisch's recovery. To travel incognito and move around. Not in some panic-stricken flight, you must understand. Panic was not – and still is not – part of my make-up. But, nevertheless, to move around.

I think that what had once been a great affinity with my own people was cooling. Patriotism – if, indeed, it ever deserved the name of 'patriotism' – had cooled considerably. And quickly. The gravy-train riders were too plentiful. The violence-for-the-sake-of-violence crowd was taking over too many facets of life. Conversely, the do-gooders were clogging up the machinery of ordinary, decent life. Music – what *I* counted as music – was being replaced by meaningless vociferation. Literature was nose-diving into hyped-up garbage.

And, of course, I was getting older.

·I travelled. I had moments of great delight. I heard the Vienna Philharmonic Orchestra, the Los Angeles Philharmonic Orchestra and the Israel Philharmonic Orchestra. I watched Kertesz and Karajan, Maazel and Mehta. Barenboim and Bernstein, Dorati and Ormandy. The years 1983 and 1984 were my 'musical years'. To be there – to be *there* – when it happened. Not some recording, however expertly made. Not some carefully balanced broadcast. But to be there! Present when some gifted genius gathered the hundred or so talents of superb musicians then, by adding his own magic of interpretation, merged the whole into a single magnificence a thousand times greater than the sum of its component parts.

I discovered a secret. That to hear great music, at its source, amounts to a great contradiction. It is to die a little but, at the same time, to have a glorious rebirth.

I rather enjoyed 1983 and 1984 and, during this period, I found my island.

THIRTY-ONE

'Davanzati?' Alva smoked the cigarette in quick, angry inhalations and exhalations. 'That boyo has been there since – since . . . even on our honeymoon.'

From the iron lung Helen Flensing asked: 'Who *is* he?'

'That's. . . .' Alva stared through the window of the side-ward. Watched, without consciously seeing. Ambulances and cars arriving and departing from the main entrance. Nurses clip-clopping busily towards and away from the single-storeyed buildings which formed the annexes. She took a longer pull at the cigarette, then said: 'That's the devil of it. He's dead. He was dead before David even knew his name. But he's always *there*.'

'You smoke too much, dear,' criticised Helen gently.

'I know. Lung cancer. Heart attacks. Maybe ingrowing toe-nails.' Alva enjoyed another long, deep pull on the cigarette, then turned from the window and demanded: 'What *is* it with men?'

'They're men,' smiled Helen.

'They're *mad*.'

'Whoever he is – or *was* – this Davanzati – he has Ralph by the throat, too . . . or so it seems.'

'David's first murder case,' said Alva heavily. 'The damn

265

thing's still undetected. It's been driving him nuts, on and off, ever since.'

'It follows.' Within the confines of her prison, Helen nodded. The impression was that if she could have shrugged she would have shrugged. 'It explains Ralph's interest. This man Fletcher committed *his* first murder. I think it stays with them.'

'All right.' Alva's irritability remained. She screwed the remainder of the cigarette into a handy saucer which held an empty cup. 'It's his child-substitute. It's his —'

'It's his pride,' interrupted Helen. 'Nothing to do with "child-substitution". It's rather like a dog fouling your private drive. You can't rest until it's been cleaned away.'

'The dog-dirt's been there a long time,' muttered Alva. 'It's damn near part of the scenery by now.'

'Hope they have luck.'

'For *my* sake,' said Alva feelingly.

Paddington (as any Londoner will tell you) has its own atmosphere. It is, of course, dominated by the presence of the railway; the lines and the station constitute its heart and its sinews. It is a place of 'mews' and 'squares' and 'terraces' and was once inhabited by second-drawer gentility – but it has slipped a little. It is now an area of hotels – many of which are fire-traps – bedsitters and flats. There are trees, but they are sickly looking efforts at making the roads look more attractive. There are lawns – public lawns – but the grass seems always to be in dire need of a lawnmower. Paddington, then, looks what it is. Not as highly regarded as it was in the past, but still clinging to tattered remnants of respectability.

That evening – early evening, and before dusk brought the threat of darkness – three men walked slowly around Cleveland Terrace, Westbourne Street, Chilworth Street and Gloucester Street. A near-perfect rectangle, which they strolled, from corner to corner, before turning right.

Two of the men were polite, but determined. The third man was annoyed, but afraid.

266

Fletcher said: 'You've no right to interview me like this. I'm straight. I've paid my debt to society.'

He had a slight American twang to his voice. His pronunciation was a little nasal.

'Of course you have,' agreed Flensing.

'*One* debt,' added Hoyle.

'What's that mean?'

'We're not on duty, Fletcher,' said Flensing mildly.

Hoyle added: 'But, we can *come* on duty . . . if that's the only way to get what we want.'

'We're – shall we say? – enjoying a day out in London. We thought we'd call and see you. Meet you on your way home from work.'

'I don't know how the devil. . . .'

'It wasn't hard.' Hoyle's tone was a shade harder than Flensing's. 'You're a married man. . . .'

'With two kids. I'd like you to remember that.'

'Your wife visited you in prison, before you were married. She has a sister. It wasn't *too* difficult.'

'*She's* a trouble-making bitch,' muttered Fletcher.

'Davanzati,' said Flensing gently.

'I don't know anybody called Davanzati.'

But the reply was too quick. Too instant. A strange name – an unusual name – but he repeated it without hesitation.

'Jacopo Davanzati,' growled Hoyle.

'I've already told you. . . .'

'Don't walk too far down *that* blind alley,' warned Hoyle. 'You'll only have a longer walk back.'

'Davanzati's dead,' said Flensing.

'Look, if you think. . . .'

'I think', said Flensing, 'you'd be wise – very wise – to assume we know the answer to every question we ask. That we know when you're lying.'

'*I* didn't kill him.' Then, with a hint of panic: 'Christ Almighty, you're not trying to. . . .'

'Just that he's dead,' said Hoyle flatly. 'You're the first to mention the word "kill".'

'And if you don't *know* him . . . ,' teased Flensing.

267

They walked all of twenty yards – around the next corner – without any of the three speaking. Fletcher was thinking. Flensing and Hoyle were waiting.

Fletcher spoke first.

'Mr Flensing, I'm straight,' he said sombrely. Quietly. Emphatically. 'I know you've heard that scores of times –'

'Hundreds,' said Hoyle.

' – but this time it's true. What I was. I'm not that any more.'

'You killed a man. Shot him to death,' said Flensing, but not unkindly.

'The world's no worse a place.'

'Possibly not. But he wasn't the only one.'

Fletcher remained silent.

Very gently Flensing said: 'There's no Statute of Limitation covering murder, Fletcher. If we dig deeply enough, I've no doubt we'll find skeletons.'

'I didn't kill Davanzati,' breathed Fletcher.

'You *knew* him.'

Fletcher nodded sadly.

'Somebody killed him.' Hoyle took up the interview as they strolled along the pavement. Then he took a risk, and added: 'Gawne knows you. *Knew* you. Gawne knew you both.'

'Gawne?'

'David Gawne. He knew you both.'

Hoyle held his breath. Praying the bluff wouldn't be called.

After a pause Fletcher said: 'Gawne's dead.'

'You've kept in touch?' Hoyle masked his relief behind the question.

'We hear things in prison.'

'Davanzati and Fletcher,' pressed Hoyle. 'Two names Gawne mentioned before he died.'

'I was. . . .' Fletcher moistened dried lips. 'I was meant to kill Gawne. I didn't.'

'And Davanzati?'

'I didn't kill him.'

'Somebody killed him.'

'Such a long time ago,' murmured Fletcher dreamily. 'God, it was another life. Before I went inside.'

'Somebody killed him,' insisted Hoyle.

Again, the stroll continued in silence. The two detectives knew their trade. Fletcher would talk. He'd already started talking. Given time – given patience – he'd tell all he knew. Given time, given steady pressure – but not too much pressure – he'd answer all questions. But not too much pressure. Too much pressure would stop him from talking. Like corking a bottle. Just enough pressure ... and in his own time.

Fletcher gulped in air and sighed.

He said: 'You're a decent man, Mr Flensing.'

'It depends,' said Flensing carefully.

'I've a good wife. Two nice kids.'

'Does she know you're a killer?' asked Flensing.

'She knows why I was inside.'

'A professional killer?'

Fletcher didn't answer.

'In your day, one of the top-drawer hit men?' pressed Flensing.

'Not top-drawer.' The smile was twisted and sad. 'The top men don't go to prison, Mr Flensing. They *never* go inside.'

'Nevertheless, an "unusual" profession,' smiled Flensing.

'She might be interested,' said Hoyle. 'A lot of people might be interested.'

They rounded the next corner, and still Fletcher said nothing. He seemed to be thinking. Contemplating pros and cons.

Then, in a rather apologetic tone, he began: 'What I know doesn't amount to much. The killing I did time for. The contract out for Gawne ... as if *I* could finish a man like Gawne! If there *are* others, they're overseas. I was always second-string. I – er – I didn't think so, at the time, but I've learned more sense.'

'Davanzati,' Hoyle reminded him.

'I was with him. Just the once. I was back-up, in case

269

things went wrong.' He gave a quick, mirthless laugh. 'I took the money ... that's all. With men like Davanzati, things don't go wrong.'

'Once,' murmured Flensing.

'What?'

'They went wrong once. *Very* wrong.'

'Eh? Oh! – yeah ... they tell me.'

'What do they tell you?' pounced Flensing.

'And we won't ask who "they" are,' promised Hoyle.

'Things. Y'know ... rumours.'

'That won't do, Fletcher.' Flensing's tone carried sadness and disappointment in equal parts. 'You can say that Inspector Hoyle has waited a long time for this moment. I, too, am anxious to know a few things. We've both travelled a long way to see you. Vague remarks won't satisfy either of us.'

'What aren't rumours ... ,' began Fletcher. He looked worried, then continued: 'These men don't exist, Mr Flensing. Y'know ... they don't even *exist*.'

'Ah, but they *do*.'

'Sure they do,' agreed Fletcher. 'It's just that —'

'We take your meaning,' interrupted Hoyle brusquely. 'Now, stop treading water, and move.'

In a very flat voice, Flensing said: 'Name some names, Fletcher. Convince us we should not tap the nearest Met man on the shoulder, and continue this conversation in the nearest cell.'

Again, they rounded a corner before Fletcher spoke.

'Davanzati,' he muttered.

'We named Davanzati first ... remember?' snapped Hoyle.

'Gawne.'

'Somebody we *don't* know, Fletcher.'

'Gawne wasn't just a killer,' murmured Fletcher. 'He was a fixer. Mainly a fixer.'

'Keep the names coming.'

'Pete Diapoulas.'

'Who the hell's – ?'

'A Syndicate gunman.' Flensing answered the question before it was fully asked. 'Bodyguard to Joe Gallo.'

'Not a *good* bodyguard.' Fletcher's tone was very contemptuous. 'Gallo got his in Umberto's Clam House. Diapoulas ended up with a slug in his arse.'

'The killer was never found,' said Flensing softly.

'No.' Fletcher bit the word off, then closed his mouth.

'You've mixed with some fine company in your time,' observed Hoyle drily.

Flensing said: 'More names, Fletcher. Unless you'd like to stop at your own.'

'I keep telling you. . . .'

'More names,' repeated Flensing.

Fletcher sighed heavily, then said: 'Gawne, Frisch, Profaci. . . .'

'Gawne's no good to us.'

Hoyle asked: 'This Profaci character?'

'A New York hoodlum.' Flensing answered the question. 'Part of the Gallo-Diapoulas thing.'

'And Frisch?'

'Like Gawne. A fixer.' Fletcher hesitated, then added: 'He used me once. Like with Davanzati. As a back-up.'

'But you weren't necessary, of course?' mocked Hoyle.

'Ask him. He'll tell you.'

'Don't worry . . . we will.'

'More names,' pressured Flensing.

It was the night train north, from King's Cross. No more than half a dozen other passengers shared the carriage, and all were well beyond listening distance. Most of them were dozing, in that comfortless, neck-aching posture of which British Rail say little. The windows were black mirrors reflecting the listless sway and weary boredom of the journey. On the table, between them, the scatter of wrappings from sandwiches surrounded the empty plastic beakers which had once held coffee.

The two men were police officers; senior CID men, with an above average knowledge of the Criminal Law. They

271

knew what they'd done. Nobody knew better. They knew the can of worms they'd deliberately opened, and they also knew that, having replaced the lid, their respective careers would come to a sudden halt should that lid ever again work loose.

Hoyle tried to speak, cleared his dry throat, then said: 'Quite a haul.'

'How many?' Flensing raised the back of his hand to his mouth to smother a yawn.

'Eight.' Hoyle flipped the pages of his notebook, then read: 'Gawne. Diapoulas. Davanzati. Profaci. Frisch. Chiaurelin. Delannoy. And, of course, Fletcher himself.'

'Killers all.' A tired, world-weary smile curved Flensing's lips. 'And don't let brother Fletcher fool you, David. He may have quietened but, in his hey-day, he was Mr Death himself. Any gun artist who can rub out a New York godfather when he's surrounded by family and bodyguard – *and* get away with it – is no amateur.'

'You think he *is* straight, these days?' Hoyle's tone gave a clue to the state of his mind. It carried a plea for reassurance. It was the cry of a man well out of his depth.

'They're not Humphrey Bogart/Robert Mitchum types.' Flensing refused the younger man comfort. 'Outwardly, they're ordinary people. They look like Fletcher looked today. Act like he acted. They just happen to have been born with this unsociable knack of being able to murder people without it troubling their conscience.'

'So we're no nearer?' The question was a little desperate.

'Nearer.' Flensing leaned forward and read, upside down, the names jotted by Hoyle. 'Forget Gawne ... he's dead. If Gawne's the man we're after, we're too late. Diapoulas? If we need to, we'll contact the FBI. That one might be as dead as Gawne. I haven't heard of him for years. More than that, he's strictly Yankee-torpedo material. I don't see him "international", like some of the others.'

'Davanzati's dead. That's the one thing we *do* know.' Hoyle made an unnecessarily savage pencil mark alongside the name. As, indeed, he had done against the names

'Gawne' and 'Diapoulas'. He said: 'Profaci?'

'One more corpse,' said Flensing flatly.

'In that case, why the devil . . . ?'

'Fletcher might have known. He might *not* have known. Profaci died in bed. Cancer. Joe Colombo took over the position of New York don in – let me see – sixty-four.'

'Therefore, Colombo?' ventured Hoyle.

'Colombo was gunned down at a rally, in seventy-one.'

'Christ! They don't live long. Fletcher's walking around on borrowed time.'

'If he *has* stepped down . . . ,' mused Flensing.

Hoyle made a mark against the name 'Profaci', then said: 'Let's move on to Frisch. Or is *he* dead?'

'That's one I *haven't* heard of,' smiled Flensing.

'Great. Great.' Hoyle's mock-enthusiasm widened Flensing's smile. 'We have his address, too . . . more or less.'

'Where he *once* lived,' corrected Flensing.

'We found Fletcher. We'll find Frisch.'

'Odd, that,' mused Flensing, and he seemed to be almost taunting his colleague. 'Frisch and Gawne. Two men – same set-up – and they lived almost next door to each other.'

'Almost fifty miles. I don't call that —'

'We're talking about a very élite bunch, David. The *crème de la crème* of the scum. Not common-or-garden tearaways.'

'Okay.' Hoyle looked both surprised and annoyed. 'Fletcher didn't name any London names. That doesn't mean. . . .'

'Nor are we talking about gangsters. "*Internationals*." That's one reason why I have doubts about the Yankee crowd. These are solo players, Inspector. Virtuosos in their own line of business. London? "The Terrorist Capital of the World"? No way! Too many snoopers. Too many tapped phones. Louts, muscle-men, mobsters, general villains . . . but not *these* people.'

'You like the bastards.' Hoyle gaped his amazement. 'Damn it, you actually *like* them!'

'Admiration, perhaps,' said Flensing gently. Reluctantly. 'The best – the very best in everything – deserves admiration.'

'Like Ripley and Gawne.'

'I didn't know them.'

'They damn well *liked* each other.'

'Would "respected" be a better word?' asked Flensing quietly.

'You can't respect a man who murders for a living, for God's sake.'

'The expertise,' suggested Flensing. 'Objectively, David. Not emotionally. Clear all emotion out of the way, accept what they do as their chosen profession. You don't agree with it ... but you must credit them with superb technical skill.'

Hoyle blew out his cheeks, then said: 'Let's go on one. Chiaurelin?'

'Wrong side of the Iron Curtain,' smiled Flensing. 'I've *heard* of him – heard rumours – he's good ... but un-get-at-able.'

'That leaves Delannoy.'

'More rumour,' said Flensing wearily. 'Five years ago – thereabouts – that he had a villa on the River Dordogne. Not too far from Argentat. We'll check things out quietly, with the Sûreté.'

As he closed the notebook, Hoyle said: 'Ralph, you are one hell of a knowledgeable copper. America, France, the Iron Curtain countries. That's covering territory.'

'Fletcher started it,' admitted Flensing. 'I arrested him, and it snowballed. His kind. The sort of men they are. How they live. That sort of thing. You ask around, and there's a hint dropped here, a suggestion there. It adds up. There's a certain amount of it recorded, if you know where to look.' The smile, with sadness at its edges, came and went. 'I have to keep myself occupied ... otherwise, I'd think of nothing but Helen.'

THIRTY-TWO

The thing stank. From the 'off' I'd had this goose-flesh feeling. One last kill – that's what Frisch had called it. Frisch, of the half-dead face and the hand that was damn near useless. Frisch, of the mumbled speech which sounded as if he had a mouthful of pebbles.

One last kill.

He moved around his bench, with one hand almost permanently in a pocket, and one leg having to be dragged around like a ball and chain.

And yet this was one bastard I yearned to kill, and had yearned to kill for a long time. Not him personally, but for what he was and what he stood for. He was the public face of the creeps who'd made the Glasgow job such a black farce. 'The Minister.' Up North for some cock-eyed political reason, and a man given to taking a morning jog every day of his life.

He was mine!

Who was paying me? Correction, who had *already* paid me?

As always, I'd never enquired too deeply but, at a guess, the lunatics who *should* have been at the Glasgow receiving end. Some paymaster from the Emerald Isle, north or south. I didn't give a damn which. The money had already been paid into the numbered account and, after this one final job, I was away.

I'd found the place and, already, workmen were swarming around what amounted to a young castle. Knocking down walls, fixing bookcases, putting in picture windows, installing hi-fi stereo systems. I'd found my island – the final, comfortable hole into which 'Lados' would disappear – but I had one debt to repay. The single cock-up of an otherwise immaculate career.

And yet that goose-flesh refused to go away.

I argued with myself. The anti-terrorist crowd, responsible for the safety of the man I'd have in the sights, made mistakes. The Special Branch men were just that – men. They could be outwitted. Short of locking a target inside a steel vault, there was no way to give tight – much less 'maximum' – security beyond the range of a handgun. Fifty yards, at the most. Beyond that, the screen had holes in it, and when it reached rifle-range the holes were big enough to crawl through. A good rifle, a good sight and rounds you could rely upon. It wasn't even going to be moderately difficult.

I still couldn't convince myself.

A simple, but highly efficient rifle; a Browning Mauser. A good, reliable sight: a Bausch & Lomb. Bullets – dum-dum bullets – virtually hand-made; and, despite his disability, given time Frisch could still give a warranty with every round.

So why the hell was I worrying?

I wouldn't know (never having been a fox) but perhaps the fox knows when the hunt gathers. Before the pack even leave their kennels. Before the horses are even taken from their stables. Maybe he *knows*. Maybe some soul-deep instinct tells him that this is going to be one day when he'd better have all his wits at needle readiness.

Maybe he feels like I felt.

Not scared. I was too old a hand to be scared. Nevertheless, the certainty was there, at the back of my mind, that this was going to be no ordinary trigger-squeeze.

Credit where due. Pollard had been right. The aiming-point couldn't be faulted. The post-and-rail fence, augmented with link-wire, formed the boundary of the estate. The broken-down deer-shelter was, of itself, no hiding-place, but the crumbling rear wall gave shelter enough for anybody standing outside the boundary fence, and the gentle downhill slope of the close-cropped grass was a perfect aiming view for anybody out to clobber somebody using the narrow tarmac road leading from the Home Farm to the main house of the estate.

One dusk (ten days before the shooting) I parked a hired car half a mile from the chosen spot, walked, then vaulted the fence. I paced it out to the curve in the road, where the target would trot past, and I made it just less than sixty yards. Even in the estimated distance, Pollard couldn't be seriously faulted.

This (as you will have noticed) was one I had to organise alone. Frisch couldn't mastermind it. I could rely on him for the equipment but, beyond that, he was shaky. His memory and his grasp of details had gone a little. Enough to make me check every possible kink for myself.

I recruited Pollard and he, in turn, was like a pup with two tails. I had to warn him.

'Pollard, this is no vicarage garden party. One slip – one very small slip – and they'll open the prison gates just about in time for us to draw our old-age pensions.'

'Oh, sure. I appreciate that. I mean —'

'*I* mean keep your damn mouth shut,' I snapped. It quietened him, and I hoped it had quietened him enough as I continued: 'I've seen the spot. I approve. But the woods on the other side of the road. Why didn't you mention *them*?'

I was finding fault. Deliberately cooling his enthusiasm.

'I – er – I didn't think it was important.'

'Because you're a mug,' I sneered. 'Because you're already handing some screw a key, and asking him to lock us both away till our bloody teeth rot.'

We were in his place – the dandified architectural nightmare he figured a hot-shot gallery-owner should call 'home' – and we'd sent his woman out to visit friends. My own resting-place was gradually becoming more austere as the favourite belongings were packed and crated for my move. Anyway, I wanted him to remember this conversation; to be reminded of it every time he entered this tarted-up room.

'Trees – forests – woods,' I spat at him. 'Timber, in other words. Something to hide behind. Pollard, the police aren't mugs, if you are. That's *just* where they'll position men who form a cordon. Because that's *just* where they'll expect some clever devil out to chop the man to hide. Creeps play Robin Hood and Sherwood Forest, and they'll be looking for creeps. That way they can come across non-creeps.'

There was much more along the same lines. The idea was to frighten him. Even to terrify him . . . but not too much. I needed him, but I needed him on his toes and *continually* on his toes.

After a pause in the tirade, and having given him time to pour two stiff whiskies, I muttered: 'Ideally, I need a back-up.'

'I'll be your back-up,' he said eagerly.

'*You*!' I made believe the thought hadn't even passed through my mind.

'Anything. Anything at all. I'm reliable and can —'

'The hell you're reliable,' I mocked.

'Yes – yes, I am. Just – y'know – just tell me what to do. I'll do it. No argument. Exactly what you say.'

'Maybe.' More make-believe. He had to be made to think I was doing him a big favour.

'Just tell me,' he pleaded.

'From behind the deer shelter,' I mused. 'That part's easy. Getting to and from the spot behind the deer-shelter – that's the tricky bit.'

'I – er- I don't see. . . .' He gulped whisky.

'I stroll casually along the road with a Browning Mauser tucked under my arm?' I mocked.

'No. No – of course not.' He took aboard more whisky. 'I thought – y'know – a car.'

'A parked car?' Again, I made the contempt very obvious, even though it was a come-on make-believe contempt. 'Nobody ever notices a parked car. Especially, nobody *remembers* a parked car at the scene of an assassination.'

'No . . . I don't mean your own car. A hired car. Maybe a stolen car.'

'*Any* car. If it's hired, somebody has to hire it. If it's nicked, somebody might see it *being* nicked.'

'Not – not at the scene,' he stumbled. 'I mean, not actually near the *scene*.'

'Within two miles.' I tasted the whisky, for the first time. 'Within at least two miles. Pollard, we are taking out a member of Her Majesty's Government. We need to be sure – *damn* sure. Sure we do the job. More important, sure we get away with it.'

'Anything,' he pleaded. 'Anything at all.'

It must be understood that Frisch, while not actually planning the killing was, nevertheless, one of the keystones in the set-up. It was Frisch to whom 'they' had made the original offer. It was Frisch who had contacted Pollard and set him to work checking out jogging patterns and double-checking the itinerary of the man I had to put the cross-wires on.

It was, therefore, Frisch who obtained things after making mumbled approval of the basic plans I'd worked out.

A van in British Telecom livery, including ladders fixed to the roof. A bicycle; a drop-handlebar model, complete with oversized paniers at the rear and twin water-bottles up front.

It was a good plan. After the basics, I added the finishing touches, and the finishing touches were going to be what made it safe.

Who the hell expects a professional killer to tool around the countryside on a flash touring cycle? Who expects him to be geared out in short shorts, open-necked shirt and cycling shoes? Who expects him to be sporting spectacles on a par with car headlights . . . even if they are of plain glass?

That was *my* get-up.

I'd cycle along a nice little country lane, in the early hours, then stop for a breather and to enjoy the scenery and, while I did so, lean the bicycle against a telegraph pole, less than three yards from the rear of a certain deer-shelter.

Meanwhile, Pollard – in appropriate dress – would be *up* another telegraph pole. Out of sight, but not too far away.

He'd have a view of the house and, when he saw movement, he'd skim down the pole, slam the ladder on to its rack and drive to the pole where the bicycle was parked.

Timing would (should!) get him to the deer-shelter at about the time the target came into view. Then open the rear doors of the van, take out the rifle and, while I'm earning my fee, Pollard shoves the bicycle into the van. Then *I'm* in the van, into appropriate telephone engineer's gear ... and away.

Fancy?

Well, maybe a little fancy, but not *too* fancy. Not as fancy as the New York penthouse killing. Not even as fancy as the Glasgow mistake.

But I had this feeling. This *damn* feeling. . . .

THIRTY-THREE

They will all cough. They will all sing. Given a weakness, given a deal, given a key word, every last one of them will talk.

Frisch was not unique.

With Frisch, the weakness was his own condition, and the fact that he'd lived with that condition far too long. It was the everlasting fear that, suddenly, like the snapping of a dry twig, the other half of his body would also die. Perhaps the fear that it would not quite die. That the part of his brain still functioning, albeit slowly and in a slightly muddled fashion, would also turn into mush. That, if the deal was not agreed, he'd end his life in zombie-like stupor in the comfortless severity of a prison hospital. That he'd lose even the slight safety-net of twenty-four-hours-a-day nursing.

It was a great fear and, because it was a great fear, it was also a great weakness.

The deal was left unspoken, but it was clearly understood by all. They wanted a man. A trigger-man. All else was, by comparison, unimportant. They would collect evidence enough to convict and, if possible – if at all possible – that evidence would not include anything likely to pinpoint the existence of Karl Frisch.

Unless, of course, Karl Frisch was the man they sought!

The key word was a name. Actually *two* names. 'Jacopo Davanzati' and 'David Fletcher'. They hinted, and more than hinted, at knowledge. They formed the basis of the deal and, at the same time, emphasised the weakness in that they underlined the fear.

That and, of course, good policing and experience enough to know when to ask questions, what questions to ask and, above all else, when to allow silence to take over.

Frisch was like the rest. Frisch talked.

And yet. . . .

Some tattered remnants of a once great pride remained. He told only what he *had* to tell. He named no names, and gave no hint of previous killings. Davanzati, perhaps – but Davanzati wasn't important . . . and they'd visited with the intention of digging into the Davanzati killing. Therefore, they guessed, and Frisch knew they guessed and was, perhaps, glad.

Davanzati!

The great Davanzati . . . but he, Frisch, had proved to be the greater, in the end.

As they drove back to Lessford, Flensing and Hoyle discussed the interview.

'Do you believe him?' asked Hoyle.

'I believe he told the truth . . . but not *all* the truth.'

'That *he* killed Davanzati?'

'It's possible. I'm damn sure he knows who did.'

'God, if *he's* the man we're after!' Hoyle's voice was heavy with disgust.

'Does he get away with it?' Flensing placed the final decision in Hoyle's lap. 'So far, we've nothing on paper?'

281

'We'd be well out on a limb.'

'Frisch would hold the only saw.' A twisted smile touched Flensing's mouth. 'I can't see him using it.'

It was something new in Hoyle's experience. To have a man as a superior in whom absolute trust could be placed and who in turn gave the same degree of trust. It made bobbying interesting ... if not easy.

'It's been such a bloody long time,' said Hoyle heavily.

Flensing chuckled quietly, as if at some secret joke. As if he, too, had faced these decisions and was now rather enjoying the witnessing of another man sweating the same sort of blood. Yet there was no malice in the chuckle. It was rather like the chuckle of a man whose friend has just seen the point of a very involved joke.

Hoyle took two cigarettes from a packet, put them both between his lips, scratched a match into life, lit the two cigarettes, then passed one on to Flensing. Flensing murmured his thanks and took a hand from the steering-wheel to accept the cigarette.

'Decision time,' said Hoyle grimly.

'It would seem so.'

'We can't ignore the tip-off about the attempt on the Minister's life. That, we *can't* ignore.'

Flensing remained silent, and allowed Hoyle to move to the next stage.

'Not much detail, though ... eh?' Hoyle drew on the cigarette. 'Just that the bloke who killed Davanzati's due to have a go at the Minister, early Sunday morning. The "where" and the "when" ... but not the "who".'

'And if he doesn't?' teased Flensing.

'We go back. We take it a step at a time.'

'You're going to let him *have* a go?' drawled Flensing. 'Assuming Frisch has given us the truth, you're prepared to risk His Nibs getting away with it?'

'No! My Christ, no!' The mere suggestion seemed to startle Hoyle. 'Assuming everything's true, it still mustn't be allowed to happen ... even if we lose our man. No....' Hoyle frowned his concentration for a moment, then

282

continued: 'It's out of our police area, but we can have a quiet word. . . .'

'I know the super likely to be in charge of security.'

'What it is to have friends in high places,' grinned Hoyle. Then, more seriously: 'No jogging *next* Sunday morning. But beyond that . . . nothing?'

The last word was a question, and Flensing answered it.

'Like catching butterflies,' agreed Flensing gently. 'Too much activity and we'll net nothing.'

'But – er – arms?' Again it was a question, but a very tentative question. '*He'll* be armed.'

'If he's there.'

'If he *is* there. He'll have a gun. I'll be guided but, to be honest, I don't *want* Alva to collect a posthumous George Cross.'

'You think you'll get one?' smiled Flensing.

'I don't even want to try.'

'I'll have a word,' promised Flensing. 'The anti-terrorist mob should be there. They'll provide a Dead-eye Dick.' Then, after a pause: 'And if it's all moonshine? If Frisch has been leading us up the garden path? What happens to the Davanzati Case?'

'It stays undetected.' There was a strange finality in Hoyle's tone. He enjoyed another inhalation of cigarette smoke, then continued, as if voicing already-reached conclusions aloud. 'Damnation, I'm not after a man like Frisch. After all these years . . . a man with one foot already in his own coffin. Not even Fletcher. Give him the benefit of the doubt. Maybe he *is* straight. Who the hell cares? Who the hell even *knows*, after all this time? Davanzati was no loss.' Then, pensively – musingly – as if accepting a reluctant truth for the first time: 'Y'know, Ralph, I don't give a damn. Not really. If it wasn't for the Minister thing, I'd say sod it. Leave it at that. I think. . . .' He gave a deep sigh. 'I *know*. It's been something of a prolonged ego trip. Lewis triggered it off. Way back. I wanted to "show" people. To prove a point. Not at first, perhaps – but that's what it became. What it still is. But not after Sunday. If it's not nailed down tight on Sunday, that's the end. Those photocopies I've kept locked away all this time – the few bits and pieces I've collected – I burn the bloody things. After Sunday, I'm back to tracing milk-bottle thieves.'

THIRTY-FOUR

It was a nice day. A nice morning. Indeed, I'd enjoyed the steady ride to the deer-shelter. If my weather lore amounted to much, we were in for a fine day; one of those days that linger on in the memory and, in time, represent all the high summers lived in a lifetime.

It was just after seven, and the sun was low enough in the east to have given problems, had I been sighting towards the east. But I wasn't, therefore all the sun did was provide longer-than-normal shadows, and I rested in the shadow from the deer-shed and eyed the slope of green across which I'd be firing.

I had my back to the wood, therefore I didn't hear him approach. He must have come from the wood – he certainly didn't come from along the lane – and he must have been there, waiting, when I arrived. He also knew his stuff. I hadn't heard a thing, and *wouldn't* have heard a thing, if he hadn't deliberately scuffed the surface of the road to attract my attention.

I think he wanted to see my face. See the fear, perhaps. Some men have this kinky desire. To watch expressions those few moments before they squeeze triggers.

The Colt .45 pistol was as steady as Gibraltar, and lined up with my navel.

'Do you need to say anything?' he asked in a flat, emotionless tone.

He wore the standard uniform which was supposed *not* to

be a uniform. Raglan-type mac; a little grimy. Lightweight felt hat; even more grimy. Shoes that needed polishing. He was a dirty little man, doing a dirty little job.

'Cat got your tongue?' he asked, and there might have been an edge to his voice.

'That's a dangerous toy you're playing with,' I remarked. And I was pleased to find my voice showed even less emotion than his.

He said, 'They think you know too much,' and he offered it as an explanation. Not an apology. Merely as if I hadn't already guessed.

'You, too,' I murmured. 'One day *you'll* know too much.'

'You're freelance.'

'Whereas you're on the staff?' I smiled.

'Something like that.'

'Don't be *too* sure,' I warned. 'Your Whitehall masters can be very jumpy.'

A cloud seemed to touch his eyes, as if I'd voiced a fear he himself had already touched. Not that it mattered. He'd do his job, then report back to be told what an obedient little killer he was.

'That's it, then?' he asked.

I might have said something. Some epoch-making last remark. But the car arrived before I could think of anything. It was a black car, and it arrived with a rush and braked as if tyres came with cornflake packets.

The grubby man holding the Colt turned and, as he did so, somebody with brass-bound lungs yelled: 'Hold-it! Police!'

But it was too late. Everything was too late.

The Colt had already sent a slug into a wing of the car, the rear door flew open and a uniformed sergeant dived out, rolled, tilted a Smith & Wesson .38 in a two-handed grip and pumped the regulation two bullets into the creep whose job it had been to kill me. I watched with professional interest. It wasn't bad shooting. The first shot blew his spine to hell. The second shot was superfluous. The grubby little bastard was dead before the twitch of his finger triggered a second round from the Colt.

Thereafter, it was pure pantomime.

Two creeps in plain clothes strolled over to me. One flashed a warrant card; a certain Detective Chief Inspector Hoyle. They asked a few questions. What was my name? What was my address? I fed them hogwash, but they believed me because I put on a scared-out-of-my-wits act.

They'd be in touch, they said.

I mustn't mention the incident to anybody, they said.

Above all, I mustn't mention it to newspaper people, they said.

I must hold myself in readiness as a witness at possible future court proceedings, they said.

And, after saying all this, they were anxious that I remove myself and allow them to perform what intricate necessities policemen think are required in such circumstances.

I hoisted myself on to the bicycle and pedalled to where Pollard was still waiting. An hour later, we'd abandoned the Telecom van and parted company.

I never saw Pollard again.

Since that murderously 'near miss' I have pondered and worked things out. Back-tracked and reached inescapable conclusions.

The mistake at Glasgow virtually created my death warrant. Of that I have no doubt. Not *my* mistake, of course, but a mistake made by 'them' in which a decent, harmless citizen was wrongfully slaughtered. The very ordinary status of the woman was the thing that scared them. They (always 'they') knew me or, if they didn't know me at the time, it was vitally important that they *get* to know me. I knew of their existence, and knew that they were far from infallible. I was dangerous, because of that knowledge, therefore I had to be removed.

I think – indeed, I'm sure – the plan to execute the Shah was an involved plot . . . and not, necessarily, to execute the Shah. The idea was that I disappear in the maelstrom of hatred and counter-hatred and if, before I disappeared, I killed the occupant of the Peacock Throne that was merely a

286

bonus – but disappear I must!

I have relaxed here, in the comfort of my new home – here on the island I own – listening to great music reproduced via immaculate equipment, and I have smiled to myself. I am beyond their reach, because I no longer exist. 'Lados' was a fiction, and by closing the book on 'Lados' I have put myself beyond their reach – beyond even *their* not inconsiderable reach.

Eventually, they will kill Pollard and, if he survives long enough, Frisch, too. Security demands it. It matters not. Their deaths will merely make certainty even more certain.

Nobody will *ever* trace *my* whereabouts. There are far too many islands in the world!

I end with a hope and a smile. That those foolish people who invested in the 'Lados' daubs profit by their lesson. They have lined my pockets well, despite the fact that they bought contemptible rubbish. The art world can be fooled, as easily as the dark world of unmentioned Whitehall 'departments' can be fooled.

I know!